THREE NOIRS
&
A BLANC

ENDORSEMENTS

This is a truly enjoyable and uplifting story. I didn't want to put it down! In a time when so many want to focus on what is twisted in our world, this is a beautiful story of grace in the lives of people who have known deep sorrow and hardship, but who have found strength in the friendship and love of one another rooted in Christ. The author's many years of pastoral ministry, as well as his own infectious sense of humor, can be seen in the story. We need more stories like this, and I look forward to the sequel.

—**Ray Van Neste,** Dean and Professor of Biblical Studies, School of Theology and Missions, Union University, Jackson, Tennessee

Three Noirs & a Blanc is a beautifully written and inviting story about the meaning of love and friendship. Weaving together the distinctive lives of friends and family members, Kelvin Moore provides an opportunity for readers not only to reflect upon the lives, connections, and circumstances of the various characters in the story, but to think more deeply about the value and true meaning of relationships, friendships, reconciliation, and family. It is genuine delight to recommend this engaging and delightful novel, which I know will be a source of joy for many.

—**David S. Dockery,** President, International Alliance for Christian Education; and President, Southwestern Baptist Theological Seminary

In this creative novel which spans at least four decades and harmonizes temporal, racial, economic, and educational diversity, Dr. Moore has incorporated how the Apostle Paul described love in his classic and inspired thirteenth chapter in 1 Corinthians. Dr. Moore's *Three Noirs & a Blanc* both entertains and challenges readers to gain a feel for and an understanding of loving, personal relationships in action. In a masterful though non-sermonizing way, Dr. Moore's novel will inspire every reader to see that love really is not about feeling—rather, love is about giving of one's time, energy, resources, and encouragement for the well-being of others.

I can't help but believe Dr. Moore's inspiration came from Jesus, who taught that he desired to be our friend—one who loved his friends by the giving of himself on behalf of others.
—**L. Manning Garrett III, PhD,** Associate Teaching Professor, Philosophy Department, University of Memphis, Jackson, Tennessee

Friends are often in short supply—and good stories about true friendship are even harder to find! Kelvin Moore's *Three Noirs & a Blanc* celebrates friendship and will inspire and motivate you to be a better friend. Read it for the joy of the story, but also for the spiritual lessons about the ultimate friend who sticks closer than a brother—Jesus.
—**Jeff Iorg**, President, Gateway Seminary

Kelvin Moore's care for people, the South, and Christ all come through loud and clear in this tender portrait of real friendship. He's done here what good novelists should do—putting flesh and blood on an idea, by way of characters you care about, in situations that are interesting. In doing so he's encouraged me to do what all Christian men should do more of—occasionally putting down our volumes of hard theology in order to think about how to relate and to care for each other as friends.
—**Ted Kluck,** Associate Professor of Communication Arts, Union University, and award-winning author of over thirty books

No lesser light than Aristotle famously said, "without friends, no one would choose to live, even if he possessed all other goods ...." Kelvin Moore's ode to friendship in the American South follows in the great tradition of friendship tales. Readers will fall in love with Lester, Laverne, and Leeroy from Chalk Bluff, Alabama. Their camaraderie and escapades will resonate with everyone who has experienced the deep joy of friendship. A refreshing memento of this rare gift in our age of paper-thin relationships.
—**C. Ben Mitchell**, Professor, Author, Friend

To anyone preparing to read *Three Noirs & a Blanc*—be forewarned! You will laugh out loud repeatedly. You will be moved to tears. You will lose sleep, because putting this book down will be a challenge. Most importantly, you will be inspired by this story about how true friendships develop and how they sustain and encourage us in good times and in bad. The tale unfolds as the circle of friends widens, drawing the reader in as well to experience the wit, the wisdom, the compassion, and the love that characterize true friendship. *Three Noirs & a Blanc* will leave you feeling like you are part of the family.
—**Barbara C. McMillin,** President, Blue Mountain Christian University, Blue Mountain, MS

Kelvin Moore has crafted a warm, witty, and tender story of four friends, drawn together by harsh circumstances of life and a common love of music and its powerful influence on the human spirit. Leeroy, Laverne, and Lester, friends and performers for more than fifty years, are joined by teenager Jake, whom they teach about life and who teaches them about not giving up. It is a heartwarming story of friendship and family whose characters work themselves into the heart of and become friends with the reader. As

Laverne would have said it, I just love me a good Kelvin Moore story.
—**Hayward Armstrong**, Minister/Missionary/Educator, Retired

Kelvin Moore's novel is about the improbable friendship of three, then four, then five, then eight extremely diverse and enormously likable characters over a period of about six years. They live in New Orleans, which for some of them is a kind of sanctuary. They go to church together. They exchange gifts. They party together. They listen to and make music. They cook and eat food. And they talk, and talk, and talk. Their many conversations include a little banter and teasing and a lot of personal sharing, and their friendship deepens as they get to know each other better. Some of their experiences are laugh-out-loud funny, others are perfectly ordinary but nevertheless meaningful, and a few are sad. The account of one of the older friends trying to describe for the benefit of one of the younger ones the mechanics of kissing—"smooth, gentle, far-off look, lips positioned, swoop, plant" —is priceless. This book proves—if any proof is needed—that goodness really is more interesting and more fun to read about than evil. I loved reading this book, and I recommend it enthusiastically.
—**Fisher Humphreys**, Birmingham, Alabama

I have known Kelvin Moore for multiple decades. I have known him as a brilliant student, excellent theologian, author, friend, and as a caring professor and pastor, but I didn't know he could tell a story like this one. *Three Noirs & a Blanc* is a delightful, engaging story of enduring friendship. It is filled with wonderful characters that I can "see" in my mind—characters who tell a story filled with joy, love, and hope. This story will make you smile on the inside and fill you with hope for the future.

This is Kelvin Moore's first novel, but I am convinced it won't be his last.

—**Waylon Bailey,** Senior Pastor, First Baptist Church. Covington, LA

In his first novel, Moore offers readers a charming slice of life narrative set in New Orleans and illustrates the value of true friendship through lived music.

—**Niles Reddick,** author of the Pulitzer-nominated novel *Drifting Too Far From The Shore,* a novella, three short fiction collections, and his newest book *If Not For You*

Kelvin Moore brings his years of experience in New Orleans to life in this tale of unlikely friendship. Weaving together the music, the food, and the atmosphere of the Big Easy, Moore captures the pathos and the strength of lives that might easily have crashed, but which soared instead. Set in the tumultuous 1960s when so many old norms were being challenged and discarded, *Three Noirs & a Blanc* is a story of faith, hope, and love.

—**Harry Lee Poe,** Charles Colson Professor of Faith and Culture, Edgar Award winner from the Mystery Writers of America

Kelvin Moore brings his characters to life with wit and grace.

—**Kathryn Cushman,** author of *The Plans We Made*

In *Three Noirs & a Blanc*, Kelvin Moore invites us into a fellowship of lifelong friends and the young man they adopt as family. Through the lens of their relationships and the music they make, we can reexamine the struggles with class, race, and faith that are part of the life we live together.

—Rebecca Poe Hays, Assistant Professor of Christian Scriptures (Hebrew Bible/Old Testament), George W. Truett Theological Seminary, Baylor University

THREE NOIRS
&
A BLANC

R. KELVIN MOORE

ELK LAKE PUBLISHING INC.

PUBLISHING THE POSITIVE
Plymouth, Massachusetts

A Christian Company
ElkLakePublishingInc.com

COPYRIGHT NOTICE

Author Represented By: AuthorizeMe Literary Agency

PUBLISHED BY: Elk Lake Publishing, Inc., 35 Dogwood Drive, Plymouth, MA 02360, 2023

LIBRARY CATALOGING DATA:

Names: Moore, R. Kelvin (R. Kelvin Moore)
Three Noirs & a Blanc / R. Kelvin Moore
380 p. 23cm × 15cm (9in × 6 in.)

ISBN-13: 9798891340367 (paperback) | 9798891340374 (hardcover) | 9798891340381 (trade paperback) | 9798891340398 (e-book)

Key Words: Friends; family; love; New Orleans; race; music; loyalty

Library of Congress Control Number: 2023946711 Fiction

DEDICATION

This work is dedicated to those I have been blessed to call friend—some related—others, while not related, just as close. You have encouraged, inspired, motivated, and educated me. We have laughed and cried together. We have celebrated accomplishments and mourned losses together. While I have bantered with you, you have given as well as you have taken, and I have enjoyed both giving and receiving.

My life has been enriched greatly by our friendship, and I shall be grateful forever.

ACKNOWLEDGMENTS

Numerous individuals, both family and friends, have inspired this work across years.

I am grateful for my biological brother and friend, Randall. One is blessed indeed to have someone like him in their life. Scripture, in Proverbs 18:24, records, "... there is a friend who sticketh closer then a brother." While I accept the truthfulness of this statement, I can't imagine someone closer than Randall.

My gratitude and thanks to Hayward Armstrong and Mary Ann Poe, for being among the first readers and making suggestions as to the final manuscript; Agent Sharon Elliot of AuthorizeMe Literary Agency, who assisted in writing and submitting the proposal; and a special thanks to Rebecca England for her initial formatting expertise. Thanks to Deb Haggerty and Elk Lake Publishing, Inc, for publishing the work of an unknown author in the area of Christian fiction. I am appreciative of Elk Lake editor Mary W. Johnson's valuable insight, candidness, and humor.

Special thanks to colleague and friend, Harry L. Poe, who encouraged me to write and publish, even as I considered abandoning all efforts. My children, Megan, Bailey, and daughter-in-law, Tabitha, are all about family and friendship, and they remind me daily of the joys of having adult children and a daughter-in-law as friends.

Finally, I am more than thankful for my wife, Cathy, who not only loves and supports me, but who has also read, edited, and critiqued almost every line I have ever written, both fiction and nonfiction. She is one of the strongest individuals I have ever known. She is much more than my wife—she is my friend.

And certainly none of this would have been possible without my walk with Christ, my truest friend.

"A friend loveth at all times ...."

Proverbs 17:17

PROLOGUE

The young man in worn clothes picked up the piece of newspaper the wind had blown against his automobile's back tire. He carried the paper to the trash bin, intending to throw it atop the greasy bags that smelled of leftover fried things, when something in the scrap of newsprint caught his attention. He carried the paper to his car, opened the driver's side back door, and sat sideways on the seat with his feet on the pavement.

He studied the scrap, then looked to the sky, closed his eyes, and murmured to himself. Then he folded the newsprint, jammed it into his shirt pocket, grabbed a beat-up case from the car's trunk, and set out for the main highway.

CHAPTER ONE

At 1:35 a.m. on a Sunday morning, on the edge of the French Quarter in New Orleans, three men stood wrapped in old heavy winter coats beside a 1951 Hudson Hornet. Leeroy had purchased the car used in 1958 and named her Hazel, as in Hazel the Hudson Hornet. At one time, the car had been a beautiful red, but now, in 1967, the car was the color of rust—for that matter, it appeared to be all rust.

Laverne and Lester shook with cold. Laverne held a flashlight for Leeroy, who bent over to use the automobile's hood as a table. The weak batteries provided enough illumination for Leeroy to see at least the denominations. The pile of bills looked substantial, but in reality there were lots of one-dollar bills and a few coins.

"How much money did we get?" Lester asked.

"Hush," Leeroy said. "Can't count and listen to you too."

"Not a multitasker, eh?" Laverne said.

"Laverne, that goes for you too," Leeroy chided. "Muzzle it."

Some folks, observing the three men standing in the light winter drizzle early on a Sunday morning, would surmise they were bums who'd just robbed a liquor store— or perhaps robbed an unsuspecting soul on the street. No one who didn't know Leeroy Edwards, Laverne Knox, and

Lester Washington would believe the three elderly friends were musicians.

They were in fact excellent musicians, now driven by circumstances to panhandle on the streets each night in hopes of earning a few dollars. No one would have guessed this trio once earned good money playing music in the finest venues in the city of New Orleans and beyond.

Lester broke the silence.

"I multitask pretty well. What 'bout you, Laverne?"

"Not me. Can't walk and chew gum at the same time."

Leeroy paused, took in a deep breath, shook his head, and began counting again.

"Oh, I'm a multitasker. I can do three or four things at the same time," Lester said, "and do 'em all well, thank you."

"Not me," Laverne said. "Can't do it at all."

"Will you two do something that's near impossible? For me?" Leeroy asked.

"What?" Laverne asked.

"Absolutely. Anything," Lester said. "Name it."

"Will you two stop flappin' your jaws for one minute?" Leeroy said, as he prepared to begin counting yet again.

"That's impossible for Lester," Laverne said.

But Lester and Laverne stopped talking, and Leeroy continued the task at hand, until finally he straightened and took a deep breath.

"Well?" asked Lester.

"Two hundred and twenty-three dollars"—he continued to count—"and seventy-eight cents. Three quarters and three …"

"Someone gave us three pennies?" asked Laverne in disbelief.

"Two *US* pennies. Other one's Canadian," answered Leeroy with a laugh, as he squinted to confirm the identity of the currency.

"And that's *with* the one hundred and fifty dollars the manager promised us?" Lester asked.

"Yep," responded Leeroy. "Divided three ways is seventy-four dollars and twenty-six cents each."

"Minus gas money for Hazel," Lester said.

"I'll take the Canadian penny and pass the thing off somewhere," Leeroy said.

"Seventy-four dollars?" asked Laverne.

"Don't forget the twenty-six cents," said Leeroy. He divided the money. "Seventy-four dollars each."

"Leeroy, take gas money," Lester said.

"I don't need gas money. I got half a tank."

Laverne and Lester suspected Leeroy was not being truthful, but no one knew for sure since Hazel's fuel gauge hadn't worked since 1962.

Leeroy gave the men their share and pocketed his.

The men continued to stand outside in the frigid December night. They rubbed their arms to improve blood flow. They shifted from foot to foot. Each knew there was no need to get inside the Hornet. Hazel's heater died not long after the fuel gauge.

An exasperated Laverne spoke.

"We got bills to pay, Lester and me. Seventy-four dollars and twenty-six cents won't go far. We got our electric bill this week—over fifty dollars, and that's with us freezing during the day. I don't need fans in the summertime, but we need a little heat in the winter. If we don't turn on the heat, we're scared the water pipes'll freeze and bust, and we sure can't afford a plumber."

Lester chimed in.

"You know that's right, Laverne. And these days, I don't know whether to buy food or medicine. I can't afford my co-pays on my heart medicine. Dang, I've eaten enough cheese sandwiches—I feel like I been constipated for weeks. I don't remember the last time I had a cup of coffee."

All three men laughed, comfortable with one another.

Lester said, "If I don't buy that medicine and take it, I'll die, and if I don't eat, I'll die."

"Heck of a predicament," Leeroy said.

Undeterred, Lester continued. "And where would you two be without me?"

"We'd die without you. Either from loneliness, sorrow, hunger, or fear for the present or the future," Laverne answered somberly.

They continued foot-shifting in the chill night air.

"Less than a hundred dollars in tips tonight. I remember when we got over five hundred on a Saturday night in tips alone. Had Saturday nights when we made more. Much more," Laverne said.

"Those days are gone. The crowd wasn't there tonight. Small, unengaged. Unenthusiastic," Leeroy said.

"The crowds died when Anthony died." Lester's voice held a tone of sadness.

"I reckon. Died with Anthony," Laverne said, as he dropped his head.

"Come on, you two," Leeroy said. "Let's call it a night and get out of this weather. There's a diner open on Elysian Fields. I'm gonna buy you both a cup of coffee."

"Oh no!" Lester responded, feigned a stumble, and placed his hands over his heart. "My heart and kidneys gonna shut down."

The three tired men climbed into Hazel the Hudson Hornet.

"How did we ever find ourselves in this situation?" Laverne mused, as he, Lester, and Leeroy drank coffee, hot and black. Lester considered coffee as nectar from the gods. None of the men felt they could splurge for anything else, and Lester and Laverne refused to take advantage of Leeroy's generosity beyond the coffee.

"In this situation? You mean struggling for every dollar and facing homelessness?" Lester said. "That what you mean?"

"Right. Sad, *sad* situation," Laverne replied, absently nudging his spoon with a finger.

"A sad situation, all right," Leeroy said.

The three nursed their coffee cups.

"Remind me, where did this thing start?" Lester asked.

The ensuing conversation was the way their talks generally went, in the style of ping pong balls bouncing off walls.

"In 1894," Leeroy answered.

"What?" This from Lester.

"In 1894, the year the three of us were born." Leeroy again.

"Not *that* beginning." From Lester.

"In 1910?" Leeroy asked.

"Remind me what happened in 1910," Laverne said.

"We walked out of Chalk Bluff," Leeroy said.

"Not that beginning either." Lester's irritation was becoming plain.

"1912?" Leeroy offered.

"Remind me what happened then." Laverne.

"We met Anthony," Leeroy said.

"*That's* the beginning to which I refer," Lester stated.

The three men reflected over their cups as each man, in time, related his own story. Each tale was one the other two knew all too well.

Each listened politely, as they always did.

CHAPTER TWO

In 1912, two years after the three friends arrived in New Orleans, eighteen-year-old Lester Washington, Leeroy Edwards, and Laverne Knox, along with twenty-four-year-old Anthony Emery, formed a band they named the Noirs. Having grown up in New Orleans, Anthony knew the French word for "black" and suggested the word as a name for their band. By this time, Lester, Leeroy, and Laverne had been playing together for as long as they could remember. When the original trio considered forming a band, they intended to call themselves Triple L, but when Anthony came along, a band named Triple L and One A didn't have quite the same allure. They became the Noirs.

Lester, Leeroy, and Laverne all grew up in Chalk Bluff, Alabama, one hundred and twenty-five miles northeast of Birmingham. They started the first grade together in the segregated South, where many Black people never went to school atall. All three men grew up "po'." In Alabama, "po'" people were poorer than the poor people.

"We were so po'," Laverne said, "we envied the poor folks."

Three a.m. and after, the men continued to drink coffee and reminisce. The waitress was generous with refills. The men smiled as she returned again and again.

Sensing their lack of financial resources after one of her refill visits to their table, she lingered a moment. Then she said, "I have an apple pie. You three want a slice?"

Embarrassed, Lester began expressing their refusal when the waitress—Carol, as Leeroy read from her name tag—overrode him.

"It was baked yesterday, so it's day-old goods now and stale. We can't sell it. Y'all can have a slice before I throw it out, if you want."

Neither Lester, Leeroy, nor Laverne spoke. Nor did they make eye contact with Carol.

She smiled. "I'll be right back."

She returned in a few minutes with three thick slices of pie. The men took their first bites, each savoring the flaky crust, the just-tender apple slices, and the aroma of cinnamon and nutmeg. Believing the pie had come from the oven minutes before, they ate without speaking, as if the fresh pie was a holy thing, and not to be disrespected by conversation.

Rain pelted the glass outside their booth. Lightning illuminated the early morning sky. Thunder shook the small restaurant. The men sat in the warm, dry diner, drank coffee, and ate blessedly delicious pie.

Finally, Lester began *his* personal story.

"The owner of the little house where my family lived gave us a piano. I *say* house—more shack than house. I always believed the owner couldn't sell the piano, and he didn't want to pay anybody to move that humongous thing. It was either move the piano or leave it in the shack. So the owner made a gift of it to us."

He took another bite of pie, chewing slowly while he reflected.

"That big upright piano was 'bout a hundred years old, I s'pect. Old and worn out fifty years earlier, yet that piano became one of our most prized possessions. The previous owner—*owners*, prob'ly—lost the stool, so my mother sat in a kitchen chair when she played. When she gave lessons to me she'd put a lard can, 'bout six inches high, in the chair. Made it more comfortable for me because then I could reach the keys easy. But the pedals? No way. My legs, minus any shoes or pants, dangled way above the pedals."

He sipped from his cup. "I asked my mother to show me a chord. Ma learned several chords somewhere—can't say I know where. To my amazement and surprise, I found playin' was easy for me. I could remember chords easy. Within weeks, I'd mastered the chords Ma knew."

Another swallow of coffee. "Then Ma came home one night with a chord book. Never knew when she got it. Never asked. I memorized the book in a few weeks. We were sittin' in the house one swelterin' August night when Ma first realized her baby boy had rhythm. She recognized her son had a gift. Leastways, that's what she said."

The other two listened quietly, having heard the story several times over the years. They never interrupted. Interrupting wasn't polite.

"My parents would listen to me play until the wee hours. Ma sang as I played them old cotton pickin' songs. She cried when I played the old gospel songs—the Negro spirituals, they called 'em," Lester said, his gaze lost in the memory.

"Nobody ever cried when I played bass," Leeroy said, "not for joy, anyway. Maybe out of pain." He gave a hearty laugh, then launched into his own story.

"I grew up in the orphanage in Chalk Bluff, 'n met you two in the first grade. Mister Verdo Willis was the orphanage manager. One of the nicest men I've ever known. Excludin' present company, of course."

He nodded to the other two, who nodded back to acknowledge the compliment.

"Mister Verdo, he believed in hard work. And we worked hard, on local farms mostly, hoeing corn and picking cotton in the summer and fall. We worked chores year-round."

He nodded, absently shifting his fork on the pie plate.

"Farm work was hard work. Most nights we came in after dark, ate supper, and went right to bed. In the summertime, we got up before sunup and started again. New day, old routine. But on the days the weather turned rainy and we couldn't work on the farms, those were days of doing chores around the orphanage, and *they* were the days for music lessons. Mister Willis gave 'em to anyone interested. I was always first in line." He chuckled and shook his head slowly. "Oh, the patience that man possessed."

The rain pounded the diner's metal roof. Leeroy's eyes grew distant. "Love the rain. Always have."

Laverne managed to get his last bite of pie onto a fork, a large piece of outer crust. He quietly relished that last bite for a moment, giving Leeroy's story proper respectful silence before beginning his own tale.

"Neither of my parents could play a musical instrument, at least not to my knowledge. Never saw them play. In all honesty, I don't know if Pa could even play a radio if he'd had one. He had no rhythm atall that I ever saw. I don't remember ever having any musical instrument in the house. Or much of anything else, either."

He shook his head. "Well, let me correct that. We never had a musical instrument until our neighbor—old man Broderick, Mister Isaiah Broderick—died, and his wife, what was her name?" He thought a moment. "Amelia. Her first name was Amelia. Miz Amelia Broderick brought her husband's guitar to me—scratched and missin' three strings, but still sound."

Laverne licked a forefinger and pressed it to the leftover pie crumbs in his plate, then cleaned the forefinger in his mouth.

"I never saw Mister Broderick play," he said. "I don't know if he *could* play. She gave the guitar to me. I took it, not knowing what I would do with the thing. She cried and asked me to never sell it."

"You still have that guitar," Lester said, as much question as statement.

"I do," Laverne said, "but I don't play it on the streets anymore 'cause it's too valuable. Sentimental value, that is. Wasn't worth a dime when Miz Broderick gave the ol' beat-up thing to me. It's worth less now, but I still own it. Never sold it. I owe that much to Miz Amelia and Mister Isaiah. Plus the guitar is the last thing I own connecting me to my Chalk Bluff family. Still scratched, but with all six strings now and a pleasant sound. Easy to play. I taught myself to play that guitar, all by ear, since I couldn't read music. Still can't. Might as well be tryin' to read Hebrew as to read music."

"You did a great job teaching yourself too," Leeroy said, as serious as a cardiac arrest.

Laverne objected. "Oh, no. I *strum* a guitar. But Anthony—now Anthony was a *guitarist*. A great guitarist."

The three turned to their memories of Anthony.

CHAPTER THREE

Anthony Emery was the only formally trained musician in the Noirs. In fact, Anthony was a college graduate, educated in music—rare for those days.

By contrast, neither Lester, Leeroy, nor Laverne ever graduated from high school. In addition to not being able to read music, Laverne couldn't read, period. Lester and Leeroy were literate, barely. Lester and Leeroy could do a little math, although Leeroy's skills outshone Lester's.

In 1910, sixteen-year-old Lester Washington, Laverne Knox, and Leeroy Edwards left Chalk Bluff, Alabama, on foot. They packed their meager possessions in flour sacks Laverne had managed to acquire. Laverne tied a piece of cord around his guitar and slung it across his back along with his flour sack.

They had no reason to stay.

Outside the diner, the rain had let up a little. The waitress came and refilled cups. Lester took a long, thoughtful swig from his cup before speaking.

"Ma 'n Pa's accident happened two weeks before we left Alabama." He paused, then continued. "Ten years back, I remember Pa was *so* excited when he told Ma about his new job. 'Makin' eighteen cents an hour,' he told Ma. 'Not as much as other people are makin', but a good wage.'"

Lester took a handkerchief from his pocket and wiped his eyes. "A few weeks after that, Ma interviewed at the same job site. She cried when the foreman hired her at sixteen cents an hour. With a combined wage of thirty-four cents an hour—why, they were on their way to achieving the American dream. They had money to buy food, pay bills, and save a little at the end of each month."

He took a deep breath. "Combined, they worked over a hundred hours a week. But they were in love. They had a son they adored. I heard 'em around the supper table, just laughin' and a-talkin' about savin' enough money for a down payment on a house."

He continued to wipe his eyes. No embarrassment. The three were family. Lester went on, both hands now clasped around his cup.

"Seventeen people died in that industrial accident, I was told. Includin' George and Roberta Washington." He was silent for a long minute, his head bowed.

"I sold the piano, along with everything else Pa and Ma owned. With those few dollars stuffed in the bib of my overalls, I started walkin' ... with you two fine gentlemen."

They nodded sagely, agreeing, commiserating. Leeroy nodded at Laverne.

"Tell us again about your momma and daddy."

Laverne Knox tipped his head in acquiescence and related the story Leeroy and Lester knew well.

"Pa died of drink—alcoholism, they call it now. I can remember only a few times when he wasn't either drinkin' or drunk or both. Drank up most of our money. Would've drunk up all of it, if Ma hadn't gone through his pockets from time to time and taken a few coins. Never took all his money, oh no. Pa would've known. A few pennies here, a nickel there."

Laverne wiped his mouth with a napkin. "You've heard of nasty drunks? Not Pa. Not Emerson Knox. He cried when he was drunk, out of shame, I s'pect. I don't hate Pa because he drank. He was sick—plain and simple. He couldn't stop drinkin' anymore than he could stop being a Black man, and the drinkin' killed him."

They all sat silent for a moment, shaking their heads, sharing the misery, until Laverne resumed his story.

"Then stress took Ma—took her mind at least. She was living in an asylum in Chalk Bluff. The last three times I visited her, she sat and stared out the window. 'Come inside, Emerson,' she said when I came in the room. I'm not Emerson, Momma. It's Laverne, your son. I'm Laverne, I would say. 'Glad to see you, Emerson,' she would say. 'Come sit beside me.'"

Laverne reached for the napkin again. He didn't own a handkerchief. A tear dripped off his cheek onto the tablecloth. It was unfair how such emotions could be this raw after all these years.

"It's Laverne, Ma. Pa ain't here. 'Oh, how I missed you, Emerson. How was work today? Is Mister Sanders well? Tell him I want to see him. I know he's holdin' my job. God bless 'im. How is Estelle and Truman?' Mister Sanders was Pa and Ma's bossman. I never knew who Estelle and Truman were—coworkers, maybe." Laverne's head dropped, and he gazed at the tabletop. "Ma never recognized me again. Never called me by my name. I couldn't bear the situation any longer. I'm ashamed now for leaving her, but I couldn't bear it. I started walking as well."

After a few minutes, Leeroy spoke.

"You both knew your parents, but I don't remember mine, nor any family for that matter. An orphanage is all I knew—all I can remember. The workers weren't bad people, but the orphanage was never what you'd call home. There was never enough to eat, and the place was always cold." They continued to think—and talk—about their life journey.

In 1910, the three young boys had little in common other than the color of their skin and poverty. They had one more commonality— the desire to get out of Chalk Bluff, Alabama.

As prearranged at school, Leeroy met Laverne and Lester under a large oak tree at the county courthouse in Chalk Bluff's city center, on a Monday morning at seven thirty.

A decision was made.

"Which way are we going?" asked Laverne.

"Yeah, Leeroy, which way we goin' to go?" asked Lester.

Leeroy bent and picked a few blades of grass, then tossed them into the air. A gentle breeze blew the blades southwest.

Leeroy pointed. "That direction. We go that way."

The three headed out, walking southwest.

"When we left Chalk Bluff, how much money did you have, Lester?" Laverne asked.

Carol the waitress filled their coffee cups and continued to smile. She didn't care if they sat in the booth all day.

Lester's response was immediate. "I had twenty-three dollars and a quarter. Most came from the sale of Ma's big chifforobe. I got twenty dollars for it—in fact, a twenty-dollar bill. The thing was made of walnut, I was told, made by Johnny Randall Elliott. Folks said he was a recognized furniture maker. The piece was nice, but I couldn't carry it, so I sold it. I cried when the new owner moved it. Ma loved that piece of furniture—it was the nicest thing we ever owned."

Lester made eye contact with Laverne. "Laverne, how much money did you have?"

"I had six dollars and a few pennies and maybe a nickel or two. Momma kept the money hidden in a cookie jar. Our emergency fund, she called it. I believed I was in an emergency, and I knew she'd never spend it."

Laverne knew the answer to his question before he asked, but he wanted to mess with Leeroy on this fine morning.

"What financial investment did you bring to our new adventure that long-ago day, *Mister* Leeroy Edwards?"

Leeroy knew the question was coming. He didn't mind Laverne asking. Unembarrassed, he smiled broadly, his perfectly-aligned white teeth accentuated by his Black skin.

"Well, *Mister* Knox, if you are asking how much money I had on that blessed day, I too know *exactly* how much money I had."

Leeroy paused for effect. Lester and Laverne waited with stoic expressions. They knew the answer.

Leeroy flung his arms wide and said, "I didn't have a *dime*."

Lester and Laverne laughed loudly. Leeroy smiled. "Not a dime. Not a nickel. Not a penny. Not even an Alabama State Fair token."

"We knew as much," Lester said.

"Heck, I stole a pair of shoes from the orphanage, or I woulda been barefooted." A pause before Leeroy continued. "But who became the *money man* of this business?"

"Can't deny that. You managed us well, long as we had money. When the money dried up, that was another matter. But that wasn't your fault," Laverne said.

"I agree," Lester said. "You became our money man and managed us well."

Another pause.

"We can blame Mister Sarcoidosis for the sad situation in which we find ourselves," Lester said, and dropped his head.

For years, Anthony had been instrumental in keeping the Noirs gainfully employed. But seven years earlier, in 1960, Anthony Emery died from sarcoidosis. With Anthony on their minds, a more somber tone enveloped them.

"So what do we do now?" Lester asked.

"At seventy-three years young and with no prospects, it appears to me we gonna sit around till we die," Laverne said. "Of something other than starvation or cold, I hope."

"No, *sir*. Not me, and not us. Not the Noirs," Leeroy declared.

"You got a suggestion?" Laverne asked.

"I *do* have a suggestion. We continue to do what we've always done. All we've ever known. We make music. We entertain people, and we get paid to do it. Maybe we won't or can't make the money we've made in the past, but we don't quit. We don't give up. Not us," Leeroy said.

"We've lost the magic, Leeroy," Lester lamented. "The magic disappeared with Anthony."

"You didn't let me finish. Not only do I have a *suggestion*, I've got a *plan*," Leeroy said.

"We're listening," Laverne said.

"Simple. We find another lead guitarist," Leeroy said.

Lester and Laverne laughed aloud.

"Simple?! Nobody gonna want to play with three old broke-down men," Lester said.

"That's the truth if the truth was ever spoken," Laverne added.

"You two might be right, but I want to try one more time. Maybe for the last time," Leeroy said. "I checked in the *Times-Picayune* newspaper. I—we—can take out an ad for five days. Won't cost much money. I'll drive Hazel to the newspaper office on Howard Street and place the ad. I've already written it. You boys want to give a listen?"

"We're listenin'," Lester said, his tone dour.

Leeroy pulled a piece of paper from his shirt pocket and began reading. In actuality, it was more of a recitation from memory of the ad his wife had helped write.

"Wanted." Leeroy harrumphed, cleared his throat, and flapped the paper. "Lead guitarist for local gigs. Apply in person, Tuesday through Saturday, 8 till 5, 25 North Galvez Street."

Leeroy paused to allow Lester and Laverne to consider his proposal. When they didn't reject his idea outright, he said, "What do we have to lose, other than the cost of the ad?"

"Nothin', I reckon," Laverne responded.

"Hazel and I, we'll go to the newspaper office on Monday. The ad will start running on Tuesday. You both know what that means?"

"Lester and I will have to be at yo' house Tuesday through Saturday, eight 'til five. *In case* a fine lead guitarist shows up and wants to audition. That what you sayin'?"

"That's correct."

A few minutes later, Laverne looked at the clock on the diner wall. The place began filling.

"Five thirty-five, men," he said. "Let's take our seventy-four dollars and twenty-six cents and go home."

The men agreed.

Leeroy paid for the coffee.

Lester, believing they owed Carol more than their appreciation, did something he felt duty demanded. He left a tip. Meager, but more than he could afford. All three men waved to her as they exited. She smiled and returned the wave.

"Y'all come back," she yelled across the now noisy establishment.

The men waved again.

They got into Hazel and headed home.

CHAPTER FOUR

Laverne and Lester lived together in a rented two-room flat above a gas station on Franklin Avenue. In addition to the two small bedrooms, the flat had a small bathroom with a washing machine. Leeroy dropped them off and turned toward home. He knew his wife, Mildred, would be off to church soon.

Leeroy got home, sat beside his wife on their sofa, pecked her on the cheek, and answered Mildred's question before she got the chance to ask.

"Seventy-four dollars and twenty-six cents."

"Well, that's seventy-four dollars and twenty-six cents more than you had when you left," she said, always the encourager and optimist.

"Minus thirty cents for three cups of coffee," Leeroy said, and smiled.

"You are one of the last of the big spenders, Leeroy Edwards."

They both laughed.

"You are right, my love." He held her hand. "And a nice waitress named Carol gave us each a slice of apple pie. Stale, she claimed. Made yesterday, she claimed. Wasn't nothin' stale about *that* pie."

"Jesus looks after his children."

After a few more minutes of conversation, they both knew what they needed to do. Leeroy collapsed onto their bed, exhausted. Mildred went to worship.

Leeroy and Hazel went to the *Times-Picayune* office the following day.

CHAPTER FIVE

Tuesday morning at six thirty, Leeroy, Laverne, and Lester were on their way to 25 North Galvez, to Leeroy's multipurpose carport. At various times, the structure served as a garage, a storage unit, a music rehearsal room, and years ago, a community gathering place, when they could afford to have the community gather there for music and food.

Now the three sat in the garage in lawn chairs, waiting for the first "fine" guitarist to arrive and audition. As they waited, they talked again about their past.

"What year did we come to New Orleans?" Lester asked.

"Nineteen ten," Laverne answered. "I remember all too well."

Upon their arrival in New Orleans, the trio purchased a used bass guitar for Leeroy for a few dollars. Along with Laverne's guitar, the men played and sang on the streets of New Orleans for what little change donors would toss in Leeroy's old hat. They'd slept on the streets, in business entryways, on the docks, and in parks during the summer. In the wintertime, they slept in men's shelters on Camp and Baronne Streets, if they could get inside. They had a few dollars to buy food. They also ate in soup kitchens and churches.

"I remember the first time you asked me if you could borrow my hat," Leeroy said to Lester. "When I asked why, you said, 'yes or no?' You were kinda short-answerin', as I recall."

"Was I? Don't remember that," Lester offered in his own defense.

"I loaned you my hat," Leeroy said, "on a Monday night. A rainy, cold Monday night when we all decided to stay put somewhere. I can't remember exactly where we were, underneath a bridge maybe, but I remember the three of us didn't play. I remember my head got cold before you got back."

"We were huddled up under one of the docks," Lester said, clarifying Leeroy's recollection. "Not a bridge. I remember. Nothing but a piece of cardboard between us and a long, wet, cold night. I took your hat and went to Decatur Street. I'd seen a piano in a bar there a few days before. I didn't see anybody playin' it. I asked the manager if I could play. He said, 'Depends.' He asked me if I *could* play. I knew what he meant. He meant did I play well or was I gonna hunt and peck a few notes. I sat down and played him something Ma taught me. I showed off, I tell you. I knew my performance was my chance, *our chance*.

"After a few minutes he said, 'You can *play* all right. You can play Monday nights, but no wages from me. I ain't gonna pay you nothin',' he said. 'Understand? Tips, but whatever tips you make is yours. A hundred percent.' I took yo' hat and put that nasty thing on the piano at eight o'clock and started playin'. Several people stopped to listen. You can't show off if you ain't got no audience, after all."

"I remember the time was after midnight but I don't remember my hat being nasty," Leeroy said, "but I do remember when you returned that 'nasty thing' you were, unfortunately, under it."

Lester smiled at the jab.

Laverne reared back in his lawn chair, stretching. "I remember the time bein' after *three*. I don't remember sleeping a wink the entire night. Cold, wet, and windy—I can still hear that wind howl. All in all a miserable night," Laverne said. "Lester, you were grinnin' like a possum because you had a pocket *full* of money."

Lester cupped his hands. "Nickels and dimes mostly. A quarter or two, and a single one-dollar bill." He laughed aloud. "I handed the money to Leeroy. In the early morning, with enough light from the street, you counted her out. Over five dollars."

"Breakfast, Lester, as I recall, was your idea," Leeroy said.

"I remember that," Lester said. "Ate biscuits and eggs with ham and gravy and drank a pot of coffee each. First hot, filling meal the three of us had in weeks. I also remember the next Monday night—again, cold, windy, and rainin'. I asked you if I could borrow the hat again. You never said a word. You smiled and said, 'please do.' I came back with another pocket of money, near seven dollars this time."

On Tuesday, Lester, Laverne, and Leeroy ate sandwiches Mildred prepared. Another cheese sandwich, Lester thought, but he would never have whispered a protest, even if it meant his life. He nodded his appreciation to Mildred as he took a sandwich. At five thirty, Leeroy drove Laverne and Lester home to Franklin Avenue without a single audition.

CHAPTER SIX

The following morning, with the three seated in lawn chairs in Leeroy's garage, Lester waxed nostalgic again.

"In nineteen twelve, at the bar where I played piano, that was where I first met Anthony. Anthony Emery. Anthony *Masters* Emery. I'd seen him in the place a few times, but we'd never spoke. He came to me as I was finishin' up and asked if he could buy me a beer. A beer, I thought. I hadn't drank a beer in years. I smelled beer every Monday night but never bought one. Sure, I told him, I'll have a beer with you. I would've given Leeroy's hat for a beer."

"Watch it," Leeroy said.

"Anthony and I talked about the weather," Lester said. "I could've told him I knew a thing or two about the weather, 'bout us living out *in* the weather, but I said nothin'. He told me he was born, raised, and lived in New Orleans. Metairie, actually. I knew from the way he talked and dressed he was well-to-do. Didn't look wealthy, but I doubt he'd ever slept on the streets or in a men's shelter. Much better off than the three of us."

Leeroy saw a car pull into his driveway.

"Could this be our first candidate?" Laverne asked.

The three eased forward in their lawn chairs. The driver backed the car into the street and drove away in the opposite direction.

"Nope. That was not our first candidate," Leeroy answered.

None of them seemed disappointed. They relaxed again in their chairs.

"Anthony told me he played guitar," Lester said, "and asked me if I wanted to play with him. You know I didn't take long makin' that decision. I said on one condition. I've two acquaintances. Notice I didn't call you boys *friends*."

Laverne and Leeroy smiled as Lester continued. "One guitarist and one bass. I told Anthony I'd *consider* playing with him if they could play too. He thought for a moment and asked, 'Do they play like you play?' Better, I said. As you two know, I lied."

Laughter from the other two this time.

"'I want to meet them,' Anthony said. 'Where are they now?' Do y'all remember where you were when we all met?"

Leeroy answered. "We were in the men's shelter on Camp Street. You brought Anthony there. Or actually Anthony brought you. He had a guitar in the trunk of his car. I had my bass, luggin' that thing around like an albatross. Laverne had a guitar. At three a.m., you woke us and we all stood on the sidewalk on Camp Street and played. Anthony started singing and we all sang. He told us he thought he could find us work, and he did."

"He did find work. Approaching fifty years, from nineteen twelve to nineteen fifty-eight, he found us work," Laverne added.

"Until he was diagnosed in '58," Lester said with a tone of unmistakable sadness.

"Sarcoidosis," Leeroy said. "I hadn't heard that word before."

"I hate that word," Lester said.

"I never want to hear that word again," Leeroy said. The other two nodded their heads in agreement.

At six that evening, Leeroy drove Lester and Laverne to Franklin Avenue. A second day, unsuccessful, in search of a guitarist.

CHAPTER SEVEN

The routine continued Thursday and Friday. Mildred made sandwiches—cheese or peanut butter. She added jelly with the peanut butter at times.

On the way home on Friday afternoon, Lester said, "We've wasted the last four days. Wasted our time and wasted your money, Leeroy. Not a single audition."

"We're kidding ourselves. Nobody's interested in playing with three old has-beens," Laverne added.

"Nobody knows we're has-beens," Leeroy answered. "Remember the ad? Nothing about us being three old past-our-prime musicians."

"People sense it. They sense desperation," Laverne said.

"*Who's* desperate?" Lester asked.

"*We're* desperate," Leeroy answered.

"Oh," said Lester, "I guess you're right. We *are* desperate, aren't we?"

"I believe I'll stay home tomorrow," Laverne said. "No sense in wasting a good Saturday sitting around in Leeroy's garage like three old idiots."

"No sir, you *won't*," Leeroy injected. "The ad said auditions Tuesday through Saturday. Tomorrow is Saturday. I'll pick you up at six thirty. *Both* of you."

"We haven't had a single person to audition," Laverne objected.

"Six. Thirty."

Leeroy was adamant. Lester and Laverne heard the determination in Leeroy's voice. Neither offered any more resistance.

After one o'clock on Saturday afternoon, Leeroy, Laverne, and Lester sat in the lawn chairs in Leeroy's garage, finishing their peanut-butter-no-jelly sandwiches. They drank water. They waited for five o'clock and the end of the audition week. Desperation and grim reality loomed over the trio like a dark cloud.

The young man was halfway up the driveway before they noticed him. He was carrying a case of some kind.

"Oh my," Lester said, sitting up in his lawn chair. "Look at this comin' here."

"You don't suppose he's come to audition? If so ..." Leeroy's words trailed off.

"That's one big White man," Laverne said.

"You mean that's one big White *boy*," Leeroy corrected. "Looks to be 'bout sixteen years old. He's just a kid."

Within moments, the "kid" stood before them. He was tall, standing over six feet four inches, and looked to weigh a bit over two hundred pounds, Lester guessed. His shoulders were broad and his waist narrow. He had the look of a person of confidence. His walk exuded it.

He wore clean blue jeans and a blue button-down shirt. His shoes were penny loafers, well worn but having the sheen of recent polish. Everything about him spoke of neatness. His shirt was tucked in his pants. His sandy blond hair was cut and combed. He was clean-shaven, assuming he was old enough to shave. His blue eyes sparked with intelligence and wit.

"Is this the audition site?"

"It is," Leeroy answered, offering no other words. He thought the White kid might simply leave.

"I found your ad in a newspaper in the parking lot where I work. Almost tossed it in the trash." The kid smiled.

"Aren't we glad that didn't happen," Leeroy said, with the faintest edge of sarcasm.

Lester couldn't help but notice the boy's hands. They were large, with the appearance of strength and the wear of hard work. A deep scar stretched across the knuckles of his right hand.

If this kid's come to audition, he can't play a guitar with those big hands, Lester thought.

The young man carried what appeared, in a previous life at least, to have been a guitar case. He set the case down and opened the lid. He removed a guitar—more rectangular box than anything else, with a rod protruding from one side which happened to have strings. The finish on the surface was faded and scratched. One tuner was broken to the point Laverne wondered if it was usable. The boy stood erect, smiled broadly, and spoke clearly.

"I'm Jake Thomas. I read you're looking for a guitarist."

Lester gave his best look of condescension as he looked over his glasses at the White boy. Laverne spoke for the trio. "Yes, we're looking for a guitarist, but I don't b'lieve you're what we're looking for."

Leeroy attempted to communicate the group's sentiments while the stranger searched the garage with his eyes. In seconds, he set the guitar aside and reached for another lawn chair, this one minus a few of the plastic strips from the bottom and back. Leeroy hoped the chair would not collapse. The three men watched for a moment in silence.

Leeroy said, "Young man, we don't mean to be rude, but the three of us are *musicians*. Has-beens, maybe, and beyond our prime, no doubt, but still musicians. I play the bass, Laverne there plays guitar, and Lester here is our pianist."

All three watched the stranger as he sat in the lawn chair in the middle of the garage. Leeroy continued. "We are known as the Noirs. Do you know what 'Noirs' means?"

The stranger momentarily retreated to retrieve his guitar. "It's French for black," he said, never looking up.

The White boy made his way back to the lawn chair and sat down, the old worn out guitar held in his large hands. He tuned his "instrument." The broken tuner worked, Laverne noted.

"That's right. We are the Noirs, the 'blacks.' Now, if you were to join us we would no longer be the 'blacks,' don't you see? No, you aren't what we're looking for, I s'pect. Again, no disrespect."

"None taken," the boy said. He continued to tune, tilting his head slightly to hear the tones.

Leeroy said, "If you were to join us, we would be what? Three Noirs and a Blanc?"

All three men roared. The stranger continued tuning, head cocked to to his left side.

"Do you know what 'Blanc' means, young man?" Leeroy asked.

"It's French for white," the boy said. He paused, flicking a string, and listening for the correct pitch. "So if I join your group we become Three Noirs and a Blanc, right?"

"That won't work. Will it, Lester?" Leeroy asked.

"Impossible. Won't work," answered Lester. "Laverne?"

"Agree, won't work," Laverne responded. "You need to keep looking for a band and we need to keep looking for a guitarist."

The boy took a deep breath, closed his eyes, waited for the space of a heartbeat, and began to play.

Leeroy, Laverne, and Lester leaned back in their lawn chairs and listened. Lester looked at Laverne and Leeroy, and the three nodded at one another.

The boy continued, one song blending into the next. The Noirs were mesmerized. No one spoke. The kid's fingers glided across the fret board, and his large hands moved effortlessly up and down the neck. He moved from song to song, from genre to genre, but the sound was the same—pure magic, from that funky old worn-out excuse for a guitar.

CHAPTER EIGHT

Lester, Leeroy, and Laverne hadn't seen Jake's kind of talent since they first met Anthony Masters Emery, approaching fifty years ago.

Laverne got up and walked to the rear of the garage. There, in a case, was his most prized possession, a Gibson guitar. He wanted to sell the guitar, but the other two had opposed it, knowing what the instrument meant to him. He took the guitar, walked to the stranger, and flashed him his friendliest smile. "Why don't you try this one ... please?"

The stranger set aside his excuse-for-a-guitar and took up the Gibson. For the next ten minutes, what came from the Gibson was solid gold. He played snippets of gospel, rhythm and blues, and jazz. Not a piece of sheet music. All from memory, all superb.

Several times, one of the men made a specific request. With one exception, he knew all the songs and played them. On the one occasion, when he didn't know the song, he asked Lester to hum a few bars. Lester did so. The boy then played the notes Lester hummed. The men couldn't hide the fact—they were impressed.

The boy ceased playing. Lester leaned forward in his lawn chair and asked a question, with no trace of his previous condescension. "What'd you say your name is?"

"Jacob Thomas. Jacob Alvin Thomas. Most people call me Jake."

"How old are you?" Leeroy blurted. "Are you out of school?"

Jake nodded. "I'm out of school."

"My name is Leeroy. Leeroy Edwards." Leeroy pointed and continued. "This is Laverne Knox, and that man is Lester Washington."

Laverne and Lester nodded at Jake.

"Three L's," Jake said.

"That's us. At one time, we even considered calling ourselves the Three L's," Leeroy said. "We're looking for a guitar player, and you're more than a guitar player. You're a *guitarist*."

"That's for sure," Laverne confirmed. Lester nodded in agreement.

"Our lives would be easier if you were Black though," Laverne said. "We weren't expecting no White man. No White kid in fact. No offense."

"None taken," Jake said.

"Nobody gonna mistake him for no Black man, that's for sure," Leeroy said. The three men laughed.

"Maybe a little black shoe polish," Lester said, making a swirling motion on his forehead.

"Maybe a *bunch* of black shoe polish," Laverne said, making the same swirling motion on his forehead. "That's one tall White boy."

Jake was not to be outdone. "Perhaps the three of you could become White," he said and smiled. "That might help. A little white shoe polish, perhaps." Jake made a swirling motion on his forehead and flashed a teasing million-dollar smile.

The three men roared with laughter.

"A sense of humor," Lester said. "I love it."

Jake grew serious. "If you offer me a job, I'll play any day except Sunday. I'll play any night except Sunday night. I don't work on Sunday, day or night."

"Well, that's going to be a problem," Lester said. "Because we play any opportunity we get, Sundays and Sunday nights included."

"Not me," Jake said. "I don't play Sun-*days* or Sunday *nights*."

With that Jake rose, handed Laverne the Gibson, and returned his guitar to his case.

"Well, thank you and best of luck to you." He picked up the case and headed away down the driveway.

"Wait a minute. We're done?" Leeroy asked. "Playing on Sunday and Sunday nights is a dealbreaker?"

"For me, yes. I don't do gigs on Sunday or Sunday nights. I'm Christian. I *worship* Jesus on Sunday and Sunday nights. I don't *work*."

With a tip of an imaginary hat, Jake walked away.

CHAPTER NINE

"Whoa, whoa. Hold up," Leeroy said.

Jake stopped and turned but didn't return to the lawn chair.

All three men looked at each other, considering carefully. They all were willing to admit the obvious. This tall White stranger might be their last hope of dying of something other than the winter's cold. He could be their last chance of dying somewhere other than on the streets or in a men's shelter. He might be their last attempt to avoid homelessness and hunger. Lester and Laverne had no one else to consider but themselves, but Leeroy had Mildred.

Leeroy spoke for the trio.

"All right. Done. No Sunday or Sunday night gigs."

"Heck," Laverne said, "we've had precious few gigs of any kind since Anthony died, and none on Sunday or Sunday night."

Jake didn't know who Anthony was and said nothing. He returned to the lawn chair, sat, and spoke.

"We cut our income four ways? Each man gets twenty-five percent? Agreed?"

"Agreed, minus money for Hazel," Lester answered.

"Who is Hazel?" Jake asked. "Your—excuse me, our—business manager?"

Laverne pointed to the car parked in the other bay. "That's Hazel—our transportation." He continued. "We cut our income four ways, minus gas money for Leeroy. For Hazel."

"That's fair," Jake said.

"Hopefully, we will make more than seventy-four dollars and twenty-six cents each," Laverne said, more to himself than anyone else.

"When do we start?" Jake asked, confused over the seventy-four dollars and twenty-six cents comment. "When's our first gig?"

"Actually," Leeroy admitted, "to date, we don't have a gig."

"No gigs?" Jake asked, raising his eyebrows.

"No gigs," Lester confirmed.

The three men thought that too would be a dealbreaker. They waited to see Jake's reaction, but he showed none. And he didn't leave.

"We thought we would play the streets," Leeroy said. "Maybe get a place on Friday, Saturday, or Sunday night off Jackson Square—or somewhere in or around the Quarter."

Jake raised his hand. Leeroy recognized his error and said hastily, "My apology, no Sunday or Sunday nights. Friday or Saturday nights. We believe we'll make a few dollars in tips, working a couple of nights a week. We've made more in the past, but the past is the past."

The men waited for the boy to respond. Leeroy thought this time he'd leave for sure.

"I don't mind the streets," Jake said. "Wouldn't be the first time for me playing there." He smiled. "Are you sure you old gentlemen will manage? I wouldn't want to keep you out too late."

"Ah, that sense of humor again," Leeroy said.

"The kid talks smack," Lester added.

"Now, Blanc, we will see how you manage when you are surrounded by three old musicians," Leeroy said.

"How did you get here, by the way?" Laverne asked.

"My car is parked around the corner."

"Where do you live?" Lester asked.

Jake paused briefly before replying. "Off Chef Menteur Highway."

The boy shook hands with the three men and exited the garage. Plans had been made.

Their desperation fading, the three Noirs watched as the White boy strolled out of sight.

CHAPTER TEN

For the next month, three times a week but never on Sundays, the four men met in Leeroy's garage/practice studio and played their music.

At the first session, the men saw Jake's car as he pulled into Leeroy's driveway.

"That a car or a boat?" Leeroy asked.

Laverne gave a low whistle. "Look at the *length* of that thang."

Jake's car was an Oldsmobile. An *old* Oldsmobile. Any identifying markers beyond "Oldsmobile" on the hood had been lost. Four long doors, with a sweeping hood and a stretch rear end. Leeroy's assessment was correct. The vehicle was long enough to be a boat.

The car appeared to have been blue once, but the hot sun in the New Orleans summers had faded the paint to a pallid gray. The tires were slick. The auto lacked hubcaps—at least, the men could see no hubcaps on their side. The window glass was missing from the automobile's left rear door, replaced by a piece of plywood over the opening. The left rear quarter panel was smashed. Albeit clean, Jake's car looked worse than Hazel.

Lester looked inside and saw the back floorboard littered with clothes.

"My, my," Lester said, "do you live in this thing?"

Jake laughed and responded, "I live off Chef Menteur, remember?"

"Oh, yes. Chef," Lester replied.

Practice began.

At noon, Mildred came with a plate of sandwiches. Cheese sandwiches. Leeroy said nothing as Mildred offered food.

"Leeroy, where are your manners? Introduce me," she said.

"Sorry, my love," Leeroy answered. "Blanc, this is my wife Mildred. My love, this is Blanc."

Mildred smiled and reached out her right hand to Jake, who stepped forward and reciprocated both the smile and the hand. "Forgive my husband," she said. "He's a bear sometimes, believe you me."

Leeroy growled. "Bear's my middle name. Leeroy 'Bear' Edwards."

Jake doubted Mildred ever tolerated Leeroy being a bear for long.

"What's your name?" Mildred asked.

"His name is Jake," Lester said.

"Jacob Alvin Thomas. Known as Jake to most," Laverne added.

"Hello, Jake. I'm sure we'll be good friends. Have a sandwich." Mildred extended the plate toward him, and Jake took one.

"Thank you," he said, "and I don't envy you living with Leeroy."

Mildred's smiled broadened as she turned to go back to the house.

"That smack again," Leeroy said. "Gonna get you in trouble one day, Blanc."

"Prob'ly so," Jake responded. "Prob'ly so."

CHAPTER ELEVEN

A month later, after their final practice for the week, Leeroy judged it was time.

"I think we're ready to go. We'll hit the street on Saturday night and see what the gods have in store." Sudden remorse hit him as he realized his irreverence. "Sorry, Blanc."

The following Saturday night at six o'clock, Leeroy picked up Lester and Laverne in Hazel. They arrived at Leeroy's garage to find Jake seated in a lawn chair. Jake put his guitar in Hazel's trunk alongside Laverne's guitar and Leeroy's bass. Lester got in the front seat with Leeroy. Laverne and Jake got in the back.

"Is the plan to set up around Jackson Square?" asked Leeroy.

"Yeah, sounds good," Lester responded. Laverne and Jake nodded approval.

Within thirty minutes, Leeroy parked Hazel off Esplanade Avenue. The four walked the few blocks to Jackson Square. Lester carried a small folding table and a canvas bag containing plastic bottles of water, while the others carried their instruments. The bottles had no labels, having been repeatedly refilled.

Jackson Square at seven thirty in the evening was a beehive of activity. All the areas in front of St. Charles Cathedral were taken, as were the areas on St. Ann Street.

"How 'bout St. Peter Street?" Lester suggested.

The group found an open spot on St. Peter, near Decatur. There was nothing more to do than swing guitars into place. Lester set up the table. Leeroy doffed his hat and placed it on the table.

"Let's see if we draw a crowd," Lester said.

"And make some money," Laverne added.

"And make some money," Lester echoed and smiled.

Jake waited for someone to announce their first number. No one said a word. Laverne began playing, Lester hummed, Leeroy added the bass, and Lester began to sing.

Jake caught up. The men played and sang songs they'd not practiced together, songs the three older men played out of habit. Jake followed Laverne's lead and contributed to the vocals whenever he knew the words.

The passion of his fellow musicians impressed Jake— passion that outshone their considerable talents. Laverne's seventy-three-year-old fingers raced across the frets with ease as he hunched over the Gibson and played. Leeroy, by contrast, played his bass guitar standing upright, often bowing his back backward when the mood struck.

Leeroy caught Jake's eye and smiled between words. Lester closed his eyes as he sang. The three Noirs were in their element, comfortable with one another. They were uncomfortable with other things sometimes, but never with one another, and never with their music.

After a few songs, Jake noticed a woman stop a few feet from the group. She stood still a few moments, listening, her eyes closed. Slowly, slowly, she began to sway, and within minutes she began dancing. A few more patrons gathered, maybe a half dozen at first. Soon a man emerged from the crowd and began dancing as well. The woman moved closer to the man and they danced together, complete strangers. The man took the woman's hand and spun her around. Then several people joined the duo. Jake saw another woman drop coins into Leeroy's hat—the first return on their investment.

Saturday night.

Three Noirs and a Blanc. Three guitars—two acoustics and a bass.

Jackson Square, New Orleans, Louisiana.

Laissez les bon temps rouler!

"Let the good times roll," Laverne said above the music.

After several songs, Jake realized how the night would go. As one song ended, he took the initiative and began playing and singing.

"Amazing grace ..."

Lester joined in, as did Leeroy and Laverne. In school, at home, and in the orphanage, the three men had grown up on those old gospel songs.

> *Amazing grace— how sweet the sound—*
>   *that saved a wretch like me!*
> *I once was lost, but now I'm found,*
>   *Was blind, but now I see.*

On a Saturday night in New Orleans, the four men continued, almost oblivious to the listening crowd.

> *Through many dangers, toils, and snares*
>   *I have already come;*
> *'Tis grace hath brought me safe thus far,*
>   *And grace will lead me home.*

As Jake began the final stanza, he stopped playing and simply sang. Laverne and Leeroy followed his lead, and Lester joined them to huddle in the middle. They rested their hands on Jake's shoulders, leaned in, harmonizing *a cappella*, all four perfectly on key.

> When we've been there ten thousand years,
> *Bright shining as the sun,*
> *We've no less days to sing God's praise*
> *Than when we first begun.*

The tears in Leeroy's eyes gleamed in the lamplight.

The group of listeners began to grow. Music could be heard from other individuals and groups playing on St. Peter, at the St. Louis Cathedral steps, and on St. Ann Street. But from that one particular spot on St. Peter, the thing that drew people close was the voices of four men. The music they made was special. Magical.

When the group finished there was absolute silence, until someone in the crowd began clapping. A chain reaction began, and thunderous applause was heard across Jackson Square. Andrew Jackson himself would have been proud. As too, would John Newton, who'd written the original poem from which the hymn was built, hundreds of years earlier.

A moment later Jake saw Laverne lean forward and bend his guitar's strings. Lester began to sing.

Once again, they were off and running.

"How much did we make?" Lester asked.

Leeroy, off Esplanade Avenue, leaning over Hazel's trunk at two thirty a.m., shushed him and continued to count.

"Three hundred fifty-two dollars and thirty-five cents," Leeroy finally reported. He held up a particular bill to the light for the others to see.

"Oh my, that's a fortune on the streets," Laverne said.

"*Aha*," Leeroy said. "Looky here."

"A twenty-dollar bill," remarked Lester. "I haven't seen one of those in a while. Let me hold ol' Andrew Jackson, Leeroy."

"Hold? Take an Old Hickory. Along with ..."

Leeroy tried to do the math. Lester calculated for him. "Eighty-eight dollars each."

"So," Leeroy said, continuing to count, "I owe you another sixty-eight dollars."

"Not bad for our first night," Laverne said.

"And as you said, on the street at that," Lester said.

"Right," Leeroy agreed.

The men put their instruments in Hazel's trunk and climbed in.

"You three men are more than musicians," Jake said, smiling. "I knew you could play, but y'all are more than musicians. You're *entertainers*."

Leeroy drove to Franklin Avenue. The car was abuzz with chatter.

"Three hundred and fifty-two dollars," Jake said, "is a good night."

Leeroy thought Jake spoke with a certain degree of knowledge about playing on the streets.

"Three hundred and fifty-two dollars *and* thirty-five cents," Leeroy corrected. "And that's a *great* night. We've worked nights for as little as a few bucks each."

They rode in silence for a time, until Leeroy said, "Have you played much on the streets, Blanc?"

"I've played on the streets."

"How old are you?"

"Seventeen."

"Born in 1950," Lester said.

"Born in 1950," Jake confirmed.

"Graduated high school then, I reckon? I haven't heard you mention anything about school," Laverne said.

No response from Jake.

"Pull over, Leeroy. Stop the car," Laverne requested.

Leeroy pulled Hazel off to the side. There was no traffic at three fifteen a.m.

"Graduated high school, I reckon?" Laverne said again.

Jake knew they weren't moving until he answered.

"No. I never graduated high school. I dropped out. Uninterested. Uncommitted. Uninspired. Unmotivated."

"You told us you graduated high school," Laverne said.

"No," Jake corrected. "I said I was *out* of school."

"Meaning—" Laverne started, but Jake interrupted him.

"I am ... *out* of school, Laverne," Jake said, and smiled.

"That's a mite sneaky," Lester said.

"Sneaky, yes. Untruthful, no. And I answered your question," Jake said.

"Listen, Blanc," Leeroy said. "This is none of my business, none of *our* business, I know, but take advice from an old Noir. Get back in school and get your diploma. Heck, go to college. You have the time, and you have the brains. We're too old, and I'm too dumb, but not you."

"You're not dumb, Leeroy. Neither are you, Lester and Laverne."

"You don't know us too well," Leeroy said, and laughed.

"I know you well enough to realize you aren't dumb."

Leeroy eased Hazel back onto the empty highway and spoke to Jake's reflection in the rear view mirror.

"Get your diploma, Blanc. A diploma—or diplomas—is your best insurance against ending up homeless, cold, and hungry. We all know firsthand."

Jake didn't ask how they knew firsthand, but he couldn't help speculating on what the three men knew about homelessness, cold, and hunger. He also considered what a high school diploma might mean for him and his future.

Approaching Lester and Laverne's flat, Jake said, "Then the Noirs and Blanc are off to a good start."

"A good start," Lester echoed. "Praying the Lord will prosper us."

"Praying the Lord to prosper us," Jake echoed.

Lester and Laverne exited the car. Jake thought the pair walked with a quicker step, and he saw the two exchange grins. Delaying or avoiding homelessness and poverty could change a person's demeanor, Jake thought.

Leeroy pulled Hazel into his garage.

Both he and Jake were encouraged.

"Until Saturday night?" Jake asked.

Reaching out, Leeroy shook hands with Jake, the boy's massive hand enveloping his. "'Til Saturday night ... Blanc."

Leeroy watched as Jake slung the guitar onto his back and began walking toward his old car, illuminated by the streetlights lining North Galvez. In seconds, Jake turned the auto, minus hubcaps, minus a glass in the left rear door, toward Chef Menteur Highway. He waved out the window. Leeroy returned the gesture.

Leeroy knew Mildred would be waiting.

CHAPTER TWELVE

For the next three months, every Saturday and sometimes, Friday night, the men played their music, mainly off Jackson Square. At times, when the square was crowded, they played Canal Street.

When the night concert ended, their after-show routine started. They walked to Hazel, with Laverne, Leeroy, and Jake carrying the musical instruments and Lester toting the table. Lester also was in charge of the bag containing the empty water bottles and the money for the night's work. Arriving at Hazel, Leeroy counted, divided, and distributed their donations. No one ever questioned why they didn't wait to count the money until they arrived back at the safety and secrecy of Leeroy's garage/practice room, perhaps because Leeroy always dropped Lester and Laverne off on Franklin before returning home.

"How much?" Lester asked, before being quieted by Leeroy.

In moments, Leeroy reported their windfall and informed each man what his individual haul would be. Still working off Hazel's trunk, Leeroy gave each his share.

Every night, without fail, their donations increased. They weren't wealthy, but they had enough. They could eat better than they had in months. They had enough for Laverne to pay the electric bill and not shiver in the wintertime, and for Lester to buy his medications. No one knew what Jake did with his money. That was none of their business. Leeroy took Mildred out to a restaurant, something they hadn't done in years.

"Nice five-star restaurant," Leeroy reported, a tone of braggadocio in his voice. "Mildred was impressed, I can tell you."

"What was the name of this five-star restaurant?" Laverne asked.

Leeroy stroked his stubbled chin before he spoke. "I can't remember. Off Poydras Street. Starts with an M. Marconi's? Marcella's? Mattina Bella? Doesn't sound right. It was a *nice* Scottish restaurant."

"McDonald's?" Laverne asked, attempting to be helpful.

"Yeah. McDonald's. That's it! *Real* nice place."

Laverne and Lester roared while Jake shook his head.

"I splurged and got her the cheeseburger. Mildred said no, but you just gotta live it up every once in a while, boys," Leeroy said.

Things were looking up for the Three Noirs and a Blanc.

Jake, Lester, Leeroy, and Laverne continued playing on the streets of New Orleans. They played in the heat of the summer, the mild weather of autumn in the Big Easy, and the cold of the winter. They all needed the income.

This particular Saturday night was busy around Jackson Square. People were in a festive spirit, Christmas only two weeks away.

Leeroy and his group waved at the men and women who were set up around the square—groups playing music, jugglers with bowling pins and other items, tarot card readers, and painters. Theirs was a fraternity and sorority of men and women who respected one another—all attempting to make a few bucks. In addition to these honest men and women, hustlers, shysters, thugs, petty thieves, and bandits were in attendance, ubiquitous in the Quarter at any time but always present on a Saturday night during the holidays.

The group of four made their way around Jackson Square, unsuccessful in their search for a place to play. Even the rear of the square, St. Louis Street, was busy.

"Nary an inch to be had," Lester concluded. "The Christmas season, I reckon."

"What's the word?" asked Jake.

"Canal Street, river end, maybe," answered Leeroy.

"If we're gonna make a dollar tonight, we best get moving," Laverne said.

"Well, let's get Hazel and move in that direction," Leeroy said.

$$\infty$$

"My, my, parking is impossible. Must *really* be the Christmas season," Leeroy said as he drove and eyed the streets for a spot to put Hazel.

"Yeah," Laverne added. "We can't get near Canal Street, for a fact."

Leeroy parked on Camp Street, near Lafayette Square, a few blocks from Canal.

"I don't like this parking place. Nor do I like this area," Laverne said. "Not atall."

"Me neither," said Lester. "It's too dark. Too dangerous. Let's find someplace else to park, Leeroy."

Jake had no time to offer an opinion before Leeroy settled the issue. "We been drivin' around in circles for fifteen minutes. Plus it's gettin' late. Grab your stuff."

"Well, if Hazel gets stolen while we're gone," Lester said, "don't blame me or Laverne."

"Okay," Leeroy said. "I'll blame Blanc." He gave a hearty Christmastime laugh.

Within thirty minutes, the four men set up on Canal, near Magazine Street. Within an hour, they'd attracted a crowd of listeners, young and old alike.

Leeroy's smooth baritone voice began. The crowd became quiet.

> *Silent night, holy night*
> *All is calm, all is bright ...*

With Jake picking the melody, the three men joined in.

> *Round yon virgin mother and child;*
> *Holy infant, so tender and mild,*
> *Sleep in heavenly peace,*
> *Sleep in heavenly peace.*
> *Silent night, holy night!*
> *Shepherds quake at the sight,*
> *Glories streams from heaven afar,*
> *Heavenly hosts sing alleluia;*
> *Christ the Savior is born!*
> *Christ the Savior is born.*

A young woman turned slowly side to side, gently rocking a newborn cradled in her arms. She glanced up from the baby, and Jake smiled at her.

> *Silent night, holy night! Son of God, love's pure light,*
> *Radiant beams from thy holy face, with the dawn of*
> *redeeming grace,*
> *Jesus, Lord at thy birth,*
> *Jesus, Lord at thy birth.*

The crowd remained silent—the atmosphere worshipful. A faint "amen" was heard from deep within the crowd.

People were in no rush to leave, although it was cold. The next day was Sunday, plus the next week was Christmas. A few walked by, while others milled around longer. Several placed money in the old hat. Someone—Lester, Leeroy, Jake, or Laverne—always managed to express their appreciation.

As long as the crowd remained, the four musicians stayed. As the night grew colder and colder, Leeroy led in their closing number.

> *We wish you a merry Christmas,*
> *We wish you a merry Christmas,*
> *We wish you a merry Christmas and a Happy New Year!*

The gathering of people clapped and wished the four men a merry Christmas.

If weight and volume meant anything, the patrons had been in a particularly generous mood, Lester thought, as he carried their haul in the bag over his shoulder.

"'Twas a good night, men," Lester said as the four made their way back down Camp toward Lafayette Square. "This here bag is almost too heavy for me to carry. *Almost*. But I shall manage."

"There she is!" exclaimed Leeroy, "I knew she would be here a-waitin'. Hazel ain't gonna leave us. Ain't she a beaut?"

"May the Lord bless Hazel. She is a beaut," Laverne said.

Hazel sat where Leeroy had parked her. Seeing her lifted their spirits, but she seemed eager to get out of the place. The three older men were alert and nervous. Camp Street was dark and deserted, with other cars parked in nearby spaces, but nary another person anywhere. Not even one uniform. Lester scowled.

Where's a New Orleans policeman or woman when you need 'em?

Lester did not offer his normal question of how much they'd made. Nobody said anything. No one wanted to count their offerings in that dark locale off Camp Street, off Canal Street, near Lafayette Square in New Orleans, Louisiana, at three o'clock in the morning. The best thing they could do was load up, get off Camp Street and get back to the safety of Franklin Avenue, Chef Menteur Highway, and 25 North Galvez.

Then they were startled by an unfamiliar voice.

"How much money you got?"

They turned to see the outlines of two men standing a few feet away, one of them much taller than the Noirs. The two had materialized suddenly and silently out of the darkness.

Lester, Leeroy, and Laverne looked for Jake. He was nowhere to be seen.

"That you, Blanc?" Leeroy asked the shadows, a noticeable hint of fear in his voice.

"Not Blanc," the shorter of the two men replied.

Lester, Leeroy, and Laverne trembled.

"You hear me, old man?" the larger shadow growled. "I *asked* you how much money you got."

"We ain't got no money," Leeroy said. " We're just three ratty old men standin' on the street in New Orleans on a Sunday morning. We're headed to the men's shelter. If we had money, you b'lieve we'd be just standin' here?"

"Just three old men," Laverne tried to help. "Three old broken broke men."

Lester clung to the bag around his shoulder with both hands. He noticed Laverne's hands shaking.

"Oh, now you's *lyin'*," the shorter man said. "Me 'n him"—he pointed to the mountain of a man looming over the Noirs—"we watched you pick up a nice piece of change tonight. Come on, man. It's Christmas. We'll let you donate to our favorite charity, which is *us*. Give us the bag."

Neither Leeroy, Lester, nor Laverne moved.

The large man shoved Lester to the ground. In a credit to his courage—not his wisdom perhaps, but certainly his courage—Lester hung onto the bag.

"Give him the bag, Lester," Leeroy said. "Ain't worth dyin' for."

It was as though Lester, immobilized by fear, didn't hear Leeroy's words, because he didn't move.

"Give him the bag, Lester," Laverne added. "Leeroy's right. Not worth your life—not worth our lives."

Hearing Laverne's words, Lester relaxed his grip and surrendered the bag.

"Smart man, listenin' to yo' friends," the tall mountain man said. He bent and rose with Lester's bag in hand. He uttered an obscenity directed at Lester, then drew back his leg and aimed a kick at him as the old man lay on Camp Street.

Without fanfare, a ghostly figure emerged from the shadows off to Leeroy's right, wielding a four-foot length of metal pipe. The apparition struck the big man a thundering blow across his lower back. The big man dropped the bag, teetering for a few seconds before his knees buckled.

He collapsed, all two hundred fifty pounds of him, and fell on top of Lester, who still lay on the ground. Lester screamed. Laverne and Leeroy gasped. In the mayhem, the ghost lost control of the pipe. They could hear it clanging away down Camp Street.

In a moment, the other would-be thief regained his wits. He wavered, thinking to leave his fellow strongarm robber in his wake. But the allure of the money was too much. Plus the pipe-swinging apparition was now minus his pipe.

In a flash, the man pulled a knife. Brandishing the six-inch blade, the man spoke to the ghost.

"You good, but that pipe don't change nothin', far's I'm concerned. Gimme the bag, or all y'all gonna die."

Jake had spotted the two strangers approaching long before the other three noticed them, and he suspected their intentions were less than honorable. He needed an edge, considering one of the two was mountainous in size. He searched the area briefly and found what he was looking for. The four-foot metal pipe would serve to even the odds.

Now, with the big man unconscious, the playing field leveled. Jake stood before the other man, ready to go one-on-one, mano-a-mano—Jacob Alvin Thomas versus the man with a six-inch blade.

"Give him the bag, Lester," Leeroy said. "Blanc, let him have the money."

"Yeah, Blanc. Lemme have the money," the man snarled, tightening his fist around the knife in his hand.

The man held the knife in an overhand grip, indicating a lack of experience in knife fighting. Jake suspected the man had flashed that same blade to other old folks—those he assumed would offer no resistance.

"Why should I give you the money?" Jake asked with a casual laugh. He moved a little closer to the man.

"Why? Because the man has a knife, and because he gonna kill us," Laverne injected calmly. "*That's* why."

"Him? He isn't going to hurt anybody," Jake said, continuing his slow shift and shuffle. He held out both arms and addressed the short man. "You wouldn't hurt anybody, now, would you?"

A look of confusion flashed across the shorter thief's face, giving Jake just enough time to reach his target spot. In one quick step, he was between the blade man and the Noirs.

The man stabbed clumsily at Jake. Jake moved faster than the Noirs could have believed possible, grabbing the man's knife arm and bending his arm violently backward. The thief gave a blood-chilling scream and dropped the knife, just before Jake loaded and landed a killer right cross on his jaw. The thief crumpled where he stood, falling a few feet away from Lester, who was still trapped underneath the unconscious mountain man.

Neither Lester, Leeroy, nor Laverne would have ever believed a boy could hit someone with such force. Lester, still struggling to get out from under the bigger thief's inert body, remembered the first time he'd seen Jacob Alvin Thomas and the deep scar across the knuckles of his right hand. Now he knew how Jake had come by the scar, and he had both appreciation and respect for what the scar meant.

The mountain man moaned as Jake rolled him off Lester and helped the old man to his feet. Leeroy and Laverne still appeared paralyzed, their feet apparently cemented to Camp Street. Jake brushed off Lester's pants and coat.

"You okay, Lester? I'm sorry for leaving you three in a pinch. As soon as I saw those two, I knew what they were after. I had to round up some sort of weapon to give me an edge." Jake retrieved the pipe from across the street and held it up. "This did the job for us, huh? We should convey our thanks and appreciation to the City of New Orleans."

Recognizing the confusion on Lester, Leeroy, and Lavern's faces, Jake turned the pipe where the trio could see and pointed to the side.

PROPERTY OF NEW ORLEANS MAINTENANCE DEPARTMENT

Jake laughed and dropped the pipe. Once more the clanging sound reverberated up and down Camp Street.

Lester, Laverne, and Leeroy could not get into Hazel fast enough.

$$\infty$$

Back at 25 North Galvez, Leeroy pulled Hazel into her bay and the men exited. The money the men had made that night seemed unimportant. No one asked about it. The bag lay in Hazel's back seat. Near-death experiences had a way of forcing one to rethink life's priorities.

Leeroy lowered the large garage door and then locked the smaller door. Jake had never known that smaller door to be locked. The four men sat in silence, knowing they'd avoided a disaster.

Jake spoke calmly, as if they'd just come home from a church picnic. "Are you three okay?"

"I've been scared in my life, lots of times. Never like that," Lester said.

"Scared me too," Leeroy said softly, rubbing his hands together.

"Jake, he could have killed you and then killed us," Laverne offered, leaning forward in his chair. "The next time, please give him—"

Jake interrupted.

"Him? The man with the knife? Ol' Blade Boy? He was all mouth. Why d'you believe he was running with the big man?" He shrugged. "Mountain Man was Blade Boy's courage. I've seen his type before. Several times. Blade Boy's a bully. You hit a bully in the mouth, and he'll run like the coward he is." Jake smiled. "You hit him hard enough, and he won't be able to run."

Leeroy visualized Blade Boy as he collapsed onto Camp Street and said, "What about that ol' Jolly Green Giant of a man, Mountain Man as you called him? What about him, Blanc?"

Jake grew serious before he replied, the smile now gone.

"Now *he* was dangerous. I've seen his type before too. I needed something against him—something to level the playing field, so to speak. And fortunate for us, the New Orleans Maintenance Department obliged. I didn't intend to kill him, but I did intend to put him out of commission for a while. I knocked the wind out of him, that's all. But his back's gonna be sore for weeks. He won't threaten anyone else for a while."

The four sat in silence. None was eager to be anywhere else. The night continued dark and cold.

Laverne broke the stillness. "Lester, let's the two of us go home, shall we? Been a night, hasn't it?"

"Yeah. A night to remember, all right. Or a night to forget. Let's go," Lester said.

The Noirs rose, Leeroy intending to drive Lester and Laverne to Franklin Avenue.

Jake rested his hand on Leeroy's shoulder. "You stay, Leeroy, and rest. I'll take Lester and Laverne home."

Leeroy took a deep breath, dropped his head, and offered no objection. Jake thought Leeroy would cry. Leeroy suddenly looked much older, Jake thought.

Jake, Lester, and Laverne stood. Leeroy got up and unlocked his garage door, his hands still shaking.

Lester and Laverne exited the garage a few steps ahead of Jake. Leeroy took Jake's arm and turned him. "Blanc?"

Jake looked into Leeroy's eyes before speaking. "Leeroy?"

"Mountain Man and Blade Boy. You said you've you seen their types before."

"Yes?"

"Where, Blanc? Where have you seen their types?"

Jake smiled. "Tell Mildred hello for me, Leeroy. I'm going to worship. See you Saturday night."

Leeroy scanned Jake's eyes, but they revealed nothing—no fear, no concern, no alarm. Nothing.

"See you Saturday night then, Blanc."

Jake stepped into the cold New Orleans morning.

He heard Leeroy lock the door behind him. The bag with the night's earnings still lay in Hazel's backseat.

CHAPTER THIRTEEN

Leeroy gave up on trying to sleep at six a.m. He'd been in bed a couple of hours but hadn't slept. He smiled to hear Mildred snoring gently. Her face looked angelic from the glow of the dusk-to-dawn light on North Galvez. He pulled the quilt up around her and tucked it, then pecked her cheek. He'd continued to toss and turn, thinking how the attempted robbery on Camp Street could have ended. Every time he closed his eyes, he saw Mountain Man standing over his lifelong friend Lester, and Blade Boy swinging the knife at his newfound friend Blanc. All four of them could have been injured. Or killed.

When troubled, Leeroy had a routine. He went to his garage and talked to Hazel. He loved Mildred, his wife of close to fifty years, more than any person or anything in the world, and often wondered where he would be without her. Prison, maybe, if not homeless or dead.

But there are some things a man can't talk about with a woman, even if she's his wife.

Hazel, on the other hand—well, he could say anything he wanted to Hazel. Not that Mildred would speak a word about Leeroy's concerns to anyone else, but Leeroy *knew* Hazel would never speak a word of his conversation to anyone.

He opened the rear door to their house, remembering the squeak he'd promised Mildred he'd oil, and went to talk to Hazel.

Leeroy sat beside his old Hudson Hornet friend. He patted her hood in a loving manner. The feel of her helped still his shaking hand. He rubbed his arthritic knees and spoke softly.

"Fear's a terrible thing, Hazel."

He sat and leaned his head back, stared at the ceiling. "Terrible thing," he murmured.

The sun shone through one of the garage's east windows. He hadn't realized he'd fallen asleep until he heard a light knock on the door. He woke to see Mildred, standing outside the door, carrying a partly visible tray. He got his knees moving enough to open the door.

Leeroy led his wife to the chair he had been using, the best lawn chair they owned. When she was comfortable, he reached for another chair.

"The door? Locked, Leeroy? Why?"

"Coffee smells good, my love," Leeroy replied, ignoring the question. In reality, he didn't remember locking the door.

Mildred handed him a cup—black, two sugars. There was a time when they couldn't afford coffee or sugar. They sat in silence and drank, two people at ease with one another after almost fifty years of marriage. A mockingbird tossed a shimmering song into the air, celebrating a new day. Traffic began moving on the street.

Mildred broke the silence. "I know you didn't sleep well."

"Did I keep you awake, my love? I'm sorry. I should have moved to the sofa."

"Mountain Man and Blade Boy, as you called them?" Mildred asked while peering at Leeroy. He smiled slightly before replying.

"I reckon so. Mountain Man and Blade Boy."

Mildred sensed something was wrong when Leeroy came into their bedroom after three a.m. Maybe his voice quaked. Maybe Mildred's inkling of trouble was nothing more than a wife's intuition. Or maybe she'd read his mind, as Leeroy often thought.

When Mildred asked, as she lay in their bed with the small bedside light on, Leeroy knew there was no need denying it. She knew something wasn't right, and Leeroy was a poor liar. He admitted he did feel better after he'd told her. Better, until they turned out the light.

Now, in the garage, when Mildred broached the topic of Mountain Man and Blade Boy, Leeroy divulged more of the night's activities.

"You should have seen Blanc, my love. He swung that piece of pipe with force, determination—with purpose. He knew what he needed to do with it. Me? I would've hit Mountain Man over the head with it, killed him, and by now I'd be on my way to prison. But Blanc? Not Blanc. A *seventeen-year-old kid*. And my love, you should've seen him step between Lester, Laverne, me, and Blade Boy. He'd have died defending us. I'm as certain of that as I'm certain the sun's gonna set tonight."

Leeroy's eyes burned. "He stood there in front of Blade Boy—as Blanc called him—a thief with a six-inch knife, and Blanc was ... calm. You'd thought he was headed to a picnic.

He disarmed Blade Boy with his bare hands." Leeroy leaned forward. "With his *bare hands*, my love."

He sank back into his chair. "I can still hear Blade Boy scream. And when Blanc hit him, one time—*wham!*—Blade Boy went down and didn't scream any more. He didn't make a sound after Blanc hit him." He looked at his wife, puzzlement on his face. "Blanc never lost his composure. How?"

"How? How what, Leeroy?"

Leeroy continued. "How does a seventeen-year-old kid know how to do that? Where did he learn that? *Why* has he learned how to do that? There's more to this White boy than we know."

She spoke quietly. "Are you scared of Jake, Leeroy?"

"Blanc? No. I'm not scared of him. I don't believe he'd harm us for all the money in the world. Nor do I think he'd harm anyone without cause. But given cause ..." Leeroy's voice trailed off, and then, he spoke again. "I'm just sayin' there's more to this White boy than we know."

Mildred offered an idea. "Why don't we invite Jake to Christmas dinner? We'll have all the trimmings this year—turkey, dressing, cranberry sauce, green beans, sweet potato pie. You know Lester and Laverne will welcome him."

"I never thought about that. Where are my manners, Miz Edwards? But I imagine Blanc prefers to eat Christmas dinner with his own family. The most festive thing we do here on Christmas Day is open a bottle of eggnog, which we *will* be doing this year."

"Leeroy Edwards, the last of the big spenders! I admit I've missed the eggnog."

Eggnog had been another unaffordable luxury in the Edwards household. Mildred sipped coffee and continued. "What do you know about Jake's family?"

Leeroy thought for a moment before answering.

"What do I know about his family? Hmmm, let me think, let me think. Nothing. Absolutely nothing. I've never heard him speak of a father, mother, siblings, uncles, aunts, cousins. Nobody. I just assumed he had them."

"Don't you find that odd? Jake not saying *something* about family? Just a hint about his father or mother or a relative?"

"Now that you've mentioned it, I do. He must have family." He paused. "Right? Blanc has to have family."

"A family would be normal, yes. Where does he live?"

"In a house off Chef Menteur Highway, he said."

"Where exactly on Chef? Do you have an address?"

"Can't remember Blanc giving an address."

They continued to sit in the garage, enjoying each other's quiet presence. After a few minutes, Mildred asked another question.

"Leeroy, why don't you call Jake by his name? Why do you call him Blanc?"

Leeroy laughed. "I don't know. Don't mean any disrespect by it. Never have—and certainly not after what he did last night. No ma'am, not after last night." He paused. "The first time Lester, Laverne, and I saw him, walking up our driveway with an excuse of a guitar case, someone remarked about the young White boy he appeared to be. That statement stuck with me, hence, Blanc. But after seeing how he dispensed with Mountain Man and Blade Boy—well, if my calling him Blanc bothered him, I suspect he'd tell me in no uncertain terms."

Another brief lull in the conversation. Unnoticed by Leeroy, Mildred napped in the lawn chair.

"I like Blanc, as do Lester and Laverne," Leeroy said suddenly, waking Mildred. "And your idea for Christmas dinner is superb, Miz Edwards. I shall follow your wise counsel and extend said invitation. King Solomon would have welcomed you into his harem, my love. For your beautiful mind, yes, but for *other* reasons as well." He smiled broadly.

"Shut your mouth, Leeroy Malcolm Edwards." Mildred said. She returned the smile as Leeroy reached for her free hand, and then glanced at her watch.

"Oh my! Look at the time. I mustn't be late for worship." Mildred hurriedly gathered the coffee cups and tray and left Leeroy in the garage alone with his thoughts.

The next Sunday, about two thirty in the morning, Leeroy drove Hazel toward 25 North Galvez. The December night was frigid. Lester had the bag containing the night's donations in his lap. After the Mountain Man and Blade Boy incident, the four decided they'd wait until they reached the safety of Leeroy's garage/practice room before counting and dividing their money. The four men were in a jovial mood. Leeroy had to admit that Blanc, in the time they'd known him and played together, had lifted their spirits to a much higher plane. Leeroy initiated the conversation.

"Blanc, what are you doing Christmas Day for dinner? Plans? Spending the day with family?"

"No plans. Eat a good meal and stay inside. Rest."

Leeroy noticed Jake mentioned nothing about family.

"You're not spending the day with your family?"

"No, I won't be spending Christmas Day with family."

"Then you're invited to have Christmas dinner with us. Noon-ish. Lester and Laverne will be there."

Jake was silent.

Lester made a casual comment. "Mildred makes the best turkey gravy you have ever eaten."

"Don't forget her sweet potato pie," added Laverne.

"I don't want to be intrusive," Jake said. "The four of you are family, and Mildred might not approve."

"What else you goin' to do, Blanc?" Leeroy said. "You said yourself you won't be spending the day with family. We'll eat and sit around afterward. Drink eggnog. Enjoy the presence of good people. Do what we do every year."

Jake considered before replying. In all fairness, he needed little nudging. Spending Christmas Day with others would be a nice change.

"Okay. I accept. I'll pick Laverne and Lester up at eleven thirty Christmas morning. Agreeable to everybody?"

Lester and Laverne nodded yes, with Laverne adding, "We'll be ready."

"Good," Leeroy said. "I'll tell Miz Edwards to set another plate. Your invitation, after all, was *her* idea. Me, I really don't like you, Blanc."

Leeroy leaned forward to look in Hazel's rear view mirror. He saw and smiled at Jake. Jake met Leeroy's eyes, returned the smile, and said, "What did a woman as wonderful as Mildred ever see in you?"

"You don't know my wife, Blanc," Leeroy said. "You've met her, but you don't *know* her."

"I don't have to know *her*," Jake said, "to know she could've done much better than *you*."

"How do you know that, Blanc?" Leeroy asked.

"Because I've met *you*," Jake said.

Lester and Laverne laughed and nodded in agreement.

"That talkin' smack again," Laverne mumbled.

CHAPTER FOURTEEN

On Christmas Day morning at 11:30, Jake picked up Laverne and Lester at their Franklin Avenue apartment. Jake was impressed with their appearance.

Both men were finely dressed, wearing white shirts, neckties of neutral colors and dress hats. Their shoes were polished to a mirror-like sheen. Jake had never seen either man wear anything other than threadbare clothes and heelless loafers, which the men admitted buying from a local Salvation Army. Their dress, accentuated by their silvery gray hair, was dignified enough for a visit to the mayor's mansion. Lester carried a single wrapped gift, and Laverne carried a bottle, wrapped, with a bow.

Lester got into the front seat, Laverne in the back.

"Hello there, gentlemen," Jake said.

Lester was willing to play his part. He leaned over and offered Jake his right hand. "I'm Mister Washington."

They shook. "And I'm Jake Thomas."

"Nice to meet you, Mister Thomas. You know Mister Knox, my traveling companion for the day, riding in the rear compartment."

"Hello, and yes, I do know Mister Knox."

"Hello, Mister Thomas," Laverne said.

Jake abandoned the charade. "Don't you two look sharp, all spiffed up, like a couple of US Senators from the great State of Louisiana. Y'all even look good enough to get buried."

They chuckled.

"I imagine you're both accustomed to riding in limousines," Jake continued. "I s'pect you'll be ashamed to be seen in my old car."

Lester and Laverne laughed. They were not ready to give up the pretense. "As a matter of fact, we *are* accustomed to riding in limousines," Laverne said, "but on Christmas Day, this fine auto-*mo*-bile will suffice."

"And I'm Jake Thomas, your proud and humble chauffeur, at your service. What's your pleasure, gentlemen? To where are you off? What is your desired destination?"

"To the Governor's Ball, 25 North Galvez, chauffeur," Lester said, "and make haste. Miz Governor doesn't like patrons to be tardy."

Lester eyed Jake. "And look at you, Jake. Have I ever seen you in anything but jeans?"

"You do look good," Laverne added.

Jake wore black slacks and a crimson turtleneck sweater, a nice touch for Christmas Day. He wore a khaki blazer with patches on the sleeves and a new pair of Oxfords. In fact, everything Jake wore was new—from his socks to the handkerchief folded and tucked in his blazer pocket. Jake could not remember having this quantity of new clothes at one time in his entire life, or indeed, such an important reason to buy them. He'd decided he wouldn't go to Christmas Day dinner with his friends without looking nice.

"I thank you both. Off to the Governor's Ball." Jake eased the Oldsmobile into Franklin Avenue traffic.

The three arrived at 25 North Galvez. Jake unfolded his six-foot-four-inch frame and emerged from the Olds. With his narrow waist and broad shoulders, he was a handsome young man. Lester and Laverne were proud *of* him and proud to be *with* him.

Leeroy met them at the door, looking equally distinguished in a white shirt, tie, and sports blazer. Once inside, Jake witnessed something he'd never seen before—Leeroy embracing Lester and Laverne.

"Merry Christmas, friends. Welcome to our home on Christmas Day," Leeroy said to Lester, then Laverne.

Jake felt awkward, not knowing how Leeroy would greet him. He knew little about physical affection. The times he'd seen his parents hug or express warmth toward each other had been rare.

Whatever awkwardness he felt dissipated as Leeroy pulled him close and wrapped his arms around him. Leeroy spoke softly. "Merry Christmas, Blanc, my friend."

"Merry Christmas, Leeroy."

Leeroy placed the gift from Lester beneath a large, beautiful Christmas tree. He carried Laverne's gift to the kitchen. Jake noticed a few wrapped gifts underneath the tree.

He looked around. Christmas trees were everywhere—not just the large tree, but numerous smaller ones, each decorated, each sparkling with lights. Trees sat on the floor, on sofa tables, and on stands. He counted four from where he stood. Before the day was over, Jake counted nine trees all told—at least one in every room. The house was aglow with Christmas lights.

Then there were the smells. Jake detected turkey roasting and the scents of sweet potato pie, cinnamon, and chocolate. He couldn't imagine what heaven smelled like, but he believed the smell would be something akin to the aromas emanating from Mildred Edwards's kitchen on Christmas Day.

The four men sat in the living room and talked, mostly about New Orleans getting their first professional football team.

Within minutes, Mildred made her appearance. Jake stood along with Leeroy, Lester, and Laverne as she entered. She wore a light blue dress with a matching jacket—unbuttoned in the front. Her shoes were black with a two-inch heel. Her single piece of jewelry, a modest necklace, complemented her dress. Jake saw no rings on her hands or in her ears.

Jake estimated Mildred's height to be five feet nine, perhaps five ten, making her taller than average for a woman. She did not appear proud or arrogant, but she did appear self-confident, a woman serene in her feminity.

She squeezed Leeroy's hand, walked past him, and moved to Lester and Laverne. She hugged both men. "Welcome, and merry Christmas."

"We wouldn't miss this for anything in the world, Mildred."

Again, Jake didn't know how Mildred would welcome him. He was an outside guest. She put Jake at ease as she hugged him. "And welcome, Jake, to our home on Christmas Day. Merry Christmas."

"Merry Christmas, Miz Edwards."

Mildred continued to smile. "Now, *Miz* Edwards was Leeroy's mother. I never met her, but Leeroy had a mother,

I'm sure. I, on the other hand, am Mildred. My friends call me Mildred, and I count you a friend."

"Thank you, Mildred. I count you as my friend as well."

The four men followed her into the kitchen.

Jake had seen little in Leeroy to lead him to believe Leeroy was a religious man, at least not until now. Leeroy took a Bible from a side counter, and opened the book to a pre-determined location. Mildred, Lester, and Laverne sat and waited, as did Jake, his hands folded in his lap. He knew this was something this *family* had done for years.

Leeroy struggled with a few words and the name of one particular governor of Syria, but Jake thought he heard the voice of God. For the rest of Jake's life, when he closed his eyes and imagined the voice of God, he heard Leeroy Edwards reading the story of the birth of Jesus.

> And it came to pass in those days, that there went out a decree from Caesar Augustus that all the world should be taxed. (And this taxing was first made when Cyrenius was governor of Syria.) And all went to be taxed, every one into his own city.
>
> And Joseph also went up from Galilee, out of the city of Nazareth, into Judaea, unto the city of David, which is called Bethlehem; (because he was of the house and lineage of David:) To be taxed with Mary his espoused wife, being great with child.
>
> And so it was, that, while they were there, the days were accomplished that she should be delivered. And she brought forth her firstborn son, and wrapped him in swaddling clothes, and laid him in a manger; because there was no room for them in the inn.
>
> And there were in the same country shepherds abiding in the field, keeping watch over their flock by night. And, lo, the angel of the Lord came upon them, and the glory of the Lord shone round about them: and they were

sore afraid. And the angel said unto them, Fear not: for, behold, I bring you good tidings of great joy, which shall be to all people. For unto you is born this day in the city of David a Saviour, which is Christ the Lord. And this shall be a sign unto you; Ye shall find the babe wrapped in swaddling clothes, lying in a manger. And suddenly there was with the angel a multitude of the heavenly host praising God, and saying, Glory to God in the highest, and on earth peace, good will toward men.

Leeroy ended with: "Hear the Word of God, as read from the Gospel of Saint Luke, chapter 2, verses one through fourteen. Amen."

"Amen," Mildred, Lester and Laverne echoed.

Leeroy closed and returned the old Bible to its spot on the side counter. Sitting at the kitchen table, with food, plates, utensils, and glasses covering every inch, Leeroy reached for Mildred's hand on his right and for Lester's on his left. Lester joined his other hand to Laverne's, while Laverne reached for Jake's. Jake understood, and extended his hand to Mildred to complete the circle.

"We thank you, great God, for the meaning of what we've read, the meaning of Christmas, the birth of Jesus, our Lord. We thank you for allowing us to share this special day with family. We pray your blessing on the meal and your blessings upon us. As taught in this passage, we pray for peace on earth, goodwill toward all. Amen."

"Amen," responded Mildred, Lester, Laverne, and Jake.

Leeroy's inclusion of Jake as family wasn't lost on anyone, especially Jake.

Mildred's reaching for a dish indicated the formalities were past and the celebration was on.

All five began filling their plates with food. The conversation became lively, with all five getting loud with laughter and storytelling. Jake relaxed and enjoyed the chaos.

∞

With the meal complete, and half the sweet potato pie eaten, Mildred stood and began gathering dishes. Leeroy looked at her, surprised.

"My love, what are you doing? You know how this works. *You* cook, *we* clean."

"Leeroy, you three have a guest to entertain. I'll get these."

"Who? Blanc? I'm about to tie an apron on him. You go in the living room and sit down."

Mildred offered no resistance. She and Leeroy exited the kitchen as Lester and Laverne began clearing the table. Within minutes, Leeroy returned. True to his word, he tied an apron around Jake's waist and gave him a cloth, with instructions.

"You wash. You know how to wash dishes, yes?"

"As a matter of fact, I do know how to wash dishes."

"Good. Start washin'."

Thirty minutes later, with the dishes washed and with Leeroy, Lester, and Laverne finishing up, Leeroy shooed Jake out of the kitchen. Jake found Mildred in the living room.

"Jake, I hope they haven't worked you too hard on Christmas Day."

"Oh, no. I don't mind. I know my way around a kitchen, including dirty pots and pans."

"Good. A man needs to be a helper to his wife in all things. I don't know where I'd be sometimes if Leeroy didn't help."

Jake waved an arm to encompass the room and beyond. "Your house is postcard pretty. I love the Christmas trees."

"I kept adding trees, until Leeroy said no more," Mildred said with a smile.

"This one's unusual," Jake said, pointing to a small tree in the corner.

"That's our traveling tree."

"I'm sorry?"

"Our traveling tree. That tree has ornaments we've collected from places where we've traveled across the years. Years ago, before Anthony died, we traveled extensively. We've seen much of the US and other parts of the world. You'll see ornaments on that tree from here in New Orleans to Bar Harbor, Maine, and Jackson Hole in Wyoming, and Hawaii, and Alaska. We've been in every state in the US except one—North Dakota."

"I figured this tree out," Jake said, indicating another decorated tree. "It's a family tree. I see pictures of you and Leeroy when you were younger and more recent ones. There's pictures of Lester and Laverne. But I don't know this young man. Who ...?"

"Our son," Mildred said.

"Pardon me?"

"Our son. Those are pictures of our son, Amos."

"I didn't know you and Leeroy have a child."

"Had." Her eyes flickered ever so slightly. "He was killed when he was fifteen."

"Mildred, I'm so sorry. I hope I haven't upset you—on Christmas Day of all days."

"Oh, hush, Jake. A mother loves talking about her child. Talking about him is part of the healing process, even after all these years. Talking about him helps ease the pain. His remembrance, for me, is both cathartic and healing."

Jake did not pry, but simply listened.

"He was born on a cold night, much like this one, on December seventh—which would eventually be Pearl Harbor Day after the bombing of Pearl Harbor in World War II. Early in our marriage, a doctor told us we'd never be able to have children, and if I should conceive and give birth to a live child, the child would probably be deformed."

She tsked and shook her head. "*Deformed.* I despise that word. Mentally retarded or physically deformed or both, the doctors said, but on that December night he was born with ten perfect fingers and ten perfect toes, as alert as could be. Nothing wrong with that child—mentally, physically, or otherwise. The doctors called him a miracle baby. We called him Amos, Amos Alonzo Edwards. Do you know what the name 'Amos' means, Jake?"

"No, ma'am, I don't."

"It means 'burden bearer.' I didn't know the meaning of the name at the time. We liked the name, but as things turned out, Amos, in his death, was both Leeroy's burden and mine to bear. His death is still a weary load, at times. But that's not Amos's fault. I don't blame him."

Mildred paused a moment, then went on.

"He was such a joy. He brought great pleasure to our lives. He was intelligent, witty. He was tall, like you, and he always stood ramrod straight. And with a talent for music— he could play the Noirs and Anthony all under the table at fifteen years old, with any instrument he chose. He once told me, 'Ma, if the instrument has strings on it, I think I can play it.'"

She paused again, summoning the strength to continue. She wrapped her arms around herself, perhaps to guard herself against the sorrow.

"He died over thirty years ago. He'd be forty-six years old now, had he lived. I visualize him today, with a wife, children, and grandchildren, filling this house with laughter and music on Christmas Day. I miss him, Jake. I miss him terribly."

Jake wondered but didn't ask. Mildred anticipated his unspoken question. "He died here, in front of this house. A drunk driver lost control of his car and swerved off the street, into our front yard."

She stopped. Jake didn't know what to say.

"Leeroy and I've considered moving, but we haven't been able to bring ourselves to leave this house. So many memories, good memories, here."

She regarded him silently for a moment, then said, "Jake, you're about the same age as our Amos when he died, I s'pect. How old are you?"

"Seventeen, ma'am."

She nodded. "Yes, about the same age. I think Leeroy sees much of our Amos in you—both of you tall, smart, witty, musical, handsome. Leeroy wouldn't ever admit it to you, but he likes you, and he's impressed with you."

"Yes, ma'am," was all Jake could manage.

Leeroy, Lester, and Laverne emerged from the kitchen, with Leeroy carrying a tray with glasses and a pitcher. Lester carried a gift, still wrapped, and handed it to Mildred, who apparently knew the contents.

"The remnants of the repast are impossible to identify, my love," Leeroy said. "Gone are the dirty pots, pans, plates, glasses, utensils. Blanc, Lester, Laverne, and I've seen to it. Dishwashers par excellence."

"I thank you all."

"Jake's a whiz with a dishcloth," Lester said.

"He's better with a dishcloth than a guitar," said Laverne, "and that's *sayin'* somethin'."

"I told you three," Jake said. "I know my way around a kitchen."

"Where did you learn your way around a kitchen, Blanc?"

Lester saved Jake from having to answer the question by changing the subject. "And we thank you, Mildred, for the wonderful meal. You outdid yourself. Every year better than the last."

Mildred unwrapped the gift. "Thank you, Lester and Laverne."

Both men smiled as Jake saw the label—a bottle of eggnog. She handed the bottle to Leeroy.

"Now, Blanc," Leeroy said, "the day is unfinished. We've eggnog to drink"—he nodded toward Lester and Laverne—"and we've one other thing to do."

Jake had never tasted eggnog before. He found he didn't care for the taste, but drank the glass out of courtesy.

Fifteen minutes later, Leeroy stood.

"One final thing before Christmas Day is complete, Blanc. We exchange gifts, something we've done for years. I could've told you, but none of us wanted you to feel obligated to purchase anything. Lester, do the honors, please."

While Lester obeyed, Mildred explained. "Jake, the time has been when gifts were meager here. Both before and after Anthony."

"I remember one year we each gave the other a gift certificate to the grocery store, and set a limit of two dollars. Remember?" Laverne said.

"I remember," Leeroy said. "At least we all thought we could go to the grocer and not starve to death for a while."

"Other years, we gave handshakes and hugs," Laverne said.

"I remember those years—plural, *years*—too," Leeroy added.

Mildred offered further explanation on the gift routine. "Leeroy and I count as one person. Lester and Laverne each get us a gift and then they get the other a gift. That way we, Leeroy, and I, counted as one, all buy and get two gifts. Leeroy and I get one gift from Lester and one gift from Laverne. They in turn, get one gift from Leeroy and me, and one from the other."

In minutes, Lester had the gifts distributed.

Leeroy exited the room and returned with what was obviously a guitar case, wrapped. He handed the gift to Jake. "From all of us, Blanc."

Jake offered no word of objection. He reached in his lapel pocket and pulled out four gifts. He handed one to Mildred, one to Leeroy, one to Lester, and one to Laverne. He'd anticipated the possibility of exchanging gifts, but had kept his gifts concealed until he was sure.

"Look at you, Blanc!" said Leeroy.

"That was unnecessary, Jake," Mildred said.

"My pleasure," Jake responded.

"Lady first," Laverne said.

Mildred opened her gifts. She saved Jake's until last—a beautiful brooch.

Jake wanted Leeroy to open Lester and Laverne's gift to him—a pair of gloves.

"I thank you both," Leeroy said.

"I'm going to ask the three of you to open my gift at the same time," Jake said.

The Noirs obliged. Leeroy, Lester, and Laverne opened their gifts. All three men expressed their appreciation. All three, in a manner or of minutes, had new tie pins in place.

"Now your turn, Jake," Laverne said.

"Oh my," Jake said, picking up the gift. "I can't imagine what this must be."

"It's a piano!" Lester offered.

"It's an accordion!" Laverne added.

"It's a set of drums," Leeroy said.

Jake expected a guitar case, but when he lifted it, he realized the gift was too heavy to be empty. He unwrapped the case and opened it, then stifled a gasp. He had never seen a more beautiful guitar. Jake recognized the brand and model and knew it was an expensive guitar, but for him the instrument was beyond price. He was speechless as he fought back tears.

"Do you like it, Blanc?"

"I do. I can't imagine a better gift for a musician to receive. And coming from friends makes it even better."

"I've never heard you play, Jake," Mildred said. "Do you mind?"

Jake strummed and found the guitar had already been tuned. He began a song he'd taught himself for playing the streets during the Christmas holidays. Within a few chords, Leeroy recognized the tune and began singing. Lester and Laverne joined in. Soon Mildred, a wonderful contralto, sang as well. With Jake playing and the other four singing inside the small house at 25 North Galvez, the entire world seemed to be at peace.

> *O come, all ye faithful,*
> *Joyful and triumphant;*
> *O come ye, O come ye to Bethlehem!*
> *Come and behold him, born the King of Angels!*
> *O come, let us adore him, O come, let us adore him,*
> *O come, let us adore him, Christ the Lord!*
> *Sing, choirs of angels,*
> *Sing in exultation;*
> *O sing, all ye citizens of heaven above!*

Glory to God, all glory in the highest!
O come, let us adore him, O come, let us adore him,
O come, let us adore him, Christ the Lord!
Yea, Lord, we greet thee,
Born this happy morning;
Jesus, to thee be all glory given;
Word of the Father, now in flesh appearing!
O come, let us adore him, O come, let us adore him,
O come, let us adore him, Christ the Lord!

"Beautiful, Jake. Thank you," Mildred said.

"My pleasure," was all he could offer in reply.

With the brooch pinned on Mildred and with the Noirs' three tie pins in place, Jake left Leeroy's with Lester and Laverne and drove toward Franklin Avenue. No one spoke a word. No one wanted this day to end.

Lester and Laverne exited the car. Lester leaned across Jake's old car and extended his right hand. "Merry Christmas, Jake."

"Merry Christmas, Lester," Jake said, extending his hand to shake Lester's and then Laverne's. "Merry Christmas, Laverne."

"Merry Christmas, Jake," Laverne replied as he patted Jake on the shoulder.

Remembering Mountain Man and Blade Boy, Jake waited for the two men to get off the street before leaving. In seconds, Laverne turned and waved, a signal he and Lester were entering their flat. The door closed.

Jake sat and thought about the day. He remembered the Christmas trees and lights—he had never seen such lights in a home. He thought about the traveling tree and was impressed at the places visited by Leeroy and Mildred. There had been the sad story of Amos Alonzo Edwards, and Jake knew how his death continued to pain Leeroy and Mildred. He could still hear Leeroy's voice, imagining it as what the voice of God must be, as Leeroy read Holy Scripture and prayed to his "great God." He could still smell the aromas of the house and hear the laughter of people as they enjoyed being with family.

Jake thought of Leeroy, Lester, and Laverne as they smiled, showing off their tiepins, and Mildred's smile as she pinned on the brooch.

Jake hadn't experienced anything like this day in a long time. For the first time in years, he felt he belonged to someone. He had friends now, even a family. He drove toward Chef Menteur Highway, pulled his car into Franklin Avenue traffic, and began to weep for joy.

CHAPTER FIFTEEN

Three days later, Leeroy met Lester and Laverne at their flat.

"Let's get lunch. I'm hungry for a chicken sandwich," Leeroy said.

Laverne spoke without hesitation. "I'm ready. A chicken sandwich sounds good to me."

"Me too," Lester said. "Where are we going?"

"Let's try Paul's Poulet on Chef Menteur,"Leeroy said. "I've never eaten there, and people at church tell Mildred the food is some kinda good."

"What the heck is a poulet?"

"French for chicken," Laverne answered. He suspected Lester knew that and was just needling him, but with Lester one could never be sure.

"Well, pardon me, Mister Knox," Lester said.

"NPR. I learned that listening to NPR."

"What the heck is an NBR?" Leeroy asked.

"*NPR*. National Public Radio. You should listen, Leeroy. You might learn something."

"I ain't listenin' to no NRB."

Laverne ignored Leeroy's final error on the topic, knowing he was simply being himself.

"Let's try Paul's Poulet," Lester said.

Leeroy waited a few minutes for the two men to dress. Lester came out first.

"I wish I knew where Blanc lives," Leeroy said, as Laverne entered the room. "We'd invite him too, but ... I don't know. Off Chef Menteur was all he said, and Chef is a long highway."

"No tellin' where that boy might live," Lester said.

Lester and Laverne grabbed old coats, old scarves, and old hats. In minutes, all three settled into Hazel with Laverne in the front. They headed to Chef Menteur and Paul's Poulet, where chicken sandwiches waited.

Leeroy turned north on Franklin and east on Highway 90, known to New Orleanians as Chef Menteur, usually shortened to just Chef. Hazel moved as she did when she was young, and soon Leeroy pulled her into an empty parking lot. At least, the front parking lot at Paul's Poulet was empty.

"Hey, there's Blanc's car," Leeroy said.

"You know that ... because?" Laverne asked with a laugh. Minus any hubcaps, minus the glass in the left rear door, and minus any paint, Jake's clunker sat in the parking lot at Paul's Poulet, tucked into a back space. Two other cars were parked in the same area.

"Good," Leeroy said. "We'll eat a sandwich with Blanc."

Entering, the three men scanned the small restaurant for their guitarist.

"Don't see 'im," Leeroy said.

The restaurant was, in fact, currently empty.

"You don't suppose there are two of those old cars in New Orleans, do you?" asked Laverne.

They all laughed before Lester said, "No, it's definitely Jake's car."

The counter was empty as the three men stepped up to order. Leeroy and Lester attempted to read the offerings.

"A man's really up against life when he can't read," Lester said.

Laverne stared in the direction of Jake's car. "At least you read enough to get by."

All three men continued to stare at either the restaurant's offerings or Jake's car. An employee of Paul's Poulet emerged from the back. Leeroy, Lester, and Laverne were oblivious to the presence of anyone else.

"Morning, gentlemen. Ready to order?"

With that, Lester, Leeroy, and Laverne knew.

"Blanc!"

Jake stood behind the counter. Ramrod straight. All six feet and four inches plus, and broad shoulders. He smiled. At that point, the men saw him as though for the first time.

He wore the standard work attire of Paul's Poulet. The men couldn't see much of his slacks behind the counter, but he wore a light blue short-sleeved shirt with a black vest on top. In white letters, *Paul's Poulet* was stitched on the right side, *Jake* on the left. What accessorized the uniform was his cap, if that was the proper name for what he wore. The headgear itself was red, but the bill was white, designed as a chicken beak, complete with large nostrils. A bright red comb arched over the top, with lighter red and black feathers emerging from the back. Lester, Laverne, and Leeroy stood and stared, all three struggling to control their emotions. Jake broke the silence, still smiling.

"Go ahead."

"Go ahead what?" Laverne managed to ask.

"Go ahead and laugh. You three aren't the first."

All three men immediately roared. Jake thought Laverne would collapse in between his howls of laughter.

"Sorry, Blanc," Laverne said, gasping for air. "I can't help myself."

Still laughing, Lester said, "You know what I keep seeing? Jake, battling Mountain Man and Blade Boy in that chicken cap."

Again they roared. Laverne launched into snort-laughing until a spell of coughing hit him, making Lester and Leeroy laugh harder. Jake took the jest in good humor. He'd seen and heard worse reactions by customers.

Jake took their orders and their money. He also delivered their orders, surprising the trio. He sat in the booth with them and pulled off the chicken cap. "What brings you three out today?"

"Chicken," Lester answered. "Chicken sandwiches and tater wedges."

"Truth be known, Blanc, Mildred threw me out of the house," Leeroy said. "She's cooking. Helping prepare a meal for her church to serve Sunday to needy New Orleanians."

"Mildred threw you out, eh? Finally came to her senses, I reckon," Jake said.

"Homeless people. Poor souls," Leeroy replied.

Laverne shuddered at the word *homeless*. The four men continued to talk. After several minutes, Laverne turned to Jake.

"Now I understand there's no other customers here, but should you be sittin' here with us? Shouldn't you be doing something? Something ... maybe ... akin to work?"

"Right," Leeroy said. "We don't want to get you fired, Blanc."

"Paul—*the* Paul, who owns this place—doesn't mind. He knows I work hard for him—*have* worked hard—for over three years."

"You been workin' here for three years, Jake?" Lester asked.

Leeroy did the math and spoke. "How did you get a job working here at the age of fourteen?"

"I lied, Leeroy. I lied on my application about my age. I know Jesus doesn't approve, and I'm not proud, but the alternative—homeless and starving—didn't appeal to me. I was a six-foot kid three years ago. Nobody, including Paul, questioned my age."

He looked up. "Speaking of Paul, here he is."

Lester, Laverne, and Leeroy saw a middle-aged man entering the restaurant. The man was well dressed. One could cut himself on the crease in his dark slacks and light blue short-sleeved shirt.

"Shouldn't you be working now," Lester asked, "with the boss man here?"

"That man gonna fire you, Jake," Laverne said.

Paul noticed Jake seated at the table and waved. Jake motioned to him.

"Paul, I want you to meet my friends. This is Lester Washington, Leeroy Edwards, and Laverne Knox. Y'all, this is Paul Evans, *the* Paul of Paul's Poulet."

Paul shook hands with all three, starting, the Noirs noticed, with Jake.

"So these are the men you told me about. Nice to meet you all. I've intended to come listen to you play, but Friday and Saturday nights are busy times here. Jake tells me good things about you. He says you're great musicians and vocalists."

In seconds, to the surprise of the Noirs, the owner of Paul's Poulet pulled up a chair at the end of their booth and sat.

"What instrument do you play, Mister Edwards?"

"Bass guitar."

"And you, Mister Knox?"

"Acoustic, same as Jake."

Paul turned to Lester, who'd anticipated the question.

"Piano. I play piano, but that's hard to do on the streets."

"I imagine so," Paul said. "I wish I could play an instrument, and I wish I could sing. In actuality, I can't do either. My church hides the hymnals from me."

"You fry a mean piece of chicken, though," Lester said.

"And the biscuits are light. They melt in your mouth," Laverne said.

"I advertise my biscuit recipe as belonging to my grandmother. Don't tell anybody—the recipe actually belonged to one of my drunken uncles."

"*One* of?" Leeroy asked.

"Oh, yes. One of three drunken uncles," Paul said. "My family put these drunken uncles, when they lived, on the front porch for all to see. We are, after all, in New Orleans, but I'm not sure advertising our biscuits as a drunken uncle's recipe makes for good business."

The men continued to talk until Jake rose. "I better get busy. I see three empty cups."

"No, you talk with your friends," Paul said, standing. He shook hands again with Lester, Leeroy, and Laverne. "Again, nice to meet you three. I'm coming to hear you play and sing. Jake tells me you set up around Jackson Square. I'll find you, and soon, I promise. You're always welcome at Paul's Poulet"—he broke into a wide smile—"where service is our proverb and chicken is our product."

With the restaurant still empty, Jake continued to sit with the Noirs. Ten minutes later, the four men heard a voice.

"More coffee, gentlemen?" Paul appeared, carrying a pot of coffee. The sharp creases could still be seen, but now a black vest covered the shirt, with *Paul's Poulet* stitched in white on the right lapel and *Paul, Head Chicken* on the left. He smiled, wearing the same chicken cap.

Again, Lester, Leeroy, and Laverne fought their emotions.

"Go ahead. Laugh," Paul said.

Lester, Leeroy, and Laverne roared again. Jake joined them. Jake didn't laugh as much at Paul as he did at Lester, Laverne, and Leeroy.

Jake saw a car pull into the lot. After three years, he knew the restaurant would soon be busy. He pulled on the cap and offered four clucks. "Work beckons."

"Till Saturday, Blanc?"

"Till Saturday."

Within thirty minutes, incoming customers searched, unsuccessfully, to find an empty seat. The Noirs knew the time had come for them to leave. Lester, Laverne, Leeroy waved to Jake.

CHAPTER SIXTEEN

Three Saturdays later, the three Noirs and Jake piled into Hazel for a night's work. With instruments stashed in Hazel's trunk, the men started toward Jackson Square.

"You sit up front, Jake," Lester said.

Offering no objection, Jake got in the front. He knew he'd arrived, because he'd never sat in Hazel's front seat. He made the most of it.

"Hey, I like sitting up here."

"Do you now, Blanc? The view here better than the view from back there, is it? What? About twenty-four inches closer?" Leeroy said.

Undeterred, Jake said, "As a matter of fact, yes, Mister Edwards. For example, I never realized Hazel once had a hood ornament. I can see the holes where an ornament used to be, with pride, no doubt. Not sure why I haven't noticed that before now. Has that been a recent development?"

"Recent?" Leeroy answered. "As recent as 1959." Laverne and Lester laughed. "I sold it that year. Needed a few bucks for something."

"How much?" Lester asked.

"How much what?" Leeroy asked, looking in his rearview mirror.

"How much did you get for it? I can't remember."

"Three dollars, as I recall. Sad. Hazel is missing an important part of her identity, and her matchless self is incomplete. Oh well." Leeroy chuckled and shrugged. "She's been without that adornment for all these years. She doesn't complain, and she doesn't seem to mind. She understands. Hard times and all." He patted the dashboard. "I love you, Hazel."

"We all love you, Hazel," Lester said.

"Not to offer a differing opinion and not to complain, but I would love you more, Hazel, if your heater worked," Laverne said.

"And there have been a few times, Hazel, when I miss your fuel gauge working," Leeroy said.

"As in last month?" Laverne said.

"As in last month," Leeroy affirmed.

"What happened last month?" Jake asked.

Lester explained. "We were headed somewhere and ran out of gas. The three of us. Can't remember where we were goin', exactly."

"Maria's," Leeroy said.

"Maria's?" Jake asked, wide-eyed and eyebrows raised. "The chicken place, Maria's? The one in Gretna?"

"Oops," Laverne uttered from the back seat.

"Sorry, Jake," Lester said, "we don't mean nothin'. We don't mean to slight Paul's Poulet."

"You bunch of traitors," Jake said, humor underlying his accusatory tone. "You bunch of worthless traitors. What did Paul's Poulet ever do to you?"

"Sorry, Blanc," Leeroy responded, "but I love Maria's barbecue sauce."

"We all like Maria's barbecue sauce," Lester added in support.

"*Love* me some Maria's barbecue sauce," Laverne said dreamily.

"Okay. That's different. Paul's doesn't do barbecue," Jake said.

Leeroy smiled at Jake. "Glad you ain't too disturbed, Blanc. You should try Maria's barbecue sauce."

Jake thought for a moment before speaking. "Maybe I will."

Saturday night was hopping. People were to be found in every niche of the French Quarter, or at least the niches the men saw. The night was early, eight o'clock, and families were everywhere—dads, moms, children, grandparents, grandchildren. The place smelled different, without the usual smells of alcohol and the Gulf. Perhaps the rain had washed the odor away, because the Quarter smelled clean, refreshed. The men found an open spot near St. Louis Cathedral and set up, lifting their instruments into place.

"I can't ever remember getting this close to the Cathedral," Lester said.

"It's a first for me too," Jake said.

With instruments swung into place and the donations table set up, Leeroy said, "Let's make some music."

"Amen, Brother Leeroy. Let's make music," Laverne said.

With that, Laverne hunched over and bent his guitar's strings. Leeroy recognized the number and swayed backward. Lester shook a tambourine he'd purchased recently from a pawn shop. The tambourine was missing one zill, but that didn't affect the instrument's tone much, not when played on the streets of New Orleans amid the din around St. Louis Cathedral. In his raspy voice, and to the absolute delight of the large crowd, Lester sang.

Goodbye Joe me gotta go me oh my oh
Me gotta go pole the pirogue down the bayou
My Yvonne the sweetest one me oh my oh
Son of me gun we'll have big fun on the bayou

Laverne, Leeroy, and Jake joined the second verse.

Thibodaux Fontaineaux the place is buzzin'
Kinfolk come to see Yvonne by the dozen
Dressed in style, go hog wild, oh me oh my o
Son of me gun we'll have big fun on the bayou
Settle down far from town get me a pirogue
And I'll catch all the fish in the bayou

Laverne, Leeroy, and Jake allowed Lester to sing solo again on the chorus. With Lester swinging the tambourine, all four finished the song, and the crowd erupted.

Jake saw him first, standing in the back of the crowd, moving to the music, clapping his hands. He caught the man's eye. Paul Evans smiled and nodded, never wavering in his sway.

Back in Leeroy's garage, Lester remarked, "A good night, I think, gentlemen."

"How much?" Laverne asked.

"Hush," Leeroy responded as he attempted to count.

Jake collapsed in one of the lawn chairs. Leeroy stopped counting, held a denomination closer to identify it before speaking. "Shut my mouth."

"That ain't a-happenin'," Lester said.

"That *would* be a first," Laverne added dryly.

"Something Canadian again?" Lester asked. "Or maybe a peso or two?"

Astonished, Leeroy answered in a tone of awe. "It's a hundred-dollar bill."

"Stop foolin'," Lester said.

"Look for yourself." Leeroy offered the bill to Lester.

"Is that right, Lester?" Laverne asked. "Tell me."

"Yes," Lester affirmed, "crisp and clean. A picture of ol' Benjamin Franklin himself. Big ol' beautiful Benny. Looks legit."

"I always liked Benny," Laverne said.

"Yes," Leeroy added, "Benny is nice. Real nice." He paused. "Wait, wait, wait. Here's another one."

"What?" Laverne asked.

"Yep," Leeroy said. "Another Benny."

He continued to pull money from the bag and sort through it. After a moment he said, "There are *four* hundred-dollar bills here."

"I haven't seen one of those in ten years. Can't remember the last one I had that belonged to me," Laverne said.

"Well, you have one now. In fact, we all have one. Come join us, Blanc."

Jake gathered his legs underneath him and joined the party.

The men continued to play every Saturday night, sometimes Friday night if Saturday's weather was predicted to be raw. On rare occasions, the men played both Friday and Saturday nights.

A month later, Jake saw him again. The man smiled as he listened to the four musicians. No one in the crowd knew Paul Evans, except perhaps those who frequented Paul's Poulet.

"There's another Ben Franklin," Leeroy said, back at the garage.

"Bless Ben," Laverne said.

Leeroy held the bills in his hands. "You three aren't going to believe this, but there are three more Bens in this bag. Another four-Ben night." He continued, speaking to Laverne. "Say hello to Ben."

Laverne was willing. "Why, hello, Ben. Good to see you again, but where have you been for the past five years?"

After Jake left to drop Laverne and Lester off at Franklin Avenue, Leeroy thought long about the night—mostly about who had left them the hundred-dollar bills, and why anyone would be so generous. Leeroy wondered if he was the only one with such thoughts.

CHAPTER SEVENTEEN

"Busy tonight," Laverne said, scanning Jackson Square early on Friday night, around seven thirty.

"Nary an inch to be had," Lester said. Every French Quarter corner to be seen was a beehive of activity.

"Do we go home and come back tomorrow night, or do we go back to Canal Street? Esplanade, maybe? Royal?" Leeroy asked. With the mention of Canal, Lester and Laverne shuddered. Mountain Man and Blade Boy had been there waiting for them.

"We've made money on Canal," Jake offered, "or Esplanade. I'm fine with either."

"I'm good to move to Canal," Lester said, "as long as we don't have to park on Camp Street. We can move toward the river."

Still thinking about the assault, Laverne said, "Let's move toward the river."

The four men moved toward the Mississippi River. In ten minutes, they found an open place and set up. Leeroy began.

> *O when the saints go marching in,*
> *O when the saints go marching in,*
> *O Lord I want to be in that number*
> *When the saints go marching in.*

Lester and Laverne joined in as Jake played.

O when the sun refused to shine
O when the sun refused to shine,
O Lord, I want to be in that number
When the sun refused to shine.
O when they crown him Lord of all,
O when they crown him Lord of all,
O Lord, I want to be in that number
When they crown him Lord of all.

Jake saw him again, curious how he'd found them, since the men had never played in this spot before. Paul smiled in Jake's direction.

After forty-five minutes, the men took a break. The crowd swelled. Lester, Laverne, or Leeroy took turns entertaining the crowd as the other men rested.

Laverne was now in his element. "Hello. Good to see you all tonight," he said.

The crowd responded with assorted hellos.

"My name is Laverne Knox. That's Lester Washington with the tambourine, Leeroy Edwards on the bass, and Jake Thomas on the guitar." Pause. "Jake is my son."

A polite groan, followed by laughter, came from the crowd.

"What about the other two? They your sons too?" a voice said from the crowd.

"Oh, no," Laverne said. "Leeroy there's my father." The crowd roared.

"You look like you're a hundred years old," the voice said again.

Jake could now identify the man—a boy, actually—small, and red-faced. He appeared to be a teenager. He also appeared to be drunk. He was loud and obnoxious—nothing the four men hadn't seen or heard before.

Laverne continued undeterred. "Speaking of age, I had a birthday—three days ago." He waved an arm in a broad theatrical gesture. "As I look around the crowd, I don't remember receiving a birthday gift from any of you. I'm still accepting gifts, but because they're late, your gift will have to be expensive." Again, laughter.

"I said you look to be a hundred years old," the red-faced boy said.

"My father there is one hundred and three. He has warts older than you, young man," Laverne said. More laughter from the crowd.

"You can't play or sing worth a plug nickel," the boy said.

"I've been tellin' these boys that for years, but they won't listen. I've encouraged these men to join the circus instead."

The more Laverne bantered with the red-faced teenager, the louder the crowd's laughter became. Some in the crowd believed the teen was a plant, added for entertainment purposes. But while the crowd laughed, the boy didn't. His face grew redder and redder. Perhaps feeling embarrassed and desiring to redeem himself, he continued to needle Laverne.

"Y'all look like you belong in the circus."

Laverne turned to look at Lester, Leeroy, and Jake. "I *told* you boys we should be playin' the circus."

"Why don't you boys go *join* a circus?" the boy said.

Laverne, Lester, and Leeroy had heard worse. Much worse. Laverne suspected alcohol dictated the boy's words. He started speaking and realized the heckler wasn't finished.

"You look like a worn-out piece of shoeleather with gum on it."

Laverne sensed he was losing control and attempted to move beyond the boy. He began playing. This gesture served as a signal for the others. Lester began shaking the tambourine. Leeroy and Jake swung instruments in place.

"I said, why in the hell don't you join a circus and get your shoeleather faces off these streets?" the boy continued.

"So I'm an old piece of shoeleather?" Laverne asked.

"Yeah," the boy said.

Laverne started to speak, but the boy interrupted him. "And an ugly one at that."

"This boy has all the answers," Laverne said.

"The omniscience of youth," Lester added.

Jake began playing again as the others caught up.

Laverne looked up in time to see the boy hurl something in his direction. Moving fast for his age, Laverne sidestepped an empty beer bottle. The sound of glass breaking on the sidewalk behind Laverne pierced the night. Several in the crowd voiced their disapproval. Street players had to tolerate mean things, but beer bottle grenades crossed the meanness line, verging on assault.

Jake had had enough, and felt now was a good time to introduce himself to the boy. The crowd agreed and cleared a path for him. But as he started to move, Jake realized his defense of Laverne was unnecessary, because just after Laverne dodged the bottle, Paul Evans moved.

Jake had never before seen Paul angry, or seen him lift anything heavier than a deep fryer full of chicken. Not until now. Paul was unrecognizable as he took the offender down.

In a matter of moments, Paul had the boy down on the street as easily as if he had unpacked a box of potatoes. Paul had the boy's right arm twisted behind him. He placed a knee in the middle of his back. The boy screamed in pain and yelled obscenities interspersed with threats.

"Get off me! I'll kill you!"

In moments, two of New Orleans's finest arrived. After hearing the full story from Paul and Laverne, corroborated by numerous bystanders, the policemen handcuffed the teen and led him away. Paul looked at Jake, but appeared to look straight through him before disappearing into the crowd. Jake was unsure where he went.

Laverne picked up where he'd left off, the same grin on his face.

"Now wasn't that fun?" he said. "Wish he'd thrown the bottle with the beer still in it."

The crowd got over the shock of what they'd witnessed as the four men played again. The crowd swayed and danced. At the next break, a man stepped forward and handed Laverne a bottle of beer.

"I'm not going to throw this bottle at you, and this bottle *ain't* empty."

The man had more beer bottles for Lester, Laverne, and Jake. Laverne toasted the crowd and took a long drink. Lester and Leeroy made the same gesture and lifted their bottle. Jake thanked the man and set the bottle on a bench near him. As the four men finished the night's playing, Jake dropped the bottle in a trash bin, still full.

"How much did we get?" Laverne said.

"I'm counting," Leeroy answered from the garage/ practice room at two thirty a.m.

Jake watched Leeroy carefully working through the cash on Hazel's hood, and the thought struck him that during all the teenager's heckling at their street gig, the three Noirs had never lost their composure. Although shaken by Blade Boy and Mountain Man, the three never appeared frustrated or discouraged.

"The guy was pushing you, Laverne," Jake said.

"Who? Ol' Leather Lung? I've heard worse. He wasn't creative atall." Laverne waved a hand in dismissal. "Shoe leather? Gum? Come on. Where's the creativity? Imagination? Throwing a beer bottle? Juvenile."

A pause. Leeroy continued to count. After a few moments he looked up. "Laverne caught a beer bottle years ago. Coming straight at his head. Grabbed that bottle like a baseball player shagging a fly ball."

"Sure did. Caught it and threw the thing back," Laverne said, grinning broadly.

"Didn't miss nary a chord," Lester laughed.

Leeroy paused again. He held a fistful of bills.

"I didn't see Mister Evans until he had Leather Lung down on the street, quick as a flash. Sure makes me see him in a different light. From now on, when I visualize him, I won't visualize that chicken cap."

"Scared the chicken crap out of Leather Lung, all right," Lester said.

"There's Ben," Leeroy reported, holding up a one-hundred-dollar bill.

"Hello, Ben," Lester said.

"Where've you been a-hidin', Ben?" Laverne asked.

"Another one. Another Ben. Number two," Leeroy reported.

"Worth getting hit with a bottle, eh, Laverne?" Lester offered.

"Close," Laverne stated, and slapped Lester on the back.

"Three. Four." Leeroy showed off the final two hundred-dollar bills.

"Another four-Franklin night," Lester said.

"'Tis indeed a sweet thing," Leeroy said. "I love me a Ben Franklin."

Leeroy tabulated the money and divided the loot. As he divided the money, he noticed Laverne deep in thought.

"A Ben Franklin for your thoughts, Laverne," Leeroy said.

Laverne thought for a moment. "Am I wrong, or on the nights when we've had four Ben Franklins in our bag, Paul Evans was in the crowd?"

Jake leaned forward in his lawn chair and nodded. "Like tonight," he said.

"Like tonight," Leeroy said.

"I hadn't thought of that, but you're right. I don't remember a four-Franklin night without seeing Mister Evans," Lester said.

"A coincidence?" Jake asked.

"May be a coincidence," Leeroy said. "And maybe ..."

"Maybe?" Jake asked.

"Maybe you need to invite Paul Evans to more of our performances."

CHAPTER EIGHTEEN

Spring and summer passed quickly. As fall approached, with a touch of coolness in the air, Laverne opened the door to their flat at midmorning to find Leeroy standing outside.

"Don't stand there palaverin' like a fool, Leeroy. Come on in," Laverne said, "even though you weren't invited. What's on your mind? Can't be much."

"Now *that's* funny. If I didn't know better, I'd feel right unwelcome this morning," Leeroy said. "I've a great mind to go home. At least Mildred pretends to like me."

"That woman could've done much better," Lester said, echoing Jake's often-heard rebuttal toward Leeroy.

Leeroy feigned pain.

"Pardon me, Mister Edwards. What's on your mind?" Lester said.

"Much nicer. Thank you," Leeroy said. "Do you realize we've been playing together with Blanc for over a year now?"

"We do realize. Laverne and I were talking about that very thing a few days ago. What are you thinking about?"

"Let's surprise Blanc and buy him a meal. I won't tell him, but he's changed my life for the better."

"A meal? Excellent idea. Count me in," Laverne said.

"I'm in. Where does Jake live?" Lester asked.

"Don't know for sure," Leeroy said, "but we know where he works. Let's drive over to Paul's Poulet and see if he's workin'. It's early in the day. Maybe Paul's isn't too busy and he'll have a sandwich with us. If not, we'll find out where Blanc lives and go by his house."

The men piled into Hazel, minus her hood ornament, and started toward Chef Menteur Highway.

"We're in luck. There's Jake's car," Lester said, pointing to a back space in the parking lot at Paul's Poulet. As before, the front parking lot at Paul's Poulet was empty.

"You know that's Jake's car ... how?" Laverne asked, smiling.

"The missing glass in the left rear door gives that car away every time," Leeroy answered.

Two other cars sat in the lot. The men assumed that to be here so early in the morning, the cars belonged to employees of Paul's Poulet. Leeroy parked Hazel in front.

The men unloaded and walked toward the main entrance. They looked every bit the aged men they were. All three were bent. Everything about them moved slowly.

"After you, Misters Washington and Knox," Leeroy said. He held the door open for his two friends to enter.

"Thank you, Mister Edwards," Laverne said.

Lester followed. "Glad to see you recognize my superiority, Mister Edwards."

"*You* will recognize *my* superiority when I shine my shoe on yo' butt," Leeroy responded. "Besides ..."

"Besides what?" Laverne said.

"Age before beauty," Leeroy said.

"I thought it was pearls before swine," Laverne responded.

Lester and Leeroy stared at Laverne, Lester trying his best not to laugh, until Laverne offered an explanation.

"NPR. You boys should listen. *And* it's in the Bible."

Leeroy grunted. "Well, *I* ain't in the Bible."

"You old enough to be," Laverne said, and with that they went in.

The restaurant was empty, with nary a patron nor a worker in sight. The three stepped to the counter and began surveying the offerings, as if they didn't know what they wanted to eat. In seconds, a young woman emerged from the back, straightening her clothing as she walked, pressing her pants with her hands. The men recognized the light blue short-sleeved shirt and black vest. They smiled at the chicken cap, the tail feathers bouncing as she walked. The young girl smiled broadly. Doubtless she'd seen lots of people smile at her cap. Her comfort level was obvious.

"Good morning. Welcome to Paul's. May I take your order?"

Leeroy read *Paul's Poulet* on the right front of her vest and then found what he was looking for on the vest's left side. "Good morning, Cora. How are you this glorious morning?"

"I'm fine. Thank you, sir." The smile never left her. She waited patiently.

The men stood with hats in hand. Leeroy said, "We're looking for Blanc."

The smile turned to a look of confusion. "Blanc?"

Laverne came to Leeroy's rescue. "Jake, ma'am. We're looking for Jake. Jake Thomas."

Cora's smile returned. "I understand. I thought you were looking for white meat, as in a sandwich."

"We are looking for white meat all right, also known as Jake Alvin Thomas," Laverne said.

Cora hesitated, a look of apprehension on her face. Lester tried to ease her anxiety.

"Forgive us, ma'am. We didn't introduce ourselves. My name is Lester Washington. This is Laverne Knox and that dangerous-looking man there is Leeroy Edwards."

Laverne and Leeroy nodded.

"We're friends of Jake's," Lester went on, "come to say hello and buy him a Paul's Poulet sandwich."

Cora's expression changed to a look of relief and understanding. "My name is Cora—I guess you read my nametag. Cora Hoelzer. It's nice to meet you. You must be the three men Jake told me about."

"We must be," Leeroy said with a wide grin.

"Jake didn't say anything about ..." She stopped.

"Us being Black?" Leeroy said.

"You being *older*, was what I was going to say," Cora said, "but no, now that you mention it, Jake didn't say anything about you being Black either. In fact, Jake told me the four of you play basketball together."

The three men laughed. Lester said, "Now, ma'am, do we look to be basketball players?"

"No, you don't. Forgive me for being candid."

Young people, at times, had difficulty talking to senior adults, but not this young woman.

"Music, ma'am. We play music together," Laverne explained.

Cora looked surprised. "Truthfully? Jake plays a musical instrument? I never knew."

"He can make a guitar sing, young lady," Lester said.

"If you close your eyes while Blanc is playing, you'll swear it's an angel," Leeroy said.

"Hmmm. Good to know," she said.

"We three old buzzards have played with two great guitarists in our time," Laverne said, "and Jake's one of them."

"What about the other great guitarist?" Cora asked.

The three men went silent.

"Oh. Forgive me for asking," she said. "I'm sorry to disappoint you, but Jake isn't here. Are you ready to order?"

"Do you mind telling us where we could find him?" Leeroy asked. "We saw his car."

All three men recognized how uneasy Leeroy's question made Cora. She shifted her weight from one foot to the other and looked uncertain. "I—uh—"

Laverne interrupted her, attempting to ease her anxiety. "Will you tell Jake three old men came to see him, and we'll come back soon? He'll know who you're talking about."

Relieved, Cora said, "Yes, I will. I'll tell him."

"Nice to meet you, Cora," Laverne said. He and Lester nodded in her direction.

"Nice to meet you three. I'll tell Jake first thing, soon's I see him."

Lester, Laverne, and Leeroy exited Paul's Poulet and started toward Hazel. Standing in the parking lot, Laverne said, "Now where do you suppose that boy is?"

"No tellin'," Lester answered. "Maybe he's out tryin' to roust up a new band."

"Can't say as I blame him," Leeroy responded, "havin' to play with the likes of you two. Let's go home. We'll come back another day."

Moving in Hazel's direction in the front parking lot, Lester veered off on a hunch and began walking toward Jake's old car instead. Once at the car, he leaned over, shaded his eyes from the morning sun and peered into the rear seat through the glass in the right rear door. He turned and motioned to Leeroy and Laverne, who joined him at the Olds, shading their eyes as well. They all stood gazing at the rear seat of Jake's car.

He lay sleeping in the seat, covered with a blanket, his feet nearest the door where the three men stood. The top of his head was visible. He looked comfortable, what they could see of him, curled in a fetal position, his knees inches away from touching the front seat.

The men stood and stared at one another. They glanced back at Jake and then stared at one another again.

Jake woke to a *peck peck peck* on the rear glass. He hesitated, hoping whoever was there would go away. He didn't move.

The pecking continued. After a few minutes, he gave up and pulled the blanket from his head, to be greeted by the New Orleans sun.

Rubbing the sleep from his eyes, he tried to focus on the origin of the pecking. Glancing in the direction of the sound, Jake saw three old men leaning over, staring at him. All three smiled broadly. One of them gave a short wave.

"What are y'all doing here?" Jake asked. He exited the car and unfolded his long frame. Lester thought their waking Jake might annoy him, but he offered no sign of vexation.

"Surprise!" Lester said. "Welcome to this cheerful celebration."

"Oh," Jake said, "a birthday? Not mine." He yawned.

"Do you realize, Blanc," Leeroy said, "we've been playing together for over a year?"

"Only a year? Seems longer," Jake said with a smile, rubbing both hands over his face and head to get rid of the sleep.

"We are here to celebrate," Laverne said. "We gonna buy you a chicken sandwich."

Jake paused for a moment before speaking. "Then a celebration we'll have. Shall we enter Paul's Poulet?"

"Let's," Laverne replied.

Jake reached in the floorboard of the rear seat and took out his shoes.

Seated in a booth at Paul's, the men talked.

"Over a year since we started playing together. Hard to believe," Lester said.

"The first time we saw you, Blanc, we didn't believe you could play a radio with hands as large as yours, but you *are* a talented musician."

"It's been a good year," Laverne said.

"A good year," Jake said. "I agree."

"A toast to a good year," Lester offered, and raised his cup, followed by the other three.

"To the Lord's richest blessing on the next year," Jake said.

Lester, Laverne, and Leeroy said "Amen," as the four touched cups together.

"Who ordered four sandwiches with potato wedges?" Cora asked.

The men turned their attention to the young waitress with a tray in hand, stacked with food.

"That would be us," Lester answered.

"I figured," she responded, "since there's no one else in here."

Lester, Laverne, and Leeroy had the opportunity to see—really see—the petite waitress. She stood about five feet, give or take an inch or two. She had an elegant olive skin tone and blonde hair cut short. She walked with unmistakable grace. She wore two sets of earrings, both on the lobes. Her hazel eyes sparkled, and when she smiled, small dimples showed on her cheeks.

In addition to the earrings, she wore a single ring on her left hand and two on the right. Leeroy noticed she was not sporting a wedding band. What truly impressed the men was her personality. She was a young lady sure of herself—much like Mildred, Leeroy thought. Her smile hinted at a mischievous personality.

"Jake, you never told me you play guitar," she said.

"Oh, no?" Jake answered, "Forgive me, Cora. I play guitar."

"Thanks," she said with a smile and the barest edge of sarcasm, detected by all four men.

Jake added, "With these three curmudgeons."

"Whoa! Don't go callin' me no curmudgeon," Leeroy said.

"My apologies."

"They introduced themselves previously," Cora said.

"So I've *you* to thank for being waked up this morning." Jake smiled in her direction.

"Oh, no," Laverne said. "She told us nothin', other than you weren't at work."

"We assumed you were goofin' off again," Leeroy said.

"Or out looking for a replacement for Leeroy," Laverne said.

"I happened to stroll over to yo' car," Lester added, "and see you."

"Curious," Jake said, "three curious old men peering into the back seat of another's automobile? Could get you hurt."

"You're right," Laverne said. "I do remember something about curiosity killing a cat."

With no one else in the restaurant and the smell of fried chicken, potato wedges, and french fries wafting through the air, Cora was in no rush. She knew once the lunch crowd arrived, she'd be busy until nine that night, so she made the most of the downtime. Perhaps it was lost on Jake, but the three Noirs could tell she liked him, just by the way she chided him.

"Let me refill those cups," she said. In moments, she returned with a pot of fresh coffee. She returned to the counter as the first customer other than Lester, Laverne and Leeroy entered. The men sat in silence. Laverne met Jake's eyes. The atmosphere grew serious.

"Why didn't you tell us you were homeless, Jake?"

Jake leaned forward and shifted his weight. He avoided looking at any of the men.

"I'm not homeless, technically. I have a roof over my head. Maybe not asphalt shingles, but a roof." He smiled.

"You told us you lived in a house off Chef Menteur Highway," Leeroy said.

"No," Jake corrected, "I never said I lived in a house. I let you assume that."

"You said you live off Chef," Leeroy countered.

Jake turned toward the street, lifted both hands, palms up, and moved both hands back and forth. "Chef Menteur Highway, gentlemen."

"Are you telling us," Lester asked, "you live in your car, parked in this lot, off Chef?"

Jake swallowed, hesitating. "Paul lets me park the car in his back lot, yes. I don't bother anyone, and I'm not costing the hard-working, tax-paying citizens of this fair community anything. Paul talked to the New Orleans Police Department. They look the other way. In fact, I've come to know several of the police personally. The men in blue—great men and women. I respect them. They respect me. I stay out of trouble and they leave me alone. No problems. No worries."

"Where do you—" Lester started.

"Bathe?" Jake finished the question for him. "Paul was kind enough to install a shower for me in a small niche in the back of the restaurant. He allows me to sleep inside when the weather gets too cold. I have a key, so I can come in and out as I please. I could sleep inside every night, but I prefer the great outdoors. When it rains, and the raindrops make music on the roof of my car—that's when real sleeping takes place."

"I was *going* to ask," Lester said, with a mild harrumph, "where you wash your clothes."

Jake turned and pointed across the street. "Ruth's Laundromat." He grinned. "I love those quarter tips."

Laverne now remembered Jake always wanted the quarters they received in tips, leaving 25 North Galvez with a pocketful, jingling as he walked. It all made sense.

Jake continued. "I iron clothes at night, after closing, on a board I picked up at a yard sale. Stashed in that closet," he said, pointing. The men knew Jake's clothes were always clean and pressed. They'd assumed his mother did both.

"Paul's been good to me, period," he said. "He's the father I lost. He invited me to live with him and his wife, but they have a large family. I've met them all. Adorable people. Beautiful wife. Six daughters. *Six.*" He gazed out the front window for a moment. "Wouldn't be right for a young man to move in with a family with all those girls. I didn't want to jeopardize my relationship with Paul. Plus, I prefer living wild and free off Chef Menteur Highway." With the last statement he smiled in Leeroy's direction.

Lester patted the table with the palm of his hand.

"Tell us about your family, Jake."

Jake swallowed hard.

CHAPTER NINETEEN

Jake had never spoken of his family to anyone. But he believed the men had earned the right to know. They had, after all, been together for over a year. They had been through Mountain Man, Blade Boy, and Leather Lung. Perhaps relating his life history to Lester, Laverne, and Leeroy would be a kind of release. Nursing the coffee cup with both hands, he looked into the depths of the cup and started his story, much of it as black and cold as the coffee itself.

"Born and raised here in New Orleans, on Pike Street, in Metairie. In a house, Leeroy, complete with asphalt shingles and walls and a driveway."

Leeroy smiled.

"Had a father, Monroe, and a mother, Elizabeth. People called her Beth. A house full of love. Mother packed my lunch before driving me to school. Dad was an accountant, Tulane University graduate, and Mother was a stay-at-home mom. The house was immaculate and smelled of red beans and rice, gumbo, fricassees, cakes, pies. I wanted for nothing and never questioned whether or not I was loved or wanted."

Jake looked out the window, his gaze on something more distant than the parking lot.

"My father loved my mother, I knew, and Dad was an excellent provider. We lived in a big house—well, a big house for just the three of us, as I had no brothers or sisters. Dad and I would play catch in our yard. We went on vacations to Las Vegas, San Francisco, New York City, Charleston, Boston—I can't remember a lot of them, because I was young. My life, looking back, was idyllic, perfect. As a child, I didn't have a care or a want in this world."

A pause. Jake gathered his thoughts as he idly swirled the coffee in his cup. He took a deep breath before continuing.

"When I was ten, my father lost his job. They told him the company was losing money. He came home one day and informed my mother. Not to worry, he told Mom. I'll start a job search Monday. But the economy in New Orleans dried up. No jobs to be found anywhere. Nothing."

He stopped and rubbed his face with both hands, then dropped his hands to the table.

"After several weeks, Mom started cleaning houses. Back-breaking work. She always came home smiling, but exhaustion was written all over her. She aged ten years in twenty-four months. I'm not sure which caused Dad more grief—his joblessness, or Mom ..." Jake's voice trailed off. His eyes remained on the coffee cup.

"Dad dropped into depression. I didn't know what depression was then, but I know now. He would sit and look into the distance, not really seeing anything. He never initiated any conversation. He'd just answer Mom's questions—or mine. We stopped playing catch. Dad shrugged me off when I asked—not in a rude manner, but I knew not to bother him. Eventually, I stopped."

He heaved a monstrous sigh. "We were given a month's notice before we lost the house—foreclosure, Mom explained. We moved into a rental—a rat-trap, roach-infested place—

that was terrible. They must have had a difficult time just to pay the few dollars in rent."

He paused, nudging the coffee cup handle with one finger, turning the cup on the saucer.

"Dad didn't eat much. He lost weight. And I'm sure Mom went hungry to ensure I had enough. One day, I came home from school to find her, but no Dad. 'He's out,' Mom said. 'No need to worry. He'll be home soon.' Later, a policeman came to our house."

Jake took another deep breath before continuing.

"They'd found Dad's body floating in a canal. The police suspected he'd been murdered by someone attempting to rob him. We lived in a dangerous part of town, the policeman said. I doubt Dad had a nickel on him, just like he didn't have a nickel at home."

Jake wiped at one eye with the heel of his hand. Laverne, Leeroy, and Lester all looked in other directions, pretending not to see.

"Mom screamed—" Jake gulped, "—when they told her about Dad's death. Her screams haunt me to this day. She and I buried him. Where she got the money, I don't know. After that, she had to work harder to provide for me."

More deep breaths, in and out—an obvious effort to maintain composure.

"I woke one morning and found her in her bed—stiff, cold, and gone. She'd died in her sleep, probably from worry and exhaustion. The city buried her. I had nothing, other than a few threadbare clothes, a single pair of old shoes, and my dad's car, the same car I have now. I came to work at Paul's a short time later."

One more pause.

"And so now, here I sit. I don't blame my father or mother. None of it was their fault. They both did the best they could until life just turned against them. Anyway, from there I dropped out of school midway through my senior year. I never knew who paid the few bills I owed. I was disciplined enough to go to school after Dad and Mom passed until I got bored, and then, I stopped going. Nobody cared whether I was in school or not. And now? Now I wear a chicken cap, work at Paul's Poulet, and live in my car. Livin' the American dream."

He smiled a gentle, rueful smile, his eyes wet. The three Noirs were silent for a time, out of respect for his story.

After a time, Lester said, "Mountain Man and Blade Boy? You learned ...?"

"How to fight on the streets ...? Yes," Jake said, finishing Lester's thought. "I'm a street fighter, self-taught, experienced. I had to be. I lost lots of fights until I learned how to handle myself. I hit hard, fast, and first, when necessary. I ran from a fight one time ... but *only* one time. I prefer standing, fighting, and losing to running. I don't enjoy the feeling of defeat." He tapped the table with an index finger. "I've fought worse than Mountain Man and Blade Boy combined. Fought 'em and beat 'em."

Jake suddenly looked bone-weary. Stunned and sad at his tale, the three men knew that in the presence of such grief, sometimes the best option was just to sit and be with the grieving person.

They sat with Jake.

"Anything for us to help with, Jake?" Lester asked.

Jake didn't answer him. They continued to sit in silence.

The men left Paul's when Jake told them he had to be at the counter in thirty minutes. None of them spoke about Jake's family for the rest of the day.

CHAPTER TWENTY

The following morning at eleven, Leeroy picked up Lester and Laverne. They drove to Leeroy's garage. Each man sat in his lawn chair and expounded on a wide range of topics. Eventually curiosity got the better of Lester.

"Why eleven a.m., Leeroy?" Lester said.

"I have my reasons—trust me."

The men turned their attention to consideration of the plight of one Jacob Alvin Thomas.

"We could give him a larger percentage of our earnings," Laverne offered.

"I'm good with the idea, but I suspect Blanc won't take the money," Leeroy said.

"There's another option," Laverne stated. "We'll invite Jake to live with us."

"Excellent idea," Lester said. "Sleeping on our sofa is better than sleeping in the back seat of his car."

Lester and Laverne waited for Leeroy to say something. Leeroy was deep in thought, contemplating, they joked, the problem of world hunger. When he did speak, Lester and Laverne were unsure who he spoke to.

"Blanc's is a sad story, indeed. A sad story," Leeroy said, as he rubbed his chin. "But I've got myself an idea."

"Whoa, look out," Lester said.

"Leeroy Edwards with an idea?" Laverne said, in a theatrically incredulous tone.

Lester sat up straight in his lawn chair and threw both arms out straight. "The world is comin' to an end, Laverne!"

Laverne matched Lester's gestures. "I'll hide the women."

"I'll hide the children." Lester said, then appeared to reconsider. "Wait. Why do you get to hide the women? Why can't I hide the women?"

"Because I called it first."

Lester and Laverne stopped bantering and waited for Leeroy to reveal his epiphany. After an agonizing several seconds, Lester grew exasperated.

"Tell us, Leeroy. What is this idea of yours?"

More delay from Leeroy. More exasperated than Lester, Laverne said, "Tell us yo' idea, Mister Edwards."

More excruciating seconds lapsed as Lester and Laverne shifted their weight in the lawn chairs. Lester and Laverne sensed Leeroy was waiting, but they didn't understand why.

Finally, Leeroy said, "My idea is coming along here ... right about ... now."

At that moment, as she did every time the men were together around lunchtime, Mildred entered the garage carrying a tray with coffee, cups, and sandwiches. The three rose to meet her. Laverne moved a lawn chair into place as Leeroy shifted his small table into the middle of the circle.

Mildred sat. She drank coffee and ate with her husband and friends.

Leeroy waited.

Within thirty minutes, with all the peanut butter and jelly sandwiches and most of the coffee consumed, Mildred asked, "How's Jake?"

A long pause occurred before Laverne answered her. "Jake's fine," he lied.

"Blanc is homeless," Leeroy blurted out.

Lester and Laverne shot Leeroy an *I can't believe you just said that* look.

The revelation shocked Mildred, the reaction Leeroy had anticipated and desired.

"What? Jake? *Homeless*?"

"Homeless," Leeroy echoed.

"How is Jake homeless?" Mildred sat speechless for a few moments. "Leeroy, you said he lived in a house on Chef."

"No. Blanc's a smooth one, my love," Leeroy said. "He said he lived *off* Chef. He never said he lived in a *house* off Chef. He lives out of his car. Sleeps in it where it's parked in the lot at Paul's Poulet. Which is off Chef."

More silence. Then Mildred said, "But his clothes are always clean and pressed ...."

"Laundromat across the street," Laverne said.

"Irons them himself in Paul's Poulet after hours," Lester added.

Leeroy anticipated Mildred's next question. Fifty years of marriage can do that between a wife and a husband, or at least it did for Leeroy and Mildred. He didn't wait for her to ask.

"Paul of Paul's Poulet was kind enough to install a shower in a back corner of the restaurant. And Paul Evans—that's Paul's last name, Evans—lets Blanc sleep inside when the nights get cold."

"I imagine Jake cooks there," Laverne said.

Neither Lester nor Leeroy had ever thought about that. Still anticipating Mildred's thoughts, Leeroy believed Paul needed defending. He continued speaking. Mildred continued to listen.

"Paul Evans ... we met him, by the way. Nice man. He invited Blanc to live with him and his family."

"Why didn't he?" Mildred asked.

"Paul Evans has a wife and a house full of girls—six daughters. Blanc didn't believe his living there would be a good idea. He didn't want to jeopardize their friendship," Lester said.

"That's Jake," Mildred said, nodding.

Leeroy waited. Mildred came back to her initial question. "How did he come to be homeless?"

For the next fifteen minutes, Leeroy, Lester, and Laverne told Jake's story to Mildred. At times, she shook her head in disbelief. As Lester neared the end of the story, at the part of Jake sleeping in his car, Mildred took a handkerchief from her apron pocket and wiped her eyes. All four sat in silence. Finally, she said, "Unbelievable. I never imagined."

She and the other three were silent for another long moment before she continued, her voice stronger than before.

"Now, we can't have this. This just isn't right. We're not being good Christians if the four of us sit around and do nothing about a homeless boy."

"We been thinkin' 'bout that too," Lester said. "Laverne and I are going to invite him to live with us. He can sleep on the sofa—it'd be better than sleepin' in his car. He'll have a roof over his head and three meals a day. He won't freeze to death, and he won't go hungry. He won't have to go back to a laundromat, or shower or iron his clothes at Paul's."

Again, Leeroy waited. He didn't have to wait long.

"Let's invite him to live with us," Mildred said. She reached over and patted Leeroy's arm to emphasize her point. "Sure, Leeroy, let's ask Jake to live here. We have the spare bedroom that hasn't been slept in since Amos—"

Her voice trailed off. She continued in a low tone, dropping her head. "Well, our spare bedroom hasn't been slept in for a long time."

Mildred's tone shifted from sadness back to excitement. "We have the space. Having a young man in the house will be nice. I know Jake. He'll help with the chores you don't do, Leeroy." With her last sentence, Mildred stopped patting his arm and swatted him.

Leeroy knew he could have initiated the idea of Jake coming to live with them. He knew Mildred would have embraced the idea with love and understanding, without reservation or hesitation. But he wanted the idea to come from her, for reasons of his own.

After a few moments, Mildred said, "I'm surprised you didn't think about Jake living with us, Leeroy."

"Don't know where my mind was, my love," Leeroy replied airily.

Out of Mildred's sight, Lester, and Laverne cut their eyes sideways at Leeroy. They knew Leeroy had known exactly what he was doing when he waited for Mildred to enter the garage.

Leeroy didn't dare look at either man.

CHAPTER TWENTY-ONE

"How much did we get?" Lester asked.

Saturday morning, sometime after three o'clock, the men assembled at Leeroy's garage. Leeroy no longer closed and locked the garage door. Lester, Laverne, and Jake sat in the lawn chairs while their accountant tabulated the night's earnings.

Leeroy ignored Lester's question while he counted. Lester, Laverne, and Jake talked among themselves.

"Divided by four ..." Leeroy muttered. He continued shuffling money, until finally he had the money divided into four neat piles atop Hazel's hood. He scooped up the piles and walked toward the three seated men.

"Another good night," Leeroy said, as he distributed dividends.

"We were lucky to get the spot off Decatur. The crowd seemed festive," Lester commented.

"And obviously generous," added Laverne, waving a wad of money.

"Thank you, Jesus," Jake said, and meant every word of it.

"Thank you, Jesus," Leeroy echoed, as genuine as Jake.

Their small talk continued. Though late, none of the men were in a rush to get home—often the case after Friday night gigs. After a Saturday night performance, Jake always hurried to the parking lot at Paul's Poulet for a few hours' sleep, a shower, and then off to Sunday worship, but early on Saturday mornings after the Friday night show, the men had little else to do.

They enjoyed the time together. Lester, Leeroy, and Laverne discoursed passionately on national politics as Jake listened. The three Noirs never agreed on their support of the American president. All four talked about local and city politics, but their real drama happened in discussions of state politics. The three Noirs had lived through the Huey P. Long Jr. era, making them experts in backroom policy making, political intrigue, greed, and corruption. Lester and Leeroy were Democrats. Laverne was a Republican.

"I wish I could think like a Democrat," Laverne goaded his friends, "but I can't git that *stupid*."

None of the four had ever voted. The thought of having to sign one's name and read a ballot frightened Laverne tremendously, and frightened Lester and Leeroy only slightly less.

Jake sat and listened as the three debated the latest political scandal. This week, they raked and dissected the state budget which, according to them, included little to no support for insolvent people. Next week, Jake knew, the discussion would be something else—an accusation against the governor, the lieutenant governor, or the attorney general. Perhaps a high-ranking official had decided to demonstrate his amorous desire toward another woman to the consternation of his wife and constituency. Jake seldom joined in the diatribe, but he didn't mind listening. He was nearly asleep when Leeroy's voice jostled him from his doze.

"Blanc. Why don't you come live with Mildred and me?"

"What?" Jake said, rubbing the sleep from his eyes.

"I said, why don't you come to live with Mildred and me?"

Jake looked across at Lester and Laverne, who looked back at him but said nothing.

"That's what I *thought* you said." Jake scrubbed at his face, then looked directly at Leeroy. "No."

"We got a spare bedroom that hasn't been used in years ..." Leeroy's voice trailed off at the memory of Amos. He paused before continuing. "Plus, Mildred needs someone to help do the chores, since I'm too lazy."

Jake knew that wasn't true. Whatever Leeroy Edwards, Laverne Knox, and Lester Washington may or may not have been, Jake knew none of the three were lazy.

"Not happening, Leeroy. But thank you for asking." Jake's tone was adamant. "I suspect all three of you've been thinking about this, and I appreciate all three of you considering me, but no."

"I ain't askin', Blanc."

"I'm sorry?"

"I ain't askin'," Leeroy repeated.

"I heard that, but ..." Jake said.

Leeroy waited for the desired result and got it as he recognized Jake's bewildered look.

"*Mildred's* askin'," Leeroy said.

"That's unfair." Jake scowled halfheartedly at Leeroy. Leeroy held up both arms, palms open and up.

"Don't tell me you're going to disappoint Mildred," Lester said.

"Never thought I'd see the day. Never," Laverne said, shaking his head in melodramatic disbelief.

"But ..."

Jake recognized defeat when he saw it.

A week later, Jake parked his car on the street in front of Mildred and Leeroy's house. Mildred smiled as she opened the door, with Leeroy behind and at her shoulder.

"Welcome Jake, to our home," she said, smiling. "To *your* home."

Jake carried two plastic bags. The bags contained everything he owned—three pairs of slacks, four dress shirts, underclothing, socks, one pair of shoes, and one dress jacket. He wore his other pair of shoes and coat.

"Let me show you to your room," Mildred said, and led Jake down the hallway to what had been Amos's room. Leeroy trailed behind, silent. Mildred entered the room and switched on a light.

"I hope you like it," she said.

The smell of fresh paint was in the air. That explained the white spots on Leeroy's hands, Jake thought.

Light streaming in from a large window illuminated the room. Jake knew the comforter on the bed was new, as were the curtains. The linoleum floor was worn but spotless. The room had a small bed with a chest of drawers to match, with a lamp, also looking to be new, sitting on the bedside table. Mildred opened a closet door. "Store your clothes in here."

Jake stood speechless, the scene taking him back to happier times when he lived in his own house, had his own room, and lived with loving parents. He hadn't anticipated the flood of memories, and he fought back tears. If Mildred or Leeroy noticed, they were too kind to let him know.

"The room is yours, Jake. Feel free to do anything you want—hang pictures, or ..." Mildred said, her voice and her smile never changing.

Leeroy entered the room quietly. He stood behind them both with hands folded in front. He, as Jake, was awash in memories.

"This room is … just the most magnificent thing I've seen in a long time," was all Jake could manage.

Mildred took one of the bags from Jake. She emptied its contents—pants and shirts—on the bed. She walked into the closet and came out with hangers, then began hanging Jake's worldly possessions. All of them.

Jake felt an overwhelming need to say something. "I can't express my gratitude for your kindness. I want to say thank you for—"

Mildred interrupted him. "Put your other things in the chest," she said, pointing.

"Yes, ma'am," Jake said. He tried to speak again, and again Mildred interrupted.

"Dinner is at six." She smiled.

"Yes, ma'am."

Jake was determined to express his appreciation and started again but was again interrupted, this time by Leeroy—the first time Leeroy had spoken since Jake's arrival.

"All of this was Mildred's idea. Me, I've never liked you, Blanc," he said with a broad grin. Leeroy's words—and Jake's response—lightened a heavy moment for all three of them.

"I'll never understand," Jake said, "what Mildred saw in you."

He slept that night in a bed, in a room, in a house—his own bed, his own room and, he felt, his own house. Dry, warm, safe, and loved, he slept better than he'd slept since the night before his mother died.

CHAPTER TWENTY-TWO

Jake rose early Sunday morning. He was unsure when Leeroy and Mildred bathed and dressed on Sunday morning, and he didn't want to be in their way. In ten minutes, he exited the bathroom, attired for the day.

Mildred moved around in the kitchen. Frying bacon had never smelled so good. He and Mildred ate alone.

"Leeroy's in the garage," Mildred explained. "He goes out there every Sunday morning. I don't bother him."

Jake made no comment and asked no questions.

"You and I'll leave about nine thirty for Bible study and worship. It starts at ten," Mildred said.

"You and I?"

Mildred patted his hand. "Leeroy doesn't go to church. Hasn't since Amos's death. Lester and Laverne don't go, either, as far as I know—again, not since Amos's death."

"That surprises me," Jake said. "I've heard all three men thank Jesus for blessings. And I remember Leeroy reading the Christmas story and praying."

"All three of them are good men, Jake, and all of them are *Christian* men, but they don't go to church." She sighed. "Amos's death rocked our little world. After Amos died, Leeroy, Laverne, and Lester turned away from organized religion. I embraced it. I don't know what I would've done without Jesus, Pastor Josiah, and the Franklin Avenue Church of God in Christ. While I encourage Leeroy and the others, I don't believe I can push them."

Mildred's sadness was unmistakable. The two finished eating in silence before she spoke again. "I always take Leeroy his breakfast on Sunday morning."

She rose and retrieved a tray. Placing bacon and eggs on a plate, she put the plate on the tray and completed the meal with a cup of coffee. She started toward the garage, but Jake stopped her. "Let me take it. Please."

Mildred offered no resistance.

Jake walked through the open garage door to find Leeroy seated in a lawn chair. He picked his bass guitar and hummed softly. Leeroy appeared to have already showered, and he sat clean-shaven and well-dressed.

"Good morning, young Blanc."

"Good morning, Leeroy."

"Did you sleep well?"

"I did, thank you. Slept the sleep of the righteous."

"Amen, Brother Blanc."

Jake offered Leeroy the tray.

"Thank you." Leeroy picked up a fork with his right hand and a piece of bacon with his left. Jake let Leeroy enjoy his eggs and bacon for a few minutes before speaking.

"Mildred tells me you don't go to church. I find that surprising."

Leeroy smiled. "I knew you were bound to find out. I grew up in an orphanage in Chalk Bluff, Alabama. Never knew any family, includin' my parents. The orphanage never had enough heat in the winter. Never enough food, year-round. Never enough anything except hunger and cold. They weren't bad people, the people who ran it. They just couldn't love all of us kids with the love we needed."

"What's that got to do with you not worshipping in a church?"

Leeroy sipped his coffee, considered, and continued. "I felt neglected, Blanc. I *was* neglected. But I never felt bad toward those folks who managed the orphanage. But I finally walked out of Chalk Bluff. Walked away from the cold and the hunger. Walked away without a dime to my name. Not a nickel. Not a penny. I grew up believing in God, in Jesus. Still do. I grew up Christian, and I *am* a Christian—born again in Christ."

He waved a dismissive hand. "I went to church with Mildred years ago, but I've little interest in church now. Haven't been interested for years."

"Not since Amos?"

Leeroy paused before speaking, avoiding eye contact with Jake.

"Not since Amos." Another pause. "Why do you find the fact that I don't go to church surprising?"

"Because you're one of the most decent people I've ever met. Period. You love Mildred, Lester, and Laverne. That's obvious. You'd give your last penny to someone in need. You're a nice person. You could never harm anyone."

"You never know," Leeroy said, and smiled.

Jake felt no need to talk around the edge of the issue as Mildred did. "I want you to worship with Mildred and me. Today."

"I won't, Blanc. Sorry. One day, perhaps, but not today."

Leeroy's determination was obvious. Jake stood, placed the other's now-empty coffee cup on the tray with the empty plate. The tray sat on Hazel's hood. Jake, undeterred, said, "I'm not asking."

Leeroy took a moment to regain his senses. "What did you say?"

"I said I'm not asking."

Leeroy opened his mouth, pointed to Jake, intending to offer an objection. Jake interrupted.

"*Mildred* is asking."

"She would never do that, Blanc. I know her too well. She would never say that to me or you."

"She didn't say it. She didn't have to. Her eyes did."

"That's unfair, Blanc," Leeroy said.

"Now you know," Jake said, holding up both arms, palms up.

"I been meanin' to ask you something."

"Ask away."

"How are *you* Christian?"

"You mean how did I become a Christian?"

"I s'pose that's what I'm askin', yes."

"My parents. I can't ever remember a time when I wasn't in church. Under their influence and guidance, I became a Christian as a child, professing my belief by faith in Christ."

Leeroy thought for a moment before speaking. "Your parents sound like good people."

"They were."

After a few moments of silence, Jake realized Leeroy was done talking on that particular subject. Jake left the garage and went into the house.

As Jake sat in the living room waiting, Mildred emerged from their bedroom dressed for worship. She looked as stunning as she had on Christmas Day. She wore a tan dress and the brooch Jake had given her, along with a white hat.

"If you don't mind riding in my car," Jake said, "I'll drive us to church."

"I don't mind," Mildred said. Jake and Mildred exited the house, walking toward the street and Jake's car.

"Odd," Mildred said. "Hazel's parked in the garage most of the time."

Hazel sat in the driveway. Her presence there surprised Jake. He had spoken with Leeroy and removed the breakfast tray from Hazel's hood not thirty minutes earlier—in the garage.

Leeroy emerged from the garage. He opened Hazel's front passenger door and swept his left arm toward the car.

"Shall we, my love? Blanc?"

"Shall we what, Leeroy?" Mildred asked, confused.

"Shall we go to church, my love. What else?" Leeroy said.

"I like your church," Jake said.

After Bible study and worship, Leeroy drove Hazel, with Mildred in the front seat and Jake in the back, home to 25 North Galvez. Lunch consisted of a baked ham, beans, and cornbread. An apple pie, baked earlier, warmed in the oven.

"Really, Jake?" Mildred asked. "You liked it?"

"I do. It's lively. Friendly. Spirited music. Your pastor is a gifted speaker."

"He's been our pastor over thirty years," Leeroy said.

"How do you know that?" Mildred asked without thinking.

"Because he performed Amos's funeral." Leeroy's voice was gentle.

Jake changed the subject. "He's educated. A doctor's degree, I think. Didn't I hear someone call him doctor?"

"A college degree and a doctorate in Hebrew and Old Testament from New Orleans Baptist Theological Seminary, I believe," Mildred said.

"I know the place," Jake said, "out on Chef Menteur Highway."

"That's it," Leeroy said. "Not far from Paul's."

"Speaking of Paul's, I need to be at work tomorrow at ten. I'm working in the kitchen."

Silence before Jake spoke again. "I can't imagine the work to get all that education. A college degree *and* a doctor's degree."

"Have you ever thought about going to college, Jake?" Mildred asked.

"Me? Oh, no. Not me. I don't have a *high school* diploma, Mildred. College? For me? No."

"What?" Mildred turned in her seat to look back at him. "Are you saying you never graduated from high school?"

"That's what I'm saying," Jake answered. Apparently Leeroy had never told her about him dropping out of school.

"But when you auditioned," she said, "Leeroy said you told them you graduated from high school."

"No. They asked if I was out of school, and I answered yes. I was and am out of school. Not the same question as if I *graduated* high school."

"Tricky, Jake," Mildred said.

Jake smiled. "Tricky, but not untruthful."

Mildred began to consider what Leeroy had already been thinking.

CHAPTER TWENTY-THREE

Three weeks later, Leeroy drove Hazel to Franklin Avenue and knocked on Lester and Laverne's door.

"I come bearing an invitation," Leeroy said, entering.

"An invitation that couldn't wait 'til eight o'clock?" Laverne asked.

"Can't wait," Leeroy said. "Too important. Lives at stake. World peace. Man the ramparts. Get the women and children into the lifeboats. Full steam ahead."

"Leeroy," Laverne said.

Leeroy continued unabated, waving his arms to emphasize his words. "Hide the silverware! Lock and load! Every man for himself. Ask not what your country can do for you—"

"*Leeroy!*" Lester shouted.

Leeroy paused for effect and laughed menacingly.

Laverne looked at Lester and rolled his eyes. Leeroy saw it, ignored it, and said, "I have mischievousness in mind."

"Oh?" Lester asked.

"That's correct, Misters Knox and Washington. Real shenanigans. First class devilry."

"Who is the object of this tomfoolery?" asked Lester.

Leeroy scanned the room to ensure they were alone.

"Quit rollin' your eyes around like marbles," Laverne said. "Ain't nobody here but us."

"Who you got mischief in mind for?" repeated Lester.

"Somebody who's getting too big for his britches," Leeroy said.

"That's all the Louisiana Republican Party as far as I'm concerned," Laverne said. "I need clarification."

"Jacob Alvin Thomas. Known as Jake to many. Aka Blanc to me."

"Why Jake?" Lester asked.

"Ol' Blanc's been talkin' smack. We don't need a reason, do we?"

Lester and Laverne agreed with Leeroy. They didn't need a reason. Leeroy laid out his plan.

The Noirs waved at Cora as they entered Paul's Poulet. She worked the floor with a pot of coffee. They waved to Paul as he worked the counter.

The restaurant was packed, with only a few seats available. The men noticed something they had never seen before—a young man talking to Cora. And it wasn't Jake.

"Who do you suspect that kid is? The one gabbin' to Cora?" Leeroy asked.

"Clueless, number one, and, number two, none of our business," Laverne said.

"Handsome lookin' gent, don't you think?"

"None of our—none of *your*—business, Leeroy," Lester said.

Leeroy sauntered up to the counter, trailed by Lester and Laverne.

"Is this a good day?" Leeroy asked Paul.

"'Tis," Paul said, looking around the busy restaurant.

"Who's the boy talking to Cora?" Leeroy asked Paul.

"Please, Leeroy, leave poor Cora alone," Lester said.

"His name is Bert. Cora told me they've been on a date a time or two," Paul said in a casual tone. "Seems nice enough."

"Give us three sandwiches," Lester said, anxious to change the subject.

Their order came as baskets—the sandwich with Paul's special sauce, his grandmother's recipe according to advertisements—with their chosen form of fried potatoes and a bottomless drink.

Lester, Laverne, and Leeroy sat to wait on their baskets. Within five minutes, Jake's voice was heard from the kitchen, where he was working the fryers. Within ten minutes, Jake, on a break, stood beside the table with the three men. Leeroy pointed toward Cora and the young man.

"I understand Cora's been datin' that feller."

"I've seen them together," Jake said. "None of my business. Or yours."

"We told him that very thing," Lester said, "but you know Leeroy."

"His name is Bert," Leeroy said.

"Oh? Bert, eh?" Jake said.

"As if you didn't know, Blanc," Leeroy said. "Why don't *you* ask Cora out on a date?"

Jake said nothing.

"You best ask that young lady out on a date," Leeroy said, "before someone puts a ring on her finger."

Jake said nothing. He'd considered the idea of asking Cora out. He'd also considered the idea of someone else putting a ring on her finger. Several times.

"I don't know," Leeroy said, slowly shaking his head. "Looks pretty serious to me."

"And you, Leeroy, are blind," Laverne said. "Ain't nothin' serious there. Only thing I see are two young people, one male and one female, sittin' in the same booth."

"On the same side of the booth," Leeroy said.

Leeroy watched Jake as the young man silently watched Cora and Bert. Bert leaned over and murmured to Cora, and she gave him a small smile. Leeroy's eyes flicked back to Jake and observed the young man's hands tighten around the dishtowel tucked into his apron until his knuckles were white.

Leeroy bit his lip, torn between his desire to say something and his reluctance to interfere, but Jake resolved the situation. After a few silent moments, he nodded to his friends at the table and then moved off to the kitchen without another glance at Cora and Bert.

Five minutes later, Paul delivered two meals for Leeroy and Lester. Cora, now behind the counter, served the other meal for Laverne. In a few minutes, Paul found Jake in the kitchen.

"Lester, Laverne, and Leeroy have a complaint about a sandwich. I tried to resolve the matter, but they insist on seeing you."

"I can't imagine those three complaining about anything."

He left the kitchen and stepped into the dining area.

Leeroy motioned for him. "Hey, Blanc. You cookin' today?"

"I am."

"Then explain this sandwich to me."

"What's wrong with it? I fried the chicken myself."

"I don't care who fried it. It tastes like rubber."

"What?"

"Rubber, I said. The sandwich tastes like rubber."

Jake gave Lester and Laverne an inquiring look.

"My sandwich is fine," Lester said.

"Paul's Poulet sandwich is some kinda good," Laverne agreed, and munched down on his meal.

"Not mine," Leeroy insisted. "Rubber, I'm telling you."

In seconds, Paul joined the four men. "What's the problem, Jake?"

"Leeroy says his sandwich tastes like rubber. I can't imagine why. Laverne and Lester's are both fine. I fried all three sandwiches in the same vat at the same time."

"Are you disputin' my word, Blanc?"

"No. Of course not, Leeroy. I wouldn't do that. I just don't understand."

"Then taste."

Leeroy turned the sandwich away from the bite he had taken. He handed the sandwich to Jake, who paused for a second before biting down on the sandwich. He pulled on the sandwich as he bit ... and consequently pulled out the chicken patty. The three men laughed, then laughed harder. Leeroy looked to be in danger of collapsing onto the restaurant floor and rolling around. Paul and Cora both joined in the fun.

Jake peered at the offending chicken patty, then whacked it against the edge of the table. The middle of Leeroy's sandwich tasted like rubber for good reason. The middle *was* rubber. Leeroy had replaced the original fried chicken patty with a rubber patty, purchased from a local magic shop. He'd home-engineered it to look like a bite had been taken from it.

Jake heard the Noirs laughing, along with Paul, Cora, and half of the people in Paul's Poulet. Apparently Paul, Cora, Lester, Laverne, and most of the patrons in Paul's Poulet were party to the trick. He'd never heard Paul laugh so hard. Cora laughed gently, but enough to make the feathers in her chicken cap seem alive.

Jake knew Leeroy was the mastermind and sole operator behind this plot. While Jake didn't mind being the butt of someone's joke, he wouldn't forget it. Nor would he let Leeroy's master prank go without a response.

Jake laughed too, enjoying both the joke and his thoughts of revenge. He laughed hard along with the others. And in fact, Cora's broad smile and easy laugh made his day.

From that moment, Jake began to regard Cora in a new light—a warm, delightful, new light.

And out of the corner of his eye, he saw Bert.

$$\infty$$

With a touch of coolness in the air, Leeroy knocked on Lester and Laverne's door at eight a.m. on Tuesday, the prearranged time.

"Are you two ready?" Leeroy asked, rubbing his hands together as he entered.

"I'm not sure your idea is a good one," Laverne said as he entered the room.

"Are you gettin' cold feet?" Leeroy asked. "We've all decided it can't hurt nothin' to ask."

"What if the man tosses us out of his office? What if you land outside his office and break yo' mouth?" Laverne said.

"Hadn't considered that," Lester said. "Laverne is right. Your idea could hurt if the man throws us out of his office."

"He *won't*," Leeroy said emphatically. "All we are trying to do is help a boy out. My grandson. He won't toss us for that."

"Your *grandson*?" Lester said. "You make that claim and he *will* toss you out of his office, and have you and *us* arrested."

"We all—all three of us—ought to be shot instead," Lester said. "We could be. Today."

"We're just trying to help." Leeroy ended the conversation by pointing to the door. "To Hazel, gentlemen."

Leeroy drove on Franklin Avenue to Interstate 10. The men cruised as though Hazel was a Ferrari, the wind whistling through open windows. Leeroy exited the interstate onto Highway 90. From Highway 90 the men exited onto Audubon Boulevard and drove toward Tulane University.

Martha Bates started her day as she did every day in the office. She arrived before seven, switched on the lights in her niche, and made coffee. She opened the door to the president's office and switched on lights. A quick glance around the area revealed everything to be in place for a busy day.

Martha had been the private secretary for the past four Tulane University presidents. She had worked diligently, professionally, punctually, and politely for over forty years. Administration, faculty, and students loved her. Her appearance, with no lines in her face and her light gray hair pulled against her head, belied her age of eighty-one years. No one had ever heard her speak the word "retirement."

Satisfied with the orderliness of the offices and with her awareness of the day's activities for Tulane's president, Martha began her daily walk across campus to get the mail. She could delegate that task, but she always enjoyed strolling across the campus in the early morning. To her, Tulane was one of the nation's most beautiful campuses.

A few minutes before seven thirty, Martha returned with an armload of mail. She'd spend the next half hour sorting and prioritizing it. Tulane's president had already arrived.

"Good morning, Doctor Sloan."

"Good morning, Martha."

Martha made her way into Sloan's office with her appointment ledger, where they discussed the president's activities for the day.

"Promises to be a busy day, Martha."

"You have a nine-fifteen appointment with New Orleans City Planner Gil Cohen, to discuss the development of property on our southwest corner."

"A small piece of property, as I recall," Sloan injected.

Martha turned a few pages in her notebook before responding. "One-quarter acre, I'm guessing, fifty feet wide by forty feet long."

"What does the city want to do with it?" Sloan asked.

"A bus stop."

"A bus stop?"

"A bus stop." Martha checked her notebook again. "Then an eleven o'clock appointment with Professor Wallace Callahan of Economics to discuss funding for a new proposal. A luncheon with representatives of the Greater New Orleans Business District at noon at Antoine's."

Sloan nodded. "That'll be an expensive lunch. At least, someone else is paying."

Martha continued. "Back here for a meeting with a representative of the the Student Government Association, another appointment at three fifteen with University Development, a dinner engagement ..."

Martha knew the president despised dinner engagements, preferring the solitude of home after a busy day, but Sloan offered no sign of displeasure.

Martha continued. "Dinner with the Ministerial Association at St. Charles Avenue Church at six."

"Topic?"

"The possible creation of a ministerial scholarship for any student desiring to serve in a ministry capacity."

"They want to give us money?"

"They do."

"Unexpected, but certainly welcomed. We'll give serious consideration to accepting their money."

Martha knew the president had memorized the schedule, making any repeat unnecessary, either now or later.

Sloan checked the time. "No appointment until nine-fifteen. That gives me time to review the reaccreditation document for the Education School."

Martha knocked on Sloan's door at eight-forty-five. Sloan put down the education reaccreditation document.

"Sorry, Doctor Sloan, but there are three men here to see you." Martha hesitated a moment. "Three somewhat—mm, unusual men."

"How so?" Sloan said. "Did they say what they want?"

"They want to speak to the president of Tulane College."

Sloan's mouth quirked to one side. "Tulane *College*? About?"

"About a student."

Anytime someone came to the president's office in regard to a student, Martha had been instructed by the president not to delay, if possible. Sloan delegated or delayed lots of matters, but she never wanted to delegate or delay *student* matters.

"Thank you, Martha. Show them in."

In seconds, Martha entered the president's office with the three men and offered introductions.

"Doctor Sloan, this is Mister Leeroy Edwards, Mister Laverne Knox, and Mister Lester Washington. Gentlemen, this is Doctor Susan Sloan, our president."

Leeroy, Lester, and Laverne stood with hats in hands. All three wore the best clothing they had, clean and pressed. Their shoes were polished to a mirror shine. The fact that a year earlier the three men were on the edge of poverty and homelessness wasn't obvious.

Susan Sloan moved from behind her massive mahogany desk and met the three men with a hearty, comfortable handshake for each, with the same grace as whenever she engaged with people of any race, age, gender, or socioeconomic background. Whether discussing sound control with an acoustical engineer, or biomedicine with an ethicist, or amiably disputing a charge with her mechanic, Dr. Sloan was at home with people—students, parents, guardians, faculty, staff.

But not every day did she have the privilege and opportunity to share her office with three distinguished-looking, unusual older men such as these.

"Please, gentlemen, sit down."

Martha brought in an additional chair, then asked for and received the trio's hats. The men stood until Sloan seated herself, and then sat in the arranged chairs in front of her desk.

Lester, Laverne, and Leeroy scanned the office in those first silent moments with Dr. Sloan. The large walnut-paneled office was filled with light from eight big windows—three on each side and two behind Sloan's mahogany desk. Three smaller work desks lined the right and rear wall. The twelve-foot ceiling made the already enormous room seem even larger.

Sloan sensed the men's discomfort and initiated the conversation. "How may I serve you, gentlemen?"

"We're here regarding a student," Lester said.

"What is the student's name, may I ask?"

"Blanc," Leeroy said.

"Jake," Lester corrected. "His name is Jake."

"Jacob Alvin Thomas," Laverne said. "His *full* name is Jacob Alvin Thomas."

"Jacob Alvin Thomas. And where is Mister Thomas from?"

"Right here in New Orleans," Lester said.

"What is his major?" Sloan asked.

Lester, Leeroy, and Laverne looked at each other, confused. Sloan tried to help. "Which department does he study in?"

Still nothing. She tried again. "Which school is he in?"

Still nothing.

"Education? Biology? Engineering? Mathematics? Another one of the professional schools, perhaps?"

"Oh, ma'am, Jake isn't in any school right now," Lester said.

Now Sloan was confused. She smiled to put the men at ease. She leaned forward in her chair and removed her glasses. "He has to be in a department or school, gentlemen."

"No ma'am, Jake isn't in any school," Lester said.

Dr. Sloan had an epiphany.

"If Mister Thomas isn't in any school or department, then Mister Thomas isn't currently a student at Tulane. Correct?"

"Correct, ma'am. Jake isn't a student anywhere," Lester answered.

Sloan was confused again. She replaced her glasses and said patiently, "I'm sorry, perhaps we can get at this from another angle. What do you want me to help you do, gentlemen?"

"We want you to help Jake get into this college," Lester said matter-of-factly.

"I will be more than happy to connect you with our recruiting office," Sloan offered.

"Ma'am, if it's all right, we came to talk with *you*," Laverne said.

"Plus we're unsure what a recruiting office does," Leeroy said.

Before Sloan could speak again, Laverne said, "Jake doesn't have a father or a mother living."

And from Leeroy, "To our knowledge, we're Blanc's family. Period."

For the next ten minutes, the three men related Jake's story. All of it. Afterward, a few moments of silence allowed President Sloan to collect her thoughts.

"And Mister Thomas is now homeless? Sleeping in his car?"

"No, ma'am," Lester said. "Jake isn't homeless now. We saw to that. He lives with Leeroy and Mildred."

Leeroy nodded toward Sloan, who looked a trifle confused.

"Mildred?"

"My wife," Leeroy said. "Blanc lives with me and my wife."

"Blanc? I heard you mention the name earlier."

For the next ten minutes, all three men, taking turns, told Sloan how they'd met Jake and how Jake became 'Blanc' to Leeroy. They spared little, including Mountain Man and Blade Boy.

Sloan said, "Let me see if I understand this. Mister Edwards, you named Jake 'Blanc' because he is *White*?"

"Yes, ma'am," Leeroy answered, "that's correct."

"I see. I'm going out on a limb here, but none of you are related to Jake. Correct?"

"Correct. None of us are related to him," Laverne said, sporting a big grin.

"I see, I see. And now Jake works for Paul's Poulet and plays music with you on the streets? Correct?"

"Yes, ma'am. He plays with us. Guitar," Laverne answered.

"He plays well," Leeroy added.

Sloan considered again before asking her next question. "How old is he?"

The men thought for a moment. Lester spoke for the trio. "He was seventeen when he came to play with us."

"Now eighteen," Leeroy said.

"From what high school did he graduate?" Sloan asked.

"Jake didn't graduate from high school, ma'am," Laverne said.

Sloan sat back in her chair. "Jake never graduated from high school?"

"Is that a problem?" Lester asked.

Sloan realized the men were uninformed as to the nature of high school and higher education. She thought about her eighteen-year-old son, a freshman at Tulane. He and Jake were the same age.

She smiled. "No, no. Not a problem, but he'll have to have a high school diploma or equivalent before being admitted to Tulane or any other institute of higher learning."

"Equivalent? What does *equivalent* mean?" Leeroy asked.

"I'm referring to what is known as a General Educational Development exam. Some refer to it as a general equivalency diploma. The exam consists of a series of tests. When the test-taker passes them, they provide certification the test-taker, Jake, possesses high-school-level academic skills. With an earned equivalency diploma, he can be admitted to college."

"So Jake needs this exam is what I'm hearing you say. Correct?" Lester asked.

"Correct," Sloan said. "And when Jake earns his equivalency diploma, you tell him to come see me about his entrance into Tulane." Sloan thought again of her son. "I'll do everything possible to help."

There was a light rap on her door. Sloan lifted her eyes to see Martha step half inside her office and speak. "Your nine-fifteen appointment is here, Doctor Sloan."

Lester, Laverne, and Leeroy rose. Lester said, "A doctor, ma'am? You're a doctor?"

"I hold a Doctor of Philosophy degree." Sloan saw the confusion on Lester's face. "I'm not a *medical* doctor."

"I never knew there was any other kind," Lester said.

Sloan shook hands with the men. "Please, gentlemen, don't hesitate to have Jake contact me for any assistance."

Martha led the men from Sloan's office. She returned their hats and watched as they exited the presidential suite.

President Susan Sloan didn't know if she would ever again see Leeroy Edwards, Laverne Knox, or Lester Washington. She didn't know if she would ever have the opportunity to meet Jacob Alvin Thomas—Leeroy's 'Blanc'—but she hoped she would have the opportunity to help all four.

With the unannounced appearance of the three men, Sloan had not been able to complete the reaccreditation document for Tulane's Education School. She could have bemoaned that point, but she didn't. In fact, when she got to bed close to midnight, she realized the meeting with three Black men who cared about a White teenager had been the highlight of her day. She seldom saw such concern for a high school dropout or a previously homeless person.

Warmed by the thought, she turned off the light on her bedside table and slept better than she had in a long time.

Back in Hazel, Lester, Laverne, and Leeroy cruised once again.

"We found him. Or we found *her*. The president of Tulane *University*. Had a tarnation of a time doin' it, but we did it," Leeroy said.

"We'll know next time," Lester said. "And how about the man we asked directions as to where we could find the president of Tulane College?"

"A *pro*-fessor, reckon?" Leeroy asked.

"Said his name was Melvin. Or Kelvin, or Kenneth. I don't know. A truck went by right then, and I couldn't hear him," Laverne said.

"Probably a professor," Lester answered, "a *pro*-fessor at Tulane College. He looked at us like we were from Mars. Probably took a good hold of his wallet when he saw us on campus, thinkin' we was about to rob him."

Leeroy and Lester laughed.

"How we goin' to get Jake to take this test?" Laverne said.

"What did the good doctor call it?" Lester asked.

"A Great Equal Diplomat test," Leeroy said.

"No, no, Leeroy," Laverne corrected, "a General Equivalency Diploma, as in high school diploma, or something akin."

"Well, Great Equal Diplomat test, or General Equivalency Diploma test, whatever, how we goin' to get Jake to take it?" Lester asked.

"I'm a-workin' on that very thing," Leeroy said as he navigated Hazel through New Orleans traffic. "I got me an idea. Something you two ain't never had—an idea. You two knuckleheads leave this here thinkin' to *Doctors* Sloan and Edwards."

"*Doctor* Sloan, I trust," Lester said. "*Doctor* Edwards? Not so much."

They rode in silence, each lost in his own thoughts.

After a time, Laverne said, "I didn't expect a woman to be college president. Not sure why."

"Nor I," Lester said.

"Have you two ever *met* a college president? Male or female?" Leeroy asked.

"Yes. One," Laverne said. He thought for a moment and then continued. "Wasn't she nice?"

"She was nice," Lester said.

"How many White women have you ever known, Lester?" Leeroy asked.

"Counting Doctor Sloan?" Lester asked.

"Yes, counting Doctor Sloan," Leeroy replied.

"Counting Doctor Sloan ... one," Laverne answered, casually, from the rear seat.

CHAPTER TWENTY-FOUR

After a busy Saturday night, Jake drove Lester and Laverne home. All three had a pocketful of cash from a good night working the streets. When the three men left at around three, Leeroy went to bed.

Mildred had been in bed for hours. She slept restlessly when Leeroy and the men played, and she woke when Leeroy entered the room. He tried undressing as quietly as possible, but he knew Mildred was awake, even though she lay facing away from him.

"You okay?" she asked quietly.

"I'm fine, love. Are you?"

"Yes, I'm fine."

Leeroy leaned over and kissed Mildred on her cheek. She still faced away from him.

"Is Jake back?"

Mildred always knew when Jake entered the house. Leeroy answered her question, even though she already knew what he would say.

"Not yet." Seeing a window of opportunity, he continued. "Lester, Laverne, and I went to see the president of Tulane College this week."

Immediately, Mildred rolled over to face him. "You did *what*?"

"We went to see the president of Tulane College."

"You mean Tulane University."

"Whatever. We—Lester, Laverne, and I—went to see the president of Tulane College, University or High School. I don't know the difference."

"What in heaven's name *for*, Leeroy?"

Leeroy didn't hear his wife. "Do you know, my love, the president of Tulane is a woman?"

"No, Leeroy, I didn't know. I assumed the president of Tulane *College* was a man. A man served in that capacity when I was in *college* there," Mildred said.

Leeroy ignored her sarcasm. "A Doctor Sloan. Susan Sloan. A doctor, imagine. Not a medical doctor, she said. A kind of doctor in phila-something. Philadelphia maybe."

"Leeroy!"

Leeroy continued unabated. "A real nice lady. You'd like her, my love."

"I look forward to meeting President Sloan, Doctor of Philadelphia, at the next ball we hold in our garage," Mildred said. Again more sarcasm, again ignored by Leeroy.

"She said she would help us."

"Help *us*? What did you and Lester and Laverne do, Leeroy?"

His name spoken an octave higher brought him back to the moment. Having gained his attention, Mildred said calmly and slowly, "Help you do *what*?"

"We went there to ask the president of Tulane University to help get Blanc into her school."

Silence before Mildred spoke again. "That's an excellent idea, Leeroy."

"All *my* idea, of course," Leeroy said. "You know Laverne and Lester. Worthless, both of 'em."

"Oh, I'm *sure* this was all your idea," Mildred said, again sarcastic.

"Blanc's smart, my love. Intelligent. After hearing a song, any song, he remembers both lyrics and music. At the age of eighteen, he manages Paul's Poulet when Paul isn't there."

A pause before Leeroy gave Mildred the bad news. "Alas, my love, Blanc can't go to Tulane College or University, or any college or university for that matter."

Mildred propped up on on elbow, her form silhouetted against their bedroom wall. "Why not?"

"Because Blanc doesn't have a high school diploma."

Mildred lay back. Leeroy continued as Mildred pondered. "Doctor Sloan said Blanc could take an exam and go to the university."

"What exam?"

"She explained it to us, and then Laverne explained what she said to Lester and me."

"And you said Laverne and Lester are worthless."

"Well, Lester is worthless. Doctor Sloan said, 'I'm referring to what is known as a General Equivalency Diploma exam, as in high school diploma. The exam consists of a series of tests that, when he passes them, provide certification that the test-taker, Blanc in this case, has high-school-level academic skills. He takes his exam and goes to a university or college.'"

Mildred said nothing.

Leeroy gave her a moment to consider before he continued. "Here, my love, is where you'll play your role."

"Me? I can't help Jake study for any exam—high school, college, or university. I wish I could, and I would if I could, but I can't."

Leeroy stretched out beside his wife. "Ah, but, my love, your role is the most vital role in all of this."

"Oh? Do tell, Leeroy. What is *my* role?"

"*You* … are to ask Blanc to take the exam and go to college."

"Me? Why would Jake listen to me?"

"Because he loves you."

"What?"

"Blanc loves you, Mildred. You're the mother he lost. I can see it. I see the love in his eyes when the two of you talk. I imagine you've seen it, too."

"Oh, hush. You're rambling like the old buzzard you are." But she did not deny what he said.

Leeroy slipped her arms around his wife and pecked Mildred on the back of her neck. "I love you too, and I loved you first."

The couple heard the back door open and close quietly. Faint footsteps were heard as the old floors squeaked. They knew Jake was home.

Within minutes, in the arms of her husband, Mildred slept. Leeroy would soon follow.

CHAPTER TWENTY-FIVE

Mildred was glad Leeroy had rediscovered church. Leeroy liked church, both Bible study and worship. He'd made friends there, and enjoyed seeing and talking with them. Their predominantly Black church had several White members, and Leeroy could no longer say, as Laverne had, that Dr. Susan Sloan was the only White woman he'd ever met. And the fact the church offered coffee and doughnuts before Bible study didn't hurt either.

Jake came into the kitchen, moving briskly.

"You're up especially early this Sunday morning, Jake," Mildred said.

"I'll meet you and Leeroy at church."

Mildred didn't ask Jake where he was going. After Leeroy's statement that Jake loved her as the mother he'd lost at an early age, she admitted to herself she loved him too. But she *wasn't* Jake's mother.

She and Leeroy gave Jake freedom to come and go. They never set a curfew for him, but he was always home in the evening before ten, unless the men were playing. Mildred trusted his judgment, but she did worry about him whenever he went out alone. She resolved her worry by reminding herself Jake had been homeless and sleeping in his car long before he came to live in their house. And according to Leeroy, Laverne, and Lester, Jake could take care of himself. Mildred trusted Jake, and she trusted Jesus.

"All right. See you at church," was all she said.

Jake started the engine in his car.

Car doesn't look like much, but she is dependable.

In fact, the Olds had never left him stranded. She had given him more flat tires than he could count, but that wasn't her fault. Since he'd purchased four tires—all used—instead of just one at a time, flats seldom happened anymore. Sure, the tires were used, but they were still better than the slick balloons he'd had on the car for years. He steered toward Franklin Avenue.

Leeroy, with Mildred sitting beside him, parked Hazel in his usual parking space at nine thirty at the Franklin Avenue Church of God in Christ, not far from Lester and Laverne's flat. The lot was nearly full. Mildred scanned the cars, looking for Jake's, but didn't find it.

Leeroy opened her door. He always opened doors for her. House doors, car doors, doors at the grocery and post office, and these days, church doors. He reached in and took Mildred's white-gloved hand as she exited Hazel.

Within minutes, they were inside the building, Leeroy cruising the crowd with a cup of coffee in one hand and a doughnut in the other. He talked with Joseph Blair—a retired cardiologist, Leeroy had learned. "One of the nicest people I've ever met," Leeroy would later tell Mildred. "He just can't help bein' White," Leeroy added, with a grin.

"Shut your mouth, Leeroy Edwards," was all Mildred said.

At nine fifty-five, individuals began moving to different parts of the church for Bible study. Still no Jake, not that Mildred could see. She began to worry.

Forty-five minutes later, Bible study gave way to worship. People moved toward the sanctuary, already half-full before the Bible study time concluded. Soon, the people would all be inside, and the sanctuary would be standing room only. Through a hallway window between her Bible study class and the sanctuary, Mildred glanced at the parking lot. Jake's car was not there.

She took Leeroy's arm. The two entered the sanctuary and started moving to their normal seats—right side, three rows from the back, on the end. Mildred took a long breath of relief when she saw Jake standing nearby, waiting for her and Leeroy. What she saw next took her breath away completely.

Lester and Laverne stood beside Jake, both with hats in hand. They looked nice, dressed in their best and clean-shaven. Mildred was surprised. Leeroy was shocked, not so much that they were in church, but because Lester seldom shaved. Sometimes he shaved before Saturday night gigs. Not often.

"Looky what we have here," Leeroy said. "Looky at Mister Washington and Mister Knox. I reckon what I've heard is true. Hell has frozen over."

Mildred silently pinched his arm. Hard. He looked at Mildred and saw her smile, a smile Leeroy knew could disarm Satan himself.

He said nothing more. He shook Jake's hand, then Lester's and Laverne's. He was glad to see his friends, his best friends, in worship.

"Welcome to the Franklin Avenue Church of God in Christ," Leeroy managed to say cheerfully, even as his arm throbbed from Mildred's tweak.

Someone was knocking.

Jake had dropped Lester and Laverne off home after their Saturday night gig ended late.

"We gettin' too old to do this," Lester told Laverne at three a.m. Sunday.

"Agree."

Now, Sunday morning at seven forty-five, someone was at their front door.

Lester gave consideration to ignoring the intruder and going back to sleep. A second knock came, louder this time. Lester considered yelling, telling the person to go away. He gave more consideration to yelling for Laverne to open the door.

Nah. The old man needs his rest.

Lester swung his legs off his bed, the metal springs creaking with age. His feet found the floor. He managed to rise and start toward the door. Lester heard a third knock— not a pounding, but louder than the second.

"Coming, coming," Lester said.

He struggled with the lock, and finally opened the door. "Jake?"

"Good morning, Lester. What a marvelous day this is," Jake said as he entered the flat.

"I don't remember inviting you to come here this early this morning, and I specifically don't remember inviting you inside the door," Lester said, "but come on in."

Jake seemed unfazed by the jab. He closed the door just as Laverne entered the room, dressed in pajama bottoms.

"Who in the sam hill blazes is beatin' on our door this early?" Laverne asked, then saw who it was. "Jake!" He was immediately serious. "Is anything wrong? Leeroy and Mildred all right?"

Lester hadn't thought about that. He too gave Jake a concerned look.

"They're both fine. No worries."

"Wouldn't surprise me if Leeroy was dead," Lester said in relief. "I *am* surprised Mildred ain't killed him before now."

The environment in the room eased. Laverne tried to rub the sleep from his eyes. "What are you doing here?"

"What are you doing here this *early*," Lester amended.

Jake saw no need to camouflage his intentions. "I've come to ask you both to go with me to worship."

Lester's eyes widened. "What?"

Laverne started back toward his bedroom. He waved at Jake. "Good night, or good morning, Jake. Come back at two and let's go to lunch instead."

"Laverne," Jake said, "I'm serious. I'm asking the two of you to go with me to church. We'll meet Leeroy and Mildred there."

Laverne reversed his intended route and sat on the sofa, where Lester joined him. Jake sat in an adjacent chair. No one spoke.

"Jake, I believe," Laverne said, "if I and that old killjoy piano player there"—he indicated Lester—"entered a church, the Lord himself would bring the walls crashing around us."

"Like the walls of Jericho collapsed on everyone there, just in reverse," Lester added. "The wall wouldn't fall *for* the Hebrews, the walls would fall *on* the Hebrews. Namely us."

"Not true," Jake said, "and you both know it."

Laverne continued. "I will say, in regard to Lester and me, I wouldn't blame the Lord for doin' it. We've earned the title of reprobates. Sad but true. And well-deserved. I can't remember going to worship since Amos died."

"Right. We haven't seen the inside of a church in years." From Lester.

"We're both Christian, Jake, professing the Lord Jesus as personal savior."

"But church? Not for us, not now," was Laverne's final answer.

Jake's voice was calm. "Have I ever asked anything from the two of you?"

"Jake ..." Lester began.

"*Have* I?"

"No. Can't say I remember you ever asking anything from us," Lester said. Laverne nodded in agreement.

"I'm asking simply for you to go with me once. That's all."

"Jake, Jake, Jake. What are we going to do with you?" Lester asked.

"Come with me."

The two men sat on the sofa. Laverne finally heaved himself upright and spoke in a tone of finality.

"I'll shower. Lester, you iron your clothes and then I'll iron mine. Jake, you go cook me and that other old reprobate that lives here something to eat."

Jake nodded. Laverne headed toward the bathroom, while Lester started for his bedroom, muttering under his breath.

Jake sauntered toward the kitchen.

CHAPTER TWENTY-SIX

Tuesday morning started with its usual syncopation. Leeroy got up at five, put on a pot of coffee, and showered. Afterward, he took his coffee to the garage. Jake woke at six and showered. All three sat down for breakfast at seven.

"I'm thinkin' about a crawfish boil, Leeroy," Mildred said, as she finished her coffee.

"Now that's a *nice* idea," Leeroy said. "We haven't done that in years."

They hadn't done it in years because they couldn't afford it.

"Maybe make a big ol' pot of gumbo and another pot of crawfish étouffée," Mildred mused.

"Oh my," Leeroy said. "Gumbo and étouffée do sound good."

Mildred continued, talking mostly to herself. "We'll invite the Blairs, Cormiers and Thibodeauxs from church. And we'll invite Pastor Josiah and his wife Tela, Music Minister Woodrow, and his wife Annie. And the Summers and the Robinsons from the neighborhood."

"Let's not invite Lester or Laverne," Leeroy said. "They'll be in the way."

"Oh, hush," she said. "They're family. Goes without sayin' they're invited."

"You know what ol' Mark Twain said about family, Blanc?" Leeroy asked.

"No, Leeroy, I don't. What did ol' Mark Twain say?"

"Family and fish both stink after three days," Leeroy said with a roar. "Or, in Lester and Laverne's case, a day and a half."

Mildred ignored him. Jake laughed.

"And Jake, why don't you invite that nice boss of yours? What's his name?" Mildred said.

"Evans," Leeroy said. "Paul Evans. Invite him, Blanc, and his wife."

"I will," Jake said.

"And Jake?" Mildred said.

"Yes, ma'am?"

"Bring a date."

Leeroy roared. "A date? Come on, Mildred, Blanc can't get a date."

Mildred swung and hit Leeroy's arm, then smiled sweetly at Jake.

They ate in silence for a time.

"What about Cora, Blanc?" Leeroy ventured.

"What about her?" Jake asked.

"Who's Cora?" Mildred asked.

"Cora works with Blanc at Paul's."

"I've thought about asking Cora out, but she's dating somebody."

The conversation paused. Then Leeroy asked, "Is she engaged, Blanc?"

"What?"

"Engaged? Is Cora engaged?"

"To my knowledge, no. But what difference—"

"Then ask her on a date," Leeroy said. "Unless, of course, you're as chicken as Paul's."

"What?"

"I don't s'pect you're chicken, Blanc. I s'pect you're worried she'll say no."

"Say no?" Jake asked.

"Can't say I blame her, when I look at the likes of you."

"Enough of that, Leeroy," Mildred admonished. "Jake, ask Cora if you want."

"Maybe I will."

The three sat in silence for a time, until Jake finally broke it with his usual breakfast table question.

"What are you two doing today?"

He expected their normal reply of "nothing," but Mildred's reply surprised him and Leeroy both.

"I believe I'll go out today. Leeroy, will you drive me?"

Leeroy, after he recovered from the initial shock, said, "Let me check my calendar and see. No, nothing on the ol' calendar for the day. Where're you goin', love?"

"*Out*," was her only reply.

At noon, Jake left for Paul's Poulet and the one-to-nine kitchen shift.

Mildred, already dressed, searched out Leeroy. "Okay, come on, chauffeur, let's go."

Leeroy dangled Hazel's keys from his fingers. "Ready to go. Where are we heading?"

"Redeemer High School."

"The one on Crescent?"

"That would be the one."

"Why?"

"Anyone ever told you that you ask too many questions?" Mildred asked.

"Yes. You," Leeroy replied.

Mildred said nothing more.

173

At a quarter past three, Mildred and Leeroy stopped by Paul's Poulet. Jake waved from the kitchen. Mildred and Leeroy drank sweet tea as Cora delivered their meal.

"Cora," Leeroy said, "this is Mildred—Mrs. Edwards, my wife. Mildred, my love, this is Cora."

"So nice to meet you," Cora said. "Jake speaks of you often and fondly."

"Nice to meet you," Mildred said.

"I hope you can come with Blanc to our crawfish boil," Leeroy said.

"Excuse me?"

Leeroy felt Mildred's cold stare and caught himself. "Nothing, nothing. Apologies."

Cora walked away with a confused look.

"Sorry, my love," Leeroy said. "Maybe Blanc *is* as chicken as Paul's."

The two ate in silence before Leeroy spoke again. "What was that all about? At Redeemer High?"

"I went there to talk to someone about Jake's high school diploma."

"Which he doesn't have."

"We talked about the test."

"Oh? Test? Right. I forgot," Leeroy lied.

"Yes. The principal spoke with me and introduced me to a person called a guidance counselor, who was helpful."

"Why did I have to stay with Hazel while you went inside?"

"I thought that was our best approach."

Feigning injured feelings, Leeroy said, his chin raised, "Well, so? As a matter of fact, I know the president of Tulane College."

"Do you want to know what I found out or not?"

"I do, my love." He chuckled. "What did you find out?"

"There are several subjects on the exam—math, social studies, science, and reading."

"All sounds like a bunch of hard learnin' to me."

"The nice man gave me this booklet."

Mildred made certain Jake was nowhere close by. She removed the booklet from her purse.

"The man said this would help Jake prepare for the exam. Once he believes he's prepared, Jake registers. The man gave me the locations of three places where the test is offered. He goes there and takes the exam."

"Sounds simple enough to me," Leeroy said.

"And to me," Mildred said. She concealed the booklet in her purse as Cora came around with a pitcher of tea.

Wednesday morning started the same as the previous day, until Mildred pulled a small booklet from her apron pocket during breakfast. She placed the booklet on the table in front of Jake, who read the title aloud.

"*McGraw Hill Preparation for the GED Test*. What is this?"

Leeroy didn't open his mouth. He let Mildred work her magic.

"For the GED exam. The GED is the equivalent of a high school diploma."

Jake thumbed through the booklet. "I've heard about the GED. In fact, Cora mentioned it to me." He read a page or two, then flipped past more pages.

"Jake, it's something you need to consider," Mildred said.

"Why?" He looked up at her. "What difference will a GED make in my life? I don't need a GED to work at Paul's. And I don't need a GED to play music on the streets."

Leeroy had to admit Blanc made a good point. He left the persuasion to Mildred.

"You need the GED," she said, "to go to college."

"Me? You're kidding, right? *College*?" He huffed. "I fry chicken and earn a few bucks playing music on the streets for a living. I slept in my car for years. You have to be smart to go to college. I'm not smart."

Leeroy leaned onto the table. Mildred recognized the intent of his movement and stayed silent, waiting for him to speak.

"Blanc, you *are* smart."

"I don't want to hear anything about being smart, Leeroy."

"You are *smart*. You remember musical chords and lyrics to dozens and dozens of songs. And I imagine, if you put your mind to it, you'd recall hundreds of them. You listen to a song, play it, and remember the instrumentals and the words too. That's intelligence."

"I may have a small gift for music, and I may be able to remember things, but that doesn't make me smart."

"That *does* mean you're smart," Mildred said, this time with more passion. "Do this, Jake. Leeroy and I will help you in any way we can. We'll create a quiet place for you to study, and there'll be fewer Saturday night gigs. We'll do everything possible, as will Lester and Laverne."

"What do Lester and Laverne know about this?"

Neither Mildred nor Leeroy responded. Leeroy thought of Dr. Susan Sloan but didn't say a word. Mildred finally said, "You and the GED exam come down to one thing."

"Which is?" Jake asked.

"Whether you want to take and pass the test or not." Mildred allowed him to consider her words, then said, "Look at me, Jake."

He obeyed.

"Do you want to better yourself, or do you want to worry? Worry about water pipes freezing in the winter because you can't afford to heat the house? Worry about having to choose what to buy—food to eat, or medicines to take? Do you want to get married someday, Jake? Have a family? Do you want to provide for them? Do you want a better life than you had, taking showers and ironing your clothes at Paul's Poulet? Livin' in your car?"

Mildred spoke passionately and forcefully. She had Jake's undivided attention, and Leeroy's as well. She asked one final time.

"Jake, do you want it?"

Then it seemed as if she was not finished after all. She held up her forefinger to emphasize her words. "Do not *ever* let me hear you say you aren't smart enough to go to college. Do you understand, Jacob Alvin Thomas?"

That brought a slight grin to Jake's face. "Yes, ma'am." He swiped across his eyes with his sleeve and smiled bigger.

Leeroy recognized Mildred's demeanor and tone. He'd heard her speak similar words to Amos—the same passion, same determination, same clarity. To Jake, Mildred spoke as a mother to her son.

She rose and began gathering breakfast dishes. Leeroy followed her lead as Jake continued to stare at the booklet.

For the next several weeks, Mildred helped Jake study. The crawfish boil was postponed. After all, Jake's future was at stake. Leeroy helped too, although he couldn't read much of the booklet. Lester and Laverne played their role and contributed where they could.

They all did what they could to help. But in the end, Jake had to be the one to take the test. Mildred was correct—preparing and taking the exam all came down to whether or not he wanted to better himself.

Jake had an affinity for learning. With eleven and a half years of education, he already knew practically everything in the booklet, but he still read and reread. Mildred asked him question after question. Leeroy, Lester, and Laverne had heard Mildred ask the questions several times, so they asked the questions too, from memory. And they heard Jake's answers over and over. They knew the correct answers, learning new things themselves by helping Jake. Jake encouraged himself by saying all he needed was a passing grade. He pressed on, encouraged by four motivated, determined people.

"I believe I'm ready," Jake said one morning.

"Pardon?" Leeroy asked.

"The GED test. I believe I'm ready."

"Then let's get you registered," was Mildred's only response. Not "Are you sure?" or "Do you want to study more?"

She picked up the phone, made the appropriate plans, and they all dressed.

At Redeemer High School, Leeroy parked Hazel between a new bright red Ford Mustang and a beautiful blue Chevy Camaro.

"Hazel will bring a touch of class to this parking lot full of clunkers," Leeroy said, speaking aloud.

He switched off the engine and got comfortable as Mildred and Jake exited the car. Mildred peered into the auto at her husband. "Aren't you coming?"

A broad smile came across Leeroy's face. He hopped out of Hazel, excited as a kid on the way to buy ice cream.

"Three weeks," Leeroy said later, in answer to Laverne's question. "Blanc takes the test in three weeks, on a Tuesday.

Long test—it'll take most of the day, and ... I don't want you two old wet blankets to do anything to distract him."

"Three weeks," Laverne said, ignoring Leeroy's attempt to rile him.

"I feel good about Jake's chances," Lester said.

"Heck," Laverne said, "I could take the exam myself, after hearing Jake's answers for the past months."

"Then why don't you?" Leeroy asked, with sarcasm.

"Because I can't read the questions," Laverne replied with a slight grin.

CHAPTER TWENTY-SEVEN

Jake couldn't sit still. It was Sunday, two days before his big test, and on this Sunday afternoon he felt the pressure. He'd never been nervous before when he took exams, but he was nervous now. Plus, he'd not been inside a classroom or taken a test in years.

Jake wasn't worried about whether he passed or failed the test. His real concern was about disappointing Mildred. He wanted to please Leeroy, Lester, and Laverne. But Mildred? He would try to move a mountain if she asked him.

As on most Sunday afternoons, after worship and lunch, Leeroy and Mildred napped. Jake sat in the living room, in the chair that had become his. He put his head down, closed his eyes, rested his head in his hands, and tried to think of something, anything other than the exam. He let his mind wander.

He recalled the first day he'd met the Noirs and acquired the nickname "Blanc" from Leeroy, and the first time the four played together, with Laverne hunched over as he played. The moment had been magic.

His introduction to Mildred had gone well. She'd impressed him and continued to do so every day. He thought of Cora and Paul, and Paul's Poulet, and then a particular memory floated up, having to do with a rubber sandwich.

Jake reconsidered the prank. Leeroy had orchestrated it, sure as the world. He particularly recalled Leeroy's laugh at his efforts to bite the fake chicken patty.

Jake thought it through. He had all the tools in Leeroy's garage to manufacture his revenge. He listened for a moment to the faint snores emerging from Leeroy and Mildred's bedroom. Then, moving quietly on the squeaky pine floors, he started his journey to take vengeance on one Leeroy Edwards.

Payback time—long overdue—had arrived.

Monday morning began as usual, with Leeroy and his cup of coffee in the garage before six. At seven, Leeroy moved toward the kitchen for breakfast. He entered the kitchen to find Mildred and Jake seated, drinking coffee as usual.

"Mornin', Leeroy," Jake said.

"Mornin', Blanc."

Leeroy moved to Mildred's side of the table and pecked her on her cheek. "Good morning, my love."

"Good morning, Leeroy."

"What are you two doing today?" Jake asked.

"Nothing," Mildred responded. "What's your work schedule?"

"Paul gave me the day off. Told me to rest before the test tomorrow."

"That was nice of him," Mildred said.

"I like Paul," Leeroy added.

"He's been generous to me in a lot of ways, financially being one of them." Jake said. "Paul's a devoted Christian, and one of the most selfless people I know. He'd give anyone his last dollar. He serves a lot of homeless people without charging them for meals and never makes a big deal of it. Never embarrasses them by making it look like charity, and never brags about it to anyone else."

"I suspect Paul thinks of you as the son he never had," Mildred said.

Jake stared at her. "I never thought about it that way."

"Nah," Leeroy said, waving a dismissive hand. "Can't be that."

Mildred and Jake ignored him.

Silence. The three finished their coffee.

"I forgot," Mildred said. "Leeroy, I need you to go to the grocery store for me and get a dozen eggs. I plan to bake a cake today."

"A cake would be nice, my love," Leeroy said. "What kind?"

"German chocolate."

"Ah. My favorite. But why can't you and I do that tomorrow, after we get Jake to Redeemer High?"

"Tomorrow would be fine, except I want to bake *today*."

Leeroy offered no more objection. He helped Mildred and Jake gather and wash dishes. As was their efficient routine, Jake washed, Leeroy dried, and Mildred put them away.

Mildred and Jake sat in the living room as Leeroy finished dressing and reached for Hazel's keys by the rear door.

"I shall return," Leeroy said. "Need anything except eggs?"

"Be careful, Leeroy," Mildred said, "and no, nothing but eggs."

"Always, my love." He motioned toward Jake. "You need to get out of the house, Blanc. How about taking a ride?"

Jake thought for a second before responding. "Sure. I'll ride along."

"Then get your shoes on, young man. Hazel the swing-low-sweet-chariot awaits."

Jake put on his shoes and got into Hazel's passenger side. Leeroy was already there, with the key in the ignition, but he hadn't yet started the engine. "Looks to be a fabulous day, Blanc. What a glorious day to be alive."

"Agreed."

"Shall we go to the grocery? Mildred's eggs await, and *I* await a German chocolate cake."

"Then let's not keep Mildred or you waiting any longer."

Leeroy started the engine. "Listen to that, Blanc. Runs as smooth as a sewing machine."

Jake, knowing nothing about sewing machines, agreed.

"Purrs like a kitten."

"Sure does."

"Slicker than a greased pig."

Jake knew less about greased pigs than he knew about sewing machines, but still concurred.

"Agreed," he said. "But Leeroy, if you don't get to the grocery, Mildred can't cook, you don't get your German chocolate cake, and I suspect your sweet Mildred isn't going to be too sweet toward you."

"Patience, Blanc, patience."

Leeroy checked the single rearview mirror. Seeing nothing, he pulled the car's transmission into reverse and turned to look out the rear window in preparation for backing out.

Hazel didn't move. Leeroy looked puzzled but said nothing. He shifted Hazel's transmission back into park and then back into reverse. Hazel still didn't move.

Leeroy scratched his chin as Jake sat silent. "Everything appears to be in order. The engine sounds fine. The transmission's engaging."

Once more Leeroy shifted Hazel into park and back into reverse. Nothing. He pressed the gas pedal harder and the engine revved, but the car didn't budge.

He switched off the engine and patted Hazel's dashboard. "Oh, well. I knew this day would come."

Jake remained silent.

Leeroy continued. "Hazel, if you never move from this garage again, I won't speak badly of you. You been a good friend for a long time. All right, Blanc, let's help our tired friend."

Leeroy and Jake emerged. Leeroy raised Hazel's hood and peered at the engine. He laughed. "I don't know why I'm doing this. I know less about cars than I know about the English language."

He lowered Hazel's hood. "Let me go tell Mildred. May we take your car, Blanc?"

"Sure."

Leeroy started out of the garage, walking along Hazel's driver's side. Reaching the rear tire, Leeroy paused and peered down.

"Odd."

"What?" Jake asked.

Leeroy edged the toe of his shoe a small distance—maybe a half inch—underneath the tire. He withdrew his shoe, rubbed his chin and head, and repeated the process. Once more, he succeeded in slipping his shoe ever so slightly not against, but *underneath* the rear tire.

"What the heck is happening here?"

Leeroy managed to get on all fours and peer underneath the automobile. From that vantage point the blocks and shims—two sets—were visible, one on each side of Hazel's rear axle. They were set so they raised the car just under an inch off the ground.

He'd been had.

He heard Jake's chuckle, and knew who did it and why. He heard Mildred laugh and saw her feet as she emerged from the shadows to stand beside Jake. Leeroy rolled to one side and lay flat on the floor of the garage, belly-laughing as Jake and Mildred made their way to his side of the car.

Leeroy sat up. "You," he said, pointing to Jake between snorts of hilarity, "are in big trouble, young man."

Mildred laughed, out of control.

"And you," Leeroy said, pointing to Mildred, "you don't get any eggs today."

She could barely speak around her own laughter. "Oh, Leeroy, Leeroy. I don't need eggs."

"What?"

Leeroy knew Mildred's request was all part of Blanc's plan. He waited for Jake and Mildred to exhaust themselves laughing. Finally he spoke.

"Blanc?"

"Sir?"

"Come help me up."

"Yes, sir."

Jake, along with Mildred, managed to get Leeroy off the floor. Appearing to be angry but fooling neither Mildred nor Jake, Leeroy said, "Well, isn't this a fine day. Now I have to get those blocks from underneath Hazel. And me an old man. What a mess."

Leeroy's dismay was a clear sham. Jake had already placed two lawn chairs nearby. Leeroy shifted one of the chairs for Mildred and sat in the other as Jake went to work.

In minutes, Jake had Hazel jacked up, the blocks removed, and Hazel's tires down on solid ground.

Jake had once read something about revenge being a sweet morsel cooked in hell. He didn't know about the cooked in hell part, but in this particular situation, the sweet morsel part fit nicely.

CHAPTER TWENTY-EIGHT

Jake thought he would drive himself to Redeemer High School on Tuesday morning for his test, but in this he was mistaken. Mildred and Leeroy came out of their bedroom dressed as though they were going to worship. Jake's big day was obviously a big day for them too.

"We'll leave at seven forty-five," Mildred said, her voice firm.

Jake thought seven forty-five was early, as Redeemer High was only a few miles away, but he offered no objection.

The trio departed at seven forty. Jake assumed the day was going to be the three of them at Redeemer High, but he was mistaken again, as a little after eight, Leeroy eased Hazel to the curb in front of Lester and Laverne's flat.

Lester and Laverne stood beside the street, waiting. No doubt Mildred had threatened both men with bodily harm if they were late. They too were dressed as though for church. Jake moved to one side as Lester and Laverne climbed inside. No one spoke as Leeroy pulled back into traffic.

They arrived at Redeemer High at eight thirty. Leeroy parked in a visitor's space. Jake had plenty of time to find the examination room—Number 18, Mildred reminded him—and get seated.

"We'll offer a little prayer, Jake. Good luck," Mildred said, and waved him off as he left for the building.

Jake started toward Number 18, hopefully toward a successful attempt to pass the GED. Who knew what passing the test could mean? He could get a job earning more money, but the thought of leaving Paul's did not excite him.

With Jake out of sight, Laverne said, "I'm nervous as a worm in a henhouse about Jake and this exam."

"I've been praying for that boy ever since this thing started," Mildred said. "I believe Jake's going to be all right."

"Heck," Leeroy added, "with my teachin' and coachin' him, he gonna do fine."

"With *all* of us helpin' him," Lester nodded and said, "he's gonna be fine."

"No need sittin' here all day," Leeroy said. "Anyone for Paul's Poulet?"

Though the time was early, Mildred, Leeroy, Lester, and Laverne needed to do something to take their minds off what Jake had before him.

"I'm game," Lester said.

"Me too," Laverne added.

When Mildred offered no objection, Leeroy started the engine. He pulled Hazel's transmission into reverse. When Hazel started backward, Leeroy turned to Mildred. "No blocks." He smiled.

Mildred smiled back nervously. Neither Lester nor Laverne had any idea what Leeroy was talking about. They looked at each other and shrugged.

Mildred, Leeroy, Laverne, and Lester sat in a booth at Paul's. They'd been there all morning and part of the afternoon, with Paul and Cora filling their coffee cups more times than they could remember. Paul didn't mind. He was glad to see them. He'd come to appreciate the three men because of what they'd done—and continued to do—for Jake. He admired Mildred for just being herself.

"What time does Jake finish?" Lester asked.

"Three o'clock," several voices answered simultaneously.

"What time is it now?" Lester inquired.

"Ten minutes later than the last time you asked," Leeroy said.

"It's one thirty-five," Cora said, coffee pot in hand.

"Well, should we get going?" Lester said. "We don't want Jake to finish and start looking for us, and us nowhere to be found."

Leeroy looked at Mildred and Laverne. Seeing no objection, he said, "Let's go."

"Tell Jake I said hello," Cora said.

"We will," Mildred responded.

"We wish him all the best," Paul added. "Let us know."

Leeroy recognized Bert in one corner. The trio often saw him in Paul's. They knew he was interested in more than Paul's chicken sandwiches.

At ten past three, Mildred, Leeroy, Lester, and Laverne waited for Jake in the Redeemer High parking lot.

"Where *is* that boy?" Lester asked.

At three thirty, still no Jake.

"I'm going to look for him," Leeroy said, opening his car door.

"No, you aren't," Mildred said and grabbed his right arm.

Leeroy closed Hazel's door once more.

"Sorry, I just remembered," Mildred explained. "Jake said the exam would be scored before he leaves."

"You mean he'll know *today*? About whether he passed or not?" Laverne asked.

"He will," Mildred answered, shifting her weight on Hazel's seat.

None of the four could get comfortable. At three forty, and then three fifty-five, still no Jake.

With the afternoon sun warming Hazel's interior, the inhabitants became drowsy. At one time or another, each nodded off, some briefly, some for a nap. Sometime after four, Leeroy roused himself, peered out the windshield, then patted Mildred on the arm.

"Hey, you three. Looky there."

Once he had their attention, he pointed. Standing in front of a different door from the one he'd entered, they saw Jake. His smile could have been seen a hundred feet away. He waved a piece of paper back and forth above his head.

"I believe our boy passed," Laverne said.

Jake ran toward Hazel like a school child to his mother's arms, and the four emerged from Hazel, stood on the sidewalk and waited.

"*I passed!*"

Lester screamed. Laverne took the paper from Jake and mimicked his gesture, holding the results high. Leeroy hopped around like a chicken on a hot sidewalk. Mildred was just grateful no one else was in the parking lot at Redeemer High. She thought they'd be arrested for disturbing the peace.

She spoke quietly. "Congratulations, Jake."

Three male students emerged from Redeemer High, all wearing basketball uniforms dark with sweat. The three appeared to be the same age as Jake.

"Jake here passed his test!" Laverne said to them.

One of the students spoke. "Congratulations to Jake. I don't know what test he passed, but good for him."

Lester said, "Paul will want to know."

"Cora," Mildred added, "said to tell you hello. Paul too."

"Load up, all!" Leeroy said, "To Paul's Poulet! The celebration awaits!"

Paul's Poulet was indeed a celebration. By the time Jake and company arrived, the dinner crowd had gathered and the place was full. Paul squeezed the five of them into a corner booth. Paul removed his chicken cap, brushed back his hair with his hand, tapped a water glass with a knife, and spoke to the entire restaurant when they quieted.

"Ladies and gentlemen. Jake here has had a major accomplishment today. He is now the proud owner of a GED." The crowd at Paul's gave a typical New Orleans response—long and loud. Several of the regulars at Paul's had known Jake all the years he'd worked there.

Paul was not finished. "In a salute to Jacob Alvin Thomas and his feat, cherry pie and ice cream for everyone is on the house!"

The party cranked to another more boisterous level. Everyone who came to Paul's that night learned of Jake's success and ate cherry pie a la mode. As closing time neared, Paul came back to Jake.

"Congratulations, Jake. I'm so proud of you."

"Thanks, Paul. I couldn't be where I am without you."

Jake wondered if Mildred was correct. Did Paul consider him the son he never had?

Cora kept the coffee coming. No one at Paul's was in any rush to leave. At eight forty-five, with closing time at nine, Mildred began moving the men toward Franklin Avenue and 25 North Galvez. Mildred exited first, on Leeroy's arm, with Lester and Laverne following. Jake was starting out when Cora caught up to him.

"I'm proud of you, Jake. You've worked so hard." Jake thought he saw tears in Cora's eyes.

"Thank you, Cora."

"Well, I've gotta run. Things to do."

"I understand. I'll see you tomorrow. I'm working the afternoon shift."

"Me too. See you here."

She tossed him a lovely smile over her shoulder as she ran back into Paul's. Jake couldn't remember ever being so happy.

Until he saw Bert.

CHAPTER TWENTY-NINE

Midmorning the following day, Mildred initiated the discussion.

"It's time we revisited our crawfish boil."

"Fabulous idea, my love."

"I've started my list of invitations—the Blairs, Cormiers, the Thibodeauxs, Pastor Josiah and his wife Tela, and our Music Minister Woodrow and his wife Annie, all from church. The Summers and the Robinsons from the neighborhood. Paul Evans and his wife. Jake, are you going to bring a date?"

Mildred hadn't forgotten. Jake remembered Leeroy's jab the last time he asked about a date. No such jab this time. Jake nodded yes.

"I'm thinking about a date."

Mildred continued. "Anyone else?"

"Let's not invite Lester or Laverne," Leeroy said. "They'll be in the way."

Mildred gave him an acid look. "You said that the last time we talked about a crawfish boil. My answer is the same as last time. They're *invited*. Now *behave*, Leeroy. You and Jake have to check our crawfish cooker and make sure we have propane in the tanks."

"I don't remember the last time the cooker was used. I'll refill the tanks and scrub the pot. Blanc and I will set up tables and chairs in the garage and on the driveway."

"I'll consider two or three nights as options. A Friday night, since you four always seem to be gone on Saturday night," Mildred said.

"Man's gotta earn a livin', my love."

"I'll cook the étouffée inside, along with a pot of gumbo. Chicken maybe, since we have crawfish and shrimp already." Mildred was now talking to herself, oblivious to Leeroy and Jake. She spoke softly. "I need a grocery list. Leeroy can buy the crawfish from a local vendor."

"Balls of fire, Blanc, this is gonna be a shindig. But I still don't believe you'll be successful in finding a date." Leeroy was going to take his jab after all.

Jake smiled but said nothing. In his mind, he rather doubted it himself. There was, after all, Bert. And Jake didn't have another candidate.

"By the way," Leeroy said, "I want to see that test paper you were wavin' around yesterday. Any observer would have thought you were waving the Declaration of Independence."

Jake retreated to his bedroom and brought out his copy to Leeroy.

"Something to be proud of, Blanc. It surely is."

"I am."

"As are we," Leeroy said.

Mildred, meanwhile, continued to make her grocery list, oblivious once more.

With the dishes washed, dried, and put away, Jake said, "I go to work at eleven. I believe I'll head that way."

"Why so early?" Leeroy asked.

Jake thought for a moment before replying. "Oh, nothing in particular."

Jake dressed and headed out. He kissed Mildred on her cheek as she continued to work on her grocery list. He nodded in Leeroy's direction.

"What are you doing today?" Jake asked as he searched for his car keys.

"Nothing," Leeroy replied.

"To Paul's Poulet then," Jake said, with a grand theatrical wave of his arm. "Where deep fryers and peanut oil awaits."

"Don't forget the chicken cap."

Jake pointed at Leeroy as he exited the house.

"Correct. Almost forget the chicken cap."

At nine thirty, Leeroy pecked Mildred on her cheek as she sat in her chair in the living room and read. Leeroy was well-dressed.

"Where are *you* going?" Mildred eyed him suspiciously.

"Out."

Mildred noticed the paper with Jake's test score tucked in Leeroy's pocket. He made a futile attempt to conceal it. She cast a hard eye in his direction. "What are you up to?"

The time was ten a.m., as agreed. Lester and Laverne were dressed nicely, matching Leeroy.

Soon after, the three men cruised the interstate, and within the half hour, Leeroy parked Hazel in one of Tulane University's lots, as near the president's office as he could park. He found a space between a BMW and Mercedes.

"Hazel sure does add class to this junkyard," Leeroy said.

Martha Bates tapped on Dr. Susan Sloan's half-closed door. Sloan sat at one of the smaller desks in her office, poring over a document. She removed her reading glasses at Martha's entrance.

"Misters Edwards, Knox, and Washington to see you, Doctor Sloan."

A smile came to Sloan as she remembered the three. "Show them in, Martha."

Lester, Laverne, and Leeroy entered the office, hats in hands. Though they'd seen the office before, they couldn't help but be impressed again. Sloan moved across the gigantic office to greet the men while Martha brought in the extra chair.

Sloan remembered them, but waited for Martha to speak. "Doctor Sloan, remember Mister Knox?"

"Of course," Sloan said, as she reached for Laverne's hand and shook it.

"Mister Edwards," Martha said, indicating Leeroy, who stepped forward to greet Sloan.

Then Sloan reached for Lester's hand and shook it. "And Mister Washington. Good morning to you all. Please sit down."

All four sat. Sloan initiated the conversation. "Good to see you three today. How may I help?"

Leeroy said, "If you recall, we came to you in regard to a young man name Blanc."

"I remember. Jake, wasn't it?"

"My apologies," Leeroy said. "Yes. Jake."

"Jacob Alvin Thomas," Lester added.

"You said Jake could get into to your college with a test," Laverne said.

"Yes, a test—passing the GED test or a high school diploma," Sloan said. "Either one."

"Well, Jake passed," Leeroy said as he removed Jake's GED test score from his pocket and slid the paper across the desk to Sloan.

"Wonderful. Please convey my congratulations to him," Sloan said, taking the paper.

All three men waited as Sloan retrieved a pair of reading glasses, one pair from four of five pairs the men could see, one pair per desk. She sat back in her chair and examined the document.

"He did more than pass it, didn't he?" she asked, not realizing one of the three men was illiterate and the other two approached the same. "Do you know Jake's actual score?"

"No, ma'am. We don't," Laverne said.

"He made a high score."

"Truth?" Lester said.

"Truth," Sloan responded. "Impressive. Good for Jake."

Leeroy cleared his throat. "You said for us to contact you if you could ever help him."

"I did say that. And I'm still committed to helping Jake."

"Will you help Jake get into your college, ma'am?" Lester asked.

"With this score, Jake can go to any college or university he chooses," Sloan said. She brooded a moment, remembering the men's story about Jake. The death of his parents. His homelessness. Sleeping in his car. She thought about her own son. "Yes, I will give oversight to Jake's application. As far as cost ..."

"Cost? You mean to tell us you have to pay to go to college?" Leeroy said.

"Yes, but with Jake's background and with this test score, he'll qualify for numerous scholarships. I doubt his university education will cost him anything."

While the three men weren't aware there was a cost to college, all three knew what Sloan meant when she referred to Jake's background.

"I'll ask Martha to get an application for you," she said. "Jake needs to complete the application. Ask him to return his application to this office in order to start classes this fall. In August."

The three men knew they'd accomplished all they could do for now. They rose. Laverne spoke for the trio. "Thank you."

"My pleasure, gentlemen. I look forward to meeting Jake."

Sloan followed the men out of her office and spoke to Martha. The administrative assistant retrieved and handed an application to Lester. With hats in hand, the men nodded to Dr. Sloan and Martha and exited the office.

"She sure is nice," Lester said.

"She is. Did you know you have to *pay* to go to college?" Laverne asked.

"I didn't," Lester answered.

"Nor I," Leeroy said, "I assumed colleges paid students for inflicting such damage on them." He laughed.

They arrived at the parking lot where Hazel waited.

Leeroy said, "I see no one stole Hazel. You know how thieves are. They steal the nicest car in the lot."

Lester looked at Laverne and rolled his eyes.

"I hope nobody scratched her," was Leeroy's last word on the subject.

CHAPTER THIRTY

"I need to finalize my grocery and invitation lists for the crawfish boil," Mildred said.

"You find a date, young Blanc?"

Jake shuddered when he thought about Cora and Bert. He ignored Leeroy and poured three fresh cups of coffee. Leeroy placed a few sheets of paper on the table before Jake, as Mildred had done with the GED booklet.

"What is this?" Jake asked as he picked up the document. He read aloud. "Application for Admission, Tulane University. An application? What am I going to do with this?"

He paused, then looked at Mildred. "What have you two done?"

"*We* haven't done anything," Mildred insisted.

Jake then turned his attention to Leeroy. "Then what have you *three* done?"

Leeroy made no attempt to deny anything. "We went to see the president of Tulane College."

"*What*?" Jake blurted out.

"University," Mildred said, her eyes on her lists.

"Excuse me," Leeroy said. "Tulane University. And the nice president, who is a lady by the way, Blanc, gave us this for you. She said she'd receive your application back and do what she could to help you get into Tulane College—excuse me again, Tulane University."

Jake turned the application over and over as he considered the possibility.

Leeroy spoke again. "She was impressed by your test score."

"You took her my *test score*?" Jake asked.

Leeroy pulled the paper containing Jake's score from his pocket and returned it to Jake.

"We did. Laverne, Lester, and me. We parked Hazel right in the middle of a parking lot that had more money in parked cars than Carter has liver pills."

Jake had no idea who Carter was nor what a liver pill was.

"And the nice lady said with your test score," Leeroy continued, "you qualify for lots of scholarship money. Mildred, did you know you have to *pay* to go to a university?"

"The university was free when I went. Didn't cost me anything."

"Such sarcasm. Did you hear that, Blanc? The things I put up with."

Leeroy said nothing about what else Dr. Sloan had told them—that Jake also qualified for scholarship monies because of his background. Jake continued turning the application over and over.

Leeroy spoke forcefully.

"You complete that application ASAP. Maybe sooner. The university president, Susan Sloan—*Doctor* Susan Sloan—we're good friends—she said classes start in August. You complete that application. Lester, Laverne, and I'll take it to Doctor Sloan."

Jake thought for a moment. "I'll complete the application. No harm in doing that. But *I'll* take the application to the president of Tulane University. This is something I'll have to do myself."

"Fine by us," Leeroy said. "Doctor Sloan is in a big, tall building on the left as you make your way onto campus off Audubon. Look for a parking lot full of long, expensive cars. Tell her secretary, Miz Bates, that Misters Edwards, Knox, and Washington sent you. That way you're sure to get the VIP treatment."

Leeroy and Jake worked in the garage and yard for most of the week. Jake mowed the lawn, a responsibility he'd taken over since moving in. He and Leeroy pulled folding tables and chairs from the garage, cleaned them, and set them up. That night, for the first time in years, the garage would once again be a community gathering place.

"I have roux made for the chicken gumbo," Mildred said. "I'll start the gumbo this afternoon. Won't take long to cook. I've got the étouffée already made and in the refrigerator. Just needs to be heated. I've got plates, bowls, flatware, cups, napkins. Missus Blair and Cormier insisted on helping, so they're bringin' desserts. All's in order in the kitchen." Mildred looked at her husband. "Leeroy?"

Leeroy reported on matters non-kitchen, representing both Jake and himself.

"Grass cut. Tables and chairs cleaned and set up. Tables covered. Propane tanks filled. Crawfish pot scrubbed, ready for crawfish. Crawfish ordered. Blanc and I'll pick them up at ten. I'll bring them back here for purging. We'll start boiling crawfish at four thirty for a six o'clock crowd arrival."

Leeroy sounded as though he was in the military.

"Drinks?" Mildred asked.

"Two coolers borrowed from church, full of ice, water, and soda," Jake reported.

"I'm afraid I'll overlook something," Mildred said.

"You should've overlooked inviting Lester and Laverne," Leeroy said.

Mildred looked at Jake and pointed toward the garage. "Get him out of my kitchen."

"Yes, ma'am."

∞

At nine fifteen a.m., Leeroy and Jake left home.

"I need to go by Franklin Avenue," Leeroy said.

Jake soon saw Lester and Laverne standing outside their flat on Franklin. Leeroy pulled Hazel to the curb.

Minutes later, Leeroy parked Hazel near one of the wharves and asked for Rafael.

"Two thirty-pound bags of crawfish for a Mister Leeroy Edwards?" Rafael announced.

"That be me. I'm *Mister* Leeroy Edwards."

"Oh my. *Mister* Edwards," Lester said softly, peering at Jake and Laverne.

"Hush," Leeroy harrumphed, but the corner of his mouth turned up in a half-smile as he did so.

Leeroy, Jake, Lester, and Laverne returned to 25 Galvez Street with sixty pounds of crawfish.

"Sixty pounds of crawfish sure seems a bunch," Leeroy said, "but that's what Mildred said."

Jake helped handle the bags as Leeroy, Lester, and Laverne divided the crawfish into four large coolers. Lester took a hose and covered them with water. Laverne added salt.

"Let's leave 'em there for a while," Leeroy said, snagging a lawn chair. Lester and Laverne followed his lead. Leeroy sat for a moment, then lifted his head and sniffed. "I smell gumbo, gentlemen."

"Yep. Smells good," Lester said.

Jake sniffed the air but smelled nothing. He thought Leeroy and Lester were imagining things.

At about three forty-five, Leeroy filled the large pot with water and ignited the propane burner beneath. Satisfied with the mixture of fuel and air, he added crab boil seasoning. By four fifteen, the water was rolling and steaming. Leeroy added onions and potatoes.

"We'll let those cook for a few minutes," Leeroy said.

Promptly at four thirty, Leeroy gave the nod to Lester and Laverne. They began adding ears of corn and crawfish.

"Put half the crawfish in, gentlemen," Leeroy directed. "That eighty-quart pot will accommodate thirty pounds of crawfish easy enough, along with the onions, taters, and corn."

He waited until the water came back to a boil and timed fifteen minutes. When the amount of time lapsed, Leeroy turned off the propane.

"We'll let 'em stay in the pot for another fifteen minutes. In the meantime, we're gonna need two of those ice chests."

Jake got busy and washed the salt and residue out of the empty ice chests as Leeroy, Lester and Laverne sat and watched. Fifteen minutes later, Jake helped Leeroy lift the basket containing the thirty-plus pounds of onions, potatoes, corn, and crawfish. Together they divided the contents into the two clean ice chests.

Leeroy started the cycle over again by adding onions and potatoes to the boiling mixture. Jake, satisfied the three men had matters under control, excused himself. He checked in with Mildred, and then showered, dressed, and left.

At five-fifty, guests started arriving. First came Curley and Mavis Cormier. Mavis had a large container of banana pudding. Then the Blairs, Joseph and Carrie. Joe carried another large Tupperware tote with two lemon ice box pies inside.

Raymond and Sally Summers soon arrived from next door. Music Minister Woodrow and his wife, Annie, came with Pastor Josiah and his wife, Tela. The Thibodeauxs, Earl and Orpah, rolled in just behind the pastor, followed by their neighbors on the other side, Silas and Romena Robinson. They were all friends. Several of them had known each other for years.

Mildred and her crew had everything perfect. The air smelled of crawfish boil, chicken gumbo, and shrimp étouffée. Soft Cajun music played from a radio in the garage.

Paul and his wife arrived, and he parked his automobile beside Hazel on the street, where she had been moved in order to provide more space inside the garage. Until the Evans's arrival, introductions were unnecessary, but Leeroy recognized that with the exception of himself, Mildred, Lester, and Laverne, no one else knew the Evanses.

Rebecca Evans was an attractive woman. She was petite, with distinguished facial features. She wore a white blouse over black slacks. What attracted Leeroy's attention was Paul. The attraction wasn't his attire for the night, which was as nice and neat as that of his wife. What attracted Leeroy's attention was what Paul Evans carried—something resembling the moonshine jugs Leeroy had seen in antique shops. The jug was wrapped with a red ribbon secured around the small neck. The presence of the jug drew Lester's attention as well, as he stood beside Leeroy.

Leeroy turned to Lester and spoke quietly. "That wrapped thang don't look good. Mildred doesn't allow alcohol in this house."

"I assumed," Lester said, "Jake had communicated the fact that this is a teetotaling bunch."

"Our pastor and minister of music are here," Leeroy added. "Mildred won't make a scene of it."

Leeroy stepped forward and took the lead. "I want to introduce all of you to Paul Evans and his wife, Rebecca." He offered context. "Mister Evans owns Paul's Poulet, where Blanc works."

He then turned to Paul, introducing him and Rebecca to the other partygoers. They both spoke and nodded to everyone. Paul still cradled the jug in his arm.

Leeroy said, "And you know Lester, Laverne, and my wife, Mildred."

Paul greeted Lester, Laverne, and Mildred, then said—not loudly, but clearly enough for all to hear, "Rebecca and I thank you for your kind invitation, and we want to present you with a token of our appreciation. Something to add spice, perhaps, to tonight's festivities."

Paul handed the jug to Mildred who, always gracious, accepted the gift and spoke, never losing her composure.

"That's kind, Mister Evans. You shouldn't have done that, but Leeroy and I thank you. I'll put this in the kitchen for later."

Leeroy knew what *later* meant—pouring the contents down the drain, after the festivities but before the sun came up.

"Please," Paul interrupted, "open it, Miz Edwards."

Mildred remained cool. "Please call me Mildred."

"All right, Mildred, and please call me Paul. Do open it."

Reluctantly, Mildred removed the ribbon. She then slowly peeled down the paper encasing the bottle. She peeked under the remaining wrapper, and her face lit up.

She quickly finished unwrapping and displayed the bottle for all to see—a stoneware moonshine jug that Paul had filled and labeled with a large official label.

Tabasco Sauce.

The crowd roared their approval. Paul shook with laughter.

"*Laissez les bons temps rouler!*" Mildred said.

"Let the good times roll!" the group responded.

Leeroy wondered where Jake went but pushed the thought out of his mind as partygoers mixed and mingled. Paul found a conversationalist in Joe Blair. The women gathered and talked, and Lester and Laverne talked to Pastor Hart, while Mildred waited for Jake before signaling to Leeroy to begin eating. Mildred wondered if Jake would be solo.

At last Leeroy turned to Mildred. "Looky here, my love. Here comes Blanc. And Blanc's ... date!"

Jake walked up the driveway slowly, wearing khaki pants and a light blue pullover. What impressed Leeroy was not only the fact that Jake *had* a date, but the *appearance* of his date. As beautiful as Rebecca Evans was, Jake's date was equally beautiful. She wore blue knee-length shorts with a bright yellow top. Leeroy met them in the driveway.

"Blanc, introduce me ..." Leeroy's voice trailed off as he peered more closely at the girl. "Cora? Is that you?"

The unmistakable smile and dimples gave her away.

"Stop that, Leeroy!" Cora said.

"I didn't recognize you without the vest and chicken cap. In fact, I've never seen you without the chicken cap, *and* ... Blanc never said he was bringing you tonight."

"Is that right, Jake?" Cora said, turning to him. "You never told them I was coming?"

"Nobody asked." Jake smiled. "Plus, my girlfriend is nobody's business except mine."

Not "date." *Girlfriend.*

The word wasn't lost on Cora or Leeroy. She continued to offer the same exquisite, disarming smile as a rose-pink blush tinted her cheeks. Her short blonde hair, lifted in front, accentuated her hazel eyes that glowed like glass with light behind it. She wore two sets of earrings in her earlobes, a single ring on her left hand, and two rings on the right.

"Blanc, do the honors," Leeroy said.

Jake knew what he meant. "Good evening, everybody. I want you to meet Cora Hoelzer." Jake then went around the half-moon circle and introduced everyone. Pleasantries were extended. Mildred nodded in Leeroy's direction.

"All right," Leeroy said, "we're ready to eat. Let me pray."

Everyone bowed. As on Christmas Day, Leeroy's prayer was brief but beautiful.

"Lord, we thank you for this day, these dear friends and family, for this incredible feast, and for this wonderful gatherin'. We pray you'll bless us, even as we may eat too much. We ask this in the mighty, joyous name of your Son, Jesus. Amen."

"Amen," the group echoed.

"Mildred?" Leeroy asked, looking in her direction. Mildred nodded, and Leeroy whooped.

"Let's eat!"

The group ate most of the sixty pounds of crawfish, along with two of Mildred's largest pots of gumbo and étouffée. They also emptied a large rice cooker's contents, along with a small mountain of potato salad and enough boiled potatoes, onions, and corn to feed most of the Ninth Ward. Then, just to round things out, they finished off a large pan of banana pudding and two lemon ice box pies. Rebecca had brought five half-gallon containers of ice cream, which was almost all consumed. They drank the biggest part of two coolers of drinks—soda and water and three gallons of tea. The large jug of Tabasco sauce sat on the corner of the head table—to be enjoyed by all.

Just before nine p.m., Pastor Josiah Hart rose. "Leeroy, would you, Lester, Laverne, and Jake mind playing a few tunes for us?"

The men needed little prodding. Folks stood, shuffled and rearranged chairs, and in minutes, Leeroy, Laverne, and Jake swung their guitars into place. Lester gently shook his one-zill-missing tambourine. Laverne leaned over and bent his guitar's strings. Jake followed, taking the party to another level. The men of the group formed a half-circle of chairs in front of the four musicians, then all sat down, clapped to the rhythm, and sang when they knew the lyrics. Cora, who had never seen or heard Jake play, also sat in front, impressed at his musical abilities.

Everyone enjoyed the music, so much so that no one noticed Paul's absence until he slipped into the garage with an electrical extension cord in his left hand. In his right hand was a rectangular case about five feet long and two feet wide. He set the case down, went to the back of the garage and returned, unrolling the extension cord behind him as he came. He opened the case and removed its contents. He unfolded its four legs, attached the electrical cord, switched on the device, and reached for an empty chair.

Then he motioned to Lester.

Lester had seen a few electric pianos, but never played one. No matter—he knew his way around a piano, electric or otherwise. He could play an expensive grand, and he could play an old upright. The tone from a grand piano sounded better than the tone generated from a worn-out upright, but that was the instrument's fault, not Lester's.

None of the Noirs could remember the last time Lester played piano with the group, but time hadn't diminished his skills. He caught up mid-song with the other three, playing as though he'd been rehearsing for this event for months. Lester's piano added a new dimension to their music, taking the group to a higher, stronger level.

Jake inched his way toward the back, to a place when he could hear and see Lester play. He marveled at Lester's fingers and hands, as agile as a much younger man's, flying across the keys.

Sylvester Thibodeaux, whose feet had not stopped keeping rhythm since the music started, rose and offered his hand to his wife, Abbey. The couple moved into the open area between the chairs and musicians and began to dance. Soon Silas Robinson and Romena followed Sylvester's lead. Paul and Rebecca soon were dancing, as were Curley and Mavis Cormier.

Cora was left sitting alone at the front of the half-circle, until Jake shrugged out of his guitar strap and leaned the instrument against the side of the garage. He took Cora by the hand as Lester, Laverne, and Leeroy continued playing.

Leeroy added his bass to Jake's guitar on the side of the garage wall and led Mildred out into the other couples' midst, leaving the music to Laverne and Lester. Everyone danced, including the Blairs and Summerses, when the music offered by Laverne's guitar and Lester's piano shifted into a slow number. Pastor Josiah, wife Tela, and Music Minister Woodrow Riles and his wife, Annie, joined in. Before the night ended, Laverne decided he wanted to dance, and he did so with most of the ladies there, starting with Mildred and Cora.

Lester wasn't interested in dancing. He focused on the keyboard. He didn't realize how much he loved playing piano, and how much he'd missed it. He provided one dance number after another, for his own pleasure as well as everybody else's.

The night was magical.

"Good night, Mildred," Sally Summers said. "What a wonderful night. We must do this again soon, at our place next time."

"Thank you for coming. Absolutely, let's do this again soon."

The party began breaking up. With the leftovers cooling in Mildred's refrigerator, and with the kitchen back in the same spotless condition as before the gala, Sally Summers and Romena Robinson set out for home, walking together as their husbands helped clean.

As the remaining wives mingled both inside and outside the house, Paul, Leeroy, Lester, Laverne, and Jake, aided by the men, made quick work of the outside. They washed down and stacked tables. They stacked chairs. Leeroy, Lester, and Laverne had already cleaned and stored the crawfish pot, propane burner, and propane tanks. Pastor Josiah volunteered to return the church's ice chests loaned to Leeroy.

The husbands and wives began their departures.

"Thank you, Leeroy, and thanks to Mildred for the invitation," Paul said, standing alone with Leeroy. "I can't remember when I've enjoyed anything more."

"Thanks for coming," Leeroy said.

Lester figured out how to refold the piano. He placed the instrument back in its case and rolled up the extension cord. He joined Leeroy and Paul and handed the cord and the instrument to Paul.

"May I ask you something without offending you, Lester?" Paul asked.

"Depends."

"Depends?"

"Depends on what it is," Lester said.

"May I give you this keyboard?"

Lester gave Paul a puzzled look. "It's brand new. That piano had never been played before."

Paul smiled before speaking. "You're correct. I bought this instrument for tonight, for you. I want you to have it. It's a gift from me and Rebecca." He looked down for a moment, then back at Lester. "I thought it would be a nice surprise for you, but I had no idea you'd make such wonderful music with it."

"Paul, I don't—" Lester started.

Leeroy eased the moment as he placed one hand on Paul's shoulder, the other on Lester's.

"Yes, Paul. You may give an instrument to an old pianist without offending him. And he showed us all tonight how grateful he is to receive it."

"Thank you, Paul," was all Lester could say.

Paul patted Lester's shoulder. "Why don't I give you and Laverne a ride home? We're going in your direction. No need for Leeroy to go out tonight."

They all agreed.

With the exception of the Evanses and Lester and Laverne, Jake and Cora were the last to leave. Jake pecked Mildred on the cheek.

"Thanks for a wonderful night, Mildred."

"Yes, Missus Edwards," Cora echoed, "thanks for a wonderful night."

"Call me Mildred, please, and you're both welcome. Thanks for coming, Cora."

Jake and Cora moved down the driveway.

Paul, Rebecca, Lester, and Laverne left. Paul opened the car door for Rebecca, while Lester and Laverne got into the rear seat. Paul pulled onto North Galvez as Leeroy and Mildred waved.

$$\infty$$

"Hazel, my dear, I hope you didn't feel lonely out here tonight."

Leeroy couldn't see in the darkness, but he imagined Mildred rolling her eyes.

"Hazel wasn't alone," Mildred said. "She had lots of company, nice company, including the Cadillac our pastor drives, to say nothing of the long black automobile Paul drives."

Leeroy moved toward Hazel, intending to stow her inside the garage for the night.

"All of 'em pieces of junk, eh, Hazel?"

Again unseen and again anticipated, Mildred rolled her eyes as Leeroy started Hazel's engine.

Around midnight, Leeroy and Mildred went to bed. The two spoke softly in the dark. They both heard the rear door open and the old pine floors' faint creaks, and they knew Jake was home and in his room.

"Oh, Leeroy. Paul forgot his electric piano," Mildred said. "I saw it against the wall in the garage, beside your guitar."

"Not forgotten, my love," Leeroy explained. "He gave it to Lester."

"What?"

"Paul bought that piano new, just for tonight," Leeroy said. "He never intended to take it home."

The two lay in silence, both enraptured by the night.

After a time, Mildred said, "Cora's a beautiful person, inside and out. And she's good for Jake. She complements him well. We should have her over for dinner sometime."

"Agree and agree. She *is* beautiful, inside and out. She's definitely good for Blanc and having her over for dinner is a fine idea ..."

Leeroy paused.

"What?" Mildred asked.

"Let's not invite Lester or Laverne. They'll get in the way."

She harrumphed. "Good night, Leeroy."

"Good night, my love."

Leeroy pecked his beloved on her cheek and spoke the final words of a near fairy-tale night. "You do know how to throw a party, my love."

Mildred settled, secure in the arms of her husband, and was asleep in minutes. Leeroy lay awake, and for a fleeting moment, thought about Bert.

CHAPTER THIRTY-ONE

Mildred woke on Monday morning, glanced at the clock on her bedside table, and leaped to her feet. She found Leeroy in the garage. He'd consumed most of a pot of coffee.

"I overslept, Leeroy. I can't remember the last time I slept past nine."

"Didn't hurt you any, my love. You were tired. No rush. Nothing pressin' today. I slept later too. I haven't been up long."

"Where's Jake?"

"Don't know. He and his car were gone when I first noticed."

"Hmm. I know for a fact he isn't working today. I wonder where that boy is," Mildred said.

Earlier, before Mildred and Leeroy woke, Jake put on a pot of coffee and dropped a single slice of bread in the toaster. As the coffee brewed, he showered and dressed. He buttered the toast and sat down with a cup of coffee, and looked over the document in front of him again. He brushed his teeth, checked his appearance in the mirror one last time, and left the house at eight.

As Leeroy had said, the parking lot was full of expensive cars. Jake found an open space and parked his automobile, minus hubcaps, minus the glass in the left rear door, between a Mercedes and a Volvo.

"Big, tall building on the left as you make your way onto campus off Audubon," Leeroy had told him. With document in hand, Jake went see Dr. Susan Sloan, President, Tulane University.

"Good morning. May I help you?" Martha Bates asked.

"Good morning. I'm Jake Thomas. I don't have an appointment, but I'm here to see Doctor Sloan, if possible. I'll make an appointment if necessary."

"An appointment isn't necessary, Mister Thomas. Doctor Sloan's been hoping to see you."

Martha stepped inside the president's office and spoke. Martha reentered her office area, followed by Sloan, who said, "Martha, please call Dorothy Ellis and ask her to join us."

Martha nodded. Susan Sloan turned her attention to Jake. "Please come in," she said, gesturing to her office.

Jake entered the cavernous office, as mesmerized as the three Noirs had been. He sat.

"You're Jake Thomas?" Dr. Sloan said, and she smiled. "Jacob Alvin Thomas, a.k.a. Blanc, according to Leeroy Edwards?"

Jake was surprised but quickly recovered. "Yes, ma'am. I understand you know Misters Edwards, Knox, and Washington."

"Indeed I do, and I was hoping to meet you. They told me a lot about you, and now you're here." She held out both hands, arms wide in an inclusive gesture. "Welcome to Tulane University."

"Leeroy, Lester, and Laverne exaggerate things at times, Doctor Sloan. You're going to be disappointed, I'm afraid."

"Oh, I doubt it."

"And do I call you President Sloan? Doctor Sloan?"

"Either is fine."

For the next few moments, Jake asked questions any student would ask as they attempted to make a decision regarding college—questions of admissions, majors, and cost. He, unlike his friends, knew college cost something and at Tulane, college was expensive. He got to the real issue.

"I suppose you know why I'm here?"

"I'm hoping you're here requesting admission to Tulane University."

"Yes, ma'am."

Jake handed her his university application. She took it and placed the application, unopened, on a desk behind her, then turned back to him. "Tell me about yourself, Jake."

Jake was unsure what Dr. Sloan wanted to know and was unsure what Leeroy, Lester and Laverne had told her. "What do you want to know? My background? My GED score?"

Jake wasn't ashamed of his family, the fact he had dropped out of high school, or the fact he'd been homeless for a period of his life. Sloan dismissed Jake's question with a waving of the hand.

"Oh, no. None of that. Misters Edwards, Knox, and Washington informed me of your history, and I already know your GED score. Which is, by the way, impressive."

"I knew they shared my results with you," Jake said.

"They did and, again, your score is impressive."

"Then what can I tell you, Doctor Sloan, that you don't already know?"

Sloan leaned forward before speaking.

"What's your passion? What do you want to do with your life, and what will you do with a degree from Tulane University? I want to know what motivates you."

Jake thought for a moment before answering.

"My passion? Serving Christ, and ... music. I love playing with Leeroy, Lester, and Laverne. My passion is people. I love and enjoy being with people—I got that from my mother. My passion is the desire to help people. I got that from my father. I guess those are the real reasons I play music with the three men. Also, the fact we all need the money."

"Academically, Jake. University-wise. College-wise. What do you enjoy, subject-wise? Math? History? Literature?"

"Science. I enjoy science. I love science and mathematics."

"And as you know, you made a perfect score on the GED science part."

"I did," Jake answered, nodding.

"You scored high on the math part. Do you know that, too?"

"I do."

The conversation was interrupted by a knock on Sloan's door. Martha Bates entered and spoke as though making an introduction. "Doctor Dorothy Ellis." Jake rose as Dorothy Ellis entered Sloan's office.

Sloan made the formal introductions. "Jake, this is Dorothy Ellis, our Vice President for Enrollment Management. Doctor Ellis, this is Jake Thomas. You and I spoke about him."

The two shook hands.

"Doctor Ellis is in charge of recruiting," Sloan said. "I've invited her here to help you consider your classes and fill out your class schedule for the fall semester."

"I'm afraid I don't understand," Jake said. "You haven't looked at my application."

"Misters Edwards, Knox, and Washington are fond of you," Sloan said. "Your history at Paul's Poulet tells me you have a healthy work ethic, and your GED score tells me you can perform on the college level. What else do I need to know?"

Jake looked dubious. Sloan tried another tack.

"As university president, Jake, I have certain ... privileges, shall we say, certain abilities. I've the authority to grant admission to a few students, every year, to the university. I admit these students without having to go through the normal channels. It's one of the perks of being a college president, a perk I take seriously. A few students have special needs. I admit students based on needs. You qualify based on needs *and* merit. Plus, Jake, I consider myself a fair judge of character. I like you, and as I've said, I'm impressed."

With a wave of her hand she added, "And I like Lester, Laverne, and Leeroy, too."

"Very few people like Leeroy," Jake said, before thinking.

Susan Sloan laughed out loud. Jake understood. As though Dr. Sloan could read his mind, she continued. "And as far as cost is concerned—tuition, as we refer to it—I've already taken care of that too. You come, you make good grades, and your education here won't cost you anything."

Sloan visualized her own son, now a sophomore at Tulane, and knew his college degree was paid for with a scholarship. She paid it forward by offering the same to

Jake. She'd always regretted not being able to do so for every student.

Sloan allowed Jake to take in the moment, then reiterated what she had already said. "I've asked Doctor Ellis here to help you register for fall classes."

Jake felt no need to ask any more questions. "Thank you, Doctor Sloan," he said.

"Then I'll leave you to Doctor Ellis."

Jake was speechless and immobile at the same time. Dorothy Ellis jostled him back to the moment. "Mister Thomas, shall we continue this in my office?"

He was about to say yes when Dr. Sloan spoke again. "Jake, before you go, I want to give you something."

Jake took Sloan's gift, a small book, without looking at it.

"Something I believe you'll enjoy," she said.

"Thank you." Jake reached for Sloan's hand. As they shook, he saw the envelope.

Application for Admission, Tulane University, Thomas, Jacob Alvin lay unopened on her desk.

Jake returned home to an empty house. He retired to this bedroom and pulled off his shoes. He reclined on his bed, put his hands behind his head and closed his eyes. His mind began the futile attempt to process the whirlwind of information he'd received earlier that morning from Drs. Sloan and Ellis.

He remembered Dr. Sloan's gift, and he got up and retrieved it. Settling back on his bed, he examined the small book. He didn't recognize the title or the author's name, which didn't surprise him. He'd never read more than a few books in his lifetime and, in all honesty, wasn't thrilled about reading this one.

The president of Tulane University obviously has high regard for this book. I should probably at least look at it.

He got comfortable and began reading.

Three hours later, he closed the book, having finished reading without ever leaving his bed. In addition to the information from Drs. Sloan and Ellis, he now had a wealth of knowledge from the book to process. He wanted to share the book with Lester, Leeroy, and Laverne. He would consider the best time for that.

CHAPTER THIRTY-TWO

Jake sat down with Mildred and Leeroy for dinner.

"If I have this right, Blanc, you're now a college student at Tulane University. Correct?"

"I'm registered for college classes, yes," Jake said, "but I don't feel much like a college student. What I feel is intimidation, mortification, and petrification. I haven't been in a classroom in years, and I haven't ever experienced anything as rigorous and demanding as I think the college classroom is going to be."

"What classes are you taking?" Mildred asked.

"Biology, chemistry, calculus. I told Doctor Ellis ..."

"Doctor Ellis?" Mildred asked.

"Doctor Sloan introduced her to me. She's Vice President for Enrollment Management at Tulane. Doctor Sloan asked her to help me. She worked with me in considering the courses I need to take. I told Doctor Sloan and Doctor Ellis I prefer science and math. Doctor Ellis looked at my GED scores in science and math and gave me her advice, and now I'm registered for a biology class, a chemistry class, a calculus class ...."

"What is calculus?" Leeroy asked.

"A math class," Jake answered.

"Then why don't you say a math class?" Leeroy asked.

"Calculus is a *type* of math," Jake answered.

Mildred flapped a dismissive hand at Leeroy. "Hush, Leeroy. Go on, Jake."

"Biology, chemistry, calculus, and history, American history. A total of fourteen hours. Doctor Ellis said she didn't want to overload me with any more hours, since I haven't been in school for a while. Most students take more hours in one semester, but Doctor Ellis said I should be able to manage with fourteen."

For the rest of the summer, the Noirs and Jake played their music Saturday nights, and occasional Friday nights. To Lester's surprise and delight, several French Quarter merchants allowed him to use electrical outlets inside their businesses, where he could plug in the piano.

Jake didn't know what college would mean for his schedule. He wanted and needed to make as much money as possible before the semester started, and he knew the Noirs could use the money too. Regardless of his classes' demands, he was determined to reserve Saturday nights for playing. He communicated this to Lester, Leeroy, and Laverne—Friday nights were an option, but Saturday nights were set. Although they were too kind to say anything, the three older men all breathed sighs of relief at the prospect of a more secure stream of income. But as August and the beginning of the semester approached, matters changed.

Leeroy, Lester, and Laverne waved at Cora as they entered Paul's Poulet. Jake worked the counter as Paul aided Cora in distributing trays of food and filling cups. All three wore the now-familiar chicken cap and black vest.

Leeroy wondered about Bert.

"How may I help you three?" Jake asked.

"You know what we want," Leeroy answered. Jake smiled before announcing the order to the kitchen workers. He punched the order into the register and told each man how much they owed. Each paid and sat, waiting for Cora or Paul to deliver their meals. Paul approached their table and sat down beside Lester, opposite Leeroy and Laverne. He removed his chicken cap.

"Afternoon, gentlemen."

"Afternoon, Paul," Leeroy said. "Getting anything out of Blanc?"

Paul laughed. "Jake is one of the four hardest working men I know."

"Who are the other three?" Leeroy asked.

"I'm sitting with them."

Leeroy ignored Paul's answer. "As I suspected. Not gettin' nothin' out of Blanc."

The four men talked about the weather and politics—local, state, and national. Paul had learned early all he had to do was criticize a political party, either Democrat or Republican, to get a quick response from one of the three men. Paul considered himself an equal opportunity offender—if you crossed his path, he felt he had the right to rattle your cage.

The men bounced from topic to topic.

"Where did you guys play Saturday night?" Paul asked.

"On Royal. Royal Street was alive Saturday night," Laverne said.

"What do y'all intend to do once Jake begins college? In regard to your music, I mean?"

"We talked about it with him," Leeroy said. "We asked him to forgo playing with us at all. The three of us played together before Blanc came, and we offered to do that again, but he wouldn't hear it. So we all four agreed to no playing on Friday nights—Saturday nights only, and only when Blanc's schedule allows."

"Which," Lester said, "we believe, will be every Saturday night unless we insist otherwise. Jake is concerned about the three of us and thinks we all need to play every Saturday night."

"You don't?" Paul asked.

"We do," Laverne said and then caught himself. "Well, it depends."

"On?"

"On how much money we make," Leeroy added with a laugh.

"That makes sense. I understand that as a businessperson," Paul said, smiling. He circled a fingertip idly on the tabletop. "I've been thinking."

"About ...?" Laverne asked.

"I'll explain in a bit," Paul said.

The conversation turned back to politics and the hot and humid August summer in New Orleans.

When Jake recognized Paul's inactivity, and with no new customers ordering chicken, he came out from behind the counter with a pot of coffee. While Cora worked the side opposite the four men, Jake worked their side. He made his way to the table where his four friends sat, and Paul pulled a chair to the end of the booth. "Sit down, Jake."

Jake looked around the restaurant. No one appeared to be in need of a refill. Cora was making conversation with a longtime customer. He glanced at the parking lot. No incoming customers. He sat.

Paul initiated the conversation. "These boys tell me, Jake, that you intend to continue playing music every Saturday night when you start college."

"Well, maybe not *every* Saturday night," Jake replied.

"I've a proposal for the four of you."

"We're listening," Lester said.

"Are y'all familiar with the Place of Jazz?"

"The Place of Jazz on Decatur?" Lester asked.

"That's the one," Paul said.

"Absolutely," Leeroy answered. "We know the Place of Jazz."

"What musician and New Orleanian *doesn't* know the Place of Jazz?" Laverne added.

The Place of Jazz had been a mainstay in New Orleans for over a century. Not just jazz, but every genre of music had been played there at one time or another. Every famous musician in New Orleans and many other musicians from other venues around the world had performed at the Place of Jazz. The owner, also famous, was loved for frequently inviting unknown musicians to take the stage. Several big names had gotten their start at the Place of Jazz.

In addition, the Place was famous for its acoustics. There was something about the high ceilings covered with tin tiles and the one-hundred-year-old-plus pine floors and marble-covered walls that created a natural amplification.

The Place was always full, and always lively.

"You interested in playing there?" Paul asked.

The four men looked at him, speechless.

Paul continued to speak. "I'll take your silence as a 'yes.' Across the years, the Place's owner, Xavier Cullum—"

"Yes, we know Xavier. Known him for years," Lester said.

"I haven't *thought* about him in years," Laverne added.

"Me neither," Lester said, "I don't know why. We should have thought about him when we were about to be homeless and starving to death."

Lester and Laverne nodded.

"He and I became friends through the Greater New Orleans Business District Association," Paul said. He paused, circling his fingertip on the tabletop again. "The night of the crawfish boil, at your place, Leeroy, I taped you four playing and singing—my apologies for not asking you. When I plugged in the electric extension cord for the piano, I also plugged in a recorder. I took the tape to Xavier. He was amazed at what he heard. Then he asked your names."

"Here comes the bad part," Leeroy said, rolling his gaze toward the ceiling. "He's gonna remember Lester and Laverne, and he'll remember you two can't play a radio."

Lester, Laverne, Jake, and Paul ignored Leeroy, and Paul continued. "When I gave the first name, Lester Washington, he named both Laverne and Leeroy."

"Well, he should have," Laverne said. "We graced the Place for a long time with our music, years ago."

"He also spoke of someone named Anthony." Paul said.

"Anthony Emery. He was our lead guitarist for years," Leeroy answered.

"Died in 1960," Laverne said.

"Xavier said when Anthony died, he assumed the band dissolved and you three went your separate ways. Actually, he said he assumed the three of you were dead."

"We ain't dead," Lester said.

"Naw, we ain't," Laverne said.

"Do we look dead?" Leeroy said. "Well, maybe Laverne."

"Go on, Paul," Jake encouraged.

"Xavier wants you to play the Place."

"Lord almighty," Leeroy said.

"Back at the Place!" Laverne said.

"I can't believe it," Lester said.

"Starting in September, Xavier wants you to play two Saturday nights a month until Christmas. Two hours a night, eight to ten. Standard fee, plus tips."

The four men paused to consider the gift that had just been handed to them. After all these years, they had no idea what the standard fee was, but they knew the opportunity could cut their workload in half, from four Saturday nights to two. The opportunity guaranteed income. They suspected they would earn more—much more—in tips. Two hours a night! No more working the streets on Saturday night, at least for the remainder of the year. No more returning to Leeroy's garage at two thirty in the morning and getting home after four. No more Mountain Man, Blade Boy, or Leather Lung. No more searing heat and bone-chilling cold.

Moreover, they'd have a piano for Lester. Sometimes, on the streets, they couldn't find an electrical outlet. While Jake, Laverne and Leeroy were all gifted musicians, Lester on the piano took the group to another dimension. They were a different group, a much better group, with Lester's piano.

Lester made eye contact with Jake, Leeroy, and Laverne before speaking. "When do we start?"

"First Saturday night in September," Paul answered.

The five men sat in silence. Finally, Leeroy turned to Paul, scratched his head, and smiled.

"Are you an *agent*?"

"Excuse me?" Paul asked.

"Working eight to ten two Saturday nights a month, guaranteed salary, plus tips. Are you our agent? You did more than inquire as to a job. You negotiated for us."

"I'm a businessperson, remember. But your agent? Oh, no. I'm your friend," Paul said, smiling.

"And a good friend you are," Leeroy said as he reached for Paul's hand.

Paul shook hands with all four.

"Customers coming in. Coffee cups to fill." Paul donned his chicken cap.

Jake stood.

"Blanc?"

"Leeroy?"

"Where's Bert?"

Laverne and Lester both groaned.

"Haven't seen ol' Bert in quite a spell," Jake answered with a broad grin. "I think maybe Cora put the—what's the word?—the *kibosh* on him."

"Well, imagine that," Leeroy said.

Jake stepped lively and returned to his post.

CHAPTER THIRTY-THREE

Before Jake's first day of college, Paul approached him as he managed the deep fryer. "What are you doing tomorrow?"

Paul knew Jake wasn't working the following day because he'd checked the schedule Cora posted. Paul had long ago relinquished the work schedule to her, relieving himself of something he'd done since opening his restaurant twenty-two years earlier.

"No plans," Jake replied. "Hang around with Leeroy and Mildred. There are always odd jobs to be done around the house and yard. It's getting harder and harder for Leeroy to do those."

"Are you free for a few hours?"

"Sure."

"I'll pick you up at nine."

"I'll be ready."

At nine the next day, Paul pulled into Leeroy's driveway. Jake rose from the table where Mildred and Leeroy lingered, told them he was going out with Paul, and left the house.

"Good morning, Paul," Jake said, as he got in Paul's car and closed the door.

"Morning, Jake. Looks to be a marvelous day."

Paul backed out of the driveway and started in the direction of New Orleans. The two made small talk as Paul maneuvered the city streets. Within thirty minutes, Paul pulled into a parking lot and parked.

"Where are we?" Jake asked.

"Brian's Men's Shop," Paul answered.

"I see that," Jake said. "Are you in need of clothes?"

"*I'm* not, but *you* are," Paul said as he switched off the automobile's engine. He ended Jake's objections by saying, "Let's buy clothes."

Paul smiled. Before Jake could offer any further objection, Paul exited the automobile and started across the parking lot. Jake followed, suspecting Paul wanted him dressed nicely for his college debut.

August and September proved to be significant months in Jake's life, and in the lives of the people who knew him. Jake began college classes in August, and he and the Noirs began playing the Place of Jazz in September.

On the Wednesday before their first performance at the Place, Paul asked Lester, Laverne, and Leeroy to join him at the diner for lunch.

"What do you believe Paul has up his sleeve?" Leeroy asked, with Lester and Laverne riding in Hazel.

"Lunch, I s'pect," Laverne answered.

"More than lunch," Leeroy said. "I smell more than fried chicken comin' from Paul's Poulet today."

"Leeroy, you have a devious mind," Lester added.

With the three men seated at Paul's Poulet, their orders taken and meals delivered, Paul came around with a pot of coffee. After he was satisfied no one else in the busy lunch crowd needed coffee, he sat with Lester, Laverne, and Leeroy.

"Morning, Paul," Leeroy said.

"Good morning to the three of you. How are matters this fine day?"

"Better now, with one of your chicken sandwiches," Leeroy added.

The men sat in silence for a few minutes as Paul scanned the restaurant for an empty coffee cup.

Lester said, "Mister Evans ..."

"Call me Paul. I insist."

"All right, Paul. Laverne, Leeroy, and I again want to express our appreciation for the opportunity to play at the Place."

"That was a nice thing to do for three tired old men," Laverne said.

"We're in your debt," Leeroy added.

"Oh no, you're not in my debt. I've heard you play, remember?" Paul said. "You're superb musicians, and your voices, the four of you, harmonize to create a beautiful sound. You each are talented in your own right, but together you're magical."

Lester, Laverne, and Leeroy had long recognized the blend of their voices. They'd expressed to one another their belief that their voices—the four of them, with Jake—blended together better, they felt, than the three of them had done with Anthony.

"You deserve the Place," Paul said. "You've earned it. I had a conversation and made the connection with Xavier, and I must tell you, Xavier's thrilled to have you there. He said the three of you, with Anthony, were hypnotic. His exact words."

"I'm not sure what that means," Leeroy said. "Is that a compliment?"

"It's a compliment," Laverne answered.

"I reckon," Leeroy responded, as Paul smiled.

The restaurant filled with the lunch crowd.

"Jake finishes his shift at two today," Paul said. "Will you three wait around till two? I promise you dessert and all the coffee you want."

"In that case—" Laverne began.

"We'll wait," Leeroy concluded.

A few minutes after two, Jake emerged from the back of the restaurant in street clothes. He joined Paul, Leeroy, Lester, and Laverne at their table. Paul had shed his work attire and was dressed in street clothes. Jake sat as Paul laid both his hands on the table and said, "Let's all take a ride."

No one spoke another word as Paul climbed behind the wheel of his car. After a period of respectful silence, Laverne said, "Paul's car is nicer than yours, Leeroy."

"I'm glad Hazel didn't hear that," Leeroy answered from the middle position in the rear seat. He continued speaking as he leaned over Jake to peer out the window. "I gave Hazel a bath yesterday."

"A bath? I can only imagine she's as beautiful as her name," Paul said.

"She is," Leeroy affirmed.

"I can't wait to see her," Paul said.

"What kind of car is this, Paul?" Leeroy asked.

"A Mercedes-Benz."

"Hazel, bathed, puts this piece of Mercedes-Benz junk to shame. No offense, Paul," Leeroy said.

"None taken."

Leeroy, attempting to peer out the window in the rear seat, practically lay atop Jake in the rear seat.

Paul sneaked a smile in Lester's direction.

"I've never driven a Mercedes-Benz auto-*mo*-bile, but I imagine this thing handles like a tank compared to Hazel," Leeroy said.

"Never driven a Mercedes?" Paul asked.

"Never driven more than three or four cars in all my life. All the other cars were Fords. Maybe a Chrysler or Chevy."

"How long have you owned Hazel?"

"Since 1958. August seventeenth, 1958," Leeroy answered.

"You remember the date?" Paul was incredulous.

"You remember the day your first child was born, don't you?"

"I do." Paul laughed. "Yes, I do."

The five rode in silence before Paul spoke again.

"Jake tells me Hazel could use a paint job. You ever thought about having Hazel repainted?"

"Blanc talks too much, and no. Never. I haven't ever considered painting Hazel. Don't mess with perfection," Leeroy answered. He kept leaning lower and lower onto Jake as if he wanted to look at something high in the afternoon sky.

"Will you get off me?" Jake said, pushing Leeroy back toward the middle.

Leeroy got the response from Jake he desired, and shoulder-bumped him, laughing.

Lester turned in his seat to admonish them. "Children, y'all behave back there."

"Else Uncle Laverne gonna have to take off his belt," Laverne said.

"Laverne, can't you keep those two in line?" Lester asked.

"One, maybe," Laverne said. "Other one's impossible."

The remainder of the trip went without fanfare or commentary. Paul eased the long car into the parking lot as Leeroy read the marquee, at least a portion of it.

"Something Men's Shop."

"Brian's Men's Shop," Jake read.

"You need clothes, Jake?" Lester asked.

"I don't."

"Why are we here?" Laverne asked.

Paul said nothing. Just as he'd done with Jake, he turned off the car's engine, got out, and started across the parking lot. Lester, Laverne, Leeroy, and Jake followed. Lester noticed the smile on Jake's face.

Paul held the door for his friends to enter Brian's. They were all well-dressed, their shirttails tucked in tidily, their clothes clean and ironed. All four men wore dark or khaki slacks. Lester and Leeroy both wore white shirts while Laverne wore a blue one. Jake wore a soft gray pullover.

"Paul!" A tall, impeccably well-dressed man approached them from the back of the store.

"Hello, Brian."

"Are these the gentlemen you told me about?"

"They are. Allow me to make introductions. Brian, this is Lester Washington, Leeroy Edwards, and Laverne Knox. And of course, you know Jake. Gentlemen, Brian Fonteneau."

The Noirs stepped forward, each accepting Fonteneau's hand while they exchanged greetings. Fonteneau turned to Jake, extended his right hand, and placed his left hand on Jake's right forearm. "Hello, Jake. Good to see you again."

"Likewise, Brian," Jake said.

Lester, Laverne, and Leeroy seemed at ease in Brian's presence. Jake suspected the three would be equally at ease in the presence of the President of the United States.

"I'm going to step across the street and eat beignets and drink coffee," Paul said.

"That new place does offer excellent beignets," Brian replied. "Not quite Café du Monde, but close enough."

"I will return, gentlemen," Paul said, and went out and across the street.

"Let's go to the back," Brian directed as he opened a door to the rear of his establishment. He turned to his two employees. "Margaret? Oslo?"

"Sir," the two responded simultaneously.

"I'll be in the back, should you need me."

"Yes, sir."

Lester, Laverne, Leeroy, and Jake stepped into the back of Brian's Men's Shop to a stunning awakening. There appeared to be more space and more merchandise in the rear of the building than in the front.

"Let's get busy. Leeroy, shall we start with you?"

"Depends on what you intend to do. Maybe you better start with Laverne and let me watch."

Brian laughed as he motioned for Leeroy to move toward the racks of clothes.

Paul ate an order of beignets, consisting of three square-shaped doughnuts minus the holes and covered with powdered sugar.

Brian was right. Not Café du Monde, but close enough.

He drank three cups of café au lait. He knew the coffee was high in caffeine—something not good for his atrial fibrillation. He knew Rebecca wouldn't approve, but he didn't drink caffeinated drinks often, and besides, Rebecca was nowhere in sight. He drank his caffeine, ate his sugar, and read the *Times-Picayune*.

Paul glanced at his watch, tipped his server, and started across the street. He opened the door to the rear of Brian's and walked into the back room. He stopped and stood in amazement, gazing on the four musicians transformed by their attire.

All four men wore identical full black tuxedos and dress shoes. The material from which the tuxes were made had a slight sheen. The white shirts with contrasting black buttons accentuated the black bowties. A sliver of white handkerchief, tucked inside a pocket, was the perfect touch, Paul thought. Their shoes were shined to a mirror gleam. Each man stood as though for a formal photo—tall, slender, handsome, heads held high. Laverne's hands gripped his jacket lapels, while the other three held their arms parallel to their bodies.

Paul had never considered the fact that Lester, Lavern, and Leeroy were almost as tall as Jake, who stood something over six feet four inches. The three Noirs' gray hair, along with Laverne's full gray beard, made the tuxedo-garbed quartet appear even more distinguished.

"Is this what you had in mind, Paul?" Brian asked.

"That's *exactly* what I had in mind. They're impressive."

"I agree, but they *are* wearing my tuxes," Brian said.

Paul laughed. "They're wearing *their* tuxes now."

"My, my," Leeroy said, shaking his head in wonder. "Lester, Laverne, you boys look good enough to get buried."

In a few minutes, the four had changed back into their original clothes. Brian placed the tuxes in protective clothing bags with the shoes in their boxes in a separate bag. The five men stepped out of the back room into the front of the store.

Brian extended his right hand. "If you need anything, gentlemen—adjustments, swaps—don't hesitate to let me know. Now if you'll excuse me, I'll see to our other customers."

With handshakes all around, Lester, Laverne, Jake, and Leeroy expressed their appreciation.

"Don't thank me," Brian said. "Thank Paul."

"Where *is* Paul?" Laverne said.

"Outside," Brian said with a brief wave. He moved off toward a waiting customer.

The four musicians, each with a tux in one hand and a shoe bag in the other, stepped outside to find Paul leaning against his car, the car's trunk raised. The four men spoke in unison to thank him for the clothing, but Paul interrupted.

"I am most happy to give these to you, and I do it in the name of Jesus, to help his plan for you move forward. Isn't he good?"

"He is good," Lester said, expressing the feelings of the group.

"Don't thank me yet," Paul said. "Let's see how Saturday night goes. You may be throwing tomatoes at me before you're done."

Paul gestured toward the trunk. The men began folding the tuxes inside, stacking the shoe boxes at each end. As the men finished loading, Paul climbed into the middle of the back seat. In moments, Leeroy stuck his head inside with a puzzled look.

"Would you, Mister Edwards," Paul said, holding up his keys, "care to drive a Mercedes-Benz?"

Leeroy smiled and took the keys. "Mister Evans, I believe I would."

"Oh, Lord," Laverne said with a moan. "That Mister Edwards gonna kill us."

"We got tuxes for burial. Four of us, at least," Lester said.

Lester got in the front with Leeroy as Jake and Laverne sat in the back with Paul. Leeroy started and revved the engine. He eased into traffic and headed toward Franklin Avenue.

Paul, mimicking Leeroy, leaned over onto Jake. He waited for Jake to respond and was not disappointed.

"What *is* it with you and Leeroy! Will you get *off* me?" Jake said, as he pushed Paul toward the middle.

Paul laughed. "How about this Mercedes auto-*mo*-bile, Mister Edwards?"

"Nice, nice. More acceleration than I'm used to. I see the fuel gauge works, and I s'pect the heater works too. And air conditionin'. Nice. And she don't handle like a boat atall, like I thought she would," Leeroy assessed. Then he added in a darker tone, "But she ain't no Hazel."

Paul, Jake, Lester, and Laverne laughed as Leeroy navigated through interstate traffic.

CHAPTER THIRTY-FOUR

"I'm as nervous as an escaped convict at a police ball," Leeroy admitted, at seven forty-five on Saturday night.

"Just another gig," Lester said.

"Gigs we been playin' for over fifty years," Laverne said, trying to calm Leeroy.

"Not just another gig," Leeroy countered. "This ain't Royal or Canal Street. This is the Place of Jazz, a place we haven't played in years. Heck, we haven't played *any* place like this in years. I ain't sure I can even hold my guitar. And the last time I checked, none of us wore tuxedos to play on the streets."

Jake checked his tux and then checked Leeroy, Lester, and Laverne. Lester tugged at his tie.

"You're fine, Leeroy," Jake said, as he assisted Lester with the offending tie.

"We all know what tonight means," Leeroy continued. "Tonight'll be the gig that dictates whether we still need to go to Royal and Canal or if Royal and Canal comes to us."

All of them had considered that.

"What does the audience look like out there?" Lester asked.

"I looked behind the curtain when the last group played," Laverne said. "Standing room only from what I could see. Every table full, every chair taken."

"Standing room?" Leeroy moaned. "Oh lordy. I'm gonna have a heart attack. I'm going to die right here. Tonight, on this stage."

"Well, like you told us, Leeroy, you look good enough to bury, so at least that's taken care of," Lester said.

"You're fine, Leeroy," Jake added. "The chords haven't moved. The C-chord is still the same C- chord."

"I know they haven't moved. I just hope I can find 'em," Leeroy muttered.

The last fifteen minutes before the show seemed like an hour. At seven fifty, the curtain lowered. Lester and Laverne stood as Leeroy and Jake paced. The previous band moved out as Lester went to the piano. Lester, Laverne, and Leeroy stepped into place. Jake bowed his head and prayed.

"I hope we don't see Mountain Man or Blade Boy," Leeroy said.

"You're just a little ray of sunshine tonight, aren't you, Leeroy?" Laverne said. "Relax, and let the night come to you."

"I hope old Leather Lung doesn't come at you with another beer bottle in his hand," Leeroy said in Laverne's direction.

"Relax, Leeroy. Regarding Leather Lung," Jake said, "I suspect Paul will be here tonight, so if he does come, Paul'll take care of Leather Lung."

"Hadn't thought about Paul," Leeroy said. "Is he here?"

"I'd bet on it," Jake said.

"Oh lordy," Leeroy said again.

At eight, the four men heard a deep bass voice.

"That's Xavier Cullum," Laverne said to Jake more than the other two. "I haven't heard that voice in years, until a few minutes ago when we met him again. But I'd recognize it anywhere."

The announcer's voice resonated across the Place. After a round of applause for the previous band, Xavier made the introduction.

"Ladies and gentlemen, I've known three of the four gentlemen in our next act for nearly fifty years. I was recently made aware of the fact that not only are they not dead"—Xavier waited for the laugher to subside before continuing—"they're still making music, after a brief hiatus. You're in for a treat tonight. They're master musicians and master performers—so here tonight, allow me to introduce you to Lester Washington, Leeroy Edwards, Laverne Knox, and Jacob Thomas."

The curtain raised to polite—but not thunderous—applause.

Xavier took his position in the audience's front row. Jake saw people dressed in everything from suits to shorts—men, women, young, old, of every race in New Orleans. As his eyes adapted to the Place, Jake saw Paul, seated, dressed in a tux. Rebecca sat on his right in a beautiful evening gown.

Mildred sat on Rebecca's right.

Mildred? In the Place? Where alcoholic beverages were sold? And on a Saturday night?

Leeroy had given no indication he knew of her presence before the curtain went up. Seeing her would surely kill off Leeroy, Jake thought. Mildred was wearing a dress he'd never seen.

Jake shifted his gaze left. In his peripheral vision, he saw Xavier Cullum. Between Xavier and Paul, looking angelic, sat Cora. Jake had not anticipated her presence.

She wore a dark dress. Not an evening gown like Rebecca's, but not Mildred's modest dress either. Cora's dress was sleeveless, v-cut, not too low, with a single strand of pearls adorning her neckline. The pearls—a contribution,

Jake suspected, from Rebecca—shone against Cora's olive complexion.

Jake seldom saw Cora wear her hair as she wore it tonight. Most of the time at Paul's Poulet, her hair was tucked underneath the chicken cap. Occasionally she wore her hair in a ponytail sticking out the back of the cap or pulled behind both ears. Tonight, she allowed her hair to fall on each side of her face. Catching Jake's eye, she waved and grinned—a broad, beautiful, white-as-her-pearls grin. Jake feared he would drop his guitar.

Lester kicked off the night's festivities with a piano intro. Leeroy, Jake, and Laverne caught up.

After the initial number, in the lull after the crowd voiced their approval, Laverne bent his guitar's strings again in a lively rhythm. Leeroy strummed his bass and swayed with the beat. Lester picked up the pace and banged out the chords, and they were off and running again.

In his raspy voice, Lester began singing. Jake, Lester, and Laverne contributed both in music and in voice.

> *O when the saints go marchin' in,*
> *O when the saints go marchin' in,*
> *O Lord I want to be in that number*
> *When the saints go marchin' in.*
>
> *O when the sun refused to shine*
> *O when the sun refused to shine,*
> *O Lord, I want to be in that number*
> *When the sun refused to shine.*
>
> *O when they crown him Lord of all,*
> *O when they crown him Lord of all,*

O Lord, I want to be in that number
When they crown him Lord of all.

O, when the saints go marchin' in,
O, when the saints go marchin' in,
Lord, I want to be in that number
When the saints go marchin' in.

Whatever nervousness Leeroy and Jake felt did not show to the appreciative gathering. For the next hour and forty-five minutes, with a brief intermission, the four friends made beautiful music at the Place ... and pulled the house down.

"Give a round of applause for Lester, Laverne, Jake, and Leeroy!" Xavier said. The crowd gave them a standing ovation as the four exited the stage. Paul, Rebecca, Mildred, and Cora met the men backstage, and all three women hugged them. An excited Paul shook their hands.

"That was *fabulous*," Paul said.

"I don't know about that," Laverne said.

"I agree with Laverne," Lester said. "Don't know about that."

"Well, *I* know," Leeroy said, "and Paul is correct. We ... were ... *fabulous*."

"Congratulations, Jake," Cora said, excited for their success. "It was magnificent."

Before he could stop himself, before he realized what he was doing, Jake bent and kissed Cora on her cheek. He felt his face go red.

"I'm sorry. I don't know what came over me. Caught up in the moment, I guess."

Jake was so red with embarrassment, one could light a match off his face. Cora didn't appear embarrassed in the least. She attempted to reassure him.

"No need to apologize, Jake."

Her smile never faded. In fact, it grew brighter.

Xavier's voice could still be heard as he informed the crowd of the next performance. Cullum made his way backstage and shook hands all around. He didn't linger, as he had other performers to introduce for the ten to midnight slot. Jake noticed Paul make eye contact with Xavier and nod. In minutes, Cullum was back on stage, introducing the ten p.m. performers.

"I've a suggestion," Paul said. "Let's go back to the diner and drink some coffee and celebrate."

They all agreed to meet there. The group of eight lingered at the Place a few minutes before giddily exiting through a rear door.

Paul and Rebecca got into the Mercedes. Leeroy opened Hazel's passenger door for Mildred. Jake opened the passenger door of the Olds for Cora as Lester and Laverne got in the back. Leeroy couldn't remember why the men had driven both Hazel and Jake's Olds to the Place.

Leeroy would, in future, remember little of that afternoon and night between three and eight o'clock.

Any bystander on Chef Menteur Highway, New Orleans, Louisiana, watching the arrivals at Paul's Poulet at ten thirty that Saturday night, would have been confused. Paul and Rebecca arrived first in the Mercedes, followed by Leeroy and Mildred in a dilapidated Hudson Hornet, followed by Jake, Cora, Lester, and Laverne in an automobile which was in considerably worse shape than the Hudson. The men all wore tuxes, Rebecca her blue evening gown and heels, Cora and Mildred in their dressed-up dresses. The group, along with their vehicles, was enough to confuse anyone.

Paul opened the restaurant and switched on the lights. He moved toward the coffee makers.

Jake began moving tables together. Rebecca assisted by moving chairs.

"Coffee will be up in five minutes," Paul said.

The group sat, and Rebecca began distributing cups. True to Paul's word, in less than five minutes, he began pouring coffee.

"You four were mesmerizing tonight," Paul said.

"I can't remember when I've enjoyed playing more," Lester said, "Ol' Leeroy was actually on key."

"I was the *only* one on key most of the night," Leeroy countered.

"I'm proud of you all," Rebecca said.

"Two weeks from tonight," Paul said, "you go back again. Back to the Place of Jazz."

"I knew y'all were talented, but I didn't imagine *that* much talent," Cora said.

"With a bonus for Blanc," Leeroy said to the group's obvious confusion. Leeroy stared at their puzzled faces. "I'm talkin' 'bout Jake givin' Cora a peck on the cheek."

Jake said, "I don't know what I was thinking."

Cora smiled the same unembarrassed grin as she had before.

Paul returned to the table with more coffee. The group sat, drank coffee, and celebrated their success.

Approaching midnight, Leeroy patted Mildred's arm.

"Let's go home, my love. I was too nervous to eat dinner. I'm going to eat a cheese sandwich, go to bed, and sleep the sleep of the righteous."

"Oh my," Laverne moaned.

"A cheese sandwich?" Rebecca said, incredulous. "Paul, can't we do better than a cheese sandwich?"

"*Leeroy*," Mildred said. "We can do better than a cheese sandwich at home."

Paul interrupted Mildred and spoke to Rebecca. "Why, yes, love, we do have something better than a cheese sandwich. Where are my manners? I'll have the fryer heated in minutes."

"Oh, no," Leeroy and Mildred said simultaneously, and then he turned to Paul. "I didn't mean to infer anything about your fryers. It's too late for that. Mildred, let's get these two old musicians named Laverne and Lester home and let's get on to 25 North Galvez." Leeroy stood.

Paul rose with Leeroy, placed his hands on Leeroy's shoulders and gently motioned him to sit back down. "I insist. It's no trouble at all."

Paul moved to the kitchen. Jake stood. Rebecca grabbed Jake's arm.

"Where are you going, young man?" she asked.

"To help Paul."

"No, you're not. Not tonight. You sit. *I'll* help Paul."

Rebecca eyed the surprise on the faces of the group. "Now, *really*. You don't believe I've been married to a man who owns a chicken restaurant for over twenty years without knowing my way around a deep fryer, do you?"

The group of eight sat, talked, and drank coffee. Jake filled their cups. He felt he could do that without being scolded.

"Chicken sandwiches up!" Paul said, emerging from the kitchen with a platter of sandwiches. Rebecca followed behind with another platter of french fries. The group of eight couldn't help but smile at the two of them.

Paul had removed his tux jacket but still wore the bowtie. He'd donned his red chicken cap. The bright red comb stood up on top, with lighter red and black feathers emerging from the back.

Rebecca, in her evening gown and high heels, had put on a vest with "Paul's Poulet" embroidered on the right front in white letters. Stitched in white letters on the left side was "Rebecca." She too wore the chicken cap.

"I didn't know you had your own vest, Rebecca," Cora said.

"Never know when I might need it," Rebecca said. "As in tonight."

She placed the platter of fries in the middle of the table and grinned mischievously. "As I said, I know my way around a deep fryer."

The group ate sandwiches and fries, and Paul kept the cups filled. Somewhere after one a.m., another automobile pulled into Paul's lot. Xavier Cullum got out.

Jake knew Xavier's presence at Paul's Poulet wasn't by chance.

"Come in, Xavier," Paul said. "May I offer you a chicken sandwich?"

"Oh no, thanks."

"Best chicken sandwich in New Orleans," Lester said.

"That sounds good, but one in the morning is too late for a chicken sandwich for me," Xavier said as he pulled a chair into the circle. "We closed the books on tonight. Thought I would bring you your earnings." He attempted to hand a check to Laverne, who pointed to Leeroy.

"Allow me to introduce you to our business manager," Laverne said.

Xavier handed the folded check to Leeroy, who tucked the check inside his left lapel pocket without looking at it.

"Shall I see you in two weeks?" Xavier asked.

Leeroy, Lester, Laverne, and Jake made eye contact. Laverne nodded and spoke for the group. "In two weeks."

"No sandwich?" Paul said. "How about cherry pie and ice cream?"

"Cherry pie and ice cream?" Xavier said.

"Too late?" Paul asked.

"For a chicken sandwich, yes," Xavier said, "but *never* too late for cherry pie and ice cream."

Paul, still in his chicken cap, turned to Rebecca in her vest and hat. "Shall we serve these fine people cherry pie and ice cream, my dear?"

Rebecca rose with Paul and said, "Now that brings back more memories."

Jake insisted on driving Cora home, with Lester and Laverne in the back seat. She gave him directions, and in less than ten minutes, Jake pulled the Olds into her driveway. Illuminated by street and porch lights, a blue Volkswagen sat parked in the carport. The house was small but tidy, its shrubs neatly trimmed. White with red shutters, it appeared to have been freshly painted. Two large live oaks framed the front entrance.

"Yours?" Jake asked.

"Mine," Cora said.

"It looks nice," Jake said.

"Thank you." Cora continued. "I'll cook for you sometime. Fried chicken, maybe?"

"The invitation sounds good, but the entrée—" Jake caught himself when he saw Cora's eyes twinkle.

She smiled her mischievous smile as if to say, *you didn't know I was joking?*

Jake parked the Olds and went around to Cora's side of the car, thinking of the time when he and his parents lived in a house. As he opened Cora's door, he realized he'd forgotten about Laverne and Lester in the rear seat. They'd both stayed silent.

Cora leaned down to look into the back seat. "Good night, Lester, Laverne."

Both men bid Cora goodnight. Jake walked her to the door and waited for her to enter. "Lock the door as soon as you get in."

"Good night, Jake. It's been a wonderful night."

Jake considered kissing her but didn't know how to go about it. Neither Mountain Man nor Blade Boy frightened him, but face-to-face with this petite woman wearing a pearl necklace, he froze.

And besides, Lester and Laverne were probably watching.

"I'm glad you came," he managed to mutter.

"Me too."

"You're beautiful," Jake said, to his own amazement.

"The pearls are Rebecca's."

"They look nice on you."

To his surprise, Cora grabbed his lapels, pulled him down, and pecked him on his right cheek. She smiled and waved in the direction of Laverne and Lester.

Jake waited until he heard the tumblers in the lock. He caressed his cheek where Cora had kissed him.

Bert's name would not be spoken again. Ever.

"Do one of you want to join me in the front seat?" Jake asked.

"I'm good," Lester said.

"Me too," Laverne said. "I kinda like being chauffeured."

Jake drove Lester and Laverne to Franklin Avenue. He parked on the street and waited for the two to emerge.

"Aren't you going to open my door, Jake?" Lester asked.

Jake turned in his seat to stare at Lester. Laverne piped up. "Aren't you going to walk us to the flat?"

"Will you get *out*?"

"Laverne will kiss you on your jaw," Lester offered.

"Won't be the same," Jake said.

"I don't mind kissing you on the jaw," Laverne said.

"Get *out*—both of you."

Lester and Laverne opened both rear doors but continued to sit in the rear seat. "Are we going to church in the morning?" Lester asked. "Excuse me, this morning?"

"We *are* up mighty late to be going to church," Laverne said.

"Will Mildred be attending church?" Jake asked.

"She will be," Lester said.

"Will Leeroy be attending church?" Jake asked.

"He will be," Laverne said, "no matter how he feels when he wakes up. Mildred'll see to it."

"Then we're attending church too," Jake said. "Until nine o'clock, then?"

"Nine o'clock," Lester and Laverne said.

Lester swung his legs out of the Olds but continued to sit. "You sure you don't want that kiss from Laverne?"

"Out. *Out!*"

Lester and Laverne managed to clamber out of the back seat, both howling with laughter. As both were illuminated by the headlamps from the Olds and the street lights, Jake saw Lester lean toward Laverne and whisper something. The two men walked the few steps to the flat, where Lester unlocked and opened the door but stood outside with Laverne. Laverne pulled Lester to him and kissed him on the jaw. The two then turned and waved to Jake much as Cora had done minutes before. Jake opened his door on the Olds.

"You two go in and rest. And be ready at nine o'clock."

Jake waited for the men to enter their flat. In his imagination, he heard the tumblers rotate in the lock. He drove home. Somewhere in the wee hours of the morning, Jake got to bed and slept the sleep of the righteous.

CHAPTER THIRTY-FIVE

At eight thirty the next morning, Jake entered Lester and Laverne's flat.

"Didn't expect to see you here this early," Laverne said. "I thought we agreed on nine o'clock?"

Lester and Laverne were dressed for worship.

"Leeroy wants us to meet him before worship," Jake informed Laverne and Lester.

They met Leeroy in the garage/practice room/gathering place. Leeroy sat in a lawn chair. He had assembled three more chairs, forming a circle. He strummed on his bass as Lester, Jake, and Laverne took their seats

Once everyone was settled, Leeroy placed his guitar in its case. He gave Xavier Cullum's check to Lester, who read the amount, his eyebrows lifting halfway up his forehead. Lester passed the check to Jake. Jake did the same and, forgetting Laverne could not read, passed the check to Laverne. Leeroy recognized Jake's mistake and informed Laverne of the amount. Laverne gave a short whistle. "We haven't seen that much money in what—ten years?"

"At least ten years," Lester added. "In the last few years of Anthony's life, we didn't make that in a single night. That money will meet our needs for weeks."

The men savored the moment. Unexpectedly, Leeroy leaned forward in his chair and started shaking. He wiped his arm across his eyes.

"What's the matter, Leeroy?" Jake asked quietly, leaning forward to meet him.

It took Leeroy a few moments to answer.

"Blanc, you don't know—you do *not* know—how close we came to living on the streets or living in a men's shelter. Before you came, it was gettin' to the point where I couldn't pay the taxes on this place, and Mildred—" His voice broke. "What would have happened to Mildred?"

Jake realized ten years of pent-up fear had come crashing down on Leeroy Edwards on this particular Sunday morning.

"We offered to help. We even insisted," Lester said quietly, "but he wouldn't hear of it."

"Y'all had bills to pay, just like me and Mildred, and food and meds to buy," Leeroy said. "I couldn't allow you to do that."

"The three of us," Laverne began, "without Mildred's knowing, were making plans to live together in our Franklin flat."

"Leaving this place ..." Leeroy coughed and cleared his throat before he went on. "After what happened to Amos, leaving here would have killed Mildred, but I didn't know what else to do. The walls were closing in on us, Blanc."

Lester said, "Our place was too small for four people, Leeroy told us. Even smaller, with one bein' a woman."

"We assured Leeroy we could all adjust," Laverne said, "and we'd have done it gladly."

Leeroy leaned back in his chair and read, aloud this time, the amount on Xavier Cullum's check. "We perform again in two weeks," he said.

"Every two weeks until January," Lester added.

"If this check is any indication, this amount of money will support Mildred and me for a long, long time," Leeroy said.

"Lester and me too," Laverne added.

Leeroy no longer fought it. He leaned forward again, put his head in his hands, and wept in deep, ripping sobs. Lester, Jake, and Laverne sat with him. No one spoke.

After a time, Lester reached out and rubbed Leeroy's shoulder. "It's all right, Leeroy. Everything gonna be all right."

Mildred emerged from the house.

"Leeroy," she called, "are you ready for worship?"

Leeroy pulled a handkerchief from his rear pocket and wiped his eyes. He stood and spoke, his voice strong. "I'm ready. In the garage, my love."

Mildred stepped into the garage. "Hello, gentlemen. I didn't expect to see all y'all before worship."

"Morning, Mildred," the men said.

Lester opened Hazel's passenger door, and Mildred got in. If she detected any struggle in her husband, she gave no sign of it. Jake, suspecting Mildred of extrasensory perception, believed she didn't want to embarrass Leeroy. Jake, Lester, and Laverne got in the back seat.

They rode in silence, and Jake sat back, considering the night before. Making music at the Place of Jazz with his friends had been wonderful. And the kisses—not one, but two kisses—were the first kisses he could ever remember from anyone other than his biological and adopted mothers.

Then he thought about earlier this morning with Lester and Laverne, seeing Leeroy weep over their Place of Jazz check—weeping in relief, because the check meant no more fear of homelessness, starvation, or separation from his beloved Mildred.

Seated on their designated pew at the Franklin Avenue Church of God in Christ, Mildred, Leeroy, Laverne, Jake, and Lester stood as the congregation read Psalm 23 responsively.

> The Lord is my shepherd; I shall not want.
> **He maketh me to lie down in green pastures: he leadeth me beside the still waters.**
> He restoreth my soul: he leadeth me in the paths of righteousness for his name's sake.
> **Yea, though I walk through the valley of the shadow of death, I will fear no evil: for thou art with me;**
> thy rod and thy staff they comfort me.
> **Thou preparest a table before me in the presence of mine enemies:**
> thou anointest my head with oil; my cup runneth over.
> **Surely goodness and mercy shall follow me all the days of my life: and I will dwell in the house of the Lord for ever.**

Goodness and mercy.

Jake knew Leeroy had learned what the words meant this morning.

God had indeed blessed him and his friends.

CHAPTER THIRTY-SIX

In August 1969, as parts of New Orleans were still digging out from under Hurricane Camille, Jake commenced his college experience, starting with a biology course. He followed biology with American history—his weakest subject. Those classes met on Monday, Wednesday, and Friday mornings. His Tuesday/Thursday schedule consisted of chemistry and calculus, again, both morning classes. Jake felt comfortable he could succeed in calculus, since he'd always been strong in math.

In addition to classes, Jake had two labs weekly. He enjoyed his classes, but he loved and thrived in the labs. His notetaking and study skills returned to him quickly. He could easily read and remember what he read from texts and from the instructors' scribbles on the class whiteboards, but he never trusted his memory. He jotted down everything his instructors said. Nights, after he helped Mildred and Leeroy clean up after dinner, he returned to the quietness of his room and rewrote his notes.

His first college exam came in his American history class. He gathered his rewritten notes before him in his room and pored over them, as he had for the past three nights. He hoped the notes were thorough and hoped he'd remember them for the following day's test.

"Got a history test today, eh?" Leeroy said.

"I do," Jake said, attempting with only minor success to hide his anxiety.

"I'm sure you'll do fine," Mildred said.

Jake did not respond. Leeroy and Mildred had expected Jake's normal query, "What are y'all doing today?" But today, Jake said nothing.

In Jake's reticence, Leeroy and Mildred sensed his anxiety.

Professor Broadus Faulkner entered the room with a stack of exams. Jake sat on the front row. He got to all his classes early to ensure getting a front seat, until he realized most students preferred sitting in the rear of a classroom, leaving the front row vacant. He felt his hands grow damp with sweat as Dr. Faulkner handed him a test.

After class, Jake worked at Paul's Poulet from six until closing. For the entire shift, his mind was on his history test. He helped two other employees clean up before leaving for 25 North Galvez. Neither Paul nor Cora had worked on this particular night, and he missed them both, most especially Cora and her smile. She always encouraged him.

Leaving Paul's, he got into his car and started the engine. When he reached to engage the transmission, he let his hands drop into his lap, rested his head on the steering wheel, and closed his eyes. A soft rain pattered and eventually pelted the car's roof, adding to his feelings of loneliness and fear.

Before meeting the trio and Mildred, loneliness had been his constant companion. In better times, he'd considered giving his loneliness a name—Beelzebub, perhaps. But while he was in the midst of it, he'd refused to name it. This feeling, this shade of aloneness, was different.

Then the fear—a new kind of fear, raw and sharp—enveloped him. He'd seldom experienced fear before. Losing both his parents, to say nothing of sleeping alone in his car's back seat and encountering numerous street thugs who saw him as an easy mark—these things had constructed within him an almost impenetrable body armor. But this fear was different.

He started shaking. He fought for control of his emotions. His eyes watered. What was happening to him?

Did I pass the exam? Maybe.

Maybe not.

Had he listed December 7, 1941, for the bombing of Pearl Harbor? He should have. Mildred had told him their son, Amos, was born on December seventh, which would eventually be called Pearl Harbor Day. Had he listed Dwight Eisenhower as the Supreme Allied Commander on D-day? He couldn't remember. Heck, he might have missed the question of Japan as the nation that bombed Pearl Harbor.

Surely I got that right.

Would Professor Faulkner agree to offer him additional work to make up any grade deficiency?

I'm not going to ask.

Either way, pass or fail college, he would pass or fail on his own.

People were counting on him. He visualized Mildred, Leeroy, Lester, and Laverne. How could he disappoint them?

Maybe I'm not smart enough to go to college. Perhaps college is not for me.

He'd fought back tears to that point. When he thought of Mildred, Leeroy, Lester, and Laverne, he closed his eyes and wept.

Jake didn't remember the drive home. The next thing he remembered was his car parked in the driveway at 25 North Galvez. He sat in the car in the darkness and considered his next move. If he failed college, he could always continue working at Paul's. He knew Paul would promote him, perhaps making him a shift manager. Construction jobs were plentiful in New Orleans. He'd heard of job openings on the docks. He reassured himself he had options. The jobs did not scare him. He'd always had a healthy work ethic. What concerned him, if he failed, was facing Mildred, Leeroy, Lester, and Laverne, not to mention Cora and Paul.

The house looked as dark as Jake felt, with not a light to be seen anywhere. He felt the tears again. Without thought, he reached across the seat for his stack of books.

Not tonight, he told himself. He wouldn't read or study— not this evening. The results of his first exam would be an indicator if he would ever again read or study as a college student.

The weight of his grimly imagined future lay on his shoulders as he walked the few steps from the driveway to the house, the rain coming now in torrents. He assumed Mildred and Leeroy would be asleep. They didn't lock the door when he was out, and he opened the door quietly and stepped inside the kitchen, still in total darkness. He did not switch on any lights, to avoid waking them.

He stood for a few moments to let his eyes adjust.

"Blanc."

Leeroy? Jake couldn't help but smile.

"Leeroy, what are you doing awake?"

"How was your exam?" Mildred asked. She was awake as well.

Jake felt his way through the kitchen to the living room. As his eyes adjusted, he could identify their shapes, each seated in their favorite chair. Jake made his way, still in the dark, to his designated seat. No one turned on a light, and Jake was glad they didn't. He told himself he wasn't ashamed of his tears, but he didn't want Mildred or Leeroy to see. That would embarrass him and sadden them.

Mildred asked again, "Did your exam go okay?"

Jake paused and fought for control of his emotions again before speaking.

"I think I missed several questions—the date for the bombing of Pearl Harbor for one, and identifying the Supreme Allied Commander on D-day."

"That's two. Not bad," Leeroy said. "Right?"

"I s'pect there were more I missed. I don't know, but I'm not optimistic."

The trio sat in darkness for several minutes, but Jake believed Mildred and Leeroy sensed his discouragement. Mildred couldn't see his swollen red eyes, but she *knew*. Jake was sure of it.

"I was in the eighth grade," she said. "Miz Collier was the teacher, and geography was the subject. I was such a poor student in every subject, but geography was my worst. I made a sixty-two, an F, on the first test. I felt bad, 'cause I had studied hard. I took the test home to my mother. I cried and cried in her arms. My mother held me tight and said 'Mildred, it's gonna be all right.' That was all she said. 'Mildred, it's gonna be all right.' I believed her, because she believed in *me*. That belief was all I needed. I passed geography, and I passed the eighth grade and the ninth and graduated from high school, the first member of my family ever to earn a high school diploma."

"You were the first member of your family to get beyond the eighth grade," Leeroy remarked.

"That's correct." She turned to Jake. "I wish I knew what to say, but I've never been to college or a university. I know little to nothing about Pearl Harbor or the Supreme Allied Commander on D-day. Nothing about notetaking, study skills, American history, chemistry." She paused for the space of a heartbeat. "But I *do* know Jacob Alvin Thomas. And I believe in you."

More silence. Then Jake stood and took the three steps to where Mildred sat. He got on his knees and leaned into her, and she took him into her arms.

Leeroy understood. Jake's strength and courage in the fight with Mountain Man and Blade Boy had been remarkable. Jake had wielded the metal pipe like a baseball player wielded a bat, without fear or hesitation. He could still see Jake maneuvering between Blade Boy and himself, Lester, and Laverne, protecting him and his friends from injury.

Jake's fearlessness and power had been obvious and impressive. Now, here in this quiet room, he saw in Jake not weakness or defeat. He saw a young man who needed his mother.

Mildred spoke quietly as her arms held Jake close. One hand patted his shoulder.

"It's gonna be all right, Jake. Gonna be all right."

The next week was one of the longest in Jake's life. On Friday, at the end of the class period, Professor Faulkner returned the history exam. Jake again felt his hands grow damp. His mouth was dry as he licked his lips. He fought back a panic attack as Faulkner announced that two people in the class of fifteen had made A's, with one perfect score of 100. Three had earned B's, five had earned C's, with five "others." Jake knew the "others" had made D's and F's.

Professor Faulkner returned the exams face down. Jake watched the other students as they turned over tests. He heard sighs of relief and breaths of disappointment. Jake left his exam face down, as Faulkner asked the class for questions and then informed them they were free to leave. Students began filing out immediately. Jake considered leaving the test, walking out of class, and driving off campus, never to return.

The classroom emptied, leaving Jake alone with his thoughts and Professor Faulkner. Jake lost track of time. He considered driving to the docks in search of a job.

"Mister Thomas, aren't you going to turn your exam over?" Faulkner asked.

The question jostled him to reality. Jake hadn't realized he was still there.

He made his decision. He left the exam on his desk face down and stood, gathering the strength to speak. "No, sir. I don't believe I will."

Jake reached and offered his right hand to Professor Faulkner. The Professor reciprocated and shook Jake's hand, puzzled.

"I apologize, sir, for wasting your time." Jake started out. The docks were calling his name.

Faulkner retrieved the exam from Jake's desk and said, "I'm afraid, Mister Thomas, before you leave, I must insist. Look at your test results." He extended the exam to Jake.

Jake, his hand shaking, took the exam and turned it over. He saw his score in red ink, circled, in the upper right-hand corner. An eighty-three?

"You made a B, Mister Thomas," Faulkner interpreted.

"A low B," Jake said. He could not believe he said it, or the fact he'd earned a B.

"It's still a B," Faulkner said.

The professor studied Jake a few moments before speaking.

"How long since you were in school, Mister Thomas?"

Jake wondered if the professor somehow knew of his situation.

"Years."

"Under your circumstances—under most any circumstances—a B is a good grade."

Jake could not believe what he saw and heard. He stood silently and stared at the exam for a full minute.

"See you Monday in class," Faulkner said, softly, more question than statement.

Maybe the docks aren't calling my name after all.

"Yes, sir. Monday. I'll be here."

"Good."

As he left the building, Jake's long week had ended. Before he could contain himself, he yelled loudly—a long, stress-releasing yell—puzzling nearby students. Jake's yell drew Faulkner to a window. The university professor smiled at the sight of his young student running across campus as though he was a kindergartener, the exam raised high in his right hand.

As for Jake, he was going home to see Mildred and Leeroy.

Perhaps Mildred had been correct.

Perhaps everything *was* gonna be all right.

As the fall semester progressed, Jake's study habits and time management skills improved. While history continued to be a challenge, his classes in biology, chemistry, and calculus were not. Math had always come easy to him, and he loved the sciences, both classroom lectures and labs.

The fall semester kept him busy. He went to class and labs all week and continued to play every other Saturday night at the Place with the Noirs. He continued to work an average of more than twenty hours a week at Paul's. Earning money while playing weekends and living with Mildred and Leeroy offered him the luxury of not having to work at Paul's out of financial necessity, but he enjoyed seeing the faithful customers, several of whom knew him by name. He enjoyed working alongside Paul. And there was the crew with whom he worked.

And then there was Cora.

Every Monday afternoon, he joined twenty other students for his biology lab. Assistant Professor Wilda Simmons led most of the labs. Some of the other Tulane biology professors would make rare appearances.

One Monday afternoon, a distinguished man with gray hair and a disarming smile, a man who Jake estimated to be in his early sixties, strolled through the lab. He wore the traditional white lab coat, his hands tucked inside the large pockets. As he approached Jake's workstation Jake read the name on his lab coat.

Michael McGinnis, MD, PhD.

Although he had never seen him before, Jake knew McGinnis was Chair of the Biology Department at Tulane and taught in both the biology department and medical school. Professor McGinnis was a legend. His presence made Jake nervous.

McGinnis stood beside Professor Simmons for several moments and observed the small group of Jake and three classmates. Neither McGinnis nor Simmons spoke. None of Jake's classmates uttered a word, as if they were in the presence of royalty. In regard to Professor Michael McGinnis, they were. As for Jake, he was glad he could breathe.

Jake saw McGinnis make eye contact with Simmons. He raised his eyebrows and nodded to Simmons. He turned and left the lab.

Two weeks later, McGinnis returned, strolling through the lab, again spending several moments observing Jake's workstation. Sometimes, Simmons would join him. Other times, he stood alone, never saying a word.

During the semester, McGinnis visited the lab on several Monday afternoons. He observed as Simmons taught and interacted with students. Simmons would ask students questions regarding the day's planned procedures. Jake seldom responded. He felt his heart leap into his throat the first time Simmons asked him for a specific response with McGinnis present. Had McGinnis and Simmons sensed his anxiety? Neither gave any indication if they had. Jake believed—hoped—he hadn't embarrassed himself.

On a Friday afternoon in early December, Jake took the last of his first semester final examinations. He felt he'd performed well and had a profound sense of pride. His pride was amplified when, two weeks later, he received his grades. He anticipated the B in history. He had not anticipated the three As in biology, chemistry, and calculus.

"We're proud of you," Mildred said.

"We need to celebrate," Leeroy added.

"Yes, let's celebrate!" Mildred agreed.

CHAPTER THIRTY-SEVEN

On Christmas morning, Jake pulled the Oldsmobile in front of Lester and Laverne's flat. Jake wasn't surprised to see Lester and Laverne bearing gifts. Nor was he surprised at their attire.

"Your chauffeur awaits your bidding," Jake said as the two entered the Olds.

Both Lester and Laverne knew the dance. "Take us to 25 North Galvez, chauffeur."

"Step on it," added Laverne. "The governor's wife doesn't suffer fools lightly, nor late-comers gladly."

Their verbal dance complete, Jake reached out his right hand to Lester. "Merry Christmas, Lester."

Lester took Jake's hand and answered, "Merry Christmas, Jake."

Before easing the Olds out into Franklin Avenue traffic, Jake offered his right hand to Laverne in the rear seat. "Merry Christmas, my friend."

Laverne clasped Jake's hand. "Merry Christmas, friend."

Jake parked the Olds on the street. The trio walked onto the narrow porch and Lester reached for the doorbell. Leeroy opened the door before Lester could announce their arrival.

Leeroy, wearing a black suit with a dark red Christmas tie, hugged the trio, wished them a merry Christmas, and invited them inside. Lester, Laverne, and Jake placed their gifts underneath the tree in the living room.

Lester and Laverne again saw the numerous Christmas trees and again enjoyed the aromas emanating from Mildred's kitchen. The four men sat in the living room, made small talk, and waited for the lady of the house to appear. She didn't keep them waiting.

Mildred entered, wearing a cobalt blue dress and the brooch Jake had given her the previous Christmas. He thought she looked both elegant and exquisite. All four men rose as she entered the room, and she hugged all four, starting with Leeroy, and bid each a merry Christmas. Each man responded likewise.

"I've got more to do in the kitchen," Mildred said—and disappeared.

"Let me see if she needs help," Jake said, and made his way to the kitchen as well. His attention was attracted by the place settings on the table. Jake counted eight, not the expected five.

"Expecting more guests? May I help?" he asked.

"Sure," she said, "you may—"

The doorbell chimed.

"You may get the door," Mildred said with a smile.

Leeroy, not surprisingly, reached the front door before Jake. Leeroy opened the door and there on the front porch were Paul, Rebecca, and Cora. Paul was well dressed, down to the handkerchief in his lapel pocket. Rebecca, as she usually did, appeared goddess-like, but Cora, both in her unexpected presence and her appearance, took Jake's breath away. Leeroy, for his part, welcomed the three into his home in the same manner he had greeted Lester, Laverne, and Jake, with hugs and warm Christmas greetings.

Within minutes, the eight sat around the crowded table in the crowded kitchen. Every inch of the table was covered with plates, glasses, and utensils, along with the platters and bowls of turkey, turkey gravy, green bean casserole, brussels sprouts, bread, dressing, potatoes, carrots, and cranberry sauce. The square table made seating of two on each side easy, even if they did rub shoulders. Mildred sat on Leeroy's right. Lester and Laverne sat in their designated places. Rebecca sat beside Paul. Jake pulled a chair away from the table and invited Cora to sit on his right.

"Thank you, Jake," Cora said, her radiant smile seeming to illuminate the room.

Each waited for the man of the house to begin. Neither Paul, Rebecca, nor Cora knew what would happen next, but Mildred, Lester, Laverne, and Jake all knew. Leeroy took the Bible, read the Christmas story, and prayed. Once he replaced the Bible on its nearby stand, he handed Mildred a plate of sliced turkey.

The group, at least five of them, knew what the passing of the turkey plate signaled. The grand observance of Christmas Day, celebrating the birth of Christ among family and friends at 25 North Galvez, had officially begun.

After dinner, Mildred, Rebecca, and Cora stacked the dishes and leftover food on a kitchen counter, making way for coffee, sweet potato pie, pecan pie, and chocolate fudge. After everyone had eaten their fill, the gentlemen cleaned up the kitchen, with the three ladies waiting in the living room. Leeroy hung aprons on both Jake and Paul and handed both of them dishcloths. Paul laughed loudly, and jokingly said he was unsure what to do with the cloth.

The men made quick work of the kitchen. Afterward, they joined the ladies in the living room, where Leeroy had previously placed additional chairs. The room was small and packed, but no one minded. Each enjoyed the presence of the others.

Leeroy soon joined the group with a tray, eight glasses, and a pitcher of eggnog. He served Mildred initially, then Rebecca and Cora, before serving the men. The group sat and waited, again on Leeroy's signal. The chatter ceased. Leeroy took his glass and sat.

"In addition to the celebration of the birth of Jesus, we come here today for another celebration," he said.

The group waited, all puzzled. Leeroy raised his glass in Jake's direction. Jake sat quietly beside Cora, unaware of Leeroy's intentions. "Our young friend, Jacob Alvin Thomas—Jake to you, Blanc to me—has completed his first semester at Tulane University."

A whoop went up from the group.

Leeroy continued. "More than just completing it, he earned one B." He paused before continuing. "Along with three A's." The roar returned, louder than the first.

He spoke again. "To Blanc for his grades, and to family and friends, on Christmas Day."

"To Blanc, family and friends," all repeated, with glasses raised.

For the next hour, the group drank eggnog and celebrated the birth of Jesus, along with three A's and a B. Lester, Leeroy, and Laverne told stories of long-ago Christmases amid much revelry. Paul and Rebecca told the group they couldn't remember when they'd laughed so much.

A slight lull in the festivities was broken by the sound of the doorbell.

"Expecting someone else, Leeroy?" Lester asked.

"Not us," Leeroy said.

Jake stepped to the front door and opened it. He failed to hide his surprise.

"Professor McGinnis?"

"Hello, Mister Thomas. I was in the area and thought I would wish you a merry Christmas." He leaned forward and peeked around Jake. "Forgive me for intruding. I didn't realize you had guests. My apologies. Merry Christmas to you, Mister Thomas, and to you all."

Michael McGinnis, Chair of Tulane University's Biology Department, stepped off the porch and started toward the street where his car was parked.

Jake said, "Professor McGinnis, wait." McGinnis paused and turned.

"You aren't intruding. Please come in."

"Oh no, I can't ..."

Mildred appeared. "Yes! Please, do come in. You're welcome here. Please, come celebrate Christmas with us."

McGinnis accepted Mildred's gracious invitation and entered the house. Jake introduced him to the group. McGinnis again offered apologies for intruding, but Mildred and Leeroy put him at ease with a seat, a glass of eggnog, and a slice of pecan pie. The festivities resumed, the group picking up where they'd left off as though McGinnis had been there from the beginning.

Thirty minutes later, McGinnis bid his farewells to all and departed. The group of eight again assembled and sat in the living room. Jake walked him to the door and out to the front porch, then returned, looking pale.

"That was a pleasant surprise," Mildred said. "What a nice man. And he happened to be driving by 25 North Galvez on Christmas Day." Mildred's implication was lost on no one, Jake included.

"He was doing more than driving by," Jake said. "He came to see me. Looked up my address in the university records."

"Did he throw you out of the university, Blanc? Surely not!"

"A student can't be thrown out of college for making a B," Lester said. "Right?"

"I wouldn't think so," Laverne said.

"That same student likewise earned three A's," Mildred said.

"Do we need to slash his tires, Blanc?" Leeroy asked, before being hushed by Mildred.

"I've seen him in our biology labs," Jake said. "I've heard him speak only a few words before today. He said Professor Simmons, our lab instructor, had told him about a promising student by the name of Jacob Thomas, and he came to the lab to see for himself. Actually, he came to several labs."

He paused before continuing. "Doctor McGinnis told me I have *intuition*."

"Is that a disease?" Leeroy asked, before again being hushed by Mildred.

"He said I have the *gift* of intuition," Jake said, "the gift of instinct. Perception. He told me lots of people peer into a microscope, read the slide, and interpret results. But he said I have the gift of anticipation, in that I anticipate what the microscope reveals before ever peering into it." He paused.

"That's a good thing, right, Blanc?"

Jake nodded. "He said I have a rare gift. Said he's known and currently knows many physicians, but few of them have the gift to diagnose medical conditions with little information. He said I should utilize my talent."

"He didn't throw you out of the university?" Lester asked.

"On the contrary. He encouraged me to consider medical school," Jake said, as casual as though he reported the weather. "Doctor Michael McGinnis sought me out, at home, on Christmas Day, to talk with me about attending medical school."

A hush fell across the group. Cora broke the silence.

"Jake, that's—why, that's *wonderful*. I believe you'll make a great doctor."

Cora's choice of verb wasn't lost on Jake. *Will* make, she'd said. Not *can* make.

Leeroy broke the seriousness in the room. "Doctor Blanc Thomas. Medicine will never be the same." He looked toward the ceiling and held up both arms in a supplicating gesture. "Lord have mercy."

"Hush, Leeroy," Mildred said. "What else did he say, Jake?"

"He said he would help."

"That was nice," Paul said. "And you know we'll help."

Jake continued. "Doctor McGinnis said if I chose to consider medical school, he would serve as my university adviser, beginning in the spring semester."

"What does a university adviser do?" asked Laverne.

"Advises students which classes to take, according to their chosen field of study."

"Did he say anything else, Blanc?" Leeroy asked.

"He did. He said he suspects I won't need any help, from him or anyone else."

The eight people sat in silence until Paul spoke. "Friends, it's been a wonderful evening, with the great gift of wonderful news. Thank y'all so much. Rebecca, Cora? Shall we go?"

Rebecca nodded as Cora stood. Jake retrieved their coats. He gave Paul his coat and Rebecca's. He assisted Cora with hers.

Paul shook hands with the men, hugged Mildred, and wished the entire group a merry Christmas. Jake, Mildred, Leeroy, Laverne, and Lester hugged Rebecca and Cora. Jake closed the door as the trio exited, with a last longing wave at Cora. Then he sat down in the living room with the remaining four.

"In all this excitement, we forgot. We haven't exchanged gifts," Mildred said.

"Of course," Lester agreed. "Laverne, will you do the honors?"

Laverne assented and proceeded to distribute the gifts.

"Lady first," Lester said. Mildred opened two gifts, one from Lester and Laverne, the other from Jake.

Jake opened two gifts, as did Lester and Laverne.

Leeroy, on the other hand, had one gift, from Lester and Laverne. He said nothing and opened it. Each one thanked the others for their gifts of handkerchiefs, a necklace, fountain pens, gloves, and scarves.

Jake left the living room and returned with another wrapped gift, smiling as he handed the gift to Leeroy. The gift's odd shape caused Leeroy to ponder its identity and purpose. Turning the gift over and over, he estimated its weight. It was heavy, about twelve inches long and six inches high. And the gift was tapered to a point on one end.

"Now what in the world do you suppose that is?" Leeroy asked no one in particular. He continued to roll the object over and over as he considered what it might be.

"Not as big as a bread box," Laverne said.

"Open your gift, Leeroy," Mildred said.

"Not a guitar," Lester said.

"Open your gift, Leeroy," Mildred said again.

"Guitar lessons, perhaps," Lester offered. "Something he needs."

"It's a piano," Laverne said.

"Leeroy, *open* it!" Mildred said.

Leeroy began unwrapping the gift, slowly, as though unpacking a valuable collectible. With a glimmer of the gift exposed, Leeroy flashed a broad grin, threw back his head and gave a loud laugh. He ripped off the remaining paper and lifted the gift, cradled like a newborn child in both hands. Mildred, Lester, and Laverne sat in absolute mystification.

"What in the name of all things decent and holy ... is ... *that*?" Lester asked, with more fervor than he intended.

"Something made of chrome," Laverne said, "a long bar with a triangle shaped object near the front."

"Pretty. But I'm clueless," Mildred offered, with a shake of her head.

Leeroy explained. "That, lady and gentlemen, is a 1951 Hudson Hornet hood ornament. Ain't she *fabulous*?"

Mildred, Lester, and Laverne joined in on Leeroy's excitement and laughed heartily. After the merriment subsided, Mildred had a question.

"Leeroy, when did you sell the original?"

"Nineteen fifty-nine."

"For how much money?" Lester asked.

"Three dollars," Leeroy answered. "Blanc, where did you find it?"

"Barney's Junkyard in Gretna. I had to look in several junkyards. That hood ornament, Mister Edwards, is a *rare* find indeed. A treasure to be treasured."

"I thank you, Jake, for this unexpected and cherished gift. I thank you all. Merry Christmas."

"Merry Christmas," they all responded.

Sometime after nine on Christmas evening, Lester and Laverne loaded into Jake's Olds. The trio left Mildred and Leeroy seated in the living room as they started toward home. Once they arrived, Lester extended his right hand to Jake.

"Merry Christmas, Jake. And congratulations on the medical school invitation—is that what they call it?"

Jake smiled. "It's as good a way to say it as any. Thank you, Lester, and merry Christmas."

Before Jake could initiate it, he felt Laverne's hand, from the rear seat, rest upon his right shoulder. Jake shook Laverne's hand as they bid each other a merry Christmas. He watched as the two men, bundled up against the cold on Christmas Day, made their way across the sidewalk and entered their flat.

Jake turned the Olds around, eased into traffic, and started home. McGinnis's words came back to him as he pondered.

Is it possible that I have the gifts to go to medical school?

Before Jake realized it, he was parked and walking up the driveway in semi-darkness. A light, perhaps in the living room, was on. Suddenly illuminated by streetlights, a figure emerged from the direction of the Hornet. Jake stopped, prepared for whatever or whoever was coming his way.

"Blanc?"

"*Leeroy*? What are you doing out here in this cold weather at—what, ten o'clock?"

Leeroy didn't respond. With his right hand, he switched on a flashlight and illuminated Hazel's hood. With his left hand, he pulled away what appeared to be a towel. He revealed the hood ornament in place, aglow from the flashlight's beam.

"Hazel is once again complete, young Blanc. I thank you."

The emotions of the day, capped off by the visit from Professor McGinnis, came rushing in on Jake. For unexplainable reasons, he felt his eyes filling up. Why? The absolute beauty of a Christmas Day with family and friends? Spending his first Christmas Day with Cora? The panic attack he felt coming on when he considered McGinnis's counsel—"a person shouldn't waste such a gift"? Whatever had caused them, Jake fought the need to wipe the tears from his eyes.

"Merry Christmas, Leeroy."

Jake knew Leeroy couldn't see his face in the darkness of the driveway. Did Leeroy have the same extrasensory perception Jake suspected Mildred possessed?

He patted Jake's arm as they stood next to the complete Hazel.

"Gonna be all right, Blanc," Leeroy rumbled softly. "It's all gonna be all right."

CHAPTER THIRTY-EIGHT

Jake arrived at Dr. Michael McGinnis's office on January 2 at ten a.m., the designated meeting time. McGinnis, a telephone receiver at his ear, motioned for Jake to enter. Jake stood and waited for the professor to complete his conversation. The few moments of waiting allowed Jake the luxury of examining the impressive office—the rich mahogany wood paneling, the oak display cases housing antique laboratory equipment, and McGinnis's magnificent dark reddish desk. The desk seemed to be nothing more than four legs, a skirt, and a top. The legs were octagon in shape and tapered from top to bottom.

Four diplomas hung on the wall behind the desk. Everyone who knew anything about Tulane's biology department knew McGinnis held the traditional undergraduate and master's degrees. What was equally as well known was the fact he held two doctoral degrees, one medical and one Doctor of Philosophy.

He turned his attention to McGinnis's bookshelves, which covered three walls from floor to ceiling. Books filled every inch of space, some of the volumes leatherbound and old. He allowed his eyes to roam over the shelves nearest him, which happened to be to the right of the office door, placing him within touching distance. But he didn't dare touch. One particular two-volume set attracted his attention. While he knew nothing about the set specifically, something about the books drew him. He leaned in to read the spines, his hands tucked behind him to avoid the temptation to pull out the books.

"You have a good eye, Mister Thomas."

"Good morning, Professor. I didn't realize you were off the phone."

McGinnis rose from behind the desk, and they shook hands. He eased one of the books from the shelf and handed it to Jake.

"A rare first edition."

Jake could now read the book title and did so aloud. "*The Descent of Man* by Darwin, Charles."

"My most prized possession. In this office, at least."

McGinnis made no attempt to take the book from Jake, but allowed him to leaf through its contents. Jake had no idea of the book's worth, but suspected it was valuable.

"That book, along with some others, was a gift to me, years ago, from one of my college biology professors. He left them to me in his will. While I'm proud of the books, I cherished his friendship more. I still cherish his memory."

Jake continued to examine the work. McGinnis made no attempt to rush him. After a few moments, Jake replaced the book into its designated slot and moved to sit down in a chair as McGinnis motioned.

"It's a beautiful book, as is your office."

"Thank you, Mister Thomas. May I call you Jacob?"

"Please call me Jake."

"Fine. Jake it is."

"Your desk is striking. I've never seen a desk like it."

"It was a piano," McGinnis said with a broad grin.

"Excuse me?"

"The desk *was* a piano." He motioned to Jake. "Come closer and look."

Jake rose from his chair and drew nearer.

"Notice this hinge, which crosses the full width of the top."

Jake nodded.

"This allowed the narrower portion to be turned back onto the other portion, exposing the keyboard. The legs have a large threaded dowel and are removable. The piano could be transported in a wagon."

"Which was when?" Jake asked.

"Hmm. A date? This is rosewood. I know rosewood got expensive around the time of the American Civil War. A piece this size made of rosewood, I suspect, was made long before the Civil War."

He hesitated for a moment as Jake returned to his chair.

"I bought the piece years ago from an antique dealer in upstate New York," McGinnis said. "My wife and I vacationed in the area. My wife fusses at me for haggling over prices of antiques. But haggling is half the fun of buying antiques. I can see her now, rolling her eyes as I spotted this piece when we were there. The dealer had an astronomical price on it. I offered less. The dealer phoned the owner of the piece and delivered my offer. I could hear the owner laughing over the phone as she delivered his rejection to me. Two years later, my wife and I were back. This piece was still there. I made another offer, this time lower than my initial offer. Same phone call. Same results, but the owner countered my offer, *and* the counter was the exact same as the offer I'd made two years previous. I was asked if I wanted it. No, I said, thinking I would buy the piece cheaper in the future. I located my wife where she was shopping in the store and told her the development. She asked if I bought it. Made her mad that I didn't. 'Don't come crying to me when we come back and the piece is sold,' she said. You know what I did, Jake?"

"Bought it?"

"Eureka! And presto, my piano-desk."

"A beautiful piece of furniture, and the story is even better."

McGinnis savored the story for a few moments before he spoke again. "Shall we get to the task at hand?"

Jake nodded.

For the next hour, McGinnis and Jake discussed his next three and a half years of undergraduate work, seven semesters. They planned Jake's path toward medical school—zoology, microbiology, and other science courses, a year of physics, two years of chemistry, and a year of calculus, along with other courses common to Tulane's core. Jake found the prospect both daunting and exhilarating.

McGinnis rose from behind the piano-desk. Jake, knowing McGinnis had other appointments, knew his time was finished. McGinnis extended his hand. "You know where I am, should you need anything, Jake."

"Yes, sir."

He shook McGinnis's hand and exited. Another student, one Jake recognized from both a lecture and lab class, sat in the outer office, waiting her turn to see the famous chair of Tulane's biology department. She smiled at Jake and said hello.

Jake nodded to her and exited the science building.

CHAPTER THIRTY-NINE

Standing on the sidewalk in front of the science building, Jake glanced at his watch. It was eleven thirty a.m.—plenty of time to get Leeroy, pick up Lester and Laverne, and get to his desired location. He turned the Olds toward home.

"Morning, Blanc," Leeroy said, climbing into the Olds.

"Morning, Mister Edwards."

"How was your meeting with the college man? What is his name?"

"Michael McGinnis. And the meeting went well. Thanks for asking."

"I assume he retracted all the talk about medical school?"

"Nope. The exact opposite, in fact. He wanted to help me consider which classes I'll need to have, just to *apply* for medical school."

"Doctor Blanc Thomas. Lord help us."

Jake had heard that before. He smiled.

"Do me a favor, Blanc?"

"Anything, Mister Edwards."

"I don't ever want you near me with any lethal dose of something in your hand."

"Scared of what I would do, eh?"

"Mortified," Leeroy replied, staring out his passenger window.

Jake laughed aloud.

The two drove in silence before Leeroy spoke again. "Where are we going?"

"We're going to pick up Lester and Laverne."

"From there?" Leeroy asked, assuming they were going somewhere else.

"Anyone ever tell you you're nosy?" Jake asked.

"Miz Edwards. Daily." Undeterred, Leeroy asked again. "Once we ronn-dey-voo with one Mister Washington and two, Mister Knox, where are we going from there?'

"Anyone ever tell you you may be an impatient person too?"

"Yep. Daily."

"Miz Edwards?"

"Miz Edwards." Leeroy gave a definitive nod.

Jake spoke no more. Leeroy asked no more questions.

Jake parked the Olds on Franklin Avenue. He stood with Leeroy as the older man knocked on the door to Lester and Laverne's flat. Lester opened the door.

"Well, don't stand there like a pair of lunatics. Come in."

"Top of the morning to you too, Mister Washington," Leeroy said, as he doffed his hat and bowed at the waist.

"Shut up, Leeroy," Lester grumped. He shook Jake's hand. "How was the big meeting with the head honcho at Tulane?"

"How did you know I was meeting with Doctor McGinnis today?"

Before Lester could answer, Laverne emerged from his bedroom.

"Morning, Leeroy. Morning, Jake. Hope your meeting with the science boss at the college went well."

Jake appeared puzzled. "Does everyone in New Orleans know about that?"

"Leeroy told us," Lester explained, pointing in the guilty party's direction. "You know Leeroy can't keep a secret. Nor can he carry a musical chord for that matter."

Leeroy smiled and shrugged his shoulders. He'd known Jake wouldn't mind if he told Lester and Laverne of the meeting with McGinnis.

"The meeting went well," Jake said. "We discussed what courses I'll need to take in order to prepare for medical school."

"Courses?" Lester asked.

"Something to eat," Leeroy said.

"Not something to eat. *Classes*. What *classes* I'll need to take," Jake explained.

"Gotcha," Lester said.

They exited the flat and moved in the direction of Jake's Olds. "Why, pray tell," Lester asked, "aren't we riding in Hazel, with her proud new hood ornament?"

"I offered," Leeroy said. "Blanc refused. Said he wanted to keep our final destination a SEE-cret."

The men piled into the Olds. On this particular occasion, Laverne took the front seat as Leeroy and Lester took the rear. Jake marveled at the fact there was never any rhyme or reason in seat selections. No hierarchy existed among the three men.

"This back seat," Leeroy remarked, "looks like someone's been livin' back here."

"At one time," Jake responded as he glanced in the rearview mirror, "someone did."

"I thought as much," Leeroy said, and gave a harrumph that was more chuckle than grunt.

"Where we goin'?" Lester asked.

"Yes, Jake, I'm curious as well," Laverne added.

"Y'all are just like Leeroy. Impatient," Jake answered. "Sit back and enjoy the ride, gentlemen, and leave the driving to ol' Jake."

The three men obeyed. Laverne rested his arm on the back of the seat. Lester sat back as though he was royalty, riding in a Rolls Royce. Leeroy sat up on the edge of the seat, behind Jake, determined not to miss anything. All four were glad to be in the presence of one another.

Jake accelerated as he merged onto interstate traffic. He crossed the Mississippi River and took the first exit as they entered Gretna. Seldom did Leeroy, Lester, or Laverne have any reason to visit the West Bank. They all indulged in rubbernecking at the sights.

"The suspense is killing me, Blanc," Leeroy said, peering through Jake's side window, his face inches from Jake's right ear.

Laverne lifted his arm from the back of the front seat, spread his fingers, and put his hand in Leeroy's face. Leeroy stuck out his tongue and licked Laverne's palm. Laverne pulled his arm off the back of the seat and rubbed it on his pants leg.

"Leeroy, I swear ..."

"I'll bite you next time."

Jake continued to maneuver the Olds. A few miles further, he turned right and made an immediate left into a parking lot. Two large buildings sandwiched a much smaller establishment, separated by two narrow alleyways—one on each side of the small building. Would-be customers couldn't see the smaller building until they pulled into the parking lot.

Nearing their destination, Leeroy, Lester, and Laverne anticipated Jake's intention. From the back seat, Leeroy read the neon sign flashing above the front entrance.

"Maria's Bar-B-Q. Famous the World Over."

With Jake's intentions revealed, Leeroy, Lester, and Laverne laughed. No doubt remembering Jake's accusations against them, Leeroy said, "Blanc, you traitor! You worthless traitor. What did Paul's Poulet ever do to you?"

"Paul doesn't do barbecue, remember?" Jake answered.

"Well, that's different," Lester admitted.

"You, Mister Edwards," Jake said, "once told me I needed to try Maria's barbecue sauce, and I said, 'maybe I will.' So, I will. Here we are. Shall we dine?"

"Let's," Laverne said.

"I love me some Maria's barbecue sauce," Leeroy said as he rubbed his hands together.

"Amen," Lester added.

CHAPTER FORTY

Jake managed to get the Olds into one of the few narrow spaces left in Maria's parking lot. Cars and trucks of every make and model filled the lot—Chevrolet trucks and BMWs, old Fords and Dodges, new Mercedes, Audis, and Volvos. This place obviously attracted patrons from every walk of life, and Jake had worked in the restaurant business long enough to know attraction was an accurate gauge of good food. He suspected whatever Maria's Bar-B-Q lacked in ambiance was more than made up for by her offerings. The men climbed out of the car and stepped inside.

Once inside, the size of the place surprised Jake. While narrow, the restaurant was deep, with a wide center aisle allowing access. Tables for two, four, six, and more, filled with diners, were seen everywhere, behind support poles and booths. The men got in line. A young female maître d' asked for a name.

"Washington," Jake said. "Mister Lester Washington."

She jotted down the name and informed the men of the wait time—about fifteen minutes. They sat and waited. None of them had any place to be on this cold, raw January day. The intoxicating smell of barbecue sauce wafted across the restaurant.

Less than ten minutes later, the men heard the call—
"Mister Lester Washington, table for four." The maître d'
showed the men to a booth. Jake and Lester slid in one
side, Jake on the inside, while Laverne and Leeroy took
the opposite bench. In seconds, another young woman
appeared with menus. She began distributing them before
Lester gestured toward Jake. "We need only one menu,
Miss, for Jake here."

The young woman blinked. "Okay, so you three know
what you're going to order?"

"We do," Leeroy said, "but give him"—he gestured
toward Jake—"a minute, please." The waitress took drink
orders and left.

"You don't need a menu, eh?" Jake said casually, as he
scanned the offerings. "Sounds like you three've been here
before."

"As Leeroy said," Lester said, "we love us some Maria's
barbecue sauce."

The waitress returned with tall glasses of iced tea. She
removed a notepad from her apron and asked, "Are we
ready to order?"

"Three barbecue chicken plates, with baked beans,
coleslaw, and rolls for the three of us," Lester said without
hesitation, pointing toward himself and then to Laverne
and Leeroy.

The waitress noted the orders and turned to Jake. "For
you?"

"The brisket looks good, as does the pulled pork. But
I'll make our order easy for you," Jake said as he folded
the menu and handed it to her. "Make that four barbecue
chicken plates, same side items."

"That's easy enough," she said, with a grin.

"Blanc here works in a restaurant himself," Leeroy said.

"Which one?"

"Paul's Poulet," Jake answered.

"On Chef Menteur Highway?"

"Correct," Jake affirmed. "Do you know it?"

"I do."

The waitress pulled the order tab from her book and turned to walk away. Then she turned halfway back again, smiling mischievously. "That's some mean fried chicken."

"Amen," Lester said quietly.

The restaurant was a beehive of activity. When one table emptied, someone cleared away dirty dishes, and the maître d' seated other customers. Jake and company drank iced tea as they waited for their food. Their waitress kept their glasses full. None of them gave the time any thought.

A short while later, their waitress arrived with two plates of food. A middle-aged man trailed behind her carrying two more plates. The waitress said, "Okay, who had the barbecue chicken plate with baked beans, coleslaw, and rolls?"

Leeroy realized she was joking with them. Without another word spoken, the waitress set two plates in front of Laverne and Leeroy. She turned, took the other two plates, and set them in front of Jake and Lester. "Need anything else?"

"Time," Leeroy answered.

Jake shot a questioning look toward Lester and Laverne, who shook their heads. Jake said. "No, nothing else, thank you."

"I'll be back later to check," she said, then turned and scurried off.

Jake couldn't remember the last time he saw so much food on a single plate. He surmised there had to be half a chicken. Plus, the plate contained two brimming bowls, one each of coleslaw and baked beans. Two large rolls adorned the top of the plate.

Lester, Laverne, and Leeroy waited patiently.

"Let's pray," Jake said.

He prayed, all said amen, and the feast began. For the next fifteen minutes, the men ate and drank what must have been a half-gallon of tea each. When the tea levels in glasses lowered, their waitress appeared with pitcher in hand. The men uttered few words beyond offering praise for Maria's Bar-B-Q—"Famous the World Over."

"I admit," Jake said, "the barbecue sauce is fabulous."

Laverne nodded agreement. "Leeroy always said if you brought that sauce in a glass, he would drink it."

"The best I've ever eaten," Jake said.

After the lunch plates had been cleared away, Jake spoke to the waitress again. "Coffee and apple pie for everyone, please."

"I'm unsure about that, Blanc," Leeroy said.

"Leeroy, I've never seen you turn down coffee or pie," Jake said, "or you, Laverne, or you, Lester."

The men said nothing. Their waitress returned with a tray stacked with coffee cups and a pot of coffee. "Four slices of apple pie coming up."

She returned with them in minutes. As scrumptious as the barbecue was, Jake liked the pie better. The men made quick work of it. The waitress gathered the empty plates. She kept the coffee coming. The lunch crowd began thinning.

Jake noticed a few empty tables. With the restaurant no longer needing their table, he believed they could linger for a while. Their waitress was in no hurry to get them out. When coffee cups emptied, she refilled them with the same soft voice and easy smile.

The men spoke of politics, local and national. They spoke of sports and the cold January weather in the Big Easy. They asked about Jake's interest in medical school and listened as he shared his passion for biology, chemistry, and people. They spoke of the Place of Jazz.

"No more coffee for me," Jake insisted, as the waitress returned with another pot.

Lester and Laverne shook their heads as Leeroy placed his right hand over his cup, an indication he too was finished.

Leeroy only said, "Stick a fork in me. I'm *done.*"

The four continued talking, their subject switching to the war raging in Vietnam and how all of them felt about it, until the issue had been thoroughly raked and furrowed.

Lester changed the subject. "I remember the first time I ate barbecue."

Leeroy and Laverne didn't utter a word. The atmosphere took on a chill. Jake sat unaware.

Lester took a deep breath and continued. "The year was 1910."

"You remember the year you first ate barbecue?" Jake asked, incredulously, as he shifted his weight to make eye contact with Lester. Leeroy and Laverne pointedly stared into their empty coffee cups. Neither spoke a word.

Lester continued. "April twenty-ninth, 1910."

"You remember the *day* you first ate barbecue?" Jake asked. He finally made eye contact with Leeroy and Laverne and thought he saw something haunting in their gaze. Again, neither man said anything.

Lester's next words froze Jake in his seat.

"It was the day after my parents died."

CHAPTER FORTY-ONE

"On April 28, 1910, Jake, my parents died in a freak industrial accident. Pa and Ma had both worked there for most of ten years. From what I knew, it was a good job. They were saving money for a down payment on a house. Ma was excited. 'Will we get a house with two bedrooms?' she asked Pa. 'Absolutely,' Pa said, 'two bedrooms is the most important part. That's what we'll look for first.' 'Finally,' Ma said, as she stroked my hair, 'Lester will have his own bedroom.' I slept on a cot in the corner of the living room. 'We're movin' the piano, aren't we?' Ma asked. 'That's the first thing we're loading onto the truck,' Pa said.

"Now, I was excited about having my own bedroom, but I wasn't as excited as Pa and Ma. For ten years they'd labored, and now their dream of home ownership was about to come true—something near impossible in Alabama in those days. A home with my own bedroom, the piano, and my dream—a backyard and neighbors. Good neighbors, I imagined."

Jake lifted his cup to his lips. Although it was empty, he needed to do something, anything. Lester took another deep breath and continued.

"Ma made my lunch and put it in a brown paper bag. She kissed my forehead as she went out the door behind Pa.

She turned to wave and she said, 'See you after school.' It's the last thing I remember her saying. The last I remember about Pa was him grabbing his old hat off a rack before he went out the front door. I remember he wore a light blue jacket. The last thing I saw of him was his backside—tall, slender, handsome man."

"I got home to an empty house, like I did every day. In fact, I can't remember ever coming home during the week when the house *wasn't* empty. I struggled through my homework. I was always a poor student. Now, I can't still read and write more than a few words." He was silent for a moment.

No one spoke a word. Time seemed suspended in the silence.

"Five o'clock," Lester said. "The time when Pa and Ma usually got home, when Ma would start preparing supper. Five o'clock came and no Pa. No Ma. I wasn't worried. They worked late all the time, sometimes as late as seven o'clock. I waited. Seven thirty. Eight. Nine o'clock. Nobody. I did the only thing I knew to do. I set up my cot in the corner of the living room about ten o'clock and I went to bed. Didn't sleep that night—not an hour, not a minute. I had never, *ever* been alone in that house at night. I got up the next morning, made my own sandwich, and put it in the same brown paper bag. And I waited for the school bus."

Lester heaved a long sigh and absently rubbed a forefinger over the rim of his saucer. "About seven thirty, before the bus came, a police car parked on the street in front of our house. A tall man in a uniform walked across to our house. I opened the door before he could knock, and I let him inside. He removed his hat and sat with me in the kitchen. He said something had happened, and then he told me.

"'What's an industrial accident?' I asked him. 'Something exploded,' he said, 'and a fire followed. The roof fell in.' 'When's Pa and Ma coming home?' I asked. He said, 'They are not coming home, son. They were caught under the roof when it fell. I'm sorry.'"

Lester looked down at his plate, his eyes unseeing. "The entire thing is still a nightmare," he said softly. "A recurring, terrible nightmare."

Jake wished he knew what to say. He opened his mouth, but the words wouldn't come.

Lester continued.

"'Your Pa and Ma are dead,' the man said. He sat with me for a few more minutes, and then asked me if I had anything to eat. I told him I had bread and mayonnaise. He went back to his car as I sat there. I couldn't move.

"I figured he'd left, but he returned to the kitchen with his own brown paper bag. He opened it and handed me a sandwich wrapped in wax paper. I hadn't had anything to eat since that mayonnaise sandwich for lunch the day before. 'It's barbecue,' the man said. 'What's barbecue?' I asked him. 'You've never eaten barbecue before?' I told him no. But that barbecue sandwich was ..." Lester's voice trailed off. He paused before continuing.

"Well, I ate it, all of it. The man asked, 'You like it?' and smiled at me. I told him I did. After a few minutes, he left."

Jake thought the story would end there. Hoped, in fact, for Lester's sake and his own, the story ended there. But Leeroy and Laverne knew better.

CHAPTER FORTY-TWO

"I never went back to school. That nice policeman—his last name was Wright—returned the next day, and the next and the next, each day with another barbecue sandwich. 'Do you have any kinfolks?' he asked. I shook my head no. 'I know this is a hard thing, but you need to think what has to be done in burying your parents,' he said. He took me to the funeral home where I chose two caskets—identical. I pointed to them. He took me to the local cemetery where I bought two burial plots. A local minister said nice words over Pa and Ma—I wish I could remember his name. He was from the Methodist church, as I recall. I had a single, simple, small tombstone erected. It said, 'George and Roberta Washington. April 28, 1910.' I paid for the funeral expenses out of the money Pa and Ma earned over those ten years gone. Money they'd saved for a house ... with a bedroom and a backyard for me."

Lester's voice trembled as he continued.

"Pa kept the money hidden in one of those mayonnaise jars inside the piano. We always had plenty of empty mayo jars. Those funeral expenses took all the money and more. I sold everything Pa and Ma had—a few pieces of old furniture—and paid the rest of the expenses. I had twenty-three dollars and twenty-five cents left over. The nice policeman came every day, always bringing barbecue and sometimes something else to eat. Never lettin' me pay for anything. He asked me what I was going to do, and I told him I didn't know. And I *didn't* know. Didn't have a clue which way to turn. I was scared to death. Less than two weeks after that, Laverne, Leeroy, and I walked out of Chalk Bluff and on to New Orleans. And I've never been back."

Lester dropped his head, and a few tears fell from his cheeks onto the tablecloth. "I regret not expressing my appreciation and saying goodbye to Mister Wright. He was a kind man."

The men sat in silence.

Jake was unsure he could speak.

"Y'all excuse me, please," Lester said as he stood and walked to the rear of the restaurant.

Jake now sat with Leeroy and Laverne. The silence was palpable. Laverne made eye contact with Jake. "Welcome to the family, Jake."

"I'm sorry," Jake managed to mutter.

"Welcome to the *immediate* family," Leeroy added as Laverne nodded.

Reading the confusion on Jake's face, Laverne explained. "The family—Lester, Leeroy, me, and now you."

"I'm confused," Jake said.

"To our knowledge, Lester has never told his story to anyone else but the two of us," Laverne said, with Leeroy nodding in agreement. "Anthony never heard that story, and Lester played with Anthony for over forty years."

"And Lester loves Mildred more than Laverne and me combined," Leeroy added, "and even *Mildred* doesn't know that story."

After a few minutes, Lester returned. "Now I've ruined a perfect day with my gloomy past. I apologize."

"Nonsense, Lester," Laverne said.

Leeroy attempted to lighten the moment. "Naw, Blanc here ruined this perfect day."

Jake again appeared puzzled, but didn't have time to say anything before Leeroy continued.

"Blanc ruined this perfect day when he wouldn't let me drive Hazel. You remember, Blanc? Hazel with her new hood ornament?"

"I remember," Jake said, with a relieved smile.

Leeroy did manage to cajole a brief smile from Lester. The men sat in silence for a few more minutes, until Jake finally said, "Lunch today is on me, gentlemen."

"That's not necessary, Jake," Laverne said.

"Let us all chip in and pay our part," Lester said.

"Absolutely," Leeroy said.

All four men reached for wallets. Jake held up one hand, palm down.

"I insist," Jake said. "The meal is on me today. I brought you here with the intention of buying lunch."

Lester, Laverne, and Leeroy conceded. "Thank you," the men offered in unison.

Jake summoned the waitress and requested their bill.

"Your bill has been paid, sir."

"*What*? By whom?" Jake asked.

She pointed. "By the man over there in the corner."

In unison, Jake, Lester, Leeroy, and Laverne turned their attention to a two-chair table in the rear of the restaurant.

"Why, that traitor," Leeroy said.

"What did Paul's Poulet ever do to Paul?" asked Laverne.

In seconds, the traitor stood at the end of the booth where the four men sat. They all expressed their appreciation to him for dining on his dime.

Then Leeroy pointed a long index finger at him and said, "You got some 'splainin' to do."

Paul smiled. "I *love* me some Maria's barbecue sauce."

CHAPTER FORTY-THREE

For Jake, the next two and a half years seemed a blur. In addition to his introduction to biology class in his first semester, he took four more biology classes, including zoology and microbiology. He took three additional chemistry courses. He had two semesters of physics and one more of calculus. Without trepidation, he expected to perform on a high level, and did.

His study skills improved with time and practice, as did his confidence. The class that made him most nervous was World History II—his last history class. He remembered the B he'd earned in World History I. With Dr. McGinnis's blessing, Jake waited until his junior year in undergraduate work to register for the class. He searched the class offerings and found the name he'd hoped for. He registered for the class offered by Professor B. Faulkner.

On the first day, Jake arrived in the classroom early. In fact, no one else had arrived. Faulkner arrived minutes after Jake, armed with a load of syllabi and books. Jake rose from his seat and assisted Faulkner as the latter struggled to open the door.

"Good morning, Mister Thomas. Thank you for holding the door."

Jake took the stack of books, placed them on a desk, turned and sat.

Faulkner said, "I see you have your familiar place, front and center."

"Good morning, Professor. I'm shocked you remember my name."

"I try to remember the names of all my students. Age makes that more and more challenging, but I must confess, remembering the names of outstanding students is easier."

"Outstanding? I earned a B in your class and was blessed to get it."

"*But* a hard-fought B. A well-earned B. I respect that. I recognized you as a determined young man as you sat in the front row with your pencil. You were a motivated, disciplined, passionate student. I respect that too. I suspected you had the intelligence to match, and I was right. I misread people at times, but I did read you correctly."

Falkner paused, then continued. "You didn't come to my class with a sense of entitlement. You came on a *quest* for knowledge, a *search* for enlightenment, for truth, and you conquered. I admire that too, Mister Thomas."

Faulkner began placing syllabi on desks and continued speaking. "What have you chosen as a field of study? Two and a half years later, what's your major, young man?"

"Biology."

"What do you want to do with that?"

"Medical school." Jake looked down at his hands. "You probably find that hard to believe."

"On the contrary, I'm not surprised at all. You'll make an excellent physician."

"Your confidence in me is encouraging, but it may be misplaced."

"Nonsense."

Other students began arriving.

Faulkner handed Jake a syllabus, leaned into him and spoke quietly.

"If you need a reference for grad school applications, you know where I am."

Faulkner addressed the class before Jake could answer. "Good morning, class, and welcome to World History II." The students mumbled their replies.

Jake thought Faulkner epitomized most of the college professors he'd had at Tulane. Intelligent, gifted teachers, compassionate, gracious, and willing to assist. Jake remembered the fear he'd had two and a half years earlier as Faulkner returned his first college exam, insisting he look at the grade. He couldn't believe then—or now—he'd earned an 83.

He earned an A in World History II. He hoped Professor Faulkner was proud.

Jake, Lester, Laverne, and Leeroy continued to play the Place of Jazz twice a month. Paul and Rebecca, Mildred, and Cora became staples on the front row for each performance, seated with Xavier Cullum.

Xavier encouraged the men to play more and offered them any schedule and any night they preferred. While Jake didn't believe he could devote any more time away from his studies, he allowed Lester, Laverne, and Leeroy to make the decision. He was inwardly relieved when Laverne told Xavier he, Lester, and Leeroy were too old to work more. Jake knew the claim wasn't true, but loved the men for recognizing the fact he needed both college and Cora time.

He continued working at Paul's, Cora being the main reason. He didn't want her working there without him. He worried about her driving home alone. He asked her to mirror their work schedules so he could follow her home at the end of each shift. Usually, he waited until she was inside her front door before blowing his car horn and driving home.

Eventually, Jake walked her to her door, rain or shine.

"You don't have to walk me to the door, Jake," Cora said, in a driving rainstorm one afternoon.

Minus an umbrella, both got soaked. Cora pecked Jake's jaw before she unlocked the door and entered. The next day, Jake presented her with a new oversized umbrella.

Cora was Jake's bright ray of sunlight, and he knew he was a better person due to her influence. He couldn't help but smile as he watched her each shift, wearing her chicken cap. Her positive disposition never changed as she greeted customers either behind the counter or with a pot of coffee.

Jake arrived at work in early December of his junior year in college to find four cards tucked inside his apron. He recognized Cora's handwriting as he read his name on one card. The names *Lester, Laverne,* and *Leeroy and Mildred* were written on the other three.

"What's this?" he asked Cora.

"Do you mind delivering those to the guys and Mildred?"

"I don't mind." He placed the cards in his jacket pocket. He made a mental note to deliver them, and to read his at the end of the shift.

The shift proved to be one of their crazy days. Usually, each shift experienced lulls when employees could take a breather. During the lulls, Jake came out from behind the counter or the kitchen to sit and talk with customers, or just to take a walk outside.

Not so on this particular day. From Cora and Jake's arrival until they turned the place over—gladly—to the afternoon and night workers, they were on their feet in the kitchen, behind the counter, and in the dining area. Somewhere in the early afternoon, Paul dropped in to say hello, recognized the madness of the day, donned his vest and cap, and hurried off to the kitchen. Paul's presence was a welcome injection of energy.

"What a day," Jake said later, as he leaned against Cora's house.

Cora unlocked her door. Jake knew she was exhausted. Being on one's feet for eight hours straight would do that. Still, her smile never left her face, nor did her positive disposition change. She pecked his cheek.

"See you tomorrow, Jake."

"See you tomorrow."

Jake waited until he heard the lock tumblers fall into place seconds later. Satisfied she was safe, he turned toward home.

Jake stopped at Lester and Laverne's flat and knocked on the door. Lester opened the door.

"Jake, my boy. What a pleasant surprise. What brings you by on this cold New Orleans day? You look exhausted. Rough day in the chicken coop?"

Jake held up two envelopes. "Mail delivery. From Cora."

Laverne silently handed his envelope to Lester, who took it without a word. Lester placed the envelopes on a sofa end table.

"Sit down, Jake," Lester said. "Take a load off."

"I would love to, but I can't. Final exams start Monday, and I need to study."

He reached for the doorknob, paused, and spoke again, without turning. "Laverne, why don't you learn to read?"

Jake had encouraged Laverne several times in the past to learn to read, without success. He didn't want to be rude or insensitive, but he thought the ability to read could add a degree of happiness and quality to Laverne's life. He turned to face Laverne and Lester.

Laverne pointed in Lester's general direction.

"Why? I've got Lester. He reads—not good, but he reads. No need for me to know how. Plus I can't learn. I'm a dumb old man."

"You aren't dumb, Laverne," Lester said. "Old, yes. Dumb, no."

Jake said no more as he opened the door and turned up his collar against the cold. He started toward home and he started thinking about the men and their inability to read. If ...

∞

Mildred and Leeroy were in their favorite living room chairs, Mildred with her crossword puzzle book and Leeroy strumming his bass, when Jake arrived and handed them their notes.

"What's this?" Mildred asked.

"Don't know," he replied.

He and Mildred opened their notes from Cora and read them.

"What is it?" Leeroy asked.

"Ah. That's nice," Mildred said, speaking more to herself than Leeroy or Jake.

"What is it?" Leeroy asked again.

"That *is* nice," Jake agreed, as he replaced the note in its envelope.

"What does it say?" Leeroy's tone bordered on plaintive.

"I have to study," Jake said, and disappeared in the direction of his bedroom.

"What *is* it?"

"I'll go finish fixing dinner," Mildred said, exiting the living room as well.

Leeroy, now sitting alone in the living room, threw up his hand in frustration and shouted at the ceiling.

"*What is it!*"

"An invitation," Jake's disembodied voice answered.

"To ...?"

Neither Jake nor Mildred said another word.

CHAPTER FORTY-FOUR

"How nice of you to invite us to your home on Christmas Day," Mildred told Cora. She and Leeroy arrived at Cora's house before Jake, Lester, and Laverne.

"I hope you aren't disappointed with having our meal here as opposed to your home," Cora said.

"I'm *not* disappointed," Mildred said genuinely. "Not at all."

Leeroy hugged Cora. "Merry Christmas, young lady."

"Merry Christmas, Leeroy. Come in, please."

Leeroy carried a container in a brown paper sack. He set the sack down in the kitchen just as the doorbell rang.

"Shall I?" Leeroy asked Cora, as he emerged from the kitchen.

"Please."

Leeroy opened the door to find Lester, Laverne, and Jake standing on the small entryway.

"Why, Lester, Laverne, and Blanc! Don't stand there lookin' like Santa's elves, come in—come in. And merry Christmas to all y'all."

"Merry Christmas, Leeroy," the trio responded.

Leeroy gathered their hats and placed them with his. The three newcomers hugged Mildred as Cora emerged from the kitchen, removing an apron. Lester and Laverne hugged Cora, and all three Noirs watched Jake bend down to kiss Cora on her cheek.

"Merry Christmas, Cora," Jake said.

"Merry Christmas, Jake."

Jake recognized many of the aromas emanating from Cora's kitchen as those he'd smelled from Mildred's kitchen on previous Christmas holidays. Cora had one Christmas tree in a corner of her small living room. Lights, ornaments, and tinsel covered every inch of the tree, from the star topper to the stand.

Jake had never been inside Cora's house. The house was small but neat. The walls were painted white, contrasting with the dark varnish of the three-inch board pine floors. The walls were adorned with a few pictures and decorative pieces.

"Shall I?" Leeroy asked again as the doorbell rang.

"Please," Cora responded.

Leeroy opened the door. Lester and Laverne held their breath, thinking Leeroy would greet the guests with another "Don't stand there like fools" or something similar. He didn't.

"Merry Christmas, Paul. Merry Christmas, Rebecca." Everyone hugged and shook hands all around, until Cora went to the kitchen and then came to the doorway.

"Dinner is ready. Let's all be seated."

Minus a dining room, the group moved to the kitchen with Cora. Her small house had a small kitchen to match, and her small kitchen became smaller when eight people entered it. She gave seating arrangements—Mildred beside Leeroy, Lester beside Laverne, Paul beside Rebecca, Jake beside her, everyone elbow to elbow. No one minded.

Cora took a Bible, which she had placed in her plate. She handed the Bible to Leeroy. "Do you mind?"

"I'm honored."

Leeroy turned to Luke 2 and read—mostly.

> And it came to pass in those days, that there went out a decree from Caesar Augustus that all the world should be taxed ... And this shall be a sign unto you; Ye shall find the babe wrapped in swaddling clothes, lying in a manger.' And suddenly there was with the angel a multitude of the heavenly host praising God, and saying, 'Glory to God in the highest, and on earth peace, good will toward men.'

When Leeroy finished, Cora took Jake's hand on her right and reached for Mildred's hand on her left. The group responded, taking the hands of others to complete the circle.

"Jake, please?" Cora said.

Jake knew what she meant and prayed.

"Father, we are grateful for this Christmas Day. We are reminded of the true meaning of this celebration, and we are grateful to celebrate the birth of our Savior and celebrate this day with family. Amen."

Jake's prayer was lost on no one. He considered everyone there to be his family. They all felt the same way.

The group waited for Cora's lead. When she reached for a platter, the meal began—and what a majestic repast they had.

"Have I told you about the time we first met Blanc?" Leeroy asked.

"Not now, Leeroy. This is Christmas Day," Mildred scolded.

"Yes, Leeroy, not now. It's Christmas Day," Jake said.

"No," Paul said, "I want to hear it."

"Me too," Cora said.

Undeterred, Leeroy begin. "We—Lester, Laverne, and I—put an ad in the *Times-Picayune*, needing a guitarist. On the last day of the auditions, this skinny White boy comes strollin' up our driveway to our studio."

"Aka Leeroy's garage," Laverne said.

Leeroy continued. "Before he got within earshot, I told Laverne and Lester he couldn't play. I told them maybe he could strum a chord or two but he couldn't play. Lester said, 'Maybe not, but he's here—our first audition.'"

"Jake's clothes," Laverne added, "all neat and pressed."

"I wondered who ironed his clothes," Lester said.

Jake smiled.

"I remember his hands," Lester said. "*Big* hands. Look at 'em. I told Laverne and Leeroy the boy couldn't play with hands that big."

"He carried what in a previous life had been a guitar case. At that particular time, I was unsure exactly *what* he carried," Leeroy said. "He stood there and smiled. 'I'm Jacob Thomas,' he said. 'I understand you're looking for a guitarist.'"

"I said," Laverne chipped in, "we are looking for a guitarist, but I don't believe you're what we're lookin' for."

"Jake grabbed a lawnchair, sat down, and started playing on this funky old box of a guitar he had in the case," Lester said. "After a few tunes, Laverne got up and got his Gibson, and handed the guitar to Jake."

Leeroy started again. "For the next ten minutes, what came from the Gibson was nothin' but solid gold—gospel, rhythm and blues, jazz. Nary a piece of sheet music. All from memory. All superb."

"We offered him a job," Laverne said. "Well, we offered him a chance to play on the streets with us, but we didn't have a job—a gig. Not then."

"'I don't work on Sundays,' Blanc said. We agreed not to work Sundays," Leeroy said.

"We agreed to split earnings four ways, minus gas money for Leeroy. For Hazel," Lester said.

"The rest, they say, is history. Now we're playin' twice a month for the Place of Jazz," Leeroy said. He raised his tea glass. "Back to the big time! To Blanc and good friends. Merry Christmas."

"To Jake and good friends. Merry Christmas!" the group echoed, touching tea glasses.

An hour later, the group had eaten most of Cora's pecan and apple pies and fruitcake. Jake kept the coffee cups full.

"That was delicious," Mildred said.

"I do know my way around a kitchen," Cora said. "I have Paul and Rebecca to thank for teaching me that."

Leeroy rose. "Gentlemen, at our house the men do the cleanup. Shall we?"

Cora protested, but Leeroy pushed her out the kitchen door into the living room. Mildred and Rebecca followed. The trio sat on the sofa while the men donned aprons and took up washcloths and dishtowels. The men made quick work of Cora's kitchen and joined the ladies in the living room.

After small talk, Leeroy went back to the kitchen, returning to the living room carrying a tray of glasses and a large pitcher for the traditional eggnog. He began pouring glasses, serving the ladies first. The group sat quietly, enjoying Christmas Day.

Cora excused herself. In minutes, she returned and handed Jake a guitar.

"This guitar belonged to my father. I'm not sure why he owned a guitar—I never saw him play, and I'm not really sure he could. Will you, please, Jake?"

Jake, Lester, Laverne, and Leeroy all recognized the instrument as a rare Martin acoustic guitar. Jake took the guitar and tuned it. He played a few chords that all recognized, and then he began to sing.

> *Silent night, holy night!*
> *All is calm, all is bright*
> *'Round yon virgin, mother and child;*
> *holy infant, so tender and mild,*
> *sleep in heavenly peace,*
> *sleep in heavenly peace.*

As Jake played, Paul coaxed Rebecca to sing. With a little persuasion, she sang the next verse in her native German. With no other sound but Jake on the vintage Martin, Leeroy thought Rebecca's was the voice of an angel.

> Stille Nacht, heilige Nacht!
> *Silent night, holy night!*
> Alles schlaft, einsam wacht
> *All is calm, all is bright*
> Nur das traute hochheilige Parr,
> *'round yon virgin mother and child;*
> Holder Knabe mit lockigem Harr,
> *holy infant, so tender and mild,*
> Schlaf in himmlischer Ruh,
> *Sleep in heavenly peace,*
> Schlaf in himmlischer Ruh.
> *Sleep in heavenly peace!*

The entire group joined in and sang.

Silent night, holy night!
Son of God, love's pure light,
radiant beams from thy holy face,
with the dawn of redeeming grace,
Jesus, Lord at thy birth,
Jesus, Lord at Thy birth.

Jake played carol after carol. Some he initiated, while others were requested. When he tired, he passed the Martin to Laverne, who played gladly, continuing the festivities. The group sang most of them. When Jake or Laverne played an unfamiliar song, those who knew the words sang while the others enjoyed the concert.

As the night progressed, after Leeroy's eggnog had been drunk and the last bit of Cora's fruitcake eaten, the group, starting with Paul and Rebecca, began to depart. Simultaneously, Mildred and Leeroy excused themselves, insisting they needed to leave as well. Jake, Lester, and Laverne exited with Leeroy and Mildred.

With them illuminated by the lights on Cora's entryway, Leeroy saw Jake kiss Cora's cheek before she closed the door, ending the festive night.

CHAPTER FORTY-FIVE

On a Sunday afternoon, Leeroy called a rare emergency meeting of the Noirs. Lester, Laverne, and Jake gathered around a small electric heater in Leeroy's garage/practice room/community gathering place. While the heater helped, it didn't ward off the outside cold completely. In moments, Leeroy joined them.

Laverne said, "Are you dying, Leeroy?"

"He looks like he been dead for years," Lester commented. "And if you *are* dyin', I want your bass."

"I'm touched you'd want my guitar, Lester," Leeroy said.

"I want to hock it," Lester said.

"In that case, and to spite you, Lester, no, I'm not dyin'."

"Are you dyin', Lester?" Laverne asked.

"I'm not."

"Are you dyin', Jake?" Laverne queried.

"To my knowledge, no," Jake answered.

"Is Mildred dyin', Leeroy?" Laverne again.

"No, Mildred isn't dying."

"I'm not dyin'," Laverne said.

"Well, we've established that no one is dying," Leeroy said. "Glad to have all that straighened out."

"If nobody's dyin'," Laverne asked, "then what are we doin' here, Leeroy?"

"Why aren't we inside your house?" Lester asked. He eased his chair closer to the heaters. "This weather is as cold as a well-digger's rump."

Leeroy ignored Lester's last question.

"Our topic today," Leeroy said, "is a matter of utmost importance. National security is at stake." Leeroy leaned into the circle. Jake sat across from him. Leeroy made eye contact with Jake. Neither Lester, Laverne, nor Jake could imagine what was on Leeroy's mind. Leeroy placed a hand on Jake's knee.

"Blanc ... are you ever gonna kiss Cora on her lips?"

"*What*?" Jake asked.

"On her lips. Are you ever going to kiss Cora on her lips?" He continued. "Have you *ever* kissed Cora on the lips?"

"Is *that* why we're here?" Lester asked. "Is this the purpose of this called emergency meeting? I should be home warm and napping."

"Jake's kissing Cora or not is none of your—none of *our* business," Laverne said. He turned to speak to Jake. "We didn't know why he called this meeting."

"I'm waiting on an answer, Blanc," Leeroy said, determined.

"He ain't gonna answer that, Leeroy," Laverne said.

"I make a motion to adjourn this special called emergency meeting," Lester said.

"I second," Laverne said. "And we apologize, Jake, for Leeroy's impropriety." Lester and Laverne rose.

Jake remained in his chair. "No."

"No *what*?" Leeroy asked.

"The answer to your question is no. I've never kissed Cora except on her cheek."

"Why in heaven not?" Leeroy asked.

Laverne and Lester sat back down. "Again, Leeroy," Laverne said, "none of our business and—"

"I don't know how," Jake interrupted.

"What do you mean, you don't know how?" Leeroy asked incredulously.

"Jake, you don't have to do this," Lester said.

"I don't mind. Leeroy, when I say I don't know how, I mean I've never kissed a girl, any girl, on the lips." Jake thought for a second before speaking again. "Any advice?"

Jake glanced at Leeroy and then in the direction of Lester and Laverne.

"Don't look at me," Lester said.

"Me neither," Laverne hastened to add.

"Well, heck fire, Blanc," Leeroy said. He paused a few seconds, shook his head, and continued. "Thankfully for you, when you come to me for such wisdom, you come to a master."

"Oh my," Lester moaned.

"Lord help us," Laverne said.

"Lord help Jake most of all," Lester added.

Jake sat patiently.

Leeroy began. "When you get ready to plant one ..."

"Plant one?" Jake asked.

"Plant one, Jake," Lester clarified, "you know. When you get ready to plant, oh say, petunias with Cora ..."

"You could plant pansies," Laverne said.

Jake knew what Leeroy meant by "plant," but he was having too much fun. "I've never planted petunias and pansies with Cora."

"Excuse me," Leeroy said, with a pointed look at Lester and Laverne.

"I know for a fact," Jake said, "Cora prefers snapdragons over both petunias and pansies. Now that's a fact."

"Fine," Lester said, "when you get ready to plant snapdragons …"

"*Excuse* me," Leeroy harrumphed.

"I prefer snapdragons," Laverne mused, "more than petunias or pansies, come to think about it. So let's plant snapdragons, not petunias. Can Jake plant snapdragons, Leeroy?"

"How about some pansies too?" Lester added.

"*Kiss!*" Leeroy yelled. He took a deep breath and continued. "When you get ready to kiss Cora …"

"That's different," Lester said.

"I would say kissing Cora is a lot different from planting petunias or pansies," Laverne said. "Wouldn't you say so, Lester?"

"I should say so," Lester said.

Leeroy had had enough of the chatter. "Well, I can see the mistake I made, inviting you two to this emergency meeting. I may have to ask you to leave."

"Not me," Lester said, "I'm not going anywhere. I want to learn to plant."

"Teach us to plant, O Wise One," Laverne said.

Jake called the group back to order by saying, "In all seriousness, I do want to learn to plant. So Leeroy, continue, please."

Leeroy made eye contact with Laverne and Lester. "Neither of you know anything about planting …"

"That's the reason we're stayin'," Lester said. "To learn."

"From a master, no less," Laverne added.

Leeroy ignored Lester and Laverne and spoke to Jake. "When you get ready to kiss Cora, you gotta be smooth. You can't grab her like grabbin' a sack of Paul's frozen french fries. Got to be smooth."

"Smooth," Jake nodded as if making mental notes. "Not french fries."

Leeroy continued. "Gentle. Cora is delicate. When you get ready to kiss her, you handle her *gently*. Like that vintage Martin guitar Cora asked you to play—the one that belonged to her dad."

"Now, that was a nice guitar," Lester said.

"Played easily," Laverne said.

"Hush," Leeroy said. He turned back to Jake. "When Cora handed that guitar to you, you took her dad's guitar as though it was a newborn baby. *Gentle*. That's how you should kiss Cora."

"Smooth and gentle," Jake said, nodding.

"Timing is important," Leeroy insisted.

"Timing." Jake nodded again.

"Cora'll have a certain look when she wants you to kiss her," Leeroy said. "It's important you recognize that look, if you want to become a master like me."

"A certain look. Got it. Such as?" Jake asked, the first question he'd asked Leeroy.

The self-proclaimed master leaned back in his lawn chair and rubbed his beard-stubbled chin. "A hard question, indeed. But a woman will get this far-off look in her eyes, or she'll lift her face toward you, or turn her head slightly."

"Why can't she just say 'kiss me'?" Jake asked.

Leeroy showed disappointment. "Blanc, you knucklehead. For Cora to say 'kiss me' destroys the moment. Destroys the great pursuit known as the love dance." He waved a cautioning forefinger. "Never will Cora say 'kiss me.' She doesn't want to have to *tell* you to kiss her. She wants you to *know* when to do it. Remember that far-off look, Blanc."

"Got it," Jake said. "Smooth, gentle, far-off look."

"Your lips ..." Leeroy started again.

"What about my lips?"

"You got to get 'em right. You can't kiss Cora with your mouth open, like you gonna take a bite from one of Paul's sandwiches—you could swallow her whole head. And you can't kiss her with lips squeezed shut like you're angry about a flat tire—if you do that, you're just buttin' heads with her. Like y'all are a couple of goats."

Jake understood the first analogy of Paul's sandwiches, but the second and third analogies of flat tires and butting heads with goats were lost on him.

"Show me."

Leeroy began configuring his lips as though he was a fish out of water, fighting for his last breath. He closed his eyes, turned his head from side to side, and smacked.

"That's about the dumbest thing I've ever seen," Laverne said.

"Maybe," Lester said, trying to be helpful, "a visual would be in order."

"A visual?" Leeroy asked.

"On Laverne," Lester explained. "Kiss Laverne."

"Don't you come near me, Leeroy Edwards."

Leeroy continued to ignore Lester and Laverne.

"Smooth, gentle, far-off look, lips positioned properly," Jake said, prompting Leeroy to continue.

"Then, when you're smooth, when you're gentle, and when she has that far-off look ..." Leeroy said.

"She lifts her face to me or turns her head slightly," Jake prompted again.

Leeroy continued. "With lips positioned ... then you got to swoop in there and plant one on her. Wham!"

"Whoa," Lester said. "*Swoop*? I don't believe that's right, Leeroy."

"And *plant*?" Laverne said. "I agree with Lester. I don't imagine kissing works like that, Leeroy."

"Sure, kissing works like that," Leeroy insisted.

"I believe Laverne and Lester are correct about this swooping thing. I can't imagine me swooping in order to plant on Cora," Jake said.

"Listen to a master," Leeroy said. "Have you *ever* swooped on the lips, Blanc?"

"Never," Jake admitted.

"How about you two Romeos?" Leeroy turned to Lester and Laverne.

"I haven't swooped and planted," Lester said, "in years."

"I was trying to remember the last time I swooped and planted," Laverne said, with a far-off gaze.

"I swooped and planted this morning," Leeroy said. "Turned up Mildred's toes."

"*Please*, Leeroy," Laverne added.

"Oh my," Lester said.

Leeroy leaned back in his chair, satisfied with his oratory masterpiece. He offered his final words on the subject. "You're welcome ... all three of you."

"Smooth, gentle, far-off look, lips positioned, swoop, plant," Jake said. "Correct?"

"Correct," Leeroy said. "Words of wisdom from a master planter. And one more thing, Blanc ...."

"Which is?"

"Cora likes you. She isn't gonna kick you."

"I'm unconvinced of that."

"I don't know about this swoop-and-plant thing," Lester said, "but I do know Leeroy is correct about Cora liking you."

"Heck, I can see it, too. And I haven't planted in years. *And* I know zero about the love dance," Laverne said.

The men sat in silence. Jake spoke quietly, appearing to make mental notes. "Smooth, gentle, far-off look, lips positioned, swoop, plant."

After a few minutes, Lester said, "How many women have you planted, Master-of-Swoop Leeroy Edwards?"

"My fair share," Leeroy said, "believe you me."

Neither Lester nor Laverne could remember Leeroy ever dating a woman other than Mildred. They knew Leeroy would die before he would ever be unfaithful to her. He would never even peck another woman on the cheek.

"How many?" Laverne insisted. Lester leaned forward on his chair, awaiting Leeroy's reply.

Leeroy smiled. "One."

Lester and Laverne roared with laughter. "Forgive us, Swoop-and-Plant Master, for doubting your acumen in the art of the love dance," Lester said.

Leeroy leaned forward in his chair. His words ended the called emergency meeting of the Noirs.

"That swoop and plant with Mildred has lasted near fifty years."

CHAPTER FORTY-SIX

Jake checked the schedule when he arrived at Paul's Poulet. He and Cora were off Friday. During a lull in the afternoon, Jake found her peeling potatoes, an endless job they all performed.

"Any plans for Friday night?" Jake asked.

"I need to clean. Dusting, sweeping, mopping," Cora said. "How about you?"

"No plans. Probably go to the grocery store with Mildred and Leeroy. They do that Friday nights."

He stood silent for a moment, struggling to find words.

"Want to see a movie?" he blurted. He halted, regained his composure, then continued. "Maybe grab a burger somewhere? Or if the weather isn't too cold, we could walk along Lake Pontchartrain."

"All of that sounds nice," Cora said with a smile.

"But if you need to dust, sweep, and mop, I understand."

"I'll do that later," Cora said. "Let's go out. That would be nice. But what about your grocery shopping?"

"I'll suggest to Leeroy and Mildred that we shop Saturday."

"All right. At four, maybe? Let's walk along the lake before dark and then eat or see a movie. Or both."

"Great. Four o'clock, then."

That shift, that day, was a blur to Jake. After confirming the date with Cora for Friday, he couldn't remember anything else about the day. Working beside Paul, he peeled a mountain of potatoes and fried enough chicken to feed half of New Orleans, but he couldn't remember doing any of it.

I'm glad I don't have an exam today. I can't remember my own name.

Jake followed Cora home after work. They both knew the routine. Cora sat in the VW and waited for him to park. He then opened her car door for her and walked her to her house. He stood as she unlocked the door. She turned to him.

Smooth, gentle, far-off look, lips positioned, swoop, plant, Jake thought.

Cora lifted her face and met Jake's eyes.

Jake pecked her on the cheek. "See you on your next shift."

"Thursday afternoon," Cora said, smiling gently.

Jake listened for the tumblers to roll before turning.

"I'm an idiot," he said aloud, as he walked back to the Olds.

Smooth, gentle, far-off look, lips positioned, swoop, plant, my eye.

"An absolute idiot."

Thursday afternoon and night at Paul's was a madhouse. Unlike Monday, Jake had no problem remembering every detail about this shift. One of the fryers stopped working at six fifteen, just as the night crowd began to arrive. The timing couldn't have been worse. Jake knew the contingency plan, and phoned Bill's Appliance for repairs. Bill arrived in minutes, but the news wasn't good. The repair man told Jake fixing the problem might take a couple of hours.

Jake relieved Cora at the counter. He preferred dealing with disappointed customers as opposed to watching Cora do it.

"I don't mind, Jake. I've dealt with rude customers before."

Jake insisted. He considered phoning Paul, but there was nothing Paul could do. Jake bowed his head and weathered the storm that emerged in Paul's Poulet that Thursday night. Cora and three other workers did the same. Thankfully those kinds of storms were rare.

Then, with Bill making repairs on the fryer, the restaurant ran out of a particular brand of soda. One of their suppliers' delivery trucks had broken down. The supplier phoned the restaurant to offer apologies and inform them he'd be there as soon as possible. An hour later, Jake still had one fryer out of commission, and still didn't have the soda.

"We have a fryer that isn't working," Jake told customer after customer. "There's an approximate fifteen-minute wait time on some orders."

A few customers waited patiently while other exited. Jake couldn't blame them. Paul's Poulet prided itself on prompt service. Fifteen minutes wasn't prompt service for many customers.

"We are out of that soda," Jake told one customer after another. "I'm sorry. May I get you something else?"

That shortage too was not received well.

One fryer down, out of a popular soda.

What else can go wrong?

The answer came sooner than he imagined.

The phone rang. Cora answered and handed the phone to Betsy, a long-term employee. Jake saw Betsy wipe her eyes as she returned to the kitchen, and as soon as he could, he followed her and inquired. Betsy's daughter, home with Betsy's mother, had fallen. Betsy's mother thought the fall was nothing but wanted her daughter to know.

"Go," Jake said.

For the second time that night, he considered calling Paul.

"I'm not going to do that," Jake said aloud.

There was nothing Paul could do about the fryer or the soda. There *was* something Paul could do in Betsy's absence—he could and would work. He knew Paul wouldn't mind coming in to the restaurant. Regarding Betsy, Paul would have made the same decision Jake made—in fact, he'd seen Paul do the same in similar situations.

In the end, Jake chose to ride out the tempest with the present crew, now down one member.

At a few minutes after nine o'clock, the final customer of the day exited Paul's Poulet. With the fryer finally working and the soda delivered, Jake locked the doors to the diner, bringing an end to a tumultuous night. He, Cora, and the two remaining coworkers collapsed in the nearest booth and rested for a few minutes before beginning their final task of the day—cleaning fryers, tables, and floors. Their work shift was far from finished.

Jake took a mop from the maintenance closet and began in the dining room. Cora and the other employees moved to the kitchen.

Jake followed Cora home, arriving there around eleven. He leaned against her house as she unlocked the door. "Have you ever had the kind of night we had tonight?" he asked.

"Nope. Something similar, but nothing like tonight. I hope we never have another one like it, either. Ever. No fryer, no soda, no Betsy. Being off tomorrow sounds good, eh?"

She turned to him.

Smooth, gentle, far-off look, lips positioned, swoop, plant. Cora lifted her face.

Jake pecked her cheek.

"Good night, Jake. See you tomorrow at four."

"Good night, Cora. Four o'clock tomorrow. Looking forward to it."

"Me too."

Jake waited for the sound of the tumblers before turning and strolling toward the Olds. He was exhausted. He couldn't remember a time when he had ever been as tired. He hesitated before starting the engine in the Olds. Had he detected that far-off look in Cora's eyes? Had she lifted her face toward him? Had she turned her head slightly? Should he have swooped? Planted?

"I am *such* an *idiot*," he said aloud.

Promptly at four on Friday, Jake rang Cora's doorbell.

"Want to come inside?" Cora asked.

"I would, but—well, I thought we might walk along the lake. The weather isn't too cold—maybe light-jacket weather—but if we're walking the lake, we should go."

"That sounds lovely," she said reaching for her jacket behind the door.

Cora wore jeans, something Jake had never seen her wear, and a long-sleeved light blue shirt. She wore simple flat shoes and what looked to be a jade necklace. He wondered if it was another loan or gift from Rebecca. If that was true, then Rebecca knew about their date, which meant in all probability Paul knew—not that it mattered to Jake.

He helped her with her jacket. She wrapped and tucked a scarf around her neck inside the black leather jacket. Her makeup was minimal—not too little and not too much, and only a touch of lipstick—but she needed very little help from any of it.

She is stunning.

"You look nice this afternoon," he said.

"I'm surprised you noticed," she said lightly. "And what do you mean, 'this afternoon'? Don't I always look nice?"

Cora's reply caught Jake off guard. "I mean I usually see you wearing a vest and a chicken cap."

"Are you saying I don't look nice wearing Paul Poulet's vest and chicken cap?"

Cora's grin gave away the fact she was teasing him.

"No, you look nice in Paul Poulet's vest and chicken cap too."

"Why, Jake Alvin Thomas, that's about the most romantic thing you've ever said to me."

Jake opened and closed the Olds's passenger door behind Cora. He maneuvered the short drive to Lake Pontchartrain and parked. They joined several couples, along with singles and families, as they walked beside the lake.

A slight wind off the water made the walk chilly. They found an empty bench and sat in silence, both enjoying the lake and each other's company. Jake felt no pressure to fill every moment with words. From her silence, Cora obviously felt the same.

"I thought we would eat at Margo's," Jake finally said, as the sun dropped below the horizon.

"I can't remember the last time I ate at Margo's."

"Shall we?"

Jake reached for Cora's hand. She linked her fingers in his and said, "Let's go."

A maître d' escorted Jake and Cora to a rear table. She returned with glasses of water and wrote as Cora and Jake placed their orders.

When they were alone, Cora said, "Jake, I've worked beside you for over four years now, but I don't know much about you. I know you lived in your car for a while, parked behind Paul's, and now you live with Mildred and Leeroy. I know you play in a band with Leeroy and Laverne and Lester. What else should I know about you?"

Jake took a deep breath and considered how much of his story he wanted to tell, realizing most of it wasn't a good dinner subject.

He began. "I was born and raised here. On Pike Street, in Metairie."

"I know the neighborhood. Beautiful. Tree-lined streets and driveways."

"It *is* a beautiful neighborhood. My father was Monroe and my mother Elizabeth. People called her Beth."

Cora noted he spoke of his parents in the past tense, but said nothing.

Jake continued. "Our house was a home full of love. As a child I didn't have a care in the world."

A pause. He gathered his thoughts and continued, the words coming in short, sharp sentences.

"When I was thirteen, my father lost his job. Became depressed. Money got tight. My parents got a thirty-day eviction notice. We lost the house to foreclosure. We moved into a rental, a rat trap roach motel."

Jake took a deep breath before continuing.

"Then a policeman came to our house one afternoon to tell us Dad's body had been found in one of the canals. Murdered, we were told. And Mom? She worked harder to provide for me. She died in her sleep not long after that, most likely from worry and sheer exhaustion. I woke up one morning and found her in her bed, already gone."

His head dropped.

"The city buried her because we—I—didn't have any money. I'm not even sure exactly where she's buried. I dropped out of school, and the Olds became my home. I came to work at Paul's not long after. Met Lester, Laverne, and Leeroy at their audition for a guitarist. They encouraged me to earn my GED and go to college. And here I am, Jacob Alvin Thomas, sitting with you tonight."

"Jake, I'm sorry. I should never have asked."

"I should be the one making apologies. My story isn't good dinner conversation."

As the evening progressed, Cora mused and said reflectively, "Jacob Alvin Thomas. I like the name."

"Thank you. Now it's your turn. Tell me who you are. I don't know much about you, other than you certainly make a delicious fruitcake. Who are you?"

Cora paused, considering, before she began her story. Then she looked up and into his eyes.

"Hello. My name is Cora Dee Hoelzer."

"Hello, Cora Dee Hoelzer. Nice name."

"Thank you. My father, Albert, named me for a daughter of Zeus."

"The heroine in James Fenimore Cooper's *Last of the Mohicans* is named Cora."

"Her too," Cora said, "I've read that book."

She absently refolded a corner of her napkin. "My father was an engineer, mechanical. My mother was a stay-at-home wife and mother. My mother was named Cecil ...."

"Cecil?"

"Cecil," Cora said with a laugh.

"C-e-c-i-l?" Jake asked.

She nodded. "My grandfather—Mother's father—wanted a boy, and he was determined to name him Cecil after a famous clan in England. When a baby girl came along, my grandfather embraced her with all his being and named *her* Cecil. My father called her 'Cee.' I was born and raised in Acacia, Mississippi, in the northwest corner of the state." Cora smiled at Jake's puzzlement at her hometown's name. "Moses and the Hebrews made the Ark of the Covenant from the acacia tree. The city fathers decided it was a good name for our town."

Jake smiled as Cora continued.

"Like you, I was raised an only child in a home full of love. I never doubted my parents' love for one another or for me. I was spoiled."

"Nothing wrong with a parent spoiling a child, if it's done the right way. In fact, parents should spoil their children."

"In the right way," Cora said.

"In the right way."

Cora continued. "I graduated high school and was on my way to Tuscaloosa and the University of Alabama in the fall, intending to major in mechanical engineering like my dad." Cora paused.

"And ...?" Jake encouraged.

Cora met Jake's eyes before continuing. Her own eyes were clear and calm.

"Two nights before graduation, my parents, Albert and Cee, went to dinner at a local restaurant they loved. They left the restaurant, and they'd almost made it home when an oncoming car crossed into their lane and hit them head on."

Jake couldn't summon enough breath to say even a whispered *oh no*.

"The patrolman who got to them first told me my father died instantly. Mom survived the crash, but she lived for only four days." Cora looked down at the table and shook her head, as if still in disbelief. "The doctors thought she'd be all right. She was conscious at first, and she and I talked about my graduation, and going on to college. I promised I would."

She swiped the back of her hands across her eyes. "On the fourth day, she took a turn for the worse. The doctors weren't sure what was happening, and they did everything they could, but she lapsed into a coma and passed peacefully shortly after that."

Jake quietly laid his hand over hers on the table. She didn't pull away.

"College lost its allure. I learned there was a large mortgage on the house, and I knew I couldn't afford to live there. I didn't want to stay in Acacia, so I sold the house. Going through my parents' personal papers, I learned my grandfather—my mother's father—had left her a home in New Orleans."

"Is that where you live now?"

She nodded. "Where I live now. After the passing of my parents, I did something I'd never done before. I left the state of Mississippi. Something else I'd never done—I rode a bus, with one suitcase, to New Orleans. From the bus station, I had yet another new experience. I rode in a taxi."

"To 873 Foxwell Street?"

"To 873 Foxwell Street."

"A house you'd never seen before." It was a statement, not a question.

"Never seen before that day, not even a picture. But my mother kept the house well-maintained, and I moved in."

She looked at Jake's hand over hers. "I was scared, Jake. I had a few dollars from selling the house and contents in Acacia, but … well, there wasn't much. I started getting bills—electricity, gas—and I had food to buy. I knew what little money I had wouldn't last long. I needed a job, so I applied to Paul's Poulet, and presto. A job." She looked at Jake. "Paul and Rebecca have been more than employers to me. They've been friends—good, good friends."

Jake patted her hand before removing his. He considered his next question before he spoke.

"How did you get to work? From 873 Foxwell Street to Paul's on Chef? Did you have the VW?"

Cora made eye contact with Jake, shook her head, and smiled. "I walked."

"You *walked*? That's at least four miles round trip."

"Nearer five. I walked. There and back."

"What about the weather? When it rained?"

"Regardless of the weather—sunny, rainy, snowy, raw, nasty. I walked. At least, until Paul realized I was walking."

"Did you ride with him?"

"No, not with him. I drove. A Volkswagen … Paul gave me."

"You mean ...?"

"Yes. The car I currently drive. Now you know why I consider Paul my second father."

Jake apologized, mortified. "I'm sorry. I shouldn't have asked that, either."

"I don't mind talking about my parents. It still hurts when I think about their accident—such needless deaths that could have been avoided." She took a deep breath. "But I'm proud of the life I've created."

"You should be."

"I feel I've accomplished *something*, at least. I have a nice house, a nice job, good friends, working with nice people. Most of them," she said airily, her voice trailing off, with a cool, twinkling stare in Jake's direction.

He returned the stare. "I've got a nice job too. Good friends, working with nice people. *Most* of them." They eyed each other only a moment before bursting into laughter.

"Enough," Cora said. "Let's change the subject."

"Let's," Jake agreed.

"Tell me about your ambitions, motivations, passions. What drives Jacob Alvin Thomas? Where do you want to be in five years? Or ten?"

"I'll tell if you will."

"You first," she said.

"I want the American dream."

For the next two hours, Jake and Cora sat and talked of passions, hopes, and desires.

"I want a wife. I want to live in a house on Pike. Not the actual house where I lived with my parents, but I want the safety and security of the Pike house and community."

"I want to go back to Acacia," Cora said. "Not physically, but I want the love of a husband as I had the love of parents."

"I want children," Jake said. "I want them to grow up and grow old. With siblings."

"Being an only child has advantages," Cora laughed, "but I missed that sibling connection as well, I think."

"Lester, Laverne, and Leeroy are brothers," Jake said. At the confused look on her face, he elaborated. "Not biological, but they *are* family. There is nothing one wouldn't do for the other. I never had that. I want that, and I want it for my children."

"I understand."

Jake noticed, a few minutes before ten o'clock, that the restaurant was empty. He motioned for their check and paid their tab. He apologized to the waitress for keeping her late.

"Time got away from me," Jake said.

"Oh, *dear*. I didn't realize it was nearly ten o'clock," Cora said.

The waitress thanked him for his generous tip.

Jake opened the door on the Olds for Cora. En route to 873 Foxwell Street, they made small talk of the weather and the next week's work schedule.

He parked on the street and walked Cora to the door, the entryway illuminated by lights from the porch.

"I can't remember when I've enjoyed an evening more," Cora said.

"Same here. Let's do it again soon?"

"An invitation's all I need."

"How about Sunday?"

"Sunday?"

"Church. Worship. Will you go to church with me?"

"Sure."

341

"Ten thirty?"

"Ten thirty."

Cora unlocked the door and turned to him.

Smooth, gentle, far-off look, lips positioned, swoop, plant. Did she turn to me? Does she have that far-off look?

Jake pecked her on the cheek.

Cora entered her house and locked the door. Hearing the tumblers roll, Jake spoke aloud.

"I'm an idiot."

The door opened.

"Jacob Alvin Thomas, are you ever going to kiss me? Really *kiss* me?"

Without thinking, Jake said, "I've never swooped or planted."

"*What?*" She switched off the porchlights, stepped outside, and closed the door behind her.

Jake briefly recalled Leeroy saying a woman never asked to be kissed.

Well, that isn't true.

CHAPTER FORTY-SEVEN

With Lester and Laverne waiting in the rear of the Olds at ten thirty on Sunday, Jake knocked on Cora's door. The door opened promptly.

"Good morning, Jake."

"Morning, Cora."

Cora wore a beautiful, simple dress. Same flat shoes.

Within thirty minutes, they joined Mildred and Leeroy at Franklin Avenue Church of God in Christ. They lined up as usual in the pew—Lester, Laverne, Leeroy, Mildred. The newcomer Cora sat beside Mildred, with Jake on Cora's right.

Music Minister Woodrow Riles led the congregation in musical worship. Pastor Josiah Hart preached. After the service, the group exited the Franklin Avenue Church of God in Christ both in awe of Jesus and encouraged by his presence.

"Lunch, anyone?" Jake asked.

"Leeroy and I are eating leftovers," Mildred said.

"Leftover meatloaf?" Leeroy asked.

"Yes, leftover meatloaf."

"Gonna be good," Leeroy said.

"Well, *I'm* game for lunch," from Lester.

"Me too," Laverne echoed.

Cora smiled. "May I tag along?"

"We'd all be honored if you would," Lester said.

"We would be," Jake confirmed.

The four got into Jake's Olds, exiting at Poncho's Restaurant on Veteran's Boulevard.

"I love me some Poncho's," Laverne said, after Jake announced his lunch choice.

"*When* have you ever eaten at Poncho's?" Lester asked.

Laverne gave him a blank look. "You're right. I've never eaten at Poncho's."

"Then how do you know you love it?" Cora asked.

"Well, I—" Laverne was taken with a sudden coughing fit. When it lessened, he said, "A few things, dear lady," he explained, "are probably better left unsaid."

The four sat in a booth, and before they could get comfortable a young man placed salsa and chips on the table.

"Now that's what I call service," Laverne said. "Jake, you should take notice."

Jake ignored Laverne as Cora grinned and said, "Yes, Jake, you should take notice."

Jake returned the grin. "I don't need any commentary from you."

"Afternoon, Cain," Lester said as he read the server's nametag.

"Son of Adam—son of Eve," Laverne said.

"Correct," Cain said with an easy smile. He distributed menus and took drink orders. Cora noticed Laverne placed his menu on the table.

"I'll be back with your drinks," the waiter said.

"We're mistaken," Cora said. "Laverne has been here before because he doesn't need a menu. He knows what he wants to order." Lester and Jake continued perusing their menus. Neither spoke.

"I put the menu down because I can't read, Cora," Laverne said.

"Pardon?"

"I can't read," Laverne repeated.

"I'm sorry," Cora said, "I didn't know. I didn't mean to embarrass you."

"Oh, no," Laverne said amiably, "you didn't embarrass me. It's just the way things are, and I'm not ashamed of it. So don't you worry."

"The tacos look good," Lester said, oblivious to Laverne and Cora's conversation.

"I was always a poor student," Laverne said, "and once I dropped out of school I completely lost the ability to read or write."

"But you still have the ability to *learn*," Jake said, seizing his opportunity.

"That's where you're wrong, young Jake. I don't. Too dumb and too old."

"The enchiladas look good," Lester said.

"I've heard you say that before, Laverne," Jake said. "I don't ever want to hear you say that again. You're *not* dumb."

"Fajitas look good," Lester said, still searching the menu. "Everything looks good. I feel like a kid in a candy store. What sounds good to you, Laverne?"

Jake turned to Cora. "He knows the music and lyrics to hundreds of songs. He quotes history from the beginning of it—names, dates, places. More than that, he *interprets* history. He holds his own in any political discussion, locally, nationally, or internationally, regardless of the topic. I've seen him support any position—Democrat, Republican, conservative, or liberal, which is a position I know he opposes—just to needle Lester and Leeroy into an argument."

"Amen," Lester said, never lifting his eyes from the menu. "He needles well."

"Does that sound like someone dumb to you?" Jake asked Cora.

"Does not," she said, with a gentle shake of her head. She made eye contact with Laverne.

Lester placed his menu on the table and addressed the topic. "The fact is, Cora, I'm near illiterate as well."

"You read well, compared to me at least," Laverne said.

"Perhaps. Leeroy is literate, I suppose. Barely," Lester said.

"You read the menu," Cora said to Lester.

Lester shook his head and laughed. "Correction. I *looked* at the menu. Not read. I looked at the pictures."

"Tacos sound good," Laverne said.

$$\infty$$

"Sopaipilla, anyone?" Jake asked as the waiter cleared the table after the meal.

"What is sopaipilla?" Lester asked.

"A sopaipilla is a fried pastry."

"Dessert?" Laverne asked.

"Dessert," Cora affirmed.

"Then let's have sopaipillas," Lester said.

"I love me some dessert," Laverne added.

Cain took their orders and returned in minutes with a plate of sopaipillas.

"I prefer them with honey," Jake said.

"Did you know," Laverne began, "if the honeybee were to disappear from the earth, many believe humankind would disappear too?"

"I don't believe that," Lester said, deciding the time for needling Laverne had arrived.

"It's true," Laverne insisted. "I heard it on the radio. Did you know there are thousands of bees in a beehive? Maybe a hundred thousand bees, but one queen bee and a few drones—which is a male bee. Did you know that?"

"Did not," Lester said.

Laverne wasn't finished. "A bee, female worker bee, will fly as far as five miles from the hive in search of nectar and pollen and return to the same hive ... with no problem. Isn't that amazing? I can't walk to the grocery with Lester without getting lost."

"Amazing," Cora said.

"I learned that listening to National Public Radio."

Laverne handed the honey squeeze bottle to Jake. He watched with interest, expecting Jake to put honey *on* the sopaipilla. Jake, realizing he had a captive audience, lifted the sopaipilla for all could see. He then bit off one corner of the deep-fried sweet and squeezed honey into the hollow sopaipilla, to Laverne and Lester's astonishment.

"Isn't that something?" Lester said.

"That's somethin', all right," Laverne said as he turned the sopaipilla over and over in his hand. Laverne, mimicking Jake, bit off one corner and squeezed honey inside. Lester followed, as did Cora. Conversation paused while they ate.

"What's the flag for?" Lester asked, as they finished the sopaipillas and wiped honey off their fingers. He pointed to the small flag, three by five inches, complete with flag pole and stand, in the center of the table.

"Serves as a summons to the waiter," Cora explained. "If you need anything, water, coffee, tea, chips, salsa, raise the flag. Our waiter—what was his name?"

"Cain," Laverne said, "as in Cain and Abel."

"Cain will see the flag raised and check to see what is needed."

"Me! Me! Me! I want to! I want to raise the flag." Lester reached across Laverne and raised the flag.

"What do *you* need? What do *we* need?" Laverne asked.

"I need to speak to Cain, the son of Adam and Evelyn," Lester said.

"Adam and *Eve*," Laverne corrected, knowing Lester knew better.

In minutes, Cain arrived and smiled. "May I help you?"

"I need," Lester began, "to tell you what an excellent job you have done today."

Cora, Jake, and Laverne nodded in agreement.

Lester continued. "Never was a glass of water, a basket of chips, or a bowl of salsa empty."

The smile on Cain's face broadened. "Thank you. That's nice of you. Not everyone is as nice as you."

"And our compliments to the chef," Lester said. "Never have I eaten a more flavorful sopaipilla."

"I will tell him," Cain said, his smile never fading.

"You have never eaten a sopaipilla in your life before today," Laverne reminded Lester after Cain left.

"He doesn't know that," Lester said, "and that sopaipilla was mighty tasty."

"'Twas!" Laverne agreed. "Mighty tasty."

Jake walked Cora to her door as Lester and Laverne sat in the back of the Olds. He pecked Cora on her cheek. She unlocked the door, waved in the direction of the Olds, and entered her house. Jake heard the tumblers roll in place before he returned to the Olds. Lester and Laverne remained in the back seat.

"One of you can sit in the front if you want."

"I'm good," Laverne said.

"I love being chauffeured," Lester said.

Jake pointed the car toward Franklin.

"That's a mighty nice young lady," Laverne said after a few moments.

"Yes, she is," Jake agreed.

"Easy to talk to," Lester added. "She has the gift of putting people at ease."

"That too," Jake said.

The trio rode in silence before Laverne spoke again. "Leeroy called an emergency meeting for this afternoon."

"I forgot," Jake said. "What time?"

"Two o'clock," Lester said.

"We have enough time to get to Leeroy's," Jake said, glancing at his watch.

"What's the meeting about?" Lester asked.

"Don't know," Laverne said and continued. "Jake?"

"Clueless," Jake said.

"Not about the distribution of funds," Laverne said.

"Right. We didn't play last night," Lester said. "Maybe he's dyin'?"

"I doubt it," Laverne said.

"Maybe he has lockjaw or a sore throat and can't talk. Maybe he fell down, broke his mouth, and he can't talk," Lester said.

"We ain't never been that lucky," Laverne said, "to say nothin' of Mildred being that lucky."

Jake passed Franklin en route to home. More silence.

"I don't understand one thing," Lester said.

"What don't you understand, Lester?" Jake asked, thinking he was still contemplating the called emergency meeting.

"I just don't understand. What does Cora see in you?"

Laverne roared with laughter and chipped in. "I don't understand that either, Jake. What does a wonderful young lady like Cora see in the likes of you?"

"That sounds like something Leeroy would say," Jake said.

"No need for you to get nasty," Laverne said.

"That's hittin' below the belt," Lester said.

"Way below the belt," Laverne said.

Jake laughed.

CHAPTER FORTY-EIGHT

Jake parked the Olds. The three men entered the garage. Leeroy was nowhere to be seen. The small electric heater had been turned on and worked hard in an attempt to ward off the outside cold, but it was fighting a losing battle. Lester, Jake, and Laverne cinched up their coats.

The men sat and waited in their normal lawn chairs beside Hazel. In minutes, Leeroy entered the garage. He sat in the final lawn chair, across from Jake, completing the circle.

"Are you dyin', Leeroy?" Lester asked.

"*What*? No, I'm not dying."

"He talks," Laverne said, "so we know he doesn't have lockjaw."

"Or laryngitis," Lester added.

"Unfortunately," Laverne said.

"Glad we got that out of the way," Leeroy said. He looked at Jake. "Blanc, talk to me."

"About what?" Jake asked, confused.

"Did you swoop? Plant?"

"I'm sorry?" Jake asked.

"Oh come on, Leeroy," Laverne said.

"Is that why we're here? *Again*?" Lester asked incredulously.

"Did you plant, Blanc?"

"Ol' Swoop-Master himself rides again," Lester said.

"This is a matter of national security," Leeroy said.

"Leeroy, Doctor of Plant and Dancer-of-Love, why don't you leave Jake and Cora alone?" Laverne said.

Leeroy ignored him. "Well? Did you, Blanc?"

"Don't answer that, Jake," Lester said.

"You two old hobgoblins haven't swooped or planted in years," Leeroy chided. "I'm asking. I'm curious. I want to know how to be more helpful."

"You've done enough, O-Swooper-and-Planter-of-One-Woman," Laverne said.

"You're asking something that's none of your business," Lester said.

"Or *our* business," Laverne added.

Jake didn't say a word. He sat expressionless.

"The next time Leeroy calls an emergency meeting, I'm going to insist on knowing the topic *before* we come here," Lester said.

"I second that, and if the topic is Jake's swoop or non-swoop, plant or non-plant, I'm not comin'," Laverne said.

"Agreed," Lester said.

Jake continued to sit silently.

"I know you went out with Cora Friday night," Leeroy said, "because we didn't go to the grocery until Saturday. You always go to the grocery store with me and Mildred, but not Friday night. And you went out all dressed up. As if you was going to church, but I know you didn't go to church. You were on a date with Cora Friday night, weren't you, Blanc?"

Jake said nothing.

"Cora was with you in church this morning," Leeroy said.

"We, Laverne and I, were with Jake in church this morning," Lester said, "and Jake didn't swoop and plant *us*."

"As were *you*, Leeroy. You were with Jake in church this morning," Laverne said. "Is Jake swooping and planting on *you*, Leeroy?"

"Smooth, gentle, far-off look, lips positioned, swoop, plant. Blanc?" Leeroy asked, undeterred. He waited.

Jake remained seated, stone-faced.

"Laverne and I apologize for him, Jake," Lester said.

"Yes, we do. Leeroy, you should be ashamed," Laverne said.

Leeroy waited, still leaning over in his lawn chair, inches away from Jake. Watching.

Jake's face cracked into the faintest of smiles. Immediately, Leeroy leaned back, raised his arms, and whooped.

"Our boy swooped! Our boy planted!"

Lester and Laverne turned to look at Jake, reading the almost-invisible smile. They too smiled and leaned back in their lawn chairs. Suddenly, the garage didn't seem as cold.

Three weeks later, Jake called an emergency meeting of the Noirs.

He drove to a convenience store and purchased four cans of soda on his way to the meeting. Leeroy, Lester, and Laverne were already seated beside Hazel when he arrived. Jake smiled as he entered, carrying a bag and a book. Lester and Laverne were in the process of giving Leeroy a hard time about something.

"Y'all don't know what y'all talkin' about," Leeroy said, motioning for Jake to sit.

"It's you, Leeroy, who doesn't know what you're a-talkin' about," Lester said.

"Which is true most of the time," Laverne added.

"You know that's right," Lester said.

Jake sat.

"What's this meeting about, Blanc?" Leeroy asked, feigning annoyance.

"Patience, Leeroy," Lester encouraged.

"I got thangs to do. Places to go, thangs to do, people to annoy."

"Where do you have to go, Leeroy?" Laverne asked.

"What people do you have to annoy? Besides us and Mildred, I mean?" Lester added.

Leeroy hesitated long enough for Laverne to jump in. "As I suspected. Nothing."

"No place to be," Lester said.

"Nobody to see," was Laverne's final word, as Leeroy sat in silence, surprising the other three.

"I want to discuss a book with you," Jake said. For the first time since Jake's arrival, Lester, Laverne, and Leeroy noticed the small book he carried.

"*The Four Loves,* written by C. S. Lewis," Jake began.

"Clive Staples Lewis," Laverne said.

Jake, Lester, and Leeroy all looked at Laverne as though he had appeared for the first time in their presence.

Laverne wasn't finished. "I learned about C. S. Lewis on NPR. You boys should listen sometime."

"I ain't a-listenin' to no NTR, I told you before," Leeroy said.

"NPR," Laverne corrected, and continued. "With the name Clive Staples, I would be called C. S. too."

Without knowing anything about C. S. Lewis, all three men nodded agreement.

Laverne continued in a nonchalant manner, as though he'd known C.S. Lewis personally. "British author and Anglican theologian. A theologian is someone helping people with the thought of God, Leeroy."

"I know what a theologian is, *LEE*-verne," Leeroy insisted.

"Taught at both of England's most prestigious colleges," Laverne said, "Oxford *and* Cambridge Universities. Best known as the writer of *The Chronicles of Narnia*, a series of seven fantasy novels written for children. Also known for *The Screwtape Letters* and *The Problem of Pain*. Wrote more than thirty books, translated into more than thirty languages, sellin' millions of copies."

"Are you finished, Mister NBR?" Leeroy asked, his voice oozing his most effective sarcastic tone.

"It's NPR," Laverne corrected again. "No, not quite, Mister Impatience. He's buried in the same grave as his brother Warren—and would you gents know the date of the death of Clives Staples Lewis?"

"On a *Monday*?" Leeroy responded with more sarcasm.

"November 22, 1963," Laverne said, "same day as—"

"The day John Fitzgerald Kennedy was assassinated," Leeroy said softly.

"Correct! Same day of President Kennedy's assassination!" Laverne said. "Give that man a SEE-gar."

Jake realized he'd lost control of the emergency called meeting. He spoke a little louder than usual to halt the banter.

"Tulane's President Sloan gave this book to me. This book has helped me understand and value friendship, *our* friendships. Lewis wrote that few people understand friendship because few people have experienced friendship."

Lester, Laverne, and Leeroy, serious now, considered the thought. Jake continued. "The insight Lewis gives us is that friendship, while unnecessary, adds value to life."

"Amen to that, Jake," Lester said.

"Preach on, Brother Blanc," Leeroy added.

Jake continued. "Lewis helped me understand in order to have a friend, you've got to *be* a friend. I've tried to be a friend to you, perhaps unsuccessfully, but you three have been friends to me. Good friends."

The moment grew quiet as Leeroy, Lester, and Laverne realized the moment was more serious than they'd thought.

Jake swiped a sleeve over his cheeks. He thumbed through the book, giving himself the excuse to divert his eyes.

"Friends walk side by side, and you three have walked side by side with me." Jake paused before speaking again. "You rescued me from homelessness." Jake glanced at Lester, Leeroy, and Laverne. None of the three men looked back at him. He chuckled softly as he added, "And all three of you helped me find my way with Cora, and one of you taught me how to swoop and plant."

"Ole Swoop Master himself," Lester said. Laverne and Leeroy laughed. Jake continued.

"You taught me generosity, independence, kindness, determination, humility, loyalty, courage, compassion, honesty, and responsibility."

Lester, Leeroy, and Laverne sat quietly, looking anywhere but at Jake.

"Our friendship is freely given to each other," Jake said, "without any anticipation of repayment. Our friendship, as Lewis wrote, is not jealous. Each one in this circle has added something to the others, and you have added much to me. As Christians, we know Jesus, our *friend*, is closer than a brother. I'm thankful for Jesus, and I'm thankful for you, my friends."

With that, Jake opened the bag. One at a time, he removed a can of soda, opened it, and handed a can to each man. Each man sat silently, none drinking, awaiting Jake's lead. He lifted his can. Lester, Laverne, and Leeroy leaned forward in their lawn chairs and mimicked.

"I'm honored, more than I have ever been honored, to call each of you my friend," Jake said.

"Likewise," Lester said, as Leeroy and Laverne nodded.

"The Apostle Paul reminds us that now these three remain—faith, hope, and love, but the greatest of these is love. I love you, my friends."

Jake looked at each of them in turn, seeing their faces—their eyes, understanding the heart of each man, and what had made each man who he was.

Laverne, Leeroy, and Lester, like Jake, struggled to control their emotions. All four touched soda cans together.

Jake swallowed hard, smiled and spoke. "To faith, hope, love—and within the circle of love—to friendship."

Lester, Leeroy, and Laverne spoke softly, simultaneously.

"To friendship."

ABOUT THE AUTHOR

R. Kelvin Moore is proud Alabamian, although this novel is set in New Orleans. He graduated from Samford University, Birmingham (BA degree) and New Orleans Baptist Theological Seminary (MDiv and PhD degrees). He grew up in a community of notable characters and master-story tellers. Since 1991, he has taught biblical studies in a college classroom (Union University, Jackson, TN) where he has been nominated numerous times as Faculty Member of the Year, receiving the recognition in 2004. He has been married to the same lady since 1984. He has two adult children and a daughter-in-law. In addition to college experience, he has almost forty (40) years of pastoral experience, both full-time and bi-vocational. Moore, a self-described fogey, has written four novels.